PRAISE FOR *Rules for Thieves*

"A smooth debut." —*Kirkus Reviews*

"This compelling debut fantasy novel with complex themes, lots of action, and a good cast of characters will appeal to fantasy readers across the spectrum." —*SLJ*

"Alexandra Ott's funny, thrilling debut, *Rules for Thieves*, will have readers flipping pages from the very first scene. Alli is a lovable, whip-smart protagonist." —*Shelf Awareness*

"The world building is magnificent and intricate, and it would be a shame if there isn't a sequel, even if Ott does wrap up the key plot points; Alli and this inviting setting both deserve another outing." —*BCCB*

PRAISE FOR *The Shadow Thieves*

"A not-to-be-missed sequel marked by action, mystery, lively dialogue, and steady character growth." —*Kirkus Reviews*

"For readers who devour Percy Jackson or Wings of Fire, this will be a welcome addition." —*SLJ*

ALSO BY ALEXANDRA OTT

Rules for Thieves
The Shadow Thieves

SEEKERS
OF THE WILD REALM

ALEXANDRA OTT

ALADDIN
New York   London   Toronto   Sydney   New Delhi

This book is a work of fiction. Any references to historical events, real people,
or real places are used fictitiously. Other names, characters, places, and events are
products of the author's imagination, and any resemblance to actual events or places
or persons, living or dead, is entirely coincidental.

ALADDIN

An imprint of Simon & Schuster Children's Publishing Division
1230 Avenue of the Americas, New York, New York 10020
First Aladdin hardcover edition June 2020
Text copyright © 2020 by Alexandra Ott
Jacket illustrations copyright © 2020 by Cathleen McAllister
All rights reserved, including the right of reproduction in whole or in part in any form.
ALADDIN and related logo are registered trademarks of Simon & Schuster, Inc.
For information about special discounts for bulk purchases, please contact
Simon & Schuster Special Sales at 1-866-506-1949 or business@simonandschuster.com.
The Simon & Schuster Speakers Bureau can bring authors to your live event.
For more information or to book an event contact the Simon & Schuster Speakers Bureau
at 1-866-248-3049 or visit our website at www.simonspeakers.com.
Jacket designed by Heather Palisi
The text of this book was set in Bembo Std.
Manufactured in the United States of America 0520 BVG
2 4 6 8 10 9 7 5 3 1
Library of Congress Cataloging-in-Publication Data
Names: Ott, Alexandra, author.
Title: Seekers of the Wild Realm / Alexandra Ott.
Description: New York : Aladdin, 2020. | Series: Seekers of the wild realm ; 1 |
Audience: Ages 8-12. | Audience: Grades 4-6. | Summary:
Twelve-year-old Bryn's only hope of becoming a Seeker like her father
is to help rival Ari train a baby dragon in exchange for sharing his training,
but holds many secrets.
Identifiers: LCCN 2019056876 (print) | LCCN 2019056877 (eBook) |
ISBN 9781534438583 (hc) | ISBN 9781534438606 (eBook)
Subjects: CYAC: Dragons—Fiction. | Magic—Fiction. | Sex role—Fiction. |
Adventure and adventurers—Fiction. | Fantasy.
Classification: LCC PZ7.1.O88 See 2020 (print) | LCC PZ7.1.O88 (eBook) |
DDC [Fic]—dc23
LC record available at https://lccn.loc.gov/2019056876
LC ebook record available at https://lccn.loc.gov/2019056877

FOR ALL THE GIRLS WITH
BIG DREAMS AND BRAVE HEARTS.
MAY YOU ALWAYS AIM FOR THE SKY.

ONE

I gaze into the clouds, but there's no sign of dragons.

Papa says they're most likely to start their morning hunt at dawn, so I always scan the skies at this time of day, when the sun is low on the horizon and the first rays of pinkish light shimmer on the surface of the sea. Spying the dragons on their morning hunt, when they leave the safety of the island to fly over the ocean, is the only way to catch a glimpse of them outside of the Realm. But aside from the occasional shadow, I never see much of anything.

"Staring at clouds again?" teases a familiar voice.

I grin at Runa. "Looking for dragons."

"Of course you were." Runa smiles. "But we have to hurry if we're going to get everything done. Didn't you say your mama gave you a long list?"

She's not wrong. It could take the whole morning to pick up all the stuff Mama asked for from the village. Which is why

I always talk my best friend into accompanying me on these boring errands. Runa makes everything more fun.

"Well, in that case . . . ," I say. "Race you!" I take off down the dirt path before she has a chance to respond.

"You cheater!" she calls, her footsteps pounding after me.

Runa's parents' farm is outside the village, all the way to the end of the lane and over the hill, so we have a long ways to go to reach the center of town. The soft earth and wet grass stick to my bare feet as I run, and the wind whips my hair from my face. The morning air is chilly, even this late in the summer, and I almost wish I'd grabbed my coat.

I crest the top of the hill and stop to catch my breath. In front of me, our little village is nestled in the crook of the bay. The ocean spreads out to the south, glimmering in the sunlight. The fishermen's boats are just visible out on the water, pursuing the day's catch. Rising hills surround the other three sides of our village, gradually giving way to even steeper plateaus and soaring mountain peaks. There, in the highlands, lies the Wild Realm.

Papa has told me all about it, of course. The mountains, the waterfalls, the forests. The crystalline lakes and spouting geysers. Not to mention the massive glaciers that lie to the north and the lava fields spread in the shadows of the volcanoes that bisect the island in a diagonal line. There's a whole world up there in the Realm, one that's uninhabitable for humans but makes the perfect home for the world's most magical creatures. One that's accessible only to Seekers, who can fly to its heights on the backs of dragons in order to collect the magical treasures that lie within.

Seekers are the only people on the island who get to access the Realm; it's forbidden to everyone else. I've never seen it, of course, but my papa was a Seeker, back before he hurt his leg, and he's told me everything about his adventures. Until I can become a Seeker myself, I'll have to be content with scanning the skies for dragons and praying I catch a glimpse of one.

"I'm going to catch you!" Runa calls. She's gaining on me. I take a quick gulp of air and launch myself down the hill.

The dirt path winds past my family's hut and the neighbor's before widening at the edge of the main village square, where the bells are announcing dawn. It's bustling—fishermen heading down to the shore, shopkeepers opening their doors, the men heading to work while the women rush to trade goods. Runa and I are neck and neck as we race toward the large tree that marks the center of the village square. We both tag it at the same time.

"I think we have to call that a tie," Runa says when she catches her breath.

"Fine," I say, panting hard. "So where do you want to go first?"

"Not the fishmonger," she says, wrinkling her nose. "Then we'd have to smell the fish all morning."

"Good point. Let's try the bakery."

Before we continue down the path, she brushes off the

hem of her skirt as if there's some dirt on it, though I don't really see anything. Even after running all this way, Runa still manages to be neat. We do look alike in some ways— we both have light-brown skin and dark-brown eyes, like everyone else in the village, and we also share raven-black hair. But where mine is an unruly mop of curls, Runa's is always in orderly braids without a single strand out of place. She never gets mud on her hems, and only gets dirt on herself when she's riding her horse or mucking out the stable. I, on the other hand, am always dirty and don't have a horse *or* a stable.

But despite our differences, we've been friends since before we could walk, and she knows me better than anyone, except maybe Papa. When I get distracted halfway to the bakery by a sprig of moss growing outside the blacksmith shop, anyone else would think it was weird, but Runa just laughs. "From staring at clouds to staring at the ground," she says.

"This is laekning moss," I say, ignoring her teasing. "It can be used in healing tonics to treat fever."

Runa's eyes light up. "Really?" she says, stepping closer. I grin. She might tease me about my fascination with plants and magical creatures, but she's just as passionate about her healing gift as I am my nature gift. "How does it work?"

"No idea," I say. "But Papa says it's rare in the summer. I should help it grow a little, and we can tell Elder Ingvar to come collect some for his tonics."

Runa steps away from the moss, and I reach for my magic.

The plant's life force is soft but strong, and I seek it out with my gift. I give it a gentle nudge with my magic, feeding the spark of its life force, and feel it grow, the energy softly swirling. The moss spreads, climbing higher up the wall.

"Come on," Runa says when I'm done. "Let's find Elder Ingvar."

We cross the village square and head toward the squat hut that houses all of Elder Ingvar's medicines and tonics, right next door to the doctor's. Inside, the hut is packed with tight rows of shelves, all covered in bottles and jars filled with healing ointments and salves and powders. The little shop feels too claustrophobic to me, but Runa loves to wander along the shelves and read all the little labels on the jars.

Elder Ingvar is talking with a customer at the back of the shop, and we wait patiently for them to finish. I recognize the customer as Olga, the elderly lady who lives near the docks.

"I can't believe they would let them come back," Elder Olga is saying. Her voice sounds strained, like she's worried about something, and Elder Ingvar frowns.

"But surely the Seekers wouldn't agree unless it was safe. . . ."

"I think they're still arguing about it. Disgraceful. You'd think the council could agree among themselves."

Even though Mama says it's rude to eavesdrop, I can't help perking up. The five people from the village who are chosen as Seekers also serve as the village council, making many of the decisions about the way things run and settling disputes. Not that there are many decisions *or* disputes in such a small village. In recent memory, their biggest decision was whether Elder Frida's potatoes were encroaching on the neighbor's rutabagas. Still, I can't help but be fascinated every time someone mentions the Seekers. If I'm going to be one someday, I want to know *everything*.

"Never should've resumed communication with them in the first place, in my opinion," Elder Olga is saying. She starts to add something else, but Elder Ingvar, who has just noticed Runa and me, clears his throat, and Elder Olga turns around to see us.

"Good morning, girls," Elder Ingvar says. "I'll be with you in a moment."

That's the end of their mysterious conversation—Elder Olga finishes her purchase and turns to leave. But as she passes us, she stops. "Stay away from the docks, girls. You hear? Nothing but trouble."

"What trouble?" I ask.

Her face darkens. "The Vondur, of course."

Runa gasps, and my eyes widen. But before we can ask anything else, she shuffles away and leaves the shop.

I turn immediately to Elder Ingvar. "What did she mean?"

His mouth is a tight line. "Nothing for you to worry about. Just talk."

"Are the Vondur back?" I ask.

Elder Ingvar looks reluctant to answer. "Rumor has it that the Seekers have given the Vondur permission to dock again at the next trading day," he says. "But it's just a rumor, nothing more."

Runa and I look at each other. The thing about living in a small village is that there are lots of rumors—but many of them are true. Conversations about the Vondur always make me a little nervous. All the mainland clans come to our island periodically to trade, except the Vondur, who have been banned. Our history with them is rocky at best. Papa says that many years ago, a ship of Vondur magicians tried to conquer our island and force the villagers out, because they wanted to take over the Wild Realm for themselves. Luckily, their magic was no match for the Seekers, who drove them away. They haven't been to the island since.

The Vondur don't have magical gifts of their own, the way us islanders do; instead, they perform dark spells by using items or creatures imbued with magic. Papa says they'd rather butcher a dragon than protect it, so that they could use its parts for their strange potions and spells. That's why the Seekers guard our island's creatures so closely. The Vondur might kill every creature on the island if they get the chance.

I can't imagine why the Council of Seekers would give the Vondur permission to trade here again. Seeker Oskar, who is the oldest and therefore head of the council, was a Seeker back when the Vondur tried to conquer the island and helped to drive them away. Could they really have become peaceful enough to trade with in such a short period of time?

They've always been known for waging war, invading their neighbors, and killing dragons.

I want to ask Elder Ingvar more, but he quickly changes the subject, asking us what we've come in for. We tell him about the moss, and he thanks us profusely before sending us on our way.

Outside the shop, I blink in the suddenly bright sunlight as Runa leads the way to the bakery.

"Do you think they're right?" I ask. "About the Vondur?"

"There are always rumors about the Vondur," Runa says. "It's probably nothing."

"But they don't usually dock here on trading day," I say. "Why would the council let them?"

Runa opens her mouth to respond, but a shout makes both of us jump. Elisa runs toward me, yelling my name.

My little sister hardly ever runs—she gets bad coughing fits that make it hard for her to breathe, and Mama strictly forbids her from running anywhere. So seeing her barreling toward me through the village square means that something's happened. Something *big*.

"Elisa?" I say. "What's wrong?"

She stops beside me, panting for breath. She's small even for six, and her hand-me-down skirt nearly drags the ground. "Seeker Oskar," she says when she catches her breath. "He came over this morning to talk to Papa. He said he's *retiring*."

Runa frowns, not getting it, but a grin slides across my face. "You're sure? He definitely said that?"

"*Yes*," Elisa says, crossing her arms in indignation.

"What's going on?" Runa asks.

"Don't you see?" I say, grinning even wider. "There are always five Seekers. So if Seeker Oskar is retiring, that means there will have to be another competition in order to replace him."

"A Seeker competition?" Runa asks, finally catching on.

"Yes! And since I'm twelve now, I'm old enough to enter! Don't you see what this means?"

"Let me guess," she says, smiling. "You're going to compete."

"I'm going to compete, and I'm going to win." I feel like dancing across the village square and shouting the news for all to hear.

This is it. The opportunity I've been waiting for.

I'm going to become a Seeker.

TWO

Elisa and I race each other home, but she slows to a walk as we reach our hut. Good thing Mama didn't see her running—

"Elisabet!" Mama calls from the kitchen window. Her voice is sharp enough to carry across the garden. "Have you been running?"

Elisa bites her lip, and I rush to her rescue by changing the subject. "Where's Papa?"

"Come inside, Brynja," Mama calls. Elisa and I enter the small, dim hut, and Mama wastes no time in scolding us. "Didn't you get the bread that I asked for? And the fish?"

"I was walking there with Runa," I say quickly, "but then Elisa came up and said—"

Mama sighs. "You'll have to go back later. Here, help me with breakfast." She hands me a ladle and steers me toward the pot of porridge hanging over the hearth. Elisa takes advantage of the distraction and slips away into the back of the hut.

"Where's Papa?" I ask again.

Mama returns to the kitchen table, where she's chopping vegetables for tonight's stew. "He's walking Seeker Oskar home," she says, in a tone of great disapproval.

"So Seeker Oskar *was* here?" Hope rises in my chest again. Maybe Elisa's right. Maybe—

"You can ask your papa about it when he gets home," Mama says, in a way that warns me not to continue the discussion.

Five minutes later, I give up on the porridge and go to the window, pushing aside the thin curtain and poking my head out. An early-morning chill greets me, the cold wind blowing in from the bay. Our garden path is bathed in golden sunlight.

"I don't see him," I say, craning my neck to peer down the lane.

"Patience," Mama says.

I bounce up and down on my heels, keeping my gaze fixed out the window. Steam rises from the pot of porridge I abandoned, but I don't leave my post to rescue it. I expect Mama to scold me, to say something dumb like "Emergencies are no excuse for ruining breakfast," but she doesn't. Minutes pass, accompanied only by the rhythmic chop of Mama's knife and the excited pounding of my heart.

A tall shadow darkens the gate at the end of the garden path. "He's here!"

Mama says something in a scolding tone, but I barely hear her. I run, my bare feet sliding across the cool, hard-packed earth beneath them. I fling open the door and race to meet my father.

Papa limps down the path, leaning heavily on his walking stick. His dark hair and beard are less tidy than usual, his eyes ringed with shadows. But he still holds his arms out for a hug as I run up, and I melt into them. His coat is covered in dew and smells of damp wool, but I don't even mind.

I take a step back, and Papa looks down at me. "I suppose Elisa told you," he says.

"Yes."

"Seeker Oskar is ill," he says softly. "He will likely recover, but he has decided to retire."

It's the best news I could have hoped for, though I should probably be sad that he has to retire. Seeker Oskar is a kind man, one of my father's closest friends, and beloved in the village. Of course I don't want him to be ill.

But I'd be lying if I said my heart isn't dancing wildly in my chest, excitement coursing through my blood. Oskar is the most elderly of the Seekers, and the only one likely to retire anytime soon. This is the opportunity I've been waiting my entire life for, and my family can't afford to wait much longer.

There are a hundred questions on the tip of my tongue, but it would be disrespectful to ask most of them now. I settle for, "How's he doing?"

"As well as can be expected," Papa says. "The healer thinks he simply needs his rest."

I hesitate, wanting to word my next question carefully. "Will they . . . will they want to find a new Seeker right away?"

Papa lays a hand on my shoulder. "Yes. Soon they will announce the next competition." He lets his hand drop. "I take it you still want to compete?"

"Of course." I frown. "Don't you want me to?" I've been telling Papa about wanting to be a Seeker for years now. I thought he wanted me to carry on his legacy.

Papa shifts his weight, leaning heavily on his walking stick, and smiles. "I think that once you set your mind to something, there is nothing in all the world that could stop you."

I grin. He takes my right hand in his left, leaning on the walking stick with his other side, and together we head up the path toward our hut. His hand is cold from the morning air, his fingers calloused.

"Your mama may not be so easily persuaded," he warns as we draw nearer to the open front door.

"I know," I say. That's a possibility I'm prepared for.

"And between you and me . . ." He lowers his voice and leans closer to my ear. "I think it may be easier to take on a whole pack of dragons than to go against your mother. You get your iron will from her, you know."

"I know that, too," I say with a sigh. Mama can be just as stubborn as I am, and it isn't easy to argue with her. But I'll convince her somehow. I *have* to enter this competition.

I was born to be a Seeker.

Papa looks like he wants to say something else, but we've reached the hut and Mama's probably listening in. I step over the threshold, my eyes adjusting to the darkness. The smell of smoke and porridge is heavy in the small room.

"Bryn," Mama says, "don't let your breakfast burn." She points to the hearth, where the pot of porridge is about to bubble over.

As I save breakfast from the fire, Papa shrugs out of his coat and tells Mama about his conversation with Oskar. He doesn't mention the competition or our conversation outside, but he doesn't have to. Mama looks at me anyway. She knows what I want.

I've been dreaming about being a Seeker ever since I was old enough to understand Papa's stories. He'd come home with pockets full of starflowers and dragon scales and tell me about flights up the mountains and over the oceans, about nursing wounded icefoxes or gyrpuffs back to health, about tracking unicorns and flying on dragons and countless other adventures.

All that stopped two years ago, when Papa hurt his leg. Since then, there have been no more stories and no more starflowers. I always knew I wanted to be a Seeker, but now I *have* to do it. Someone has to bring the starflowers back.

Mama retrieves four bowls from the drying rack and lines them up on the table. "Serve breakfast while I fetch Elisa," she says to me. Papa crosses the room, his boots thudding against the earth, and hangs his coat by the fire as Mama ducks under the clothesline dividing the kitchen from the sleeping areas.

I ladle four bowls of porridge and set the table for breakfast, sliding into my seat at Papa's right. A minute later Mama and Elisa emerge from the bedroom. Elisa's breathing is raspier now than it was earlier. She had another coughing fit last night, a bad one. Mama's been trying to use the last of our medicine sparingly, but she was forced to break out more starflower paste to ease my sister's breathing.

Elisa slides into the chair across from me, already chattering excitedly to Papa. He smiles and laughs with her, hiding the worry in his eyes. Maybe he's wondering what I'm wondering—how much starflower medicine we have left and what we'll do when we run out.

Back when Papa was a Seeker, we never worried about it. Mama would serve Elisa tea steeped in starflower leaves every morning to keep the coughs away, and she'd grind the petals into a thick paste, which we'd carry in little jars at all times in case of a fit. Elisa's had trouble with her lungs since she was born, but I never thought about it as a real problem before. The starflowers don't cure the coughs completely or fix her lungs forever, but the medicine helps her breathe when the fits get bad. Our supply seemed endless, until Papa got hurt and the starflowers stopped coming. Now there's no more tea, and our supply of paste is dwindling.

It's up to me to become a Seeker just like Papa did, so we can have starflowers again.

As Mama and Papa chat with Elisa, I let my mind drift to thoughts of the competition. There hasn't been one since Papa got hurt two years ago, and I wasn't old enough then to compete. I watched the finals just like everyone else in the village, but I wasn't allowed to see any of the training beforehand. I'm not sure what it will be like or how hard it will be. I share Papa's nature gift, and that's got to count for something. But the gift alone isn't enough. I have to be skilled in all areas of magic to win.

But I'm Seeker Jakob's daughter. If anyone can be a Seeker, it's me.

I've known it since I was five, when I first discovered my gift. Some kids find theirs even earlier, so I was a little worried that mine would never come. But then it happened.

Runa and I were playing on her family's farm when her sheepdog started barking at the edge of the trees. We followed him into the woods and heard a strange sound. It was a high-pitched whine, like a dog, and we eventually found the clump of bushes it was coming from. Runa was scared to investigate, but I stepped slowly toward the bush and peered between the leaves, only to see a pair of big brown eyes staring back at me. It was a little sea-wolf cub, all alone.

I had never seen a sea wolf before, since they were supposed to live in the Wild Realm, but I knew what it was. I'd seen Papa's drawings of sea wolves in his sketchbook. They're typically smaller than regular wolves, and they have reddish-brown fur instead of gray. This little one was small even for a cub, so small I probably could've lifted it with one hand, and its fur was definitely brown. Energy radiated from it, like nothing I'd ever felt before. Its life spark was so bright, so intense, that I knew this creature was magical.

"Why's it all alone?" Runa asked. "Do you think it's abandoned?"

"I don't know," I said. "We should tell my papa. He'll know what to do."

"But if we leave, how will we find him again?" Runa asked.

With more confidence than I felt, I said, "I'll find him again. I can feel him."

So we ran to fetch Papa and brought him back to the woods. As I'd suspected, Papa was very concerned about the sea-wolf cub being all alone and so far from his home in the Realm. But, as Runa had predicted, it was hard to find the exact place where we'd seen the cub. I closed my eyes and focused as hard as I could, trying to sense the energy I'd felt before. And to my surprise, I *did* sense something. Faint at first and then stronger. I directed Papa and Runa to it, and after a moment Papa smiled. He could sense it too, but he pretended not to and let me lead the way.

In the end I led Papa straight to the bush where the cub was hiding with my eyes closed.

"Bryn," Papa said softly, "look."

I opened my eyes. Green light was dancing along my hands. The color of my magic.

"I think we've found your gift," Papa said. His smile was huge. "A nature gift, just like mine. And a strong one at that. You were right about this cub."

The green light of Papa's own gift swirled in the air as he used his magic to reach out to the cub, letting it sense his presence and know that we didn't mean it any harm.

"What are you doing so far from home, little fella?" Papa said to it. "You must be lost."

"How could it have left the Realm?" I asked him.

"Sea wolves prefer the ocean to land," he said. "They'll stay on shore only to sleep, care for their young, or nurse an injury. The packs regularly climb down from the Realm to make their way to the sea, where they hunt for seafood. They can swim incredible distances and hold their breath underwater for hours, you know. This little one probably wandered off while the pack was in transit, and now he's lost. He shouldn't be this far south."

After a moment Papa reached into the bush and carefully lifted the cub out, wrapping it firmly in his coat. "Never do this without training, girls," he said to me and Runa. "Sea wolves can bite and claw you if they feel threatened."

"Are you taking him back to the Realm?" I asked.

"Yes," Papa said. "The other Seekers will help me find his home. Sea wolves are very loyal to members of their packs— I'm sure this little one's packmates will be looking for him."

I watched the wolf cub as he peeped out of Papa's coat, staring at me. He was so cute, with tufted fur and puppy-dog eyes. My gift mixed with the cub's own energy, filling the air with magic. I'd never felt such a powerful connection as I did in that moment.

"Can I go with you?" I asked Papa as we walked out of the woods. "I want to see the cub find his pack."

"I'm sorry, Bryn," Papa said. "But you know the rules. Only Seekers can go into the Realm."

"Why?" I asked.

"Because," Papa said gently, "the Realm belongs to the magical creatures who live there, not to us. If too many people tried to travel there and take the magic of the Realm for themselves, it could ruin the land forever."

"But I'm just one person," I said, "and I'd be there for a *minute*."

"I know," Papa said gently, "but we all follow the rules. If I let you come into the Realm once, then you'll just want to come back again and again. And what about Runa? She found the cub too, so it wouldn't be fair not to bring her along. And if I bring guests into the Realm, then it would only be fair to let the other Seekers do that too. . . . Do you see? If we start making exceptions, then the rules will have no meaning. This is why everyone agrees that only Seekers may enter the Realm."

"Okay," I said, "then make me a Seeker."

Papa laughed. "All in good time, Bryn. You have to be at least twelve years old to be a Seeker. And besides, there can only be five at once."

"Why?"

"Five is nature's number—the number of the five gifts. Long ago, when our people first settled in this village, it was believed that five was the proper number to maintain balance within the Realm, and so they appointed five Seekers, one with each of the five gifts."

"But we don't do that anymore. You have a nature gift, and so does Seeker Oskar. That's two Seekers with the same gift, not one of each."

"That's true," Papa says. "Some of the gifts are rarer than others, so we don't always have each of the five gifts represented at the same time. But there have always been five Seekers, and we always follow that tradition."

"Well, it's a dumb tradition," I said.

The sea-wolf cub made a little whimpering sound, and Papa gently stroked its back to soothe it. "Don't worry," he said to me. "With such a strong nature gift, you'll be a Seeker in no time."

I believed him then, and I believe him now. Ever since that day, becoming a Seeker is all I've ever wanted. And I know, deep down in my heart, that I was meant to do it. I connected with that little sea-wolf cub so easily, so naturally, and it was the best connection I've ever felt.

There's just one teeny-tiny problem with my becoming a Seeker, the part of our tradition that Papa didn't tell me that day in the woods, but that I soon figured out.

Only boys have ever been Seekers.

What I didn't really understand when I was five is that the men in our village do most of the jobs—they are the fishermen and the shopkeepers and the blacksmiths and the doctors. Some people in our village say that it's because men have stronger magic and are better suited to jobs that are considered harder, while women's magic is supposedly better suited to household work. But that doesn't make any sense to me. I mean, I've met most of the boys in the village, and there's no way their magic is stronger than mine. I think the real reason is just that it's always been this way and people don't know how else to do it.

But some traditions are in need of changing. Besides, once people in the village see what my magic can do, they'll know what I know—that nobody's going to make a better Seeker than me.

THREE

I wake early the next morning, filled with anticipation. They'll probably announce the Seeker competition today.

"Wild child," Mama says with a sigh, swatting me away from the stove, "take all that energy outside."

Grateful for the escape, I leave the breakfast dishes on the table and dash out to the garden. Clouds roll in over the horizon, promising another summer rain. I rush down the path, heading into the center of the village.

I stop in the middle of the main square, where a massive old birch tree marks the very center of town. This is the place where the announcement will be made.

I'm not the only one who's waiting. Johann and his little brother, Aron, dart in and out of the square, pelting each other with bilberries. They both work as village criers, so they're likely waiting for the news.

I'm not thrilled to see them. I tried to be a crier too, once, but the villagers always listened to the boys and didn't take me seriously. I might've kept at it anyway, but Mama made me stop, since she didn't approve of me "running wild around town," as she put it. Johann and Aron have been smug about it ever since, so I mostly try to avoid them as much as possible.

Another potential competitor lurks across the street, gazing toward the birch tree and shielding his eyes from the sun. Tomas is fourteen, the perfect age to audition. The minimum is twelve, since most people's gifts fully mature around that age. It's technically open to anyone older than that, but most boys in the village start working full-time by fifteen or sixteen, and then they usually can't abandon their jobs for several weeks in order to train for the competition. Tomas will likely be one of the oldest competitors, which could be an advantage for him. And he's one of the best young healers in the village, not to mention Seeker Freyr's son. There's no way he won't compete.

I lean against the tree and settle in, but I don't have to wait long. A few minutes later, a Seeker makes his way up the path toward the square, his long, forest-green cloak sweeping the ground. It's Seeker Larus, who will be the oldest Seeker once Oskar retires and therefore the new head of the council.

Johann and Aron suddenly drop to attention, abandoning their berries and moving closer to the tree. Tomas crosses the street to join us.

"Move, Bryn," he says, brushing past me. "They're about to announce the Seeker competition, and you're in the way."

I grit my teeth. "That's why I'm here."

Tomas's eyebrows draw up. "So it's true, then. You really think you're going to compete?"

"Why can't I?"

"Because you're a girl, duh," says Johann as he draws closer.

"So? I'm a naturalist, and I'm good at it."

"But girls don't use magic that much. They don't even have jobs," Johann says.

Tomas shakes his head slowly, but before he speaks, his attention is drawn away by the arrival of Seeker Larus.

"I have an announcement," Seeker Larus says gravely to the brothers. He hands Johann a small vial that glows blue from within. Crushed starflower, as payment for his services. "Make sure everyone in the village hears, all right?"

"Of course," Johann says, drawing himself up proudly. "What's the announcement?"

Tomas and I lean in, straining to hear.

"There will be a competition," Seeker Larus says slowly, "to determine our next Seeker."

He pauses, and the boys nod eagerly for him to continue. "There will be three rounds of competition. Three trials that must be passed. Each one will be held in the arena; the first will be held one week from today, the second one week after that, and so on. Some competitors will be eliminated after each of the first two trials, while the final will determine our next Seeker. To prepare potential Seekers for the competition, Seeker Agnar will hold training sessions every afternoon in the arena. Anyone who wishes to compete is strongly encouraged to attend the training. The first session will be held today."

He smiles down at the boys, who grin back. "Spread the word."

The brothers take off, running through the square and shouting the news. Passing villagers stop to listen, and shopkeepers emerge from indoors to see what all the fuss is about.

I glance over at Tomas, who nods at me. "Guess I'll see you at training, then," he says.

"Guess so."

He nods again and strides away.

I take a deep breath and break into a sprint.

One of the village women yells at me as I pass—probably telling me to stop running—but the wind rushing past my ears whips her words away.

I arrive at our hut in record time, leaping over the garden gate and dashing up the path. Papa looks up from the bed of potatoes, squinting into the sun. "Where are you going in such a hurry?" he asks, but he's smiling. He already knows why I'm running.

"They announced the competition," I shout, throwing open the hut's door and dashing inside.

Elisa sits at the table, braiding her doll's hair. "What's wrong?" she asks.

I pause to catch my breath. "I have news!"

"What news?"

Mama emerges from the sleeping area, carrying an armful of laundry. "Bryn," she says sharply, "have you been running?"

I inhale deeply, trying to steady my breathing. "No."

"Are you lying to your mother?"

I pause. "Yes."

"Brynja," she scolds, "how many times—"

"They announced the Seeker competition!"

Mama doesn't react right away. She lowers the pile of laundry into the nearest chair.

"The first training session is this afternoon in the arena," I say quickly when Mama doesn't speak. "Can I go? Pretty please can I go?"

Elisa sets down her doll, her eyes darting back and forth between Mama and me.

"I don't suppose there's any dissuading you," Mama says finally. "Dissuading" is the word she uses when she really means telling me not to do something. She "dissuades" a lot.

"Thank you thank you thank you!" I give Mama a hug. Elisa laughs, and I dance around the tiny kitchen.

"Does this mean you're going to be a Seeker, Bryn?" Elisa asks.

"I have to win the competition first."

"Of course you'll win," Elisa says. "Will you get to ride the dragons like Papa did?"

"Yep! I'll get to fly them into the Realm and—"

Elisa frowns. "But then you'll go away all the time and we'll never play anymore."

"Sure we will," I say. "We can play dolls every night if you want. Just not while I'm at training."

Elisa pushes her doll pointedly in my direction. "You're not at training *now*."

I sigh, dropping into the chair beside her. "Okay, we can play now. But then I have to go to training. I can't be late on the first day."

Mama purses her lips and doesn't say anything. She crosses the room and steps out the front door. Going to talk to Papa, probably.

As I help Elisa braid her doll's hair, I glance out the window. My parents' shadows are visible in the garden, but I can't hear what they're saying.

Whatever it is, Mama isn't happy about it when she comes back inside. She strides toward the bedroom without saying anything, disappearing behind the clothesline.

"Bryn." Papa stands in the doorway, his shadow looming over the threshold. "Come help me in the garden for a minute, please."

I leave Elisa and her doll and step warily outside. Papa limps over to the stone bench propped at the side of the low fence. "Yes, Papa?" I say quietly, taking a slow step forward.

He lowers himself wearily onto the bench. "So I hear your Seeker training begins today."

"You already told me I could do it," I say, fear twisting knots inside my stomach.

"I did." Papa smiles. "And I believe that you will win that competition easily, if that's what you want."

"Of course it's what I want."

"Are you sure?" When I don't answer—because the answer is obvious—he sighs. "Your mother has some . . . concerns. And she's not wrong, Bryn."

I swallow hard. "What kinds of concerns?"

"You know your mother. She worries about your safety."

I roll my eyes. "It's perfectly safe."

"Bryn . . ."

"Your injury was an accident. You said yourself it hardly ever happens. 'A well-trained Seeker is in no danger from the creatures of the Realm.' That's what you told me once."

"I did say that," Papa says slowly, "but . . ."

"And I'll be really, really careful. I promise."

"I know you will."

"And I'll work really hard at training, and—"

"I know." Papa sighs again, like he's steeling himself for whatever he's about to say. "Not everyone in the village will be happy about you competing."

I look down at the dirt, thinking about what Johann said earlier. "I know not everyone thinks girls are good at magic. But they'll change their minds. Once they see . . ."

"People can be set in their ways."

I'm not totally sure what he means, but it doesn't matter. "I'll just have to prove them wrong, then."

Papa studies me silently.

"I don't care what people say about it," I continue, my voice firm. "They'll change their minds. There's no rule that says girls can't be Seekers. They have to let me try."

"That they do," Papa says, smiling. "Your mother and I just worry that it will be . . . more challenging than you expect. And we don't want you to be disappointed."

"I know."

"Just . . . be prepared for what may come."

"All right," I say, rocking back impatiently on my heels. "Is that all?"

Papa smiles. "That's all."

"I have to leave now, then." I pause. "Have any advice for my first day?"

He laughs. "You know Seekers aren't supposed to provide an unfair advantage to anyone."

I bite my lip. Papa technically isn't a Seeker anymore, so that rule doesn't really apply. He won't get a say in any of the judging. But I can't say that out loud—it might hurt his feelings.

Papa reaches into his pocket and withdraws a small, square object wrapped carefully in linen. His most prized possession: a sketchbook. He says that paper is more common on the mainland, but here on the island it's rare, since we have no way to manufacture it. Papa managed to barter for a few pieces from a trading ship years ago. He then bound the precious pages into a sketchbook with a thin strip of leather.

He gingerly unwraps the covering, as he's done so many times before, and gestures for me to sit beside him. As I settle onto the bench, he carefully flips through the sketchbook.

I've seen his drawings hundreds of times, but they never fail to amaze me. In bold strokes of ash and charcoal, Papa has brought each of the Realm's creatures to life upon the page. On one, a phoenix rises from a sea of fire, its wings tipped in flame; on another, a majestic unicorn rears up, tossing her mane.

"Let's see how well you've been paying attention," Papa teases, flipping to another page. "Do you remember what I told you about firecats?"

I gaze at the familiar sketch. A massive cat prowls across the page, fire dancing along its paws and lighting the tip of its tail, a crest of flames running along its head and back.

"One of the Realm's largest creatures, aside from dragons," I say promptly. "All firecats produce magical flames from their paws and tails, and males also have fiery crests, which can be used to fight off predators."

"Very good," Papa says. "But what else should a Seeker know about approaching them?"

"They must be approached slowly," I recite. "Firecats can run faster than the human eye can see, and will often flee if startled or spooked. Seekers must never enter their dens, which they guard against intruders with their magical fire. They don't kill unless provoked but can be deadly if mishandled. They've even been known to cast balls of fire toward enemies."

"And if you find a firecat, what else might you find?"

I have to think about this one for a second, but then I remember. "Firecats often make their dens near volcanic hot springs—that's their water source. And hot springs are also home to gulurberries and other magical plants."

Papa nods and flips to the next sketch. A creature with a long, coiled body like a serpent stretches across the page, webbed crests dotting its length. A pair of horns springs from its forehead. Its two sets of short legs end in webbed feet, and its jaw stretches wide, revealing a forked tongue and pointy teeth.

"A vatnavera," I say immediately. "Dwells only in fresh-water glacial lakes. A shape-shifter that can change elements of its appearance including size and shape, but usually resembles a horned serpent. Eats mostly fish and has never been known to harm a human, though it may grow to massive size and sharpen its teeth to scare them away."

"What else might they do if frightened?" Papa prompts.

"Shrink really small so they can hide."

"And what's one thing Seekers must watch for in order to care for them?"

"Make sure that their lakes don't grow too warm," I say. "They're unaffected by cold but don't like heat and avoid sunlight. Lakes that are too close to the volcanic region may overheat and need to be cooled."

"And what magical items can be gathered from them?"

This one's easy. "They sometimes shed their scales when

they shape-shift, depending on what form they take. Vatna-vera scales are softer than dragon scales, so they don't make for good weapons or shields like dragon scales do, but they still have magical properties in potions when combined with certain herbs and plants."

Papa smiles. "You don't need any advice," he says. "You're ready."

"Thank you." With one last, longing glance at the sketch-book, I stand. "I'd better get going. I'll see you at dinner!"

"Don't be late," he calls. As I run through the gate and onto the path, his laughter fills the air behind me.

The arena lies a few miles outside the edge of the village, in a low clearing near the shoreline. Mountains border it to the north, their peaks rising so high that from this distance I can't even see the tops.

The arena itself is built from massive chunks of stone that fell from the mountains during a rockslide caused by a volcanic eruption many years ago—or so the stories say. The villagers of old constructed tiered benches to encircle the arena's edges, allowing spectators to observe the competitions. But for now the benches remain empty.

I enter the arena under the curved stone archway. A small crowd of boys stands around in the center of the massive open space. There's no sign of any of the Seekers. But then, I'm still very early. The sun isn't directly overhead yet, so it's not quite noon.

I keep to the edge of the arena, taking a minute to size up my competition.

Most of the boys are showing off, using their magic to do flashy tricks. Johann is utilizing the strength of his warrior gift to levitate heavy rocks and send them spinning through the air. The other boys shout and applaud like it's a big deal, but I'm not worried. While warrior gifts look impressive on the surface, they don't give you much of an advantage when it comes to tracking, healing, or caring for animals. Besides, Seeker Agnar has the warrior gift too, so I doubt they'll want another. They need a naturalist more. Which means they'll probably focus on naturalist skills over warrior skills during the competition, and it will probably influence the Seekers as they judge the results.

One of the older village boys, fourteen-year-old Emil, raises his hands and forms a shimmery shield of purple magic in the air, letting Johann's rocks bounce off it. A defender gift. They are important for Seekers, since they have to pre-serve the shields that encircle the boundaries of the Realm, so he might be decent competition. But Seeker Ludvik is a defender, so they don't really need a second. Besides, I have a feeling Emil is too energetic to stay focused on any one task for long. He'll probably get bored and wander off before training even finishes.

Tomas is here, of course. He lounges casually beside the nearest bench, as if he couldn't care less about this whole thing, but I know better. I saw how eager he was when the announcement was made. He's a healer, and unlike the other boys, he might actually know a thing or two about magical creatures. Plus his father, Seeker Freyr, has probably taught him as much as my father has taught me. The Seekers are supposed to remain impartial while judging the competition, but having a father on the council will likely help him.

There are a few other boys as well, but none that I'd consider major competition. I'm the only naturalist in sight—the nature gift is rare enough that I'm the only one of the right age. That will work in my favor, for sure.

"Hey, it's Bryn," Johann shouts, pointing at me. He and Emil laugh, and heads turn in my direction.

"What's *she* doing here?" someone asks loudly.

Several of the boys whisper to each other, and someone laughs.

Heat floods my face. I was hoping they wouldn't act weird about this and would just accept that I'm here. Maybe I can convince them if I just act like I belong. I tilt my chin, holding my head up, and stride forward, joining the boys in the center of the space.

"What are you doing here, Bryn?" one of the boys asks. "Don't you know this is the Seeker training?"

I ignore him, crossing my arms firmly over my chest.

He shouts something else, but I turn away, forcing myself not to pay attention.

Across the arena, a short figure approaches from under

the archway. Another competitor, most likely, but probably not anyone I need to worry about—

Or not.

It's Ari.

Unlike the rest of us, Ari isn't a naturalist, a defender, a healer, or a warrior. His magical specialty is called empathy, and it's the rarest of the five gifts. There's never been an empath Seeker during my lifetime. But it's a talent that could certainly serve him well.

Empaths can sense the energy of other living beings even better than naturalists can. They can feel the emotions of others, meaning they can tell when someone is sad or hungry or in pain. While naturalists can detect the life sparks of plants and creatures and help nurture them with their magic, empaths are more closely attuned to what people and animals are feeling. And that could be an incredibly useful gift when working with the beings of the Realm. Ari will be able to detect and communicate with magical creatures more directly than any of the rest of us. He'll be able to sense their needs. Some people say that empaths can influence the emotions of others, too.

A tiny knot of fear lodges in my stomach. If there's anyone other than a naturalist who the Seekers might want to consider, it's Ari.

He's my biggest threat.

He makes his way slowly across the arena, joining the rest of us in the center. A few of the boys greet him, but mostly they look away. Ari isn't particularly popular among the village kids—he keeps to himself.

He glances in my direction, but if he's startled to see a girl here, he doesn't let on. He tucks his hands casually in the pockets of his jacket and scuffs a pattern in the dirt beneath his feet.

"*This* is our competition?" Emil sneers. "A girl and an empath? This is going to be so easy!"

Johann laughs, and so do a couple of others. My heart races, but Ari doesn't look up. I try to channel some of his calm. *I don't care. I don't care. I don't care. . . .*

Emil shouts something else, but he's cut off by Tomas, who is gazing toward the entrance of the arena. "Shut up," he says. "Seeker Agnar's here."

Sure enough, Seeker Agnar is striding briskly toward us, his long green cloak flapping. Agnar is the youngest of the current Seekers, only eighteen, with a short-cropped beard and trim dark hair.

He's the man who replaced my father.

Ari looks up from the dirt, glances at Seeker Agnar, and frowns, his mouth twisting into a strange line.

"Welcome," Seeker Agnar says, drawing to a slow halt in front of us. "I'm pleased to see so many fresh faces here today." He scans the group, his eyes lingering on each of us—

His eyes lock with mine, and he freezes. "Jakob's daughter," he says quietly. "What are you doing here?"

My mouth goes dry. Everyone swivels to stare at me.

I will myself to speak clearly and firmly. Once I explain, he'll understand. "I'm here to train," I say. "I'm going to compete to be a Seeker."

For a long moment, only silence meets my words.

"But you're a girl," one of the boys says. I don't see which one—I keep my gaze fixed on Seeker Agnar, waiting to see what he'll say.

When he doesn't speak, I raise my voice. "There's no rule that says girls can't be Seekers."

"There's never been one before," Emil scoffs.

"There's no rule that says I can't compete," I say louder, hoping my voice will stay steady.

Silence.

A shiver of fear races up my spine. I thought for sure the Seekers wouldn't care about letting me compete . . . but what if they do? Was this what Papa was trying to warn me about?

"That may be true," Seeker Agnar says at last. "But I cannot in good conscience encourage you to do so."

It feels like all the air has been forced from my lungs. Before I can respond, he continues.

"This work is not for the faint of heart. The magical creatures of our island can be dangerous. I would expect you of all people to know that, Jakob's daughter."

Tears well up behind my eyes, but I refuse to let them fall. "I can do it just as well as the boys," I say, but this time my voice *does* waver. "I'm a naturalist—"

"Your father would never forgive me if I let any harm

come to you," Seeker Agnar continues. "It's too dangerous. I'm sorry."

"But I—"

"That's my final word on the matter," Seeker Agnar says firmly, turning away from me. "I suggest you go home."

Everyone stares at me, and I blink rapidly, trying to hold the tears back. I didn't expect this, and I don't know what to do now. I can't move. I can't speak.

"Now, boys, let's begin. . . ." Seeker Agnar leads the way across the arena to begin training. One by one, the boys follow him, leaving me behind in the dust.

Choking on the lump in my throat, I finally find the strength to move.

I turn on my heel and run from the arena.

FOUR

I'm not sure where I'm running, but I bypass the path to the village, not wanting anyone to see me. I head for the shoreline instead, picking my way over the rocks until I reach the beach.

The sea is quiet today, and for once I wish it wasn't. I want the waves to slam against the shore, to reflect the turmoil happening inside me. I taste salt water, and it takes a second to realize it isn't from the sea. It's from the tears streaming down my cheeks.

Papa tried to warn me it would be hard, but I never expected this. I never expected them not to even let me *try*. Papa always told me I'd be a Seeker one day if I wanted to be. And while Mama worries about my safety, she never said I couldn't do it just because I'm a girl. She and Papa always told me—

Oh no. Papa. What am I going to say to him? He was so proud that I wanted to follow in his footsteps, even if it worried him too. What will I say now? How can I tell him I failed before I even started?

And Elisa. She always believed I could do it. What will I tell her? Next time she has a coughing fit, how can I explain that we don't have enough starflowers because I couldn't get any? Because I wasn't good enough?

No, that isn't right. I *am* good enough. Seeker Agnar just wouldn't give me a chance to prove it.

I wipe my cheek with the back of my hand, looking out over the water. It stretches on for miles in every direction, large enough to swallow our little island whole. I wanted to see the end of it someday. But there are only two ways to cross the sea—on boats or on dragons.

I know which one I prefer. But it will never happen now.

Somewhere out to sea, a funnel of water shoots into the air. The spray is followed by a low, rumbling bellow. Whales, probably.

No, not whales. The water is churning in a strange, unnatural pattern. Sarvalurs.

I rush forward, stepping into the surf, squinting against the sunlight. *There.* A single dorsal fin, rising above the waves for a split second before diving back under, the water swirling in its wake. Sarvalurs are large sea creatures, much like ordinary whales, but once infused with our island's magic, they seem to have the ability to control the ocean's water, creating currents and waves and even floods. Legend says that if fishermen offer them food, they will help guide the ships with their currents and even lead them safely through storms.

It's not unusual to see sarvalurs in our ocean, but it still feels special every time. A reminder that our island is home to dozens of creatures, in land and sky and sea, magical and not. Papa always says we humans are really just spectators, given a front-row seat to view the most beautiful, incredible animals in the world. It's our island's magic that gives birth to dragons, unicorns, phoenixes, icefoxes, gyrpuffs, sea wolves, vatnaveras, firecats, and more.

But I think Papa's wrong about us being spectators. Most people who live in the village will never see any of those creatures. They might catch a glimpse of a dragon's wing in the sky or spot the fin of a mighty sea creature in the ocean or hear the song of a phoenix overhead. But they'll never *really* get to see them. Only Seekers get that chance.

And Seekers aren't just spectators. They're guardians, healers, trackers, magicians. They care for the animals and their habitats. They ride dragons as they soar. They bring back medicine and other supplies for our village, like starflowers. Seeker magic protects both our village and the wildlife of our island. They keep everything in balance.

There's nothing else I want to do, nothing else I *can* do. Girls in the village usually don't have jobs when they grow up. They're supposed to cook and clean and sew and run their households, but I'm not interested in any of that. How can I be happy watching generations of boys become Seekers while

I stay within the confines of the village? I don't want to live so close to the most incredible creatures in the world without getting to *see* them. The connection I had with that sea-wolf cub meant something, even if it lasted for only a minute. I want to be a Seeker more than I've ever wanted anything.

I don't care what Seeker Agnar says. I don't care if he refuses to train me. I don't need him. He can't stop me from competing. I have a week to prepare for the first trial. I already know more about being a Seeker than almost everyone else, and I already have a strong nature gift. I can beat the others even without official training. I *will* beat them. Somehow.

I can't give up.

I wipe my eyes dry, gaze at the spot where the sarvalur disappeared, and wave goodbye to it.

Then I turn and make my way back over the rocks toward the arena, anger and sadness giving way to something stronger: determination.

I walk through the village with my head held high, not looking at anyone. Luckily the boys are still in the arena, and nobody else knows what happened. I'll have to deal with the pitying stares of the villagers at some point, but not yet.

I pass the turn toward home but don't stop. I'm not ready to talk to my parents or Elisa. My feet steer me over the hill, toward Runa's farm, and I let them. I need my best friend right now.

I find her in her family's sheep pasture, guiding one of

the lambs to join the rest of the flock along with Hundur, the sheepdog. Hundur wags his tail excitedly when he sees me, but he doesn't abandon his job, following the little lamb as she stumbles forward. I reach out to the lamb with my magic and offer a tiny, encouraging nudge.

"Hey," Runa says, surprise coloring her voice, "I thought you'd be at . . . ?"

"Seeker training?" I say. "Yeah, well, apparently Seeker Agnar doesn't let girls train."

Runa's jaw drops. "You're kidding! I thought you said there wasn't a rule—"

"That's the thing. There isn't a rule. But Seeker Agnar is in charge of the training sessions, and I guess he can throw me out if wants."

Runa frowns. "I'm so sorry, Bryn. I know how important this was to you."

"Don't be sorry," I say firmly. "It isn't over yet. This is just a minor setback."

Runa's brow furrows. "What do you mean?"

"They can't stop me from competing. I'm still going to do it. I have one week to get in shape before the first round of the contest. And if they won't train me, I'll just have to train myself."

"Um," Runa says. "Bryn, how are you going to . . . ?"

"I haven't figured it all out yet," I admit.

"But isn't the training, like, important? I thought the whole point of the competition was to see who's trained the best."

I deflate. "You think I can't do it? That I won't win?"

"It's not that," Runa says, biting her lip. "I think it's great, really. I know you'd be the best Seeker. You know more about the Realm than anybody."

"But?"

She looks at the ground. "But there's never been one before. A girl Seeker. Do you really think they'll let you win?"

"Of course. I'll just have to be the first girl—that's all."

Runa doesn't look convinced, but she lets it go. "Do you think it will be hard? The competition?"

"I don't know," I say. "I mean, having a nature gift is definitely going to help." I reach toward Hundur with my magic, seeking out the bright, burning spark of life within him. I give it a gentle nudge with my gift. He wags his tail as he continues herding the little lamb, his natural magic brushing up against mine.

"Obviously," Runa says, grinning. Everyone in the village can feel bits of the magic's current regardless of which of the five gifts they have. Runa's gift is healing, not nature, but she can still sense when I'm using my magic.

"But your gift would come in handy for the healing parts," I add.

"Obviously," Runa says again. She loves to goad me about her magic being better than mine. We're a little bit competitive. And by a little, I mean a lot.

"Hey, you should compete too!" I say, brightening at

the thought. It might not seem so scary with my best friend by my side. "We could practice together. That could be our training."

Runa wrinkles her nose. "Wouldn't we be competing against each other, then?"

"Well, yeah, but it would be fun."

"In other words, you don't think I'd be able to beat you, so you wouldn't care if I tried," she says wryly.

"I didn't *say* that. . . ."

"But you thought it." She grins. "It's fine, Bryn. Believe it or not, I have no interest in being a Seeker."

"I don't believe it. Why wouldn't you want to see the glaciers and volcanoes? And ride dragons? And find starflowers and phoenix ash and gyrpuff eggs and—"

Runa shrugs. "I like animals and all, but I'm not as athletic as you are, remember."

"But you're a great healer!"

"That's not all there is to the job, though."

"Well, no . . ."

She smiles. "I'll leave all the running and fighting and flying and everything to you."

"Okay, well, your loss."

She laughs. "But you can totally ask me for help with the healing if you want."

"What makes you think I need help?"

She gives me a pointed look.

"Okay, *maybe* I'll ask you if I have any questions. *If.*"

"You'll probably be up against the best young healers in the village," she reminds me. "Tomas is pretty good."

"I won't be up against the best young healer in the village, because you won't be there."

"Second best, then."

I grin. "Teach me your ways, O great healer."

She laughs. "I don't know anything about magical creatures, though. You're on your own there."

"I'll figure it out. I don't think healing will matter that much anyway. Oskar was a naturalist like me. They already have two healers on the council. They'll want to replace him with another naturalist."

"Maybe," she says. "But I bet healing will be an important part of the competition. Seekers have to care for any injured creatures as well as tracking them down. Healing was in the competition a lot last ti—oh, sorry." She stops abruptly, looking away.

"It's fine." It's not like I don't know that they replaced my father two years ago. That was the last time there was a Seeker competition, and it's the only one Runa and I are old enough to remember. I tried to pay attention during the contest because I knew it would be my turn someday, but it was hard. I didn't want to think about them replacing Papa. I cried through most of the competition and all of the ceremony afterward.

It wasn't the council's fault, of course. What happened was nobody's fault. It was an accident—Papa was trying to help a dragon that had gotten trapped during a rockslide, but the dragon was so frightened it lashed out at him, and he fell from the cliff. Another dragon caught him, which saved his life, but his leg took most of the impact and fractured when he landed on the dragon's back. It never healed right afterward, despite the efforts of the village's best healers, and he couldn't continue being a Seeker. The council's decision to replace him was nothing personal—they always need five Seekers.

But it was still hard to watch.

"Do you think you'll have to ride dragons or something? During the competition?" Runa asks, bringing me back to the present.

"Not right away, no. They'll want to start with simpler stuff."

"Makes sense. They wouldn't want anyone getting hurt on the first—oh, sorry!"

"It's *fine*," I say again. "Really, Runa, it's okay to talk about."

"How's he doing?" she asks quietly.

"Okay. I mean, he still uses his walking stick to get around, but other than that he's good as new. Really."

I don't mention the part about how he can't do any of the jobs in the village that the other men do. Or that we're running low on just about everything—food and clothes and firewood and starflowers—because Papa's barely scraping by, working odd jobs around the village.

Everyone helps out, of course. Our neighbors ask him

to fix leaks in their hut or help them with their gardens, whatever needs doing, often in exchange for a more-than-fair trade. And his fellow Seekers have even been bringing us starflowers occasionally, and trading them for less than they were worth. But starflowers can be hard to come by, even for Seekers, and they need them for their own families too. There aren't always many left over for us.

The problem is that starflowers only grow within the Realm, where the island's magic is strongest. Collecting starflowers and other treasures and trading them to villagers who need them is how Seekers earn their living. It's what Papa did, before he got hurt. But now we don't have much worth trading.

I used to complain about only Seekers being allowed in the Realm all the time, when I begged Papa to take me with him every day. His explanation for our traditions the day we found the sea-wolf cub did nothing to deter me.

"Why do only Seekers get to go?" I grumbled. "I want to see it too!"

Papa always laughed. "Maybe you will someday."

"Why can't I go *now*?"

"The balance of magic on our island is delicate," Papa explained. "If too many people go into the Realm, they'll upset that balance."

As I got older, I began to understand what he meant. Working with magic is tricky. Like the time a few years ago when I tried to help Mama in the garden by making the life forces of the turnips bigger, thinking I could make them grow faster. But I overdid it. The turnips required so much magic to sustain their new giant life force that they started draining magic from the plants around them, and everything else in the garden died.

The Realm is like that, but on a much bigger scale. There are so many intersecting life forces, so much magical energy, that even the tiniest changes can have unintended consequences. If I did the same thing to a plant in the Realm that I did to our turnips, the results could've been a whole lot worse than the loss of a few garden vegetables. And the more people go into the Realm, especially without training, the more disastrous it would be.

But part of me still thinks it's unfair, that only five people on our island will ever get to see its wonders, to care for its creatures, or to collect treasures like starflowers, which many desperately need. It's even less fair that those Seekers have always been boys.

But once I become a Seeker myself, I can find whatever we need. I can fly into the canyons and onto the mountains of the Wild Realm, where the starflowers grow.

Not to mention the fact that I'll get to see unicorns and icefoxes and phoenixes and all the other magical creatures that populate the Realm. Including real, actual dragons.

It's a sacred duty, to be chosen to enter the Realm. Once I become Seeker, I'll join a short list of people from our village who have been given the honor. And considering how young most of the current Seekers are right now, there might not be another competition for years. By the time another is held, I'll probably be too old.

This is my one and only chance.

"Do you think . . . ?" I ask Runa, but I can't finish the sentence.

"What?"

"Do you really think I can do it? Like, seriously?"

"Of course I do."

"Seriously."

"Yes. You're one of the best magicians our age in the village, you fight just as well as the boys, and you know more about magical creatures than anybody else, thanks to your father. There's no way you won't make it!"

"But earlier you said—"

"Forget what I said. It doesn't matter. You're right. There's no rule saying you can't compete. They have to let you. And you and I both know you're way better than the boys."

"You think so?"

"I know so."

I grin. "Thanks."

She gives my shoulder a playful nudge. "What are friends for?"

"For helping me figure out how I'm going to train myself for the competition if they won't let me train with the boys," I say pointedly. "I have to make sure I'm prepared for whatever the competition is going to throw at me."

"Like a dragon."

"Right."

"Um," Runa says again. "No offense, but this doesn't sound like the most well-thought-out plan ever."

"It isn't. I've had only five minutes to think about it. But I have a week. That's plenty of time to figure out how I'm going to train by myself. And you'll help me, right?"

"Of course I will." Runa bites her lip. "As long as that doesn't involve, like, getting eaten by a dragon. Or burned to death by a firecat. Or—"

I laugh. "I promise not to let you get eaten, maimed, or burned by any magical creatures."

"Or gored by a unicorn horn—"

"Runa! Unicorns don't *gore* people. They're gentle animals."

"But they could. Those horns look awfully sharp."

She grins, and I giggle. Trust Runa to know how to make me laugh, even when things seem bad.

Hundur, having successfully guided the lamb back to the rest of the flock, bounds over to me, wagging his tail. I grin and rub him behind the ears. "Good dog," I say. "You'll help me with training too, won't you, Hundur?"

"Oh, sure," Runa says, rolling her eyes. "He's a regular predatory sea wolf. One who loves having his belly rubbed."

I laugh. "Maybe we could attach a stick to his head and he could stand in for a unicorn?"

"Right, because grace and majesty are really his strong suits."

I giggle. "Well, okay, maybe we'll have to come up with something else for him to do. But I'll figure it out!"

Runa shakes her head. "What have I gotten myself into?"

I nudge her shoulder. "You know you love me."

"Some of the time," she grumbles, nudging me back.

"Just think. Without me, you'd never get into any trouble at all."

"Very true." She smiles. "Everything with you is an adventure, that's for sure."

"And this is going to be the best one yet! You'll see."

Runa grumbles some more, but I can't stop grinning. With my best friend to help me, I know I can do this. I'm going to be a Seeker, no matter what Seeker Agnar or anybody else says.

I just have to figure out how.

FIVE

I stay with Runa for the rest of the afternoon, helping her do chores. Her mother invites me to join them for dinner, but I reluctantly decline. Mama and Papa will worry if I don't go back soon. Somehow, I'm going to have to face them.

As the sun makes its way west, the last of its light streaking across the sea, I run over the hill and down the path toward our hut.

The smell of fish fills my nose as I step inside. Cod stew again. Ever since Papa got hurt, we eat lots of simple, inexpensive meals. Before, we'd get chicken or beef sometimes, and even a lamb on special occasions. But now it's just fish, fish, fish. And usually chopped up in a stew, along with vegetables from our garden, to make the fish last longer. I know I shouldn't complain. But it's one more thing that I'm going to change around here as soon as I become Seeker. I'll be able to sell some gyrpuff eggs or unicorn hair or even extra starflowers, and then we'll have enough money to eat lamb for days. When I become a Seeker, cod stew will be the first thing to go.

Mama bustles around the kitchen, laying the meal out on the table. Elisa helps, carrying over some spoons. "Where have you been?" Mama says as I walk in. "You're late."

"How was Seeker training?" Elisa asks, her eyes wide, but Mama shoos me away before I can answer.

"Fetch your father for dinner," Mama says. "He's down the street at Viktor's."

I gulp. Viktor is Johann and Aron's father, and Johann might be back from training. Has he told his family what happened to me? Has Papa heard the news already?

"Hurry now," Mama says, "but don't run." I sigh and head back outside.

It's a short run from our hut to Viktor's, and I'm hardly even out of breath when I arrive. Papa is in the front garden, repairing a few loose boards in their chicken coop. There's no reason Viktor or one of his sons couldn't do that themselves, but Viktor has been hiring Papa to do lots of little tasks around his hut. Just one of the ways our neighbors have been helping us. Papa says there's nothing wrong with accepting help, but it still makes my insides prickle. We won't rely on the pity of our neighbors once I become Seeker. I'll make sure of it.

There's no sign of Johann or Aron around, luckily. Maybe Papa hasn't heard about training yet.

"Papa," I call. "Dinner's ready."

He glances up from his work. "Bryn," he says, smiling, "how was training?"

He must not know. I open my mouth, prepared to tell him what happened.

And nothing comes out.

I swallow hard. Papa waits expectantly, concern creasing his brow.

"It was fine," I hear myself say. Papa doesn't look convinced, so I add quickly, "Some of the boys were kind of jerks. But I don't care. I did way better than all of them."

Papa smiles. "That's my girl," he says, and a guilty knot twists in my stomach. I never lie to my father.

I've never been ashamed to tell him the truth before.

"We'll have to celebrate your first day of training," Papa says. He rises slowly, gripping the edge of the chicken coop for balance and reaching for his cane. "What are we having for dinner?"

"Cod stew again," I say, wrinkling my nose.

Papa laughs. "Well, there's no reason we can't make it a celebration anyway."

I can think of several very good reasons. Like the fact that I don't feel like celebrating. Or the fact that I just lied to my father and I don't know how to take it back.

Abruptly, a terrible thought occurs to me. Papa is friends with the Seekers, especially Larus and Ludvik. What if Papa talks to them about the competition? What if he asks them how I'm doing in training, and they tell him the truth?

"Papa," I say quickly, "you're not going to talk to any of the Seekers about the competition, are you?"

He glances down at me and misinterprets my concern. "I'm not going to try to influence their decision, of course. That wouldn't be fair."

"But will you talk to them about it at all?"

He frowns, not understanding. "I suppose I might casually check in on how a certain competitor is doing. . . ."

"Please don't," I say quickly. "It's . . . No offense, but it's embarrassing. Nobody else's parents will be popping in to check up on them. I'm already one of the youngest competitors, and I don't want them to think of me that way. Like I'm too young to do it by myself and need my papa to watch out for me. I want to do it on my own."

He studies me for a moment. "All right. If that's what you want."

"Thank you." I swallow down the guilt rising inside me and force a smile. "Can we convince Mama to make bilberry pie for dessert?"

Papa laughs again, resting his free hand on my shoulder. "I suspect we might need to pick some bilberries first."

"They're starting to come into season," I say, putting as much fake cheer into my voice as I can. "I've seen a few around."

"Perhaps we should wait a while, until they're fully in

season," Papa says. "But I can think of something else we might have to celebrate in three weeks, can't you?"

I fake-smile again. "I might have something in mind."

Papa squeezes my shoulder, and I swallow the lump in my throat. He believes in me. Elisa needs me. And I want to be a Seeker more than anything. I have to win that competition, no matter what.

Once I become a Seeker, it won't matter that I lied.

Dinner passes in a blur, with Elisa pestering me for details about training and me deflecting her questions. Mama unknowingly helps me out, changing the subject often. She's still not happy about me competing, though she'd never say so. For tonight, at least, I'm grateful that she wants to talk about something else.

I won't lie to them forever. Just for now, just until I figure out what I'm going to do. I need something more convincing than what I told Runa. I need a plan, one my parents will approve of. If I can come to them with confidence and a surefire strategy, they won't worry so much. And I won't be so ashamed to tell them the truth.

The problem is, I don't have a surefire strategy. I don't know exactly what I'm missing at Seeker Agnar's training session, but I'm sure it involves working with some of our island's magical creatures and learning the spells that Seekers will need to know. I have no one to teach me the magic. And even though I know a lot about our island's animals, that knowledge isn't a replacement for actually working with them. I have no access to anything, not without a dragon that can fly me into the Realm.

I don't know what I'm going to do.

Mama seems to sense my distraction; she only makes me do half the dishes before letting me loose. I play dolls with Elisa for a couple of minutes, but I'm so unfocused that she grumbles and goes off to play by herself in our bed. Papa has returned to his own bed to rest his leg, and Mama is ever present in the kitchen; there's nowhere else in our hut to be alone to think. With no other options, I head outside.

"Don't leave the garden," Mama calls after me. "It's almost bedtime. Don't make me track you down!"

"I won't," I call back, trudging over to the garden bench. It's mostly dark now, and there's not much to do but sit. I rest my chin in my hands, staring down at our potato plants. My magic might be useful for making these plants grow and connecting with animals, but it isn't going to help me get over the mountains and into the Realm. Without access to either the Realm or Seeker Agnar's training sessions, there's just no way I can work with magical creatures for real.

I reach idly toward the nearest plant with my magic, nudging its life force with mine and watching it grow instantly. I twirl my finger, letting the leaves unfurl.

"Neat trick," says a voice.

I jump, looking around. A figure walks through our gate. In the darkness, it takes me a long moment to recognize him. Ari. The empath, and my biggest competition.

I frown. Ari and I have barely exchanged two words before now that I can recall, and he's never visited our hut. His family lives closer to the center of the village, and we don't cross paths much, even though we're about the same age.

"What are you doing here?" I ask. It comes out sounding harsher than I intended, and he flinches a little.

"I, um . . ." He stops, looking down at the potatoes.

This can't be good. Is he here about what happened in training today? Heat rises in my cheeks. Whether he's here to mock me or pity me, either is embarrassing. I don't want that kind of attention. I don't want to be singled out. Though I suppose it's too late for that.

"I need to talk to you," he says finally. "About Seeker training."

"I don't want to hear it," I say. "Unless you can make Seeker Agnar change his mind, I really don't think you can help me."

"That's the thing," he says quickly. "I can't make Agnar change his mind. But I *do* think I can help you."

I hesitate. Ari knows the other boys in the village as well as I do. He has to know that I'm his biggest rival. He should be thrilled I got kicked out of training. "And why would you want to do that? You're auditioning too. I'm your competition. Unless you don't think a girl can be a real challenge?" I glare at him, daring him to say it.

"It's not that," he says quickly. "You'd be helping me out too, honestly. It would be . . . mutually beneficial."

"*What* would be beneficial?"

He pauses, glancing in the direction of my hut. "Can your family hear us out here?" he whispers.

My suspicion deepens. "No, we're too far from the house." On second thought, I add, "Although they'd hear me if I shout for help."

Ari keeps his voice low. "You're not giving up on becoming a Seeker, are you?"

I have to admit I'm surprised. I didn't think Ari knew me that well. But then again, my stubbornness is probably legendary around here. And maybe he's using his empathy gift on me somehow, though I don't really know how that works. "No, of course not."

"Good," he says. "I know you need a way to train. And I need someone to help me out with something while I'm at training in the afternoons. So I was thinking . . . if you can help me, then I'll help you. Whatever we learn in training that day, I'll show you. I can teach you the spells and stuff and go over what Seeker Agnar tells us."

This offer is way too good to be true. Whatever his motive is, it can't be beneficial for me.

I rise from the bench, drawing myself up to my full height. "No offense, Ari," I say. "But I don't trust you. I don't think there's anything I'd want to help you out with. Sorry."

"Wait," he says quickly. "You'll want to hear about this."

"Just tell me, then. What is it?"

Ari hesitates, casting another glance at my hut before speaking. "I have a dragon," he says. "And I need you to help me hide it."

SIX

It takes me a second to find my voice. "You're joking."

"I'm not."

"I—" I don't believe him. It can't be possible. "Where exactly did you find a *dragon*?" It's not like they just wander around the village. While they're free to fly in and out of the Realm, the Seekers use their boundary spells to prevent them from entering the village and surrounding bay, both to keep the villagers safe from dragons and to keep dragons safe from the villagers. They might pass overhead on their way to the sea, but they don't land.

Ari seems to shrivel a little in the face of my disbelief. "I hatched it."

"You *what*?"

He sighs. "It was in an egg. I found the egg and tried to keep it safe, and a few days later it hatched. And now there's a baby dragon."

"Why didn't you report it to the Seekers? It should be in the Realm."

"I know, but . . ." Ari glances toward my hut. "Look, it's a long story, and that's not really the point. The point is, there's a baby dragon that isn't in the Realm, and you and I are the only ones who know about it. I need someone to help me look after it, especially while I'm at Seeker training every day. And you need a way to practice dealing with dragons if you're going to train for the competition. So we can help each other out."

My head is spinning. It feels like this has to be some kind of joke. How is it that Ari just so happens to have a *dragon*? I don't know whether to believe him.

"I know you don't believe me," he says. "I swear I'm telling the truth. Just . . . come with me. See it for yourself."

"I can't right now. My parents won't let me stay out this late."

"Can you sneak out?"

I hesitate. This is probably a terrible idea.

But if there really *is* a dragon . . .

"I'll try. Where should I meet you?"

He tilts his head in the direction of Runa's. "How about the farm on the other side of the hill? It's out that way, and no one will see us there at night."

I nod. "Okay. I'll meet you at the sheep pasture as soon as I can sneak away."

"Okay." He pauses. "Er, thanks, Bryn."

"Ari?" I say as he turns to walk away. "You'd better not be making this up."

It's kind of hard to see in the dark, but I'm pretty sure he smiles. "You'll see."

He crosses the garden in a few quick strides, vaults over the gate, and melts into the shadows beyond.

Sneaking out is harder than I thought.

I curl up in bed and close my eyes, pretending to sleep, while I wait for the rest of my family to doze off. But Mama spends ages in the kitchen after tucking me and Elisa in, and my sister keeps waking up coughing. She tosses and turns beside me in the bed we share, her breathing labored. In the bed across the room, Papa snores loudly.

Finally, after what must have been an eternity, Mama enters the sleeping area. I close my eyes quickly, the light of her candle dancing before my lids. Mama's footsteps are soft as she approaches our bed, checking on us, and I try to lie as still as I can.

A blanket rustles as Mama slides it higher over Elisa's shoulders. Finally, her footsteps sound again, and the flickering candlelight retreats.

I count to one hundred in my head, hoping Mama will fall asleep quickly. Papa's snoring deepens, and Elisa has finally quieted beside me. I think it's safe.

I slip slowly from bed, making sure not to disturb Elisa. The dirt floor is cool under my feet, and I shiver as I tiptoe across the sleeping area. I don't dare glance over at Mama and Papa. I grab a coat from the clothesline—it's impossible to tell whose coat it is in the dark—and creep into the kitchen.

The door creaks loudly as it opens, and I freeze, holding my breath. When I don't hear anything, I slip out through the crack and slowly pull the door closed behind me.

The moonlight guides me through the garden as I shrug on the coat, which turns out to be one of Mama's, and it trails down to my knees. I tuck my braids into the coat's hood and yank it up over my head, both to keep out the chill and to keep anyone I might pass from recognizing me.

Now I run.

As I crest the hill, it's clear I don't need to worry about being recognized. No one is outside, at least not out here. There are no boats out on the water, no villagers walking the paths, no sign of anyone at all. Runa's farm stretches out below me, dark and quiet.

I reach the sheep pasture and jump the fence. Mama's coat snags on the top of the post, and I carefully tug it free, my breath clouding the air as the wind picks up.

"Bryn? Is that you?" a voice whispers behind me.

I turn. Ari strides toward me, his black clothing blending so well with the darkness that I didn't even see him in the pasture.

"Good thing it's me," I whisper back. "If it wasn't, you just gave away the fact that I'm meeting you here."

"Sorry. I couldn't tell . . ."

I drop my hood, revealing my face. "So where's this dragon of yours?"

"This way. Come on."

We run along the edge of the pasture, keeping our distance from the sheep. Yellow light dances across Ari's fingertips as he uses his gift, and I call on my gift as well to help illuminate the night. After a few miles, we reach the end of the fields and the dirt lane gives out, disappearing into the undergrowth. We're on the far side of the bay now, and no one ever bothered clearing a path this far. Water stretches to the south and east. The highlands of the Wild Realm lie to the north. But to the west . . .

A tiny sliver of rocky beach is nestled against the side of the cliffs. It looks closer than it actually is—we have to pick our way through the overgrown brush for what must be ten more minutes before we finally reach it, the soil underfoot gradually giving way to solid rock. The crashing of the sea and the wind in our ears are the only sounds.

"How much farther?" I ask.

"Nearly there," Ari huffs, slowing his pace. "See those caves up there?" He points at the cliffs.

"Um, no." I cross my arms over my chest. "If this is some kind of trick—"

"Reach out with your gift," he says. "Can't you feel her?"

My magic is like a second pulse under my skin, flowing through my body with every beat of my heart. It's always there, but it usually lies dormant until I reach for it. Like I do now. I concentrate on that second pulse, on the feel of the current in my blood, and push it outward. A green light, the color as soft as leaves on a spring day, emanates from my hands as I release the magic from them.

Instantly I sense the other life forces surrounding me. This is my specialty as a naturalist—to detect and interact with the magic of other living things—and nowhere is it more exhilarating than out in the wild. There's so much life *everywhere*, in the trees and the bushes and the birds, the insects and the undergrowth and the—

Oh. *Now* I feel it.

A massive spark of energy, bigger than anything I've ever felt before, is thrumming somewhere ahead of us. It's so overwhelmingly bright that I pull away from it, tugging my magic back. Tentatively, I release the tiniest tendril of my gift, letting it sense the presence of whatever-it-is and guide me forward.

I sense some magic emanating from Ari, too, though his feels funny—I'm not used to sensing empathy gifts. He must be using his magic to feel the whatever-it-is too. Without speaking, we move forward in the same direction.

Once we get closer to the cliffs, I begin to understand. The rock wall is studded with ledges of varying heights, some easily wide enough to walk on. It isn't hard to climb from one ledge to the next and walk along the sides of the rock until, about halfway up, we reach the caves.

"Not that one," Ari says unnecessarily as we pass the

first small cave. The strong, bright energy is still somewhere ahead of us.

We ascend another ledge and discover another cave entrance, this one much, much wider and taller. Big enough to fit . . . a dragon.

Inside the cave, it's mostly just empty space, stretching out into the darkness. The spark of energy feels even stronger as we get closer, becoming impossible to miss. "Where—"

Ari whistles three high, clear notes, and the darkness *moves*.

Ari and I duck as something massive bursts from the ledge above our heads and barrels toward us. I raise my hands to call on my gift, filling the cave with green light.

Hovering over us, suspended ten feet in the air, is the most beautiful dragon I have ever seen.

She's clearly not fully grown, but already she's as tall as a horse and twice as long. Silver, pearlescent scales, some easily as big as my hand, cover all of her body except her wings, which are light and thin like a bat's. A row of pointy spines runs from her neck to the tip of her long tail. Her head is massive, with a pointed snout and two big, gleaming yellow eyes. Each of her four feet ends in five taloned toes, every claw sharp and curved.

With a few slow beats of her wings, the dragon descends, landing about thirty feet away from us. Her scales shimmer, and her eyes are bright. Her life force is a big, burning flame of energy as it brushes against my gift, so strong that simply being near it almost knocks me off my feet.

"This is her," Ari says unnecessarily.

"She's so—"

But before I can say the word "beautiful," the dragon lowers her head, opens her mouth wide to reveal rows of massive, pointed teeth, and charges right at us.

SEVEN

My heart pounds so hard I think it's going to burst out of my chest. I reach instinctively for my magic, wanting to shield myself somehow as the dragon bears down on us—

She skids across the cave, small stones flying up around her claws, and practically pounces on Ari like a dog greeting its owner, her chin knocking him flat on his back.

"Easy, easy," Ari says, reaching up and running one hand under her chin. "I missed you too. Careful . . . easy. That's a good dragon."

The dragon tilts her head back, letting Ari rub further under her chin. Her tail snaps against the ground in . . . contentment?

Ari manages to roll over and stand, stepping carefully around the dragon's claws. "She gets a little overexcited," he says, looking somewhat sheepishly at me. "She's been growing really fast, and she hasn't quite figured out yet that she's too big to keep doing that."

"Oh," I say. At the sound of my voice, the dragon's eyes dart toward me. "Um, hello, dragon." I want to look at Ari, but I'm afraid to take my eyes off her. "Does she have a name?" I say to him.

"Not yet. I haven't figured out what to call her."

I understand the dilemma. It seems impossible to find a word for a creature so massive, so incredible, so *magical*. Her life force is like nothing I've ever felt before, sparks of energy flying off it in different directions.

The dragon snorts, still staring at me.

"I know you've never met another person before," Ari says gently to the dragon. "But you like people, remember? This is Bryn. She's going to be your friend too."

The dragon snorts again. I'm not sure if that's a good thing or a bad thing. I've never had to read dragon body language before.

But I'm Seeker Jakob's daughter, and soon to be the next Seeker of the Wild Realm. I can handle this. Papa taught me what to do.

When approaching a strange dragon for the first time, move slowly. Keep your hands down at your sides. Keep your breathing steady and soft—dragons associate breath with fire and may feel threatened if they sense a big exhale. Back away from dragons that bare their teeth or snarl. Only approach dragons whose spines are relaxed.

I glance at the dragon's back. Her spines are lowered,

almost level with her scales, rather than sticking up defensively. She's relaxed.

I take a slow, careful step forward, barely breathing, my
hands pressed flat to my sides. The dragon watches me.

"It's okay, Bryn," Ari says. "I can sense her emotions,
remember? She's curious, but she doesn't feel threatened."

I don't know if I trust Ari's gift or not. Maybe he's wrong.
Maybe he's lying. Maybe he lured me all the way up here so
I'd get eaten by a dragon. That would certainly be a way to
get rid of the competition.

The dragon's spines stay relaxed. I take another step forward.

She's even more exquisite up close. I can make out the
patterns of color in her scales—she's not really solid silver,
but shimmers with all the colors of the rainbow when you
look closer. Her wings are tucked carefully at her sides, her
massive claws gently kneading the earth.

"Hello," I whisper.

She blinks at me, and suddenly something sharp tugs at
my magic. I gasp as my gift is pulled forward, nearly knocking me over. The green glow of my gift fills the air, colliding
with sparks of bright silver. The dragon's magic.

"She uses her magic to get to know yours," Ari explains
belatedly.

Where my gift touches hers, it swirls and bursts in bright
explosions of light. My magic feels warmer suddenly, and
stronger, like I have all the life force in the world.

The dragon's tail thumps excitedly against the ground, and she releases her hold on my gift. I stagger as magic floods back into my body all at once.

"Whoa," I say.

"She likes you," Ari says.

The dragon lowers her head and rests it on top of her front feet, her curiosity about me apparently satisfied.

"Don't take a nap," Ari says to her. "We have work to do."

The dragon huffs.

"How . . . ?" I start, trying to figure out what to ask Ari first. "I mean, *how*?"

"How am I keeping a dragon hidden outside the village?" Ari guesses. "Or how did I find her?"

"Both."

"I already told you about the egg."

"You didn't tell me where you got the egg."

Ari sits down in front of the dragon. I don't sense much magic coming from him, but a soft yellow pulse plays across his hands, so he must be doing something. I sit down carefully, making sure I can keep both him and the dragon in my sight. I don't trust either one of them yet.

And the dragon is too beautiful to look away from.

Ari seems to be deciding what to say. I get the feeling that he's unsure whether to trust me, just like I'm unsure whether to trust him. Neither of us knows the other well to begin with, and being rivals for the competition makes this even more fraught.

"Let's just say that I found the egg and leave it at that, okay?" he says finally. Apparently I have not be deemed trustworthy.

"You're going to have to give me a little more than that," I say. "In fact, you're going to have to give me one good reason why I shouldn't tell the Seekers about this dragon right now. She belongs in the Realm, in safety, where she can be with other dragons."

"I know that. And I *will* take her to the Realm eventually."

"So why not now?"

"It's complicated."

I raise my eyebrows. "Sorry, but that's not a good enough answer."

"Look, I—I have a good reason for not telling the Seekers, at least not yet. I can't tell you what that is, and you're just going to have to trust me on that."

"I don't. Why should I trust you when you don't trust me?"

Ari looks down at his hands, watching the soft golden light of his gift play over them. "I think there's one thing that both of us can agree on. We both want to be Seekers because we love magical creatures. Right?"

"Sure." There are also a million other reasons, but I don't correct him. I want to see where he's going with this.

He looks up, his eyes meeting mine. "So you can trust me when I tell you that I want to do what's best for this dragon and keep her safe. And right now that means not telling anyone about her. Not until I figure something out."

"So you want me to, what, just not tell anyone that you're hiding a dragon outside the village?"

"Yes."

"And you won't tell me why?"

"No."

I frown. Hiding magical creatures goes against all of our village's rules. It's dangerous for the villagers if someone should stumble upon a dragon and dangerous for the dragon if she gets hurt. So many things could go wrong.

And if Ari and I get caught secretly hiding this dragon, we'll be in big, big trouble.

Which is why I shouldn't agree. But it's that fact, more than anything, that makes me believe he must have a reason. There *must* be a good reason he's hiding the dragon if he's willing to risk getting caught. He's probably not doing this just to have an advantage in the Seeker competition.

Though, admittedly, that's exactly why *I'm* doing it.

Maybe Ari's right. Maybe he really is keeping the dragon safe by keeping it secret, and maybe he just doesn't trust me enough yet to tell me the truth. In his position, I probably wouldn't trust me either. But it still doesn't feel right, not when it goes against everything I've ever been taught about caring for magical creatures.

What would Papa do?

Papa's priority would be the dragon, of course. He'd do whatever was best for her.

But how can I know what's best for her when I don't

know what it is that Ari's supposedly protecting her from?

But maybe I don't have to make this decision right this second. I can try to find out more from Ari, get to know the dragon, get more information. That seems smart. Once I know Ari better, maybe he'll tell me more. Or maybe I'll realize that he can't be trusted and go to the Seekers. In the meantime, I'll keep a close watch over the dragon.

There are several glaring problems with this plan, one of which is the fact that I'm now equally guilty of hiding the dragon and will get in just as much trouble as Ari will if anyone finds out. But there's also a major advantage, one that I can't overlook: caring for this dragon is exactly the kind of training I need to win the competition. It's not just caring for the dragon herself, either.

Because once she learns to fly and can carry passengers, she could take us into the Realm.

"Okay," I begin. "Let's say that, for the moment, I agree to help care for her and keep it a secret. What exactly would I have to do?"

"It's pretty simple, really. She mostly sleeps at night and hunts in the mornings, so it's really only in the afternoons that she needs to be watched; I'm a little worried about her getting bored and wandering off when I'm not around."

"So you haven't warded this place at all?" Not having any kinds of spells to keep the dragon here is asking for trouble.

Ari holds up one hand, the golden light sparking across it. "I'm not much good with boundary spells."

I have to admit that I'm not either. While technically anyone in the village can attempt a boundary spell, only those with the defender gift will find it easy. I knew I'd have to learn it for the competition, but I thought I'd have proper training first.

"How is she able to be so close to the village in the first place?" I ask. "Shouldn't the Seekers' boundary spells that protect the village prevent any dragon from coming so close?"

Ari nods. "I think it's because she was actually hatched here. If she were born in the Realm and then tried to travel here, the boundary spells would stop her. But she was just an egg when she was brought out."

I want to press him for details on how, exactly, a dragon egg was taken out of the Realm and brought here, but for now I decide to let it go. "So how are you going to set the spells to keep her from wandering into town?"

"I should be able to do it once they teach us in training," Ari says. "I just need to learn how."

"So what do I do in the meantime?"

"She doesn't really wander off as long as there's some-one here to entertain her. Just show up and keep an eye on her while I'm at training, make sure she's eating, that sort of thing."

"How exactly have you been feeding her?"

Ari tilts his head in the direction of the cave's opening, and I nod. That makes sense. Dragons typically go for larger fish and sea creatures in the ocean. They're strong swimmers who can dive deep and hold their breath for ages, hunting prey in the depths of the sea. Of course, they'd also eat large land animals if we'd let them, which is why Seekers are careful to maintain the protective spells around the territories of other creatures in the Realm, as well as the village and surrounding farms. Wouldn't want dragons carrying off our sheep.

"But she flies back here when she's done hunting?" I ask. "She doesn't get closer to the village?"

"She doesn't fly yet. She mostly just swims to hunt fish."

"What do you mean? I saw her flying when we walked up."

"She hovers sometimes," Ari says. "But it's mostly straight up and down. I don't know how to teach her to move around once she's airborne."

I don't know how to do that either. Papa never said anything about teaching baby dragons to fly. They're supposed to have their parents around for that.

"Poor dragon," I say. "She's an orphan."

"Maybe not. Maybe her parents are up in the Realm, searching for her. They'll be reunited eventually."

"Maybe. But now she's all alone."

"No, she isn't. She has me. And now you, if you're up for the job."

"Of course I'm up for it," I say indignantly, and Ari grins.

"Somehow I had a feeling you'd say that."

"So what else do you need me to do?"

"Here," he says, getting to his feet in one quick movement, "let's wake her up and I'll show you."

"Um," I say. Waking a sleeping dragon does not seem like a good idea.

But Ari is already approaching her. He kneels down in front of her head and gently rubs her nose, right between her nostrils. "Hey, dragon. Time to wake up. We need to show Bryn your tricks."

The dragon cracks one eye open, assesses Ari, and closes it again.

"Come on," Ari says, giving her scales a pat.

The dragon huffs through her nose, blowing Ari's springy curls back, and I tense. If she added flames to that breath, she could easily have set him on fire.

Ari seems unconcerned. He reaches into his coat pocket, rummaging for something. "Look, dragon. I brought you bilberries," he says in a singsong voice.

The dragon's eyes fly open. In the space of a breath she raises her head, stretching to her full height. Her tail slams into the ground so hard it trembles under my feet.

"She loves these things," Ari says, placing a small red berry between his fingertips.

"I can see that." The dragon is flicking her tongue in and out of her mouth.

"Let's show Bryn what we've been working on," Ari says to her. He takes a few slow steps backward. *Stay.*

"Ari," I say, "dragons are not dogs. They're much more

intelligent. You can't expect them to follow commands like that."

"But Seekers train dragons all the time," Ari argues.

"Right, but only because they form a mutually beneficial partnership with the humans who train them," I say, quoting Papa.

"This *is* mutually beneficial. In this case, she wants the berry, and I want her to learn to stay put so that she doesn't get into trouble when we're not around."

"I don't think—"

"Watch." Ari takes a few more steps. The dragon is watching him *very* intently, her tongue still flicking in and out, but she doesn't move.

"Good dragon," Ari says. "Now, *catch*." He lobs the berry up into the air.

The dragon's wings snap open, and she leaps forward so fast I have to scramble out of her way. She shoves up from the ground, her wings beating frantically, with so much force that the tremors knock me off my feet. Above me, the dragon stretches her jaws and snatches the berry out of the air.

Now that I'm slightly less overwhelmed by the sight of a dragon, I can see what Ari means about her not really flying. She hovers in place in the air, swallowing the berry, her wings flapping somewhat jerkily. Then she drops to the ground directly below, and I have to roll hastily to the side to avoid being swiped by her tail.

"This game keeps her entertained for *hours*," Ari says. "So just bring some bilberries with you and you'll be fine."

I brush the dirt off Mama's coat and stand up, a little shaky on my feet. "Does she know any other words yet?"

"I don't think so. We've just been working on 'stay.' She doesn't really like that one."

"I told you, dragons are too intelligent to want to stay on command."

"Well, she might not *want* to, but until either of us learns how to put up a decent boundary spell, she's just going to have to learn to stay put." Ari tosses another berry, and the dragon snatches it up quickly, not even needing to go airborne this time. Her tail thuds the ground again in satisfaction, and I brace myself against the impact. Getting knocked off my feet twice in a row would be embarrassing.

"She really needs a name," I say. "We shouldn't just keep calling her 'dragon.'"

"What did you have in mind?"

I glance at the dragon, who's now lowered her head in Ari's direction and is snuffling for more berries. Her silver scales gleam in the moonlight.

"Something . . . something about her color," I say. "It's so unique, the way she kind of shimmers. She needs something that fits how unique she is."

Ari sweeps a loose clump of curls behind his ear, considering. "Like 'moon' or something? 'Cause she's shimmery and silver?"

"Something like that," I agree, "though Moon doesn't seem quite right."

"Star?" he suggests.

"Closer," I say, "but Runa has a horse named Starlight, so we need something different. More unique."

"Who's Runa? That's the girl who lives on the farm we met at, right?"

"Right." I forget how little time Ari spends with the rest of the kids in the village. Everyone knows everyone in the village, but Ari is mostly a stranger. A question mark.

Which reminds me how little I should trust him.

"How about something in the old language?" Ari asks, distracting me from that thought.

"Huh?"

"For a name," he says, giving me a quizzical look.

"Oh. That could work." The old language feels fitting for such an ancient species as dragons. Nobody except for the village elders speaks much of the old language anymore, though, so I don't know many words. "Do you know any of the names?"

"Svana?" he says. "I think it means 'swan.'"

I glance at the dragon again. She's huffing at Ari, demanding more berries. "Still not right," I say. "She's not exactly *graceful* like a swan, is she?"

Ari ducks a blast of hot air as she snorts at him, his curls ruffling. "Fair point," he says.

"How about . . . ?" I close my eyes, trying to think of

an inspiration. I want something related to nature—I picture a landscape bathed in moonlight, where the flowers shine. "How about Lilja?" I pronounce it just like they did in the old language—*Lil-ya*. "It means 'lily,'" I explain. It was my grandmother's name, according to Papa. I never met her, but he told me stories about what a strong naturalist she was, and I always thought her name was fitting.

"Lilja," Ari repeats, looking at the dragon. At the sound of the name, she tilts her head and blinks at him. She's probably just trying to figure out how to get more berries, but still, her attention seems like a good sign.

"You know," I say, "because lilies are natural and beautiful and—"

"I like it," he says, cutting off my awkward explanation. "Lilja it is."

The dragon—Lilja—snorts again, and we both laugh.

"See, I knew you'd be the perfect person to help me out with this," Ari says. "You've already come up with a name in five minutes, when I've had days and couldn't think of anything."

"It's true," I joke. "You *clearly* need my help."

"I was thinking," Ari continues, ignoring the jab, "that you could watch her while I'm at training, but then when will we meet up to train together? I promised to teach you everything they show us in the training sessions."

It's a testament to how distracting Lilja is that I'd completely forgotten about that. I'm supposed to be getting Ari's help to win the competition. I can't lose sight of that goal. "Well," I say, "I'll come here when my parents think I'm at training, but of course you won't be here because you *will* be at training . . . but they'll expect me for dinner afterward. So . . ."

"Think you can sneak away again?"

I frown. "It will have to be at night like this, after they're asleep. They won't just let me disappear for hours without explanation."

Ari shrugs. "I can get away from my mother at night easily enough. How about you?"

It *was* easy to sneak away, I suppose. It was a little nerve-racking in the moment, but no one woke up. . . .

"I guess I can do it," I say hesitantly. The idea still doesn't thrill me. I've never done anything like this before, and now suddenly I'm lying to my parents and sneaking out at night all in the same day.

But it's for the competition. To become a Seeker. Right now nothing is more important.

"Actually, yeah, I'm sure I can do it," I say firmly.

Ari nods. "It's settled, then. Just keep on eye on Lilja tomorrow afternoon while I'm gone. I'll take the dinner shift, and you can meet me here tomorrow night as soon as you can get away."

"Won't your mother miss you at dinner?" I ask.

"We don't eat together, because she works in the evenings. I'll just grab something right after training and eat it here."

I'd nearly forgotten about that. Ari's mother actually has a job, unlike most of the women in the village. I'm not sure what happened to his dad; he's lived with only his mother for as long as I can remember. She works at the village bakery.

"Why does she work at night?" I ask. "The bakery is open during the day." Once the question is out of my mouth, I wonder if it might be rude. It seems like the kind of thing Mama would chastise me for saying. *Don't be nosy, Bryn*, says her voice in my head.

But Ari doesn't seem fazed. "They bake most of the goods early so that they'll be ready for sale in the morning," he explains. "She bakes at night, and Olga sells to customers during the day."

"Oh," I say. "That makes sense." I'm having trouble imagining Ari's life—living alone with only his mother and having her gone at night. It sounds . . . lonely.

Ari is distracted by Lilja, who's tapping the end of her snout against his side, trying to find berries in his coat. He backs up, and she follows, half chasing him around the cave. It looks like this could go on awhile.

"Well," I say, "if that's all I need to know, I guess I'd better get going."

"Yeah," Ari says, sounding reluctant. "I guess you'd better."

"You know, because my parents might wake up and . . ."

"Yeah, you're right. Not sure there's much else to do tonight anyway."

"Are you going to head home too?"

Ari shakes his head, his curls flopping. "I'll wait here awhile longer, make sure she gets back to sleep. Wouldn't want her wandering off at night."

"Right," I say. "Well . . ." For some reason I don't want to leave. Probably it's because I'm in the presence of a real, beautiful dragon, a creature I've dreamed about seeing for my entire life.

But also, if I'm being honest, I think I'm a little reluctant to leave Ari alone.

Which is silly. He's been doing this by himself for who knows how long—a few weeks at least, judging by Lilja's size. There's no reason he needs my help right now. And anyway, why should I care when I clearly can't trust him? He hasn't told me the truth about anything, and I still don't know if he's going to keep his word and help train me. He could be planning to lie to me about what happens in training, to make sure I can't beat him during the competition.

He's my rival, and I can't lose sight of that. If meeting Lilja has taught me anything, it's that I want to be a Seeker more than ever. I can only imagine getting to work with her and more creatures like her every day.

I don't care about Ari. I don't care. I don't care. I don't care.

He's backing away from me, laughing at Lilja as she pursues him.

"Bye," I call to him, turning my back quickly so I don't lose my resolve.

"See you tomorrow, Bryn."

I walk briskly out of the cave without looking back.

EIGHT

I don't sleep at all that night.

I can't stop picturing Lilja. How incredible she is, how strong her magic is. I can't stop wondering what it will be like to train her each day, to watch her while Ari is gone, to fly to the heights of the Realm on her back.

And I can't stop thinking about Ari and wondering if I can trust him.

In the morning, Mama notices how tired I am right away. "What's wrong?" she asks instantly. "Are you ill?"

"No, Mama."

She looks skeptical.

Papa smiles at me. "Too excited about training to sleep?"

"Right," I say, latching on to this excuse. "I couldn't stop thinking about it. . . ."

Mama's mouth twists into a frown. "You'll never make any

progress at that training of yours if you're too tired to keep your eyes open."

"I'm not that tired. I'm awake, look." I stretch my eyes open wide. Elisa giggles, and I bat my eyes at her, making her laugh harder.

Mama gives Papa an "I told you so" look. Papa shrugs at her and digs into his breakfast.

"Well," Mama says finally, "don't think that this training of yours and staying up all night is going to excuse you from chores."

"Of course not," I mutter.

"You'd better get going if you don't want to be late."

"Late?" I don't remember needing to be anywhere—

"The docks?" Mama says. "Don't you always meet Runa there on trading day?"

"Oh!" I completely forgot about trading day. Once a month, the ships from the mainland arrive at the docks. Our trading partners—the Ermandi, Laekens, and Midjans—each send a ship packed with all the goods they've brought to trade. Runa and I love to go. Since we've never left the island, trading day is the only time we get to meet people from other lands and learn about their treasures. It's always fun, even if we can't afford to trade anything ourselves.

I rush through the rest of my breakfast and hurry to the village square, where Runa is waiting for me beneath the tree. "What took you so long?" she says.

"I have *loads* to tell you." I can't help but grin. "You're never going to believe it."

We walk together through the small alleyways of the village, skirting around rows of shops and houses and aiming for the docks. As we walk, I tell her everything: Ari appearing in my garden, the deal we made, and the hidden dragon. I whisper as quietly as possible so we won't be overheard, but now seems to be a safe time to talk—everyone has already gone down to the docks, and the streets are deserted.

"I can't believe it," Runa says. "You met an *actual* dragon."

"I know!"

"Do you think Ari's really going to help you train?" A frown creases her brow.

"I don't know whether to trust him or not," I admit. "But I don't have much to lose."

Runa nods in acknowledgment. We fall silent as we reach the docks, the crowds forcing us to end the conversation. Dozens of people have already assembled on the big wooden platforms that jut into the sea. Ordinarily, only the smaller docks are in use, for our village's fishing boats. But today three massive ships fill the harbor.

"So where do you want to go first?" I ask.

Runa's eyes light up. "The Laekens, of course."

I groan. "I should've known."

"The Ermandi can be next, I promise," she says, and I can't help but smile. Runa knows me too well.

The Laeken ship is the smallest of the three, but what

it lacks in size it makes up for in beauty. Its wood has been intricately painted with swirling designs—whorls of red, blue, green, and yellow that match the colorful patterns on their sails. The Laeken are known for their art, and Runa could spend hours admiring the vivid paints and soft brushes they bring from the mainland.

"Hello, Runa," says an elderly woman in a red shawl as we approach the tent that's being hastily pitched on the dock beside the Laeken ship. Elder Margret has been the chief Laeken tradeswoman for years. "Hello, Brynja," she adds when she sees me.

"Good morning, Elder Margret," we chorus.

"Do you have anything new this month?" Runa asks excitedly. "I've still been thinking about that orange tonic from last time."

More than the art supplies the Laeken bring, Runa loves to look at all their herbs and ointments and medicines. While the Laekens don't have magic like the people of our island do, they're known for their skill with healing. Runa loves to ask Elder Margret about all the new ways they've found to treat burns or coughs or colds. Personally, though, I have to say that rows of bottles filled with funny-smelling goo don't appeal to me much.

As Runa admires the latest Laeken wares, I cast a glance at the ship at the next dock over. The Ermandi have the largest one, befitting the largest mainland clan. I never know what to expect from the Ermandi ship, but it's always something new and exciting. Last month, one of their tradesmen showed me a mainland plant I'd never seen the likes of before—it had tall thick stems, cone-shaped leaves, and petals the color of a sunrise. I might not have any interest in plants after they've been bottled up in jars and sold as tonics, but I love them when they're still growing. That plant had a magical energy I'd never felt before, soft and bright all at once.

I take a step closer to the Ermandi ship, but someone in the crowd jostles me, and I bump into a boy walking past. "Sorry," I say.

The boy looks up and pauses. It's Tomas. After a moment of awkward silence, he says, "Brave of you." But he doesn't say it like a compliment; his mouth twists into a sneer.

"What do you mean?"

"Showing your face in public. After Agnar kicked you out of training, I figured you'd be off crying somewhere."

I'm so taken by surprise that I just stand there for a second. But I recover as best I can, drawing myself up to my full height. "Well, you figured wrong. I've been too busy training instead."

Now he's the one who's surprised. "Training?"

"For the competition, of course."

He blinks. "You can't compete."

"Of course I can. I was kicked out of *training*, not the competition."

"But Seeker Agnar said—"

"Seeker Agnar isn't the whole council. He isn't even the

head of it. Unless all of the Seekers pass a rule that says girls can't compete, there's no reason I can't."

Tomas opens his mouth, but he seems to think better of whatever he was about to say and shakes his head. "Well, I hope you *do* show up. It will be hilarious watching you try to keep up with no training."

"I'm pretty sure I'll be the one laughing," I say, "when I beat all of you."

"Sure. If a dragon doesn't eat you first."

"I—"

"Bryn!" Runa calls, interrupting me. She appears at my elbow, and her eyes are wide. Something is wrong—something bigger than Tomas. "Bryn, we have to go," she says.

"What? Why?"

Runa hardly glances at Tomas. "It's the Vondur," she says. "One of their ships is coming here. Right now!"

"*What?*"

Tomas laughs suddenly, causing both of us to look up at him. "You haven't heard?" he says. "The council had a big fight about it. The Vondur keep asking them if they can bring a ship—they claim they just want to trade. Oskar was always one of the Seekers who was most opposed to letting the Vondur come back, but now that he's gone, Seeker Agnar and my father persuaded Larus that it was the right decision. Ludvik still opposes it, but he was outnumbered."

"Why would your father want that? Why would *anyone* want that?" Runa asks.

Tomas shrugs. "It's been ages since the Vondur were last here. Maybe they've changed. And this could be a good economic opportunity for the island, trading with them."

"Yeah, but letting their ships into our waters puts them really close to the dragons when they're hunting," I say. "The same dragons that the Vondur love to kill."

Tomas shrugs again. "According to my father, the new Vondur chief promised the council that they wouldn't harm any magical creatures in close proximity to the island. I guess the council believed them."

"Bryn," Runa says, tugging on my sleeve. "I really think we should go. If our parents find out we were here when the Vondur showed up, they'll kill us."

"Assuming the Vondur don't kill you first," Tomas says with a smirk. "Yes, run along home, little girls."

"You—" I start, clenching my hand into a fist, but Runa grabs my arm and drags me away.

"Save the fighting for the competition," she says, towing me along.

As we follow the path uphill, back to the center of town, I turn and look beyond the docks, out to sea. There, on the horizon, I catch a glimpse of white sails crowned with bright-red flags.

The Vondur ships have arrived.

I find Papa in the garden, where he's practicing magic with Elisa. She has a defender gift like Mama, rather than a nature gift, but Papa still likes to help her nurture her magic. Even though she's only been developing her powers for a few years, she's already strong. Some people have gifts that develop fast that way.

"Papa," I say, "did you know about the Vondur?"

Papa straightens up. "What do you mean?"

"Their ships. They were coming to trading day. Runa and I left before they got there. Tomas—Seeker Freyr's son—says the council decided to let them come."

Papa's expression is unreadable. "I didn't realize they'd be arriving so soon," he says. "But yes, I knew the council was discussing it. And with Oskar gone, it seemed only a matter of time. Some of the younger Seekers have been very . . . *insistent* on the issue lately."

"But why? Aren't the Vondur dangerous?"

Papa doesn't respond for a moment. "They are not known for being peaceful. But things change."

"Do *you* think they've changed?"

He steps toward me, leaning heavily on his cane, and places one hand on my shoulder. "It's not for you to worry about."

"But if I'm training to be a Seeker, then I *should* worry about it," I insist. "The Vondur kill magical creatures. You said so yourself. What if the Realm isn't safe?"

"When you become a Seeker, you can discuss it with the others. For now, though, you should focus on your training. Isn't that where you're supposed to be right now?"

Oh. Right. I forgot Papa doesn't know that I got kicked out.

"Right," I say. "I was just headed that way. . . ."

"Can I come too?" Elisa asks, and I wince.

"I think your mama needs your help here," Papa says to her gently. Elisa must have been coughing a lot last night. Otherwise Papa wouldn't try to keep her at home. He usually encourages us to be adventurous.

I can't help but picture the jar of starflower paste on the kitchen counter. When I saw it at breakfast this morning, less than a fourth of the jar was full.

Papa starts to head inside, but then I remember what I meant to ask him. "Hey, Papa . . ."

"Yes?"

"I was wondering: How do baby dragons learn to fly?"

Papa leans back on his heels, considering. He doesn't find the question remotely unusual, or at least doesn't seem to. I ask about magical creatures all the time. "They usually learn to stretch their wings within a week after hatching," he says. "They'll hover a bit for a few weeks after that, getting used to being in the air. They start truly flying anywhere from three to six weeks old."

I don't know how old Lilja is, though I'd guess from her size that she's at least two or three weeks. "But how do they learn to fly? Is it just instinct? Do they just *do* it? Or do I—I mean, Seekers—have to train them somehow?"

"Much of it is instinct, it seems," he says. "Though they also learn from watching the adult dragons, of course."

I swallow hard. That's what I was afraid of. "But what if there weren't any adult dragons to learn from? What if, say, a dragon egg hatched and the baby was alone? Would it still figure out how to fly on its own?"

Papa frowns, scratching his beard. "Interesting question. How much of it is innate and how much of it is learned? I can't say for sure, since I've never seen a dragon that was raised on its own like that. We always have a plentiful population in the Realm."

"I know," I say impatiently, "but just in theory . . . ?"

"In theory, yes, I expect the dragon would figure flight out on its own eventually, though it might take longer."

"Okay," I say. "That's what I was wondering. Thanks."

"You'd better hurry along to your training. Perhaps you'll even get your first magical creature introduction today!"

I force a smile. The boys will get a magical creature introduction, not me. Though I suppose I have the advantage now, what with spending the whole afternoon in the company of a baby dragon.

"Hey, Papa? Is there anything else special a Seeker would need to do to care for a baby dragon? Like, if its parent dragons weren't there?"

Papa raises his eyebrows. "Why the sudden interest in baby dragons?"

"Um, no reason. Just something Ari and I were talking about in training."

"You should start posing your questions to Seeker Agnar

during training, so that the others can learn from them as well. I'm not supposed to give you any unfair advantage, remember?"

"I know, Papa." I have a ton more questions, but I don't know how to ask them without making him suspicious. He's right—I *should* be discussing all of this in training.

Guilt twists in my gut, but I ignore it. Lying is necessary, just for now, just this once. Papa would understand.

I hope.

Papa and Elisa cheerfully wave me off to training, while Mama huffs and reminds me not to be late for dinner. I wave goodbye, ignoring the sickening lurch in my stomach, and head off down the lane like I'm walking toward the village. As soon as I'm out of sight of the hut, I turn around and cut back, keeping to the trees until I'm past the hut again and headed toward Runa's farm.

I find the beach again easily enough. I can't quite remember which cave Lilja is in, but it doesn't matter. I reach out with my gift, searching for Lilja's magic, and find her almost instantly. That strong a life force is impossible to miss, and I head straight toward it.

Inside the cave, I spot Lilja right away, curled up in a beam of sunlight that's streaming through a crack in the rocks. She's even more beautiful in the daylight, with her scales almost sparkling.

She senses my presence and leaps up, her massive clawed feet thudding into the stone. I wince. We're going to have to teach her to step a little more lightly, or she's bound to cause an earthquake or something when she gets bigger.

I imitate the three-note whistle that Ari used last night, just to make sure she doesn't see me as a threat. "Hi, Lilja," I say as she bounds in my direction. "Remember me?"

She slams her tail to the ground in response.

"Nice to see you, too," I say. "Did you have a good morning?"

She blinks.

"I'll take that as a yes. Okay, how about we do some training?"

Another blink. Her spikes are flattened against her back, and she doesn't look aggressive, so I decide to take that as a positive response. I reach into my pocket, pulling out a single bilberry.

She perks up instantly, her ears swiveling in my direction, her head lowering toward the berry.

"Not yet," I say. "Okay, Lilja. *Stay.*"

She flicks her tongue out, eyeing the berry.

"Stay," I repeat, and back up.

She takes a step forward, her claw studding the earth barely a foot in front of me.

"No, *stay*," I repeat, taking another step back.

She puts her other foot forward, getting closer.

How did Ari do this last night? He made it look so easy.

"Lilja," I scold. "I know you know what that word means. Now *stay.*"

I leap backward in three quick steps, and Lilja lunges,

her jaws open wide. I fling the berry away, not wanting her to bite my whole hand off, and she follows it with her head, snapping it off the ground with a flick of her tongue.

I groan in frustration. "Okay. Let's pause for a second." Papa would *not* be impressed with my skills so far. It's been only five minutes and I already almost lost an appendage.

I try to think back to how Ari pulled this off last night. What did he do that I'm not?

I close my eyes and picture him walking backward, saying "stay," the berry clinched between his yellow-tinged fingers—

Yellow. From his magic. *That's* it.

I don't have Ari's gift, and I don't know how he uses it. But I do know how to use mine.

I've been letting it loose, allowing my gift to collide with Lilja's sparking life force, but I haven't been doing anything with it. Time to change that.

I release more of my gift, watching the green light of natural magic bloom across my fingertips, and reach toward Lilja. She starts as my magic touches hers, diverting her attention from the berry for a split second. I let myself feel her energy, despite how overwhelming it is, trying to get a sense for how it flows. It's like a ball of silver flame, sparking with life. I allow my gift to flow around the edges of hers like the smallest trickle of water: gentle, coaxing, soft. Lilja's head tilts to the side, and she lowers her ears. As I continue smoothing my gift over the surface of her magic, her claws loosen their grip in the dirt.

"There you go," I say softly. "You've calmed down a little now, haven't you? Okay, now we can focus."

I raise the berry again, and her ears shoot right back up, her excitement returning, but I wait for several heartbeats until she steadies again.

"Lilja," I say, not loosening my magic's gentle grip on hers, "*stay*."

I back up a step.

The dragon doesn't move.

I take another step. Her ears shift forward and her eyes follow me carefully, but she's not overly excited this time. She's paying attention.

I take another step. And another. And another.

I'm halfway across the cave before she moves, sliding one foot slowly forward, testing me.

"Stay," I repeat, and she stops.

I don't want to test my luck, so I take only one more step backward. She doesn't move.

"Okay," I say. "Good dragon. Now, *catch*!"

I toss the berry in her direction, and Lilja lunges for it so fast her movement is a blur. I don't even see the moment when she catches the berry, but her neck moves as she swallows, turning back toward me. A few sparks shoot off her energy again as she gets excited for another.

I repeat the trick, making sure she's calm first, then backing away a little more. I get almost to the far end of the cave this time before she tries to move again. It's slow going, having to wait for her to calm down each time, but it works.

Still, I don't want to push her too hard, so I only make her stay once more before tossing a few more berries and letting her catch them. She thuds her tail happily against the ground as she swipes them from the air.

"Okay, Lilja, you're doing great," I say. "But we need to work on this whole flying thing now, all right?"

She isn't really paying attention. Her eyes are on my coat pocket, the source of the delicious berries.

I frown. I'm still not sure how to encourage her to fly. It's not like I can demonstrate. But maybe I can give her a nudge with my magic somehow. It's worked so far.

Besides, what kind of Seeker am I if I can't handle teaching a baby dragon some tricks?

"Okay, Lil, we're going to go really high for this next one. Are you ready?"

She lowers her head and scoots toward me as I produce another berry from my pocket. I step back and toss the berry into the air as high as I can.

Lilja shoves against the ground and lurches into the air, flapping her wings, but she doesn't fly directly toward the berry. She hovers vertically and stretches her long neck out to grab it, then thuds back down to the ground.

I sigh in defeat.

Maybe training a dragon is going to be harder than I thought.

NINE

The rest of my first afternoon with Lilja passes quickly. She has thoroughly mastered the "stay" trick, but I can't coax her into doing more than hovering in the air for a few seconds.

By the time Ari shows up, I'm completely frustrated, and Lilja is now ignoring me and trying to curl up and take a nap. "So I see it's going well," Ari says dryly, taking one look at my face.

"This is the most stubborn dragon in the history of the world," I inform him. "How was official Seeker training?"

"Pretty basic stuff for the second day," Ari says. "We practiced sensing living beings with our gifts."

"Really? That's all?" I've been doing that since I was five. Though maybe it's easier for me, as a naturalist. I can see how someone with a warrior gift would have a harder time with it.

"Yeah," Ari says, shrugging, and I can tell he finds it easy too. "Seeker Agnar did share some useful tips, though. I can show you tonight if you want."

I nod. "Okay. And I was thinking maybe we should try to get Lilja out of the cave tonight. Maybe we could get her down to the beach? We might be able to get her to fly more easily if she has open air to maneuver. This cave is big, but it probably seems pretty small to a dragon."

"Good idea," he says. "So, you'll meet me on the beach when you can sneak away?"

"Yeah, I . . ." I stop. Thinking of sneaking away made me realize that I have no idea what time it is. I run to the front of the cave and peer out the opening to look at the sky. The sun is already setting. "Oh no," I say. "I think I'm going to be late." Dusk is still a ways off, but I also have a long run to get home.

"Go ahead," Ari says. "I can take it from here."

"Thanks," I say. "See you tonight!"

Of course I end up being late for dinner, and of course Mama gets her revenge by keeping me busy with chores for the rest of the night. By the time Mama sends me and Elisa off to bed, I could sleep for a week. But I can't. I have more important things to do.

Sneaking out of the hut is slightly less nerve-racking this time, though it still takes forever for the rest of my family to fall asleep. Cold wind greets me as I creep outside, buttoning my coat tightly. The moon is large tonight, a few days shy of being full, but it's mostly obscured by thick clouds, making it hard to see as I leap over the garden gate and run up the lane and over the hill.

By the time I reach the beach, Ari has already lured Lilja out of her cave. He's tossing berries and coaxing her to fly, but he's having little luck. I linger at the edge of the beach, planning just to watch them for a minute, but Lilja senses my presence and runs over immediately.

There are very few things that scare me, but the sight of a massive dragon with sharp teeth running toward me does, admittedly, make my heart race. Lilja stops just short of knocking me over and gives me a welcoming sniff.

I pat her nose in greeting. "How are you doing, Lil? Ready to start flying?"

"I think we have a defective dragon," Ari grumbles, approaching us. "She just won't do it."

"Maybe she's not ready."

"Maybe." Ari pauses. "So, ready to train?"

"Born ready."

Ari tosses a few berries toward the other end of the beach, and Lilja bounds after them. "That ought to keep her busy for a second at least. Okay, so . . . Sorry, I've never really taught anyone anything before. I'm not sure how to start."

"It's fine," I say. "Just tell me what Seeker Agnar told the rest of you."

"Well, he talked about calling on your gift, which of course you already know how to do. . . . But the part that I liked was when he talked about rhythm."

"Rhythm?"

"Like . . . Let me show you. Close your eyes."

I give him a skeptical look but follow his instructions. "Now what?"

"So, he explained it like this. First, just focus on yourself. Listen to the sound of your breathing, or focus on your heartbeat. Don't think, just listen. You're supposed to get, like, in tune with your own natural rhythm."

"Um, okay . . ." I feel a bit ridiculous, just standing there with my eyes closed, but I try it anyway. I take a deep breath and listen to it.

"Even breaths," Ari says. "Fall into a rhythm with it."

After a minute, I start to relax a little, and my breathing falls into a more even pattern. "Now what?" I whisper.

"Now do the same thing, but with what's around you. Let your gift spread out, and try to find a rhythm in something nearby."

I push my gift out, and it flows eagerly from my fingertips. "Like this?"

"Not so fast," Ari says. "Just a little bit at a time."

I reel it in and try again. My gift hovers only a few inches from my fingertips. "Like this?"

"Yes."

"But I don't feel anything."

"It takes a minute. Just like when you were listening to your breathing. Just wait."

With a sigh, I close my eyes again. For a long moment, I

still don't feel anything. But—a tiny little pulse beats somewhere below me. I didn't feel it at first, but there *is* a rhythm to its life force, a tiny movement that vibrates the air. "I feel something!"

"Without opening your eyes, try to guess what it is," Ari says.

"Well, it's coming from the ground. . . . I think it has a heartbeat, so it isn't a plant. It's . . . It's moving pretty quickly over the rock, scurrying. Definitely an insect. A little one."

"Now open your eyes," Ari says.

I look down at the ground. If I hadn't searched for the life force first, I never would've noticed the tiny beetle, whose coloring blends in with the rocks. I wouldn't even have known it was there.

"Whoa," I say. "Pretty neat trick. But, um, I hope they don't expect us to do that *every* time we need to use our gifts to sense something. Because that took *forever*."

Ari laughs. "I doubt it. Most of the guys in training couldn't even do it right."

"So that's it? That's the whole lesson?"

"I mean, we spent the rest of training just practicing sensing stuff. Seeker Agnar hid a bunch of plants around the arena, and we had a kind of scavenger hunt to find all of them. Not really something you need to practice, I guess, since you can already do that."

"Hmm." I'm not sure whether to believe Ari or not. How do I know if that's really what happened in training? What if he's holding out on me?

Ari, of course, immediately senses my skepticism. His empathy gift at work, I'm sure. "If you don't believe me, you can ask one of the other boys to train you instead. Although I don't think any of *them* has a secret dragon."

"I just may do that. I'm starting to think your secret dragon is more trouble than she's worth." I nod toward Lilja, who's happily sniffing a boulder as if pondering eating it for dinner.

"Go ahead, then." Ari's tone is light. "But don't expect any of the others to actually help you win the competition."

I bristle. "I could win it without your help, thank you very much."

"You're not going to win it regardless. *I'm* going to win." Coming from Johann or Tomas, this might have sounded mean, but Ari grins at me when he says it, his tone teasing, and I get that he's just trying to joke around. Still, I can't let that kind of comment go unchallenged.

"In your dreams," I say. "As if an empath could beat a naturalist."

Ari opens his mouth, but whatever he's about to say is cut off by a loud *thud*.

Lilja, having thoroughly sniffed every inch of sand and rock on the beach, is now staring out at the sea and slamming her tail down against the ground, only to lift it and slam it back down again. *Thud. Thud. Thud.*

"What are you doing, Lil?" I yell as both Ari and I run toward her. The ground trembles beneath our feet.

"She wants to fly out there," Ari says. *Thud. Thud. Thud.* "It's probably some kind of instinct, knowing that there's food out there, and she's frustrated that she can't get it. I can feel it."

Sure enough, the yellow sparks of his gift are dancing around his fingertips. "Can you calm her down?" I ask.

"I can try." The light of his gift glows brighter. "I need to quiet her down before—"

"The other dragons," I say, tilting my head toward the sky.

"No, I meant the villagers. I thought they might hear—"

"No, look! Other dragons! There." I point straight up.

The palest rays of moonlight illuminate the sky, and silhouetted against them are the unmistakable shapes of wings, tails, spikes, clawed feet—

"Whoa," Ari says.

Fully grown dragons practically make Lilja look like an ordinary lizard. Their wingspans can be as long as fifty or sixty feet, their bodies blotting out the sky. I try to count their shadows, but it's hard to tell as they move so fast overhead. One, two, three . . .

Beside me, Lilja makes a strange keening sound in her throat that I've never heard before. As I turn toward her, she leaps forward, her claws scrabbling against the rocky beach. Her wings snap out, and with a few quick strides she launches herself into the air.

"Yes!" Ari shouts. "She's doing it!"

He's right. Lilja isn't just hovering this time. She's flapping her wings hard, stretching her long neck forward, trying to move faster and higher. She sways a little, still trying to get the hang of it, her feet paddling ungracefully in the air like a dog trying to swim. As the larger dragons fly directly overhead, the sound of their wings pounding like drumbeats in our ears, Lilja finally manages to surge forward, getting closer to the cliffs. Ari and I whoop and cheer as she soars. It really, really worked. Our baby dragon has learned to fly. She's really going to—

"Look out, Lilja!" Ari calls, and a second later I see the problem. A second too late. Lilja's wildly swinging tail slams into the cliff's face and snags on a tree. A bigger, stronger dragon could simply tug themselves free, but Lilja is caught so off-balance that she nearly tumbles from the air, dropping rapidly. The tree snaps in half with a loud crack, dragged down by Lilja's weight as she plummets. I start to rush toward her, wanting to help in some way, but Ari waves his arms frantically, stopping me.

"Get out of the way," he yells. We both scramble backward as Lilja tumbles toward the beach.

At the last minute, she finds some balance, her wings flapping wildly, and she manages to land on her feet with an earthshaking thump that probably woke up the whole island, let alone the village. Vibrations tremble underneath us, knocking me to the ground.

I stumble to my feet and rush across the beach toward Lilja, who is shaking her head and looking dazed.

"Are you okay, Lilja?" I ask, as if she'll answer me. I reach for her life spark with my gift.

Ari's hands glow yellow with his. "She's all right," he says. "Not in pain, just confused."

"Maybe we should check her for injuries just in case." I approach her side and run my hand down her smooth scales.

"What, you don't trust my gift?"

I have to stop myself from saying "not really" out loud. As I rub Lilja's side, she twists her head around to look at me, her yellow eyes wide.

"It's okay, little dragon," I tell her. "You almost got the hang of it. Just one more try, okay?" The spines along her back slowly flutter downward as she relaxes. I wonder what it would be like to actually ride her, like Seekers do every day. She's not so tall yet, really. It would be easy to . . .

"Hey, Ari, do you think she'd let us ride her?"

I don't turn to look at him, but I don't need to see his expression to sense his disapproval. "Are you kidding? She just crash-landed and you want to go for a ride?"

"She didn't crash. She landed on her feet."

"A technicality."

"An important fact."

Ari groans. "You can't be serious."

"I don't mean that she'd have to take us anywhere yet. I just wonder if she'd let one of us sit up there. Even just while she's walking around. She's got to get used to us, right? If she's going to take us into the Realm."

"Now isn't the best time, Bryn——"

"Ready, Lilja?" I slide my hands as high up her side as I can reach, tightening my grip along her back, and haul myself up. Ari makes various disapproving noises as I swing my legs around, using the ridge of one of her spines to steady myself. Lilja remains relatively still and doesn't make a sound, as if I'm no more than a butterfly landing on her back.

I sit up straight and look down at Ari, whose mouth is hanging open. "See?" I say, more than a little smugly. But inwardly, I can't believe it. I'm really doing it. I'm sitting on a real, actual dragon, with real, smooth dragon scales beneath me. I wiggle around a little, resting against an indentation in her spine right above one of her spikes, my hands finding purchase on it. "You want to walk around, Lilja?" I say softly. "Get used to me being up here for a bit?"

In response, Lilja's wings snap open. Ari ducks, narrowly avoiding being hit in the face, as I grip her scales tighter to stay balanced.

"Um," I say, "let's take this slow, Lil——"

Her wings begin to move.

"Lilja?"

Abruptly Ari leaps forward, grabs hold of her scales, and swings himself up behind me. "If you're about to fly some-where, I am *not* missing this."

"Maybe we should rethink——" I start, but I don't finish.

Lilja bounds forward as if she were just waiting for both

of us to climb aboard before she could take off. Her wings beat faster, and faster, and faster—

It's all Ari and I can do to cling to her back as Lilja launches herself into the air, leaving the beach far below with just a few beats of her massive wings.

Ari yells something behind me, but the wind snatches his words away as we climb higher into the sky, higher than I've ever been in my life.

Lilja turns in the direction that the larger dragons flew from earlier. The direction of their home.

With Ari and me clinging to her back, our dragon heads straight for the Wild Realm.

TEN

Flying is incredible.

I can't hear anything over the rush of the wind in my ears and the steady beat of Lilja's wings, but I can *feel* everything: Lilja's scales beneath my hands, the cold mist in the air against my skin, and the sensation of *soaring*, of going higher and higher and higher until there's nothing between me and the sky.

Despite the dampness in the air, it's a clear enough night to get a good view. The only thing better than the feeling of flying is seeing the Wild Realm spreading out below us, the landscape tinged with shades of deep blue and black and gray, illuminated only by the moon and stars. I have only ever glimpsed these mountains from their base, but now Lilja flies us directly over them, and it's like we've entered another world. I have never seen the island like this before, and it's even more stunning than I imagined.

The landscape is shadowy and uneven, filled with rolling hills and mountain peaks and low valleys. Lakes glimmer in the moonlight; the dark blurs of forests stretch out as far as the eye can see. Somewhere ahead lie the volcanoes, surrounded by fields of hardened lava, as well as the solid glaciers as tall and thick as the mountains.

I lean forward, trying to peer over Lilja's head to see where we're going, and something tugs sharply on my hair. I glance back at Ari, who looks apologetic. "You didn't hear me over the wind," he shouts. Even though he's sitting right behind me, it's still difficult to hear him.

"Sorry," I say back, raising my voice. "What's wrong?"

He cups his hands around his mouth. "We need to get her to land!"

"Why?" There's still so much more of the Realm to see. . . .

"She's never flown this far before. If she keeps going, she'll get too tired to take us back."

Oops. I didn't think of that, but I should have. I'm still not sure why Ari's so concerned about Lilja being in the Realm, though. He hasn't told me why she isn't supposed to be here, and I can't think of a good reason.

Ari yells something else, but his words are snatched away by the wind. "What?" I shout back, leaning closer in his direction.

"I said, we have to get you back before your parents wake up!"

He's right. I hate it, but he's right. What will Mama and

Papa think when they wake up and I'm not in bed? And what could I possibly tell them to explain where I went? If Mama finds out, she'll never let me become a Seeker. We have a few hours, at most, to see the Realm before we'll have to take Lilja back to the beach and return to the village.

"How do we get her to land?" I ask.

"We need to guide her with magic, the way Seekers do."

Right. I should've thought of that.

I turn around, close my eyes, and reach for my magic. Within seconds, Lilja's energy surrounds me, as bright as ever. I give her life spark a tiny nudge with my gift, urging her to fly lower. Lilja turns her head slightly, snorts, and proceeds to ignore me.

"Lilja," I say, gritting my teeth as I try to keep a grip on my gift. "Don't be stubborn. Come on, let's check out what's on the ground."

As I give her another nudge, something warm and soft brushes up against my magic. The yellow light of Ari's gift blends with the green of mine and the silver spark of Lilja's life force. It feels like a soothing sip of tea after a long day, or curling up beneath a warm blanket at night. It's somehow heavy and cozy all at once, and my eyelids almost droop in response. Lilja's energy grows noticeably dimmer, like she's getting sleepy too.

I understand what Ari's trying to do—make Lilja sleepy so that she'll want to land and rest for a while. It's a good idea, but it's working too well. "You're overdoing it," I yell. "She's going to get too sleepy before she can land, and so am I!"

I think Ari yells, "Sorry," but it's hard to tell. His magic pulls back from mine a bit, and I give Lilja a firmer nudge with my gift. She turns her head again, hesitates, and angles her body toward the ground, flying lower. I open my eyes and grip her spine tightly as we descend.

Only now does it occur to me that *Lilja* might not know how to land, since she's never done this before.

We might be about to crash.

As Lilja drops lower, a new sound is audible over the wind—a thunderous roar below us. I lean forward, trying to see around Lilja's wings, and catch glimpses of the ground—or rather, glimpses of water. Lilja is aiming for a wide clearing surrounding a lake. At the far end of the clearing, towering cliffs drop off, and a massive waterfall cascades from the rocks, the water plummeting into the lake below. The roar of the waterfall gets louder and louder as we descend, and I give Lilja a nudge with my gift, encouraging her to turn in the direction of the shore so she can land smoothly. But Lilja snorts again and ignores me. As we drop through the air, she passes right over the shoreline and heads straight toward the lake.

Ari figures it out at the same moment I do. "She's headed for the water!"

At this point, we're descending too fast for me to try to coax her anywhere with my magic. It's too late.

"Hold your breath," I yell. I suck in a gulp of air as Lilja dives into the lake and water rushes up to meet us.

I try to hold on to Lilja's back, but it's no use—the impact sends me spinning, water rushing all around me. I open my eyes, but it's so dark and the water is so turbulent that I can't see anything. I reach for my gift. Lilja's life force is somewhere below me. There are small sparks everywhere, probably fish and plants, but it feels like there are trees above me. I start swimming, aiming for those sparks. The surface has got to be somewhere above. . . .

My lungs burn. I swim faster, straining for the surface, trying desperately not to inhale and choke. The water churns. It's so cold that every part of me feels numb. I need air. Air. Air.

I rise what must be six feet, my limbs thrashing, my magic flung in every direction, seeking the surface. I can't breathe, I can't breathe, I can't—

Lilja's life force suddenly engulfs me, and something hard presses against my back, propelling me forward. In seconds, I rise through the water and the surface breaks around me.

I gulp for air, gasping and spluttering. Something solid rests beneath my back, lifting me out of the lake. I blink water from my eyes, but it's hard to make anything out in the darkness. The waterfall is somewhere behind me, its roar muffled by all the water clogging my ears. I wrap my arms over my chest, shivering with cold.

"Bryn?" a voice calls. "Bryn, are you okay?"

There's so much magical energy around me, more than

I've ever felt before, and it's making my head spin. Carefully I pull my gift closer to myself, trying not to sense so much at once. Then, just like I did the first time I met Lilja and had to get used to her spark, I release a tiny tendril of my gift.

The feeling of magic is still incredibly overwhelming, but there isn't any one source. It's like it's in the air all around me, and in the earth, and in the water. . . .

Of course. I'm in the Wild Realm now. The source of all magic. This is what the Realm feels like.

As I regain my breath, I release a little more magic. The now-familiar feeling of Lilja is below me, almost as if—

Oh.

I'm sitting on her nose.

I glance down. Her silver scales are bright in the moon-light, shimmery with water. I'm sitting directly on her snout, my legs dangling off into the water. Lilja must have pushed me up to the surface with her head.

She saved me.

"Bryn!"

I look around again, and this time the shadows come into focus. A figure stands at the edge of the lake, not clear enough to actually see, but from that funny empath-life-source feeling, it must be Ari. It occurs to me that he's been shouting my name for a while.

"I'm okay," I yell back, immediately followed by a cough. Recovering my breath, I slide carefully off Lilja's nose and into the water. The dragon's yellow eyes are wide as she looks at me. "Thanks, Lil," I say, rubbing the end of her nose. "Thanks for saving me. But no more water landings from now on, okay?"

She taps me with the end of her snout, nudging me toward the edge of the lake.

"It's okay," I say. "I'm all right." But now that I think about it, I am very, very cold. This water is freezing.

I turn away from Lilja and swim to shore.

Ari waits at the edge and offers me a hand up when I reach the embankment. I let him pull me to my feet and then stop to catch my breath again.

Like me, Ari is drenched. Water drips from his curls, and he's taken off his heavy, waterlogged coat. "Are you okay?" he asks again. "I couldn't find you in the water, and then when you took so long to surface . . ."

"Lilja found me," I say quickly. That's twice tonight that I've felt so embarrassed in front of Ari. I really shouldn't be showing my competitors what a bad swimmer I am. The fact that he got to the surface perfectly fine on his own makes it worse.

To distract myself from the heat rising in my cheeks, I shrug off my coat and wring it out as best I can, the water puddling at my feet. Fat droplets fall from the end of my braid, and my boots are soaked all the way through, as well as the rest of my clothing. I quickly put my coat back on. Even though it's summertime and we're not in the northern part of the Realm, it's still much colder up here in the highlands than it is in the village, and the water is frigid.

I have to hope that the flight back home will help dry me off. Mama will certainly notice if I'm still soaking wet when she wakes up. Maybe I can hide these clothes somewhere. . . .

"Well," Ari says, interrupting my thoughts. "This is it."

I follow his gaze. The black surface of the lake shimmers with pinpricks of light from the stars above. Only the curve of Lilja's back and the top of her head are visible above the surface. The waterfall towers what must be a hundred feet above us, pouring over the jagged cliffs. A clearing stretches off to our right, filled with flowers and bordered by tall, thick trees. Framing everything are the sharp peaks of the mountains in the distance, with the sea lying somewhere beyond them. It's the most beautiful landscape I've ever seen.

We really *are* in the Wild Realm.

"Look, Bryn," Ari says, pointing across the lake. A dozen tiny pinpricks of light are flashing in and out. "Fireflies."

"I wonder what else might be around here," I say. As pretty as the fireflies are, they're common outside the Realm too. I want to see something *magical*. "I wish it weren't so dark," I add. "Then we could see more." I let my gift shine brightly around my fingertips, trying to illuminate as much as I can, and glance toward the clearing, where I can just barely make out the shapes of flowers in the distance. "I wonder if . . ."

I walk away from Ari, winding around the edge of the lake and heading into the grassy clearing. I call my gift into my fingertips, letting its green light shine as brightly as I can to illuminate the ground in front of me.

Most of the flowers look—and feel, with the sense of my gift—like ordinary, non-magical plants. Wild thyme, arctic poppies, and what looks like purple saxifrage and mountain avens are grouped together, along with bunches of white-tipped cotton grass and dandelions. But I sense a few clusters of flowers with stronger, more magical life forces—plants infused with the magic of the Realm that can only grow here. Fireflies cluster nearer to these plants than any of the others. I step closer to one of them, my wet boots squelching, and lean in for a better inspection.

"Fairy clovers," I whisper, my eyes widening. They're fragile little plants, with short stems and four wide leaves that, according to legend, look like fairy wings. The fairy bit is probably nonsense—Papa says fairies have never been spotted in the Realm, contrary to legend—but I do know that if you chop up a handful and mix them with herbs, you can make a magic tonic that cures headaches. I've seen the village herbal-ist give Papa a whole bottle of Mama's favorite skin ointment or two flasks of salt in exchange for only a handful of these clovers.

"Did you find something?" Ari calls, coming up behind me. I tense. For a second I'm defensive—I found the clo-vers, and I don't want to share them. But that isn't really fair. Without Ari, I never could've flown here in the first place. And there are more than enough plants here for both of us.

"Fairy clovers," I explain, pointing. I reach into my coat, searching for the pocketknife Papa gave me for my eleventh birthday. "The herbalist will make a good trade for those."

"We can't," Ari says.

I stop digging through my pocket, looking up at him. "What are you talking about? They're right here."

"Think about it, Bryn. Neither of us is a Seeker yet. Neither of us is supposed to be here. You can't just march into the herbalist's shop with a handful of fairy clovers. How will you explain how you got them?"

I shrug. "I can just say that Papa's had them for a while. He still trades things he found in the Realm sometimes." But even as I say it, I know Ari's right. If Papa had found clovers in the Realm years ago, they'd be dried and yellowed after being plucked from their roots. Their magic would have faded. These are bright and fresh and brimming with life.

With great reluctance, I step back. "Fine. We won't take the clovers. But I really need to find some more starflowers—not to trade, but for medicine. Will you help me look?"

I expect him to refuse for some reason. But he doesn't. "Of course. Where do starflowers usually grow? They're forest flowers, right?"

I hate that he knows that. "Yes. I don't actually think we'll see any this far south. Papa says they're most common in the northern forests. But they do bloom at night, so now's the perfect time to try to spot some."

"We have to hurry," Ari says, "but we can look for a

bit." He glances back at the lake, where Lilja has disappeared under the surface. "She's hunting, I think. So she'll be fine for a while."

"Should we let her do that?" I ask. "We don't want her to eat any magical creatures in that lake."

"Yeah, but we must be within the dragons' normal territory. Otherwise Lilja wouldn't even be able to enter this part of the Realm. If the Seekers haven't put up boundary spells to keep dragons away, then it must be okay for her to hunt here."

A fair, noncompetitive person would probably say that Ari has made a smart observation. I am not that person. "Whatever. I guess we can look for a minute."

Leaving the fairy clovers behind, we circle around the clearing, not wanting to trample the flowers, and reach the tree line. A tangle of trees towers ten feet above our heads. Beyond them is nothing but darkness.

Ari and I exchange a glance, but he looks sharply away. Without a word, we step forward at the same time and enter one of the forests of the Realm.

ELEVEN

There are sounds in this forest that I've never heard before. In the woods near the village, we might hear the occasional rustle of a rabbit in the brush, the chirps of a bird, a snapped twig or two. But here in the Realm, there is so much *more*. It seems as if every tree branch, every bush, every leaf is rustling as the creatures of this forest move through it. These woods are brimming with life.

I'm tempted to cast my gift out wider, to see if I can figure out what kinds of creatures are nearby. But I'm already tired from using my magic so much tonight, and now Ari and I have to use our gifts to cast some light. We both hold our hands out in front of us to illuminate as much as we can, the yellow of his magic and the green of mine casting strange shadows on the ground in front of us. I shiver in the cold night air, my wet clothes still sticking to my skin.

"Do you recognize any of these plants?" Ari asks as we wade

deeper into the trees. "Seeker Agnar hasn't discussed plants at all in training yet."

I smile, hoping Ari can't see me in the dark. While Papa mostly draws magical creatures in his sketchbook, there are a few pages devoted to plants, too. I can already recite the magical properties of half a dozen. I shouldn't say that, though. Better for my rivals not to know my strengths. "It's hard to tell what anything is in the dark," I say, which is the truth anyway. "The trees look mostly like birches and poplars. Nothing interesting there. But those thick clumps of bushes look like briarwood, and I think those flowery vines are figroses."

"What do those do?"

I hesitate, ducking under a low-hanging branch. I suppose he'll learn all this in training anyway, but I don't want him to know what I know. "Briarwood is a prickly shrub, just like ordinary briars, but it's called that because, here in the Realm, its long wood branches soak up magic. It's both stronger and lighter than ordinary wood, and . . ." I stop myself before continuing. It's *hard* not to share all the things that I know, but I need to be careful. "I think it has other properties that woodcarvers like," I finish. "It's hard to collect in large quantities, though, since briarwood bushes are so small. I think." In my head, I recite the rest of its properties: naturally smooth, responds well to gifts, easy to carve, durable, sturdy . . .

"And the figroses?" Ari asks. "I've never heard of those."

I'm pretty sure he's looking right at me, but I can't stop myself from smiling. "Figroses are more interesting. Their fruits are sweet and can be used in medicines." I deliberately leave out the most important fact: There is one magical creature in particular that loves to eat figroses. One of the most magical and mysterious of all. But I'm not about to give Ari any help in tracking them.

"You know a lot about plants," he says. I can't tell whether he sounds impressed or not.

I shrug, then remember he can't see it in the dark. "My papa taught me a little."

"Must be nice," Ari says. "To learn about being a Seeker from him."

Again, I can't read his tone. Is he jealous or being snide? Is he suggesting that I couldn't become a Seeker on my own? That I'm getting an unfair advantage? "Must be nice learning about being a Seeker in training every day," I say curtly.

Ari's head snaps toward me. "I didn't mean—"

Something prickles at the edges of my gift, and I stop abruptly. "Shh," I whisper.

Ari stops too, and the sparks of yellow around his fingertips glow more brightly as he increases the use of his magic. I do the same, drawing on more of my gift so I can get a better sense of what, exactly, is in front of us.

It's a soft energy, but it isn't faint—in fact, it's really strong. Strong like Lilja's, but calmer. The sensation reminds me of the taste of Mama's bilberry pies, which are just the right amount of sweet and sugary. But underneath that, there's something deep and wild. This is truly a creature of the Realm: strong and untamed.

I'm practically holding my breath as I inch my gift a little closer, trying to sense more. Whatever this creature is, it's shy. Unlike Lilja, who lets her magic run right up to me, this creature is pulling back, like—

Of course.

I know exactly what kind of creature is shy and sweet, lives in wooded territories, and loves to eat the figroses that are currently growing all around us.

It's a unicorn.

Ari sucks in a surprised breath at the same time I do, but neither of dares to speak. Unicorns are notoriously wary of humans and even make themselves invisible in the presence of strangers. We have to be very careful not to scare it.

But I'm not about to let this opportunity go to waste.

I pull some of my magic back, trying to give the unicorn space so it doesn't feel threatened. At the same time, I reach slowly into the damp pocket of my coat, rummaging around.

"What are you doing?" Ari whispers, barely loud enough to hear.

"We need an offering," I whisper back. I'm not sure how much Ari knows about unicorns, but I don't dare explain further in case our voices scare it away. Papa's told me how to approach one dozens of times. *Make an offering,* he would say. *Unicorns will only approach humans if you offer them a gift. Even then, they may vanish rather than approach. They won't go near individuals they deem to be unsavory. You can always tell the quality of a person's character by whether a unicorn trusts them.*

I don't have anything in my pockets except a few bilberries that managed to survive the plunge into the lake, my knife, a single knitted glove with a hole in one finger, and a spare strip of cloth I use to tie back my hair. But none of those would make a good offering. Beside me, Ari is checking his pockets too, but he withdraws his empty hands and shakes his head.

I'm about to grab the bilberries and see if they're as popular with unicorns as they are with baby dragons when the answer occurs to me. Moving slowly, I step toward the nearest figrose plant. My foot snaps a twig and I wince, but the life force of the unicorn doesn't fade or disappear. I think it's watching me.

I channel my magic into the plant, until it grows larger and its petals unfurl. Carefully, I draw my pocketknife and cut one of the figrose blooms from the stem. I peel the petals apart gingerly—they might be worth something to the village herbalist if they're intact—and pluck the small round fruit from inside. Pocketing the petals and my knife, I let the fruit rest in the palm of my hand and take a few slow, slooow steps forward.

"Careful," Ari whispers unnecessarily. I hardly dare to breathe. I take another step. Two. Three. Judging by its life force, the unicorn can't be more than four feet in front of me—

A shape materializes out of thin air. I see its body first—the same size and shape as an ordinary horse, but with a gleaming silver coat that reflects the moonlight shining through the trees. Its mane is just as silver, the hair thick and tangled. Finally the rest of the head appears: bright, beautiful eyes the color of the ocean after a storm, a long snout, and a single, polished silver horn protruding from its forehead.

It's the most beautiful thing I've ever seen.

I've completely forgotten how to breathe, let alone what I'm supposed to be doing, but the unicorn hasn't forgotten. It tilts its head in my direction and sniffs, fixing its gaze on my open hand, which is still cradling the fruit. Slowly, I extend my arm closer to it, letting it sniff the fruit a few more times.

I don't know if unicorns understand speech, but Papa says they're highly intelligent, so I whisper, "A gift for you."

I don't dare step any closer to the unicorn, but then Ari says, "It's okay, Bryn. With my gift I can tell she's calm. She's decided not to run now."

I take one last, tiny step and hold my hand up to her snout. The unicorn blinks, lowers her head, and snaps the fruit from my hand in one bite.

As she chews, I take another step closer to her side, glancing at her beautiful mane. Unicorns have a lot of magical properties, including in their horns and their blood, but of course it isn't possible to collect those things from a living unicorn without harming it. There *is* one item Seekers can collect from unicorns, though.

"Is she still calm?" I whisper to Ari as the unicorn finishes chewing.

"Yeah. It doesn't feel like she's going to run."

I just have to hope his empathy gift is right. Unicorns are very reluctant to let people touch them, especially people they just met. So what I'm about to do is really stupid.

I lift my hand again, making sure her eye is fixed on me so she knows what to expect. I lightly touch her mane, prepared to back away if she gets scared, but she just watches me calmly, so I stroke her mane, letting my fingers brush over the silvery strands. It's the softest hair I've ever felt, softer even than the wool of Runa's lambs. I try to run my fingers gently through the strands, but it's so tangled that I don't have much luck brushing it. It doesn't matter, though. My plan works.

A few of the twisted strands break off, leaving me with three short, silver unicorn hairs in my hand.

The unicorn has lost patience with me, stepping away and tossing her head. I move back, and the unicorn vanishes in a blink, making herself invisible. I sense her life spark fading into the distance as she trots away, disappearing into the darkened woods.

I wrap my fingers around the silver hairs and walk back to Ari, who's standing openmouthed a few feet away. "That was the coolest thing I've ever seen," he says, and my cheeks flush warmly again, but this time with pride.

"I can't believe that happened," I say, but I'm grinning. I tuck the precious strands of hair into my pocket. I can't trade them right away—Ari's right about people in the village being suspicious if I suddenly have items from the Realm I shouldn't have—but they'll be worth a lot someday, once I become a Seeker. Unicorn hair is so rare and magically powerful that even these few tiny strands are valuable.

"Her magic . . . ," Ari says. "I've never felt anything like that before."

"Me neither. I can't wait to tell my little sister. She *loves* unicorns." As soon as I say it, I stop smiling. I can't tell Elisa, at least not yet. No one can know that Ari and I went into the Realm tonight. "We'd better head back," I say, glancing up at the sky. I don't think I'm imagining that it's getting lighter.

"We haven't found your starflowers yet."

"I know, but I don't think we'll find any here. These aren't the kinds of plants they usually grow with. We need to try one of the northern forests."

"I'm surprised we found a unicorn this far south," Ari says. "Don't they prefer the northern forests?"

"Usually," I say, "but they tend to travel a bit farther south in the summer. The icefoxes in the northern forests come out of their dens at this time of year and eat more of the plants, so the unicorns tend to migrate to the south to find more food."

"Really?" Ari says. "I didn't know that."

Oops. I bite my tongue. I really need to stop giving the enemy information.

But for some reason I'm having difficulty thinking of Ari as the enemy.

As we walk, it occurs to me that it would be useful to learn more about how Ari's gift works. I've seen him use it now, but I'm still not totally sure what the extent of an empath's abilities are. And that will be good to know during the competition.

"Hey, Ari," I say, trying to sound casual as we duck under a tree limb, "how much did you know about what the unicorn was feeling? Like, when you told me she wasn't going to run, how did you know?"

Ari takes a second before answering. "How much do you know about empathy gifts?"

"Not much," I admit.

"It's similar to your gift, really," he says. "But I can't make plants grow or use elements or anything like you can. And when it comes to animals and people, it's more . . . I guess you'd say the empathy gift is really focused on emotions—I mean, obviously you know that already, but . . ." He stops, flustered, and takes a second to think before starting again. "What I mean is, being an empath is like being a specialist. We do exactly one thing, but we do it well. Being a naturalist means having a broader range of powers, but not being as aware of nuances in life forces." I frown, and he adds quickly, "I don't mean that as an insult to naturalists. It's just . . . I don't think you sense life forces in the same way that I do."

"So how do you sense them, then?"

Ari clears his throat, stepping carefully around a clump of thick briarwood bushes. "I think, from what I've seen of naturalists, that you guys see each life spark as all one thing. Like, Lilja has a distinct life force, right? You can know she's nearby without seeing her."

"Yes," I say, "but so can you."

"Right, but . . . I don't *only* sense that. Lilja's life force isn't all one sensation to me; it doesn't feel the same all the time. There's something about it that's distinctly *her* and that stays the same—that's what you sense. But I feel more. When she's afraid of something, her force gets all spiky and alert. Most of the time she's excited, with her energy flying around all over the place, but I can also tell the difference between when she's hungry and sleepy and calm. And sometimes she's more than one thing at once—both hungry and excited, for example, when she wants some bilberries. Being an empath means picking up on all those tiny little feelings that make up her larger life force. And it also means being able to *shape* those feelings if I want. Like, if she needs to be calmer instead of scared, I can try to smooth the spiky parts of her energy so that they're calm instead."

"Wow," I say. "You're right, naturalists don't sense any of that stuff. I can pick up on things about her energy—like, I can tell that there's a lot more energy when she's excited than when she's tired. And I can try to direct her energy in one way or another, like how I was nudging her with my gift when we flew. But I haven't ever felt any of that other stuff."

We're both quiet for a minute. I'm not sure how much further I can push Ari—he shouldn't be telling me all this about his gift when we're going to be competing against each other. But it's useful for me to know, and anyway I'm really curious. "Can you do all of that stuff with people, too?"

"Some of it," he says, sounding wary. "People are harder. But the better I know someone, the easier it is to pick up on their emotions."

"Naturalists are kind of like that too," I say. "We can identify people's unique life forces if we spend enough time around them. But it's more like sensing their gifts than their emotions. And it's hard to even detect other people's magic unless I concentrate and cast my gift out really far."

After a second, the meaning of what Ari just said hits me. *The better I know someone, the easier it is . . .*

The more time I spend with Ari, the easier it's going to be for him to sense—and maybe even manipulate—my emotions. The thought makes me shiver. I still don't know him well enough to really trust him, and I have no idea what's going to happen during the competition. What if he decides to take me out of the running by using his gift against me? Could he affect my emotions during the auditions? Make me too tired to run, or too confused to focus, or too sick, or . . .

He's even more dangerous than I thought. I need to be careful. In fact, I should probably call this whole thing off and not meet with him in secret anymore.

Except I can't do that, because Elisa needs starflowers, and Lilja needs supervision in the afternoons, and I need to learn what I'm missing in training. If I hadn't teamed up with Ari in the first place, I wouldn't be standing in the Realm right now with unicorn hairs and figrose petals in my pocket.

But we can't stay a team forever, because only one of us can win.

TWELVE

B y the time Ari and I emerge from the forest, the sky is definitely getting lighter as the first ray of dawn creeps over the mountains. We find Lilja sitting at the edge of the lake beside a pile of fish, which she snaps up one or two at a time and swallows whole.

"Well, guess she figured out how to hunt here on her own," I say.

"Let's just hope that isn't some kind of magical endangered Realm fish or something."

I laugh. "Pretty sure they're just trout."

"We can only hope," Ari says, grinning.

"Okay, Lilja, snack time's over," I say, clapping my hands to get her attention. She glances up at me, a fish tail dangling from her mouth. "Time to go back to the beach."

Lilja slurps the tail into her mouth.

"I'm not kidding, Lil. Time to go."

She pauses, looking at us, then turns away and snaps up another fish.

I look at Ari. "Maybe we should climb on her back again so she'll get the hint?"

He shrugs. "Worth a shot."

Only now does it occur to me that we might not be able to get Lilja to leave the Realm. What do we do if she doesn't listen to us? We'll be stuck here with no way to get home. Our families won't know where we went. I suppose the Seekers might find us eventually, but the Realm is a big place, and they wouldn't even know to look for us here.

Possibly we should have thought this through a little bit better.

There's nothing to be done about it now, though, except try to convince Lilja to leave, so Ari and I climb onto her back once again. Reluctantly, I let him sit in the front this time, since it's only fair.

Lilja huffs when she feels us sit on her spine, but she doesn't stop eating her fish. "What are her emotions right now?" I ask Ari. "Is she confused, or just being stubborn?"

"Definitely stubborn," Ari says. "We got her attention when we sat down, but she's mostly still thinking about her fish."

"What should we do?"

"Wait. She's almost done eating, and then I think she'll pay attention to us."

I sigh. "We've got to work on your training, Lil. You can't just—"

"Do you hear that?" Ari asks suddenly.

"Hear what?"

Ari releases more of his gift, sensing something. "Someone's here!"

Immediately I release my own gift, copying him. But there's so much magic in the Realm, so many different life forces, that it takes me a second to figure out what he's feeling. There—something strange. An energy like nothing I've ever felt before. It's definitely magic, but it doesn't feel natural. Not like that of the Realm's creatures, or like any gift. "What *is* that?"

"We have to go," Ari whispers. "Before they sense us!"

Whoever it is, they're not that far away from us. Not far away at all. If the Realm weren't so full of magic, we would have sensed them sooner. "It might be too late," I say, panic rising in my chest. "If it's one of the Seekers, they could sense Lilja a mile off."

"I don't think it's a Seeker," Ari says, and there's something in his tone that I don't understand.

"Who, then?"

"Not now. We need to go. They shouldn't think anything unusual about a dragon being in the Realm if they sense Lilja. But we need to make sure they don't sense *us*."

"Ari. Whatever that magic is, it's coming closer!" I say. The energy is moving toward us, and it definitely feels human—but it's also wrong, not like a normal gift at all. It's fighting with the other life forces around it, clashing against them rather than melding into them. "If we get Lilja in the air, they'll see her. If it's a Seeker, they'll know that a silver baby dragon isn't one who lives here."

"It's not a Seeker," he says again, but he frowns. "She should run. Until we get far enough away."

Lilja is finally picking up on our distress. She stretches her jaws and flutters her wings, her energy picking up.

"She's ready," Ari says, and her wings snap wide, preparing for takeoff. "Stop using your gift," he adds. "The more you use, the easier it will be for them to sense you."

"But then I can't steer Lilja!"

"We don't need to steer her. We just need her to *run*."

As I pull the rest of my magic back, I feel it—Ari's gift collides with Lilja's energy, but he isn't calming her down this time.

He's making her feel afraid.

Lilja's spine stiffens, and she bolts forward so suddenly I nearly fall. Ari grabs my arm, holding me steady, as Lilja bursts through the trees and leaps forward, running as fast as I've ever seen her go.

Both Ari and I have stopped using our gifts, so we have no control over what Lilja does next. She runs through the forest at breakneck speed, wings tucked tightly against her sides, and it's all Ari and I can do to hang on for dear life. As soon as the trees fade away and she enters another clearing, she snaps her wings open and leaps into the air, nearly dislodging both of us from her back.

"Um, I think you might have scared her a little too much!" I yell at Ari as Lilja takes flight.

"No kidding!" he yells back.

With every frantic beat of her wings, Lilja soars toward her cave, leaving the Realm, and the figure in the forest, far behind.

We pass over the mountains, and the bay lies before us, the ocean a smooth stretch of blue tinged by dawn. Rather than having Lilja land on the beach again, though, I steer her toward the cliffs. Now that we're far away from the mysterious energy, I let my gift guide me, flinging it out wide so I can sense the landscape. It's hard to tell how things are laid out with so much rock everywhere, but there are enough scattered life sparks—of the occasional grass or tree or weed—that I can sense the rough shape of things. It takes a couple of tries, but after a minute of steering Lilja around the cliffs with my gift, I detect her cave and nudge her toward it. Lilja doesn't need much coaxing to land on the ledge about halfway up the rock wall above the beach, right in front of the entrance to the cave. Luckily, she doesn't crash us into any large bodies of water this time.

"Here you go, Lil," I say as she thuds to the ground, her claws scraping against the rock. "Home sweet home."

"How'd you do that?" Ari asks. His windswept curls are sticking up in every direction, and his eyes are wide.

"Do what? Get her to land?"

"And find the cave," he says.

I shrug. "Naturalists can sense plants, too, remember? It's not so hard to figure out how the land is shaped when you can sense everything that grows on it."

Ari looks thoughtful. "Sorry about earlier," he says. "When we were flying into the Realm, and I made her too tired with my gift, and then when I made her too scared just now. I haven't exactly tried any of this on a dragon before. I didn't know how much to—"

"It's fine," I say. "It was a good idea. The execution just needed some work. But now you'll know how to do it in the future, right?"

He shrugs and looks away. He seems embarrassed, like I was earlier when I forgot about how Seekers steer dragons and then again when I nearly drowned, so I want to say something to make him feel better.

"Flying was *amazing*, right?" I say finally.

Ari glances up, a small smile creeping onto his face. "Amazing," he agrees. "I've never felt so . . . alive."

"Or so free," I say, nodding. "Yeah."

We share smiles, and for a second it feels nice—almost like we're friends. But we can't be. Only one of us is going to be a Seeker. After this competition is over, only one of us will get to fly dragons every day. And the other will never get to do it again, once Lilja goes to live in the Realm.

Only one can win.

I turn away from Ari and slide carefully off Lilja's back, landing on my feet beside the cliff's wall. I walk toward Lilja's head, stepping carefully around her claws. Her eyelids are drooping a little, and she huffs a breath when she sees me.

"Thanks for the ride, Lil," I say, giving her snout a pat, "but it's time for bed now, okay?" Behind me, there's a thump as Ari climbs down too. Lilja gives the cave a quick sniff, apparently deems it satisfactory, and curls up against the far wall, closing her eyes immediately for a nap.

Ari and I look at each other.

"So what *was* that back there?" I say quietly. "And what makes you think it wasn't a Seeker?"

Ari hesitates. "I don't think I can tell you that."

My eyes narrow. "You're keeping too many secrets. You won't tell me anything about how you found Lilja or why you're hiding her or—"

"I can't tell you, okay? Don't you trust me?"

I pause, but on instinct, I tell the truth. "Yes. I do. But why don't *you* trust *me*?"

For a moment Ari doesn't answer. "If I tell you this," he says, "you have to promise not to tell anyone. Especially not your papa."

"What? Why?"

"It'll all make sense in a minute. Just—promise."

"Okay, fine. I promise. What *is* it?"

Ari sits down, leaning against the cave wall across from Lilja, and I do the same. The dragon's eyes are closed, and her breathing is slow and even as she falls asleep.

I wait, and finally Ari speaks again.

"The night that I found Lilja's egg . . . Well, I didn't just find it. I was out on the docks late because my mother had asked me to bring something up to the bakery, and the docks are on the way. I saw someone wearing a Seeker's green cloak with a hood pulled up over their face, carrying something in a burlap sack. I knew immediately that something was wrong—with my gift, I could sense that this person was feeling secretive and fearful and greedy. So I followed him.

"The Seeker—or the person wearing a Seeker's cloak—went down to the docks, and there was a little boat there. Like one of the fishermen's short-range rowboats, not something I would've ordinarily even noticed. But there were a couple of people in the boat, all wearing dark cloaks, and I couldn't see any of them well. All of their energy felt—wrong. Dark. Like a different kind of magic."

"Like what we just felt in the Realm?"

"Yes."

"What do you think it is?"

He hesitates again, and I want to wring the words out of him. "The Vondur," he says finally.

I let that sink in for a minute. "You're sure? You think there was just a *Vondur* in the Realm?"

"Or someone using Vondur magic, at the very least."

"That's impossible. How could they . . . ?"

"Think about it, Bryn. You know what we just felt back there. You *know* that it didn't feel like natural magic. It's

Vondur spells that feel like that. I don't know how, but that's what it was."

"And the Vondur . . . were trying to steal Lilja's egg the night you found her?"

Ari nods. "I could only hear snatches of conversation, but whoever was in the Seeker's cloak was showing them something in the burlap sack. It seemed like they were making some sort of deal. So of course, I suspected that if this person really was a Seeker, they were carrying something from the Realm and trading it away to the Vondur. And I didn't want that to happen.

"So I used my gift to cause a distraction. I tried to make the Seeker feel suddenly sick, and it worked. He started vomiting over the edge of the dock, and while he was distracted I grabbed the sack and ran. When I got home and looked inside, I found Lilja's egg."

"Whoa," I say. "I didn't know your gift could do something like that."

"Neither did I," Ari says quietly. "I'd never tried to hurt someone like that before."

"But I don't understand. If those were Vondur, how'd they get into a fishing boat?"

Lilja snorts a little in her sleep, and Ari glances over at her before continuing.

"I was wondering that too. So I climbed one of the hills by the arena, where you have a pretty good view of the ocean past the bay. After a while, the people in the boat gave up on looking for me, got back in the boat, and rowed out of the bay. And around the edge of the cliffs, I could see a ship waiting for them. One with Vondur flags above the sails."

I lean back into a pile of feathers, unwilling to believe what I'm hearing. "So you're saying . . . the Vondur have been sailing as close to the island as they can and then coming ashore on rowboats at night so no one will notice them?"

"That's what it looked like. And it also looked like *someone* was trying to trade Lilja's egg to them. If I hadn't gotten to it first, Lilja would be with the Vondur right now."

I shudder. "But why haven't you told anyone this? Ari, this is *huge*!"

"I know. But the person I saw . . . I'm sure they were in a Seeker's cloak. Which doesn't necessarily mean it was a Seeker, but . . ."

"But not many people have one of those cloaks."

"Right. And the fact that we just felt Vondur magic in the Realm, which no one is supposed to have access to but the Seekers . . . I don't know. I think one of the Seekers has to be involved in this somehow. So who can I tell? I can't trust anyone on the council.

"That's why I've been hiding Lilja on my own. I need to figure out who's trading with the Vondur, and I need to find some kind of proof to turn them in. Otherwise, who would believe me? I mean, I'm accusing the *Seekers*, and I'm just the weird empath kid. No one will listen unless I have real evidence."

"Lilja is evidence."

He shakes his head. "They'll just say I was cheating to try to win the competition or something. It isn't enough."

"You should've told me sooner. I can help! We can figure it out together."

Ari hesitates. "I didn't know if I could tell you, because . . ."

"Because what?"

"Bryn. Your papa used to *be* a Seeker. He has one of those cloaks. I didn't know if—"

I shake my head before he can even finish his sentence. "No. My papa would *never* do that."

"I'm not saying he would. I'm just saying—at the very least, he's friends with all of the Seekers. If you tell him about this, what if he tips them off without realizing it? I don't trust anyone who's too close to the Seekers right now."

The accusation immediately makes me defensive, but my head is spinning, and I have to admit that in Ari's position I'd be suspicious too. I just can't believe that any of the Seekers would do something like this. They're practically the most trusted people in the village. The council makes most of the decisions about what's best for the village because the Seekers are trusted to do that. "But who do you think it was? Do you have any suspicions?" I ask. "I mean, if it *is* somehow one of the Seekers . . ."

"Well, I never saw this person's face. His cloak was up, and it was dark. But I'm wondering about Agnar and Freyr. They're the two Seekers who were most in favor of letting the Vondur start trading with us again, or so the rumors say. I haven't had any interaction with Freyr, so I can't say if it's him. Agnar . . . In training, something about his emotions has always felt kind of *off* to me, like he's hiding something. And it seems like he's avoiding me in training, like he never gets too close. But I could be reading too much into it because I don't like him."

"Fair enough," I say. "I'm not exactly his biggest fan either, but that doesn't mean he's trading with the Vondur, necessarily."

"You know the Seekers better than I do," Ari says, suddenly perking up. "Because of your papa, right? So who would *you* suspect?"

"Honestly? No one. Seeker Larus has been on the council for decades, so there's no way he'd just suddenly decide to start trading dragons to the Vondur. Same with the others— Ludvik and Freyr have both been on the council for years. I think it's more likely that someone stole a Seeker's cloak— or was wearing something that kinda looks like a Seeker's cloak."

"But in that case, it could have been anyone," Ari says.

"Right."

"But then how would anyone who's not a Seeker get hold of a dragon egg? How'd they get into the Realm?" he points out, and I don't have an answer.

We both stare dejectedly at the cave walls for a moment. All of this is still sinking in, but at least Ari's secretiveness is starting to make sense. "This is why you insisted on keeping Lilja out of the Realm," I say. "Because if one of the Seekers *is* the person you saw, they might just smuggle her out again."

"Exactly. I don't know if it's safe to tell the Seekers about her when one of them might have been the person trying to trade her off in the first place."

"We should tell my papa," I say. "He'd know what to do."

"No. We can't tell anyone until we know for sure who it is."

"But I know we can trust—"

"You promised, Bryn!"

I glare at him. "Fine, but only if we're actually able to figure out who this person is. If we can't get the evidence you want, we need to go to the Seekers anyway. This is too big to keep to ourselves."

"We can find the proof. I know it."

"What's your plan?"

He reaches into his pockets and pulls out a handful of small objects. I lean in closer. Silver dragon scales shimmer in his palm.

"Lilja shed a few," he explains, "and I picked them up."

"But what for? What are you going to do with them?"

"Now that the Vondur are participating in trading days, I was planning to stockpile a few things from the Realm—harmless little things. Absolutely no magical creatures, but items like this that the Vondur will value, that clearly came from the Realm. That way I can build up a relationship with the Vondur traders and get information from them. If they think I'm just like this other person, someone willing to trade magical creatures to them, they might tell me more."

I frown. "*Might.* Maybe."

"Do you have any better ideas?"

"Not right this second."

"Well, think about it, then. We can try to figure this out together."

"Okay," I say finally. "But if none of our plans work, then we tell my papa. Deal?"

"Deal."

Ari smiles at me, but I can't bring myself to return it. Our alliance just got a whole lot more complicated, and I can't help but feel like we're in over our heads. But maybe he's right about one thing: we need to find out more about what's going on.

There's just one problem. "We can't go back to the Realm, can we?" I ask quietly.

"I was thinking the same thing," Ari says. "I don't think we should. Whoever or whatever that was, clearly someone's in the Realm who isn't supposed to be there. And that means they could catch us."

"And Lilja."

"And Lilja," he agrees, nodding. "If that was the Vondur, we can't have them finding out where we're hiding her."

He's right, but I hate it. This really complicates our plan to prepare for the competition—we'll have to train outside of the Realm. And I don't know how I'm going to get star-flowers for Elisa now.

Not to mention the fact that everything we saw in the Realm tonight was incredible and I'm dying to see more.

But we'll have to figure all of that out later.

"We'll come back here tomorrow, right?" I say to Ari. "We can at least train on the beach or something."

"All right."

Ari and I get to our feet quietly, careful not to disturb Lilja, and exit the cave. We climb down the sloping ledge along the side of the cliff. We don't speak much, except to point out better hand- and footholds to each other as we climb.

By the time my feet hit the sand, my body aches with tiredness. The sun is rising higher every minute, and I haven't slept a second the entire night. But we still have to go all the way back to the village, and if we don't hurry, I'll never make it before Mama wakes up.

So we run.

Halfway up the lane to Runa's farm, we both have to stop to catch our breath. While we're stopped, Ari turns to me, a funny expression on his face. "Can I ask you something?"

"You just did."

He ignores me. "Why do you need starflowers?"

I glare at him. "Not that it's any of your business, but I need them for my sister. She has problems with her lungs sometimes. She has coughing fits and trouble breathing at night. Starflowers can be used in medicine that helps her a lot. When I'm a Seeker, I'll be able to get as many as we need, the way my papa did."

"Can't you just get some of the other Seekers to trade them?" Ari asks. "When I become Seeker, I'll bring you some."

"*You* aren't going to be Seeker, because I'm going to win."

Ari grins. "Not if I win first."

"We'll see about that," I say. "Who is it that tamed a unicorn, again?"

Ari groans. "You didn't *tame* a unicorn. You fed it some fruit. And brushed its hair. Big difference."

"And how many unicorns have *you* fed, Ari?"

"I don't think feeding unicorns is going to be part of the competition."

"No, but knowing how to approach them and get their hairs might be. And who is it who's done that, again?"

He sighs. "You're never going to let this go, are you?"

"Nope." I smirk. "You'll be calling me Seeker Bryn in no time."

"You're forgetting about the part where you were only able to approach the unicorn because I used my gift to tell you whether she was calm."

"I could've figured that out myself. You're not the only one who can sense life forces."

Ari smirks. "No, I'm just better at it than everyone else."

I roll my eyes. "Whatever. Your gift isn't all that special."

"I know you don't really mean that," Ari says, stepping

over a fallen tree branch as we crest the top of the hill. "I know, because I can use my gift to tell."

He's only joking, but it makes me think back to what he said earlier, and I can't help but ask, "Can you really tell when people are lying?"

Ari's smile fades. "Usually, yes. People's emotions don't feel right when they lie."

I bite my lip. Good thing my parents aren't empaths. But keeping my distance from Ari is proving to be much harder than I thought.

Ari looks away suddenly. "Shouldn't have told you that," he mumbles.

At first I think he means that he shouldn't be giving away the secrets of his gift to his competitors, which he shouldn't. But he still won't look at me, like there's more to it than that. "Did I say something wrong?" I ask.

"No. You just felt it."

"Um, what?"

Ari glances down at the dirt and shrugs. "People always get freaked out when I start telling them about my gift. Nobody likes that I can read them so well. Nobody likes that I know their feelings. Or their secrets."

"Oh," I say quietly.

"People always pull away from me when they find out what I can do, or when they assume I can read their minds or something. Like you did, just now." He shrugs again like it's no big deal, but I don't have to be an empath to see that it is.

"I didn't do that," I protest.

"You did it earlier, too."

I'm not sure which moment he's referring to, but admittedly there were several when I thought about needing to be careful around him. I shouldn't explain, but the way he looks right now is so . . . lonely. I've always known that Ari doesn't spend much time with the other kids in the village, but I assumed that was by choice. It never occurred to me that Ari might not be keeping to himself on purpose.

So I tell him the truth. "It's not really about your gift," I say. "I don't care that you're an empath. Or I wouldn't normally. But I *do* care about becoming a Seeker. I want to win this competition more than I've ever wanted anything. And you're the competition. Your gift is going to help you a lot. I'm trying to be careful around you, because I don't want to give you anything that could be used against me later."

Ari finally looks up. "You think I would do that?"

"I think I don't know you very well. And I think you want to win."

Ari nods. "That's fair. But maybe you should also think about this: even if I weren't an empath, I'd know how you felt when you were kicked out of training. Because I get left out of things all the time, and I feel the same way. I didn't just ask you to help me with Lilja because it's convenient or because I'm planning to betray you or something later. I asked you because I think you deserve a fair shot at this just like the rest of us." He smiles a little. "I don't need to cheat or backstab my friends to have an advantage in this contest. When I win, that will be fair too."

I'm suddenly having trouble breathing again, but I don't think it's from running this time. We've reached the bottom of the hill, and my family's hut is looming down the path. "That was a nice speech and all," I say finally, "but there's one crucial thing wrong with it. Fairly or not, you're not going to win. Because I'm going to beat you." I smile to let him know I'm teasing, even though I mean every word, and he smiles back.

"See you tomorrow, then," he says.

"See you."

As Ari continues down the path toward the village, I turn toward home, leap over the garden gate, and—

Someone rises from the garden bench and steps out of the shadows, looking right at me.

Thirteen

I freeze, my heart pounding. Is it Mama or Papa? Elisa?

"Where have you been?" the shadow asks, stepping forward.

Runa.

I exhale. "You scared me! I thought you were my parents."

"I saw you and Ari on your way toward my house," she says. "I thought I'd run up here and wait for you so we could talk alone."

She gestures to the garden bench, and we both sit down. "What's wrong?" I ask. "Why do you want to talk?"

"I wanted to warn you," she says. "About Tomas and Johann."

I frown. Aside from my confrontation with Tomas on trading day, I've barely given any of the other competitors a second thought. Except Ari, of course.

"When I was in the village today, I overheard them

talking. They were whispering and looking kind of guilty about something, so I tried to eavesdrop. I heard Tomas say your name and tell Johann that you were still planning to compete. Then Johann said something dumb about how you couldn't win because girls don't have strong magic." Runa rolls her eyes.

"Figures," I say. "But that doesn't matter. I'll just prove him wrong."

"I know, but . . ." Runa pauses. "Then Tomas said something else, so soft I could hardly hear him. And Johann was, like, nodding in agreement. And then Tomas said, 'Make sure she loses.'"

"Meaning what?"

"I don't know. But it sounded like . . . I don't know, like they were plotting something. I thought I should warn you."

"Thanks. It's probably nothing, but I'll keep an eye out."

"So where have you been all this time?" she asks, looking pointedly at the dawn sky. "What were you and Ari doing?"

I tuck one leg up on the bench, turning sideways so I can see her better. Quietly, so as not to wake my family, I tell her all about how Ari and I flew Lilja into the Realm.

One of the things I love about Runa is that she's a great listener. She gasps in all the right places and is just as excited as I am about the Realm.

"That sounds *so* awesome," she says when I finish describing the unicorn encounter.

"Sure you don't want to change your mind about training

with me?" I say with a grin. "It's not too late for you to compete!"

"I'm sure," she says, grinning back, "although a unicorn
is pretty tempting."

We talk for a few more minutes, but eventually Runa
notices that I can barely keep my eyes open and shoos me off
to bed, sounding more than a little like Mama.

"I want updates on all your Realm adventures!" she says
as she leaves the garden.

"You'll be the first and only person to know," I say, waving goodbye.

I tiptoe inside the hut as quietly as I can. I hang my coat on
the clothesline to dry, then slip into the sleeping area. I take off
my boots, which are caked in mud—I'll have to wash them later
when Mama isn't looking. For now, I hide them beneath the
bed, then slip under the covers and pull the blankets over me.

The second my head hits the pillow, I realize I've never
been more tired in my entire life. It will be so good to sleep,
just for a little while. . . .

The next thing I know, Mama is shaking me awake.
"Time to make breakfast, Bryn!"

I'm pretty sure I've been asleep for only about five minutes.

I take a deep breath, remind myself that becoming a
Seeker will be worth this someday, and stumble out of bed.

The morning does not go well.

I'm so tired that I can barely focus on my chores. I burn

the oatmeal, spill half the bucket of well water on the kitchen floor, and get into a fight with Elisa over which spoon she's going to use. By the time breakfast is over, Mama has lost all patience with me.

"I don't think you should go to this training of yours today," she says. "Clearly you're exhausted. They're working you too hard."

"Mama! That's not fair." It comes out as more of a whine than I intended, and Mama's eyebrows rise sharply.

"Don't argue with me, Brynja."

"But it isn't fair! You just don't want me to compete. You're looking for an excuse not to let me go." I say it without thinking and instantly regret it. Arguing with Mama is never a smart decision.

"Go to your room," she says, and for once I do the smart thing and don't argue. I stomp into the sleeping area and throw myself down on the bed.

Of course, not going to training isn't as much of a punishment as Mama thinks it is. I haven't been going to the official training anyway. But this *does* mean I won't be able to watch Lilja this afternoon or practice anything with her. I guess I can still sneak out tonight and meet Ari, though. Maybe it isn't such a bad idea to just lie here and close my eyes. . . .

At one point Elisa's footsteps pad toward me, but Mama calls her away and she retreats back to the kitchen. The front door opens and closes a few times, and I can hear Mama scrubbing dishes. I'm supposed to help, but I don't.

A few minutes later, a new set of footsteps approach, soft and almost silent. Mama.

She sits on the end of the bed, but I don't look up.

"Sulking is not helping your cause, you know," she says, but for once she doesn't sound stern.

I turn my head so that the pillow doesn't muffle my words. "Why don't you want me to do this?"

Mama sighs. "It's not about that. Clearly there's something else going on, or you wouldn't be so upset. Did something happen at training? Are the boys . . . ? Are they getting along with you?"

That makes me open my eyes. "Some of them have been kind of mean," I say, thinking of what Tomas said on trading day. "But I'm making friends with Ari."

She pauses, considering. "I know this isn't easy. I'm worried about . . . about how the other kids might treat you. That's what I don't want you to have to face."

I frown. "I thought you were just worried about me getting hurt."

"I am," Mama says, nodding, "but you're a smart girl, and you have your father's talents. I know you could become a great Seeker. But I am not so certain that this village will give you that chance."

I roll onto my back, looking up at her. "What do you mean?"

Mama scoots closer to me, resting one hand on my knee.

"Did I ever tell you about the time I wanted to become a sailor?"

I giggle. *"You?"*

Mama smiles. "Yes, me. I was a little girl, maybe even younger than Elisa. One day, when my mama wasn't feeling well, my papa took me out on his boat with my brothers. You remember when I told you that your grandfather was a fisherman?"

"Yes."

"Well. I thought his boat was the most spectacular thing I'd ever seen. I loved being out on the water, with nothing around but sea and sky. My father taught me how to fasten the sails and even let me stand at the wheel and pretend to steer the boat. I thought it was the most fun I'd ever had. After that day, I told everyone who would listen that I was going to become a sailor."

I sniff. "Why didn't you?"

She looks down at the quilt, one of her fingers tracing a pattern in the stitching. "Most of the village kids laughed, including my brothers, and told me I'd never become a sailor. 'Girls don't sail,' they said. 'The ocean is no place for you.'"

My eyes widen. "What did you do?"

Mama smiles. "I fought with them. Once I got kicked out of the butcher's shop for pulling another girl's braid after she teased me. I got into fistfights with my brothers. I told everyone who would listen that I was going to be a sailor, and I'd punch anyone who didn't believe me."

I can't help but laugh, trying to picture my mother getting

into fights. I've never seen her do anything improper, ever.

"It's true," Mama says, laughing a little herself. "I was often in trouble, as you can imagine."

"What happened?"

Mama pauses. "One day, when I came home with a black eye, my mother sat me down, and she explained to me that our village works in certain ways. That it's only boys who become fishermen and shopkeepers and sailors."

"And Seekers," I say.

Mama nods. "And Seekers. So I gave up my dream of becoming a sailor. I thought it was impossible."

"But that's not fair. You should've gotten to sail if you wanted."

"That's right." Her smile is sad. "It isn't fair, the way that our village works. But I wasn't as brave as you are. I'm glad that you're fighting for what you want and that you won't quit as easily as I did. I think you can be the one to change things in this village. But I wish you didn't have to. I wish you didn't have to fight even harder than I did, but I think you will."

"You're right," I say quietly. "It's already been harder than I thought it would be." I hesitate. The truth about getting kicked out of training is on the tip of my tongue. But I still can't bring myself to say it. "I don't care. I don't care how hard it is. I still want it."

Mama smiles and pats my knee. "I know."

"So you're okay with me becoming a Seeker?"

"It wouldn't have been my first choice for you," Mama says carefully. "But I want you to be happy."

I sit up. "I'm sorry you didn't get to become a sailor like you wanted."

Mama laughs. "Don't worry about that. I would have changed my mind eventually anyway. Sailing involves far too many fish." She wrinkles her nose, and I giggle.

"But if that *were* what you wanted, you shouldn't have had to give it up," I say.

"Yes. But you know what? I think once people in this village see a girl become a Seeker for the first time, they'll start to believe that girls can be other things too."

I smile. "I hope so."

Mama gives my knee a final pat and stands. "But that isn't going to happen if you don't get some rest and adjust that attitude, you understand? I *will* pull you out of this competition if I have to."

"Yes, Mama."

"Now come help me finish the dishes."

"Yes, Mama." But as soon as she disappears into the kitchen, I smile.

By the time the afternoon rolls around, I have redeemed myself enough in Mama's eyes that she gives me permission to leave. As soon as I'm out of sight of the hut, I rush to Lilja's cave as fast I can.

Lilja nearly knocks me over when she sees me and

ALEXANDRA OTT

immediately hunts for berries. I'm pretty sure she'd eat my whole coat if I let her; she sniffs the pocket hungrily.

"Calm down," I say. "Behave yourself."

She blinks up at me, her eyes huge and round and pleading. I sigh and toss her a berry.

I intended to spend this time training with Lilja, but about halfway through I get so tired that I curl up beside her and take a little nap. When I wake up a few hours later, I find Lilja eating the berries, which had fallen out of my coat pocket. She's snapped up most of my supply by the time Ari arrives, his coat collar turned up against the sea spray.

"Everything going okay here?" he asks.

"This dragon is addicted to berries," I say. "We've created a monster."

Ari laughs. "I think it's food in general that she's a bit obsessed with."

"A bit?" I joke. "She doesn't care about anything else. If she's not eating, she's looking for food."

"She's a creature of limited interests," Ari admits, smiling. "How'd training go?"

"Well, I've either got good news or bad news," he says. "Depending on how you feel about gyrpuffs."

I sit up straight. "You learned about gyrpuffs? For real?"

He laughs. "I had a feeling you'd be in favor."

"Who doesn't like gyrpuffs? They're incredible!"

"If you say so," Ari says. "I don't know much about them myself, except what I've heard from the Seekers. Agnar had us learning about how to track them and find their nests today."

"Oh, that's easy enough. Their nests are pretty distinctive."

"Well, tonight should be easy, then." Ari smiles.

I eye him with deep suspicion. "What exactly do you have in mind?"

"Seeker Agnar created a bunch of fake trails in the arena today to have us practice tracking. I thought maybe we could set up something similar on the beach tonight, and then you can practice too."

"If only we could go into the Realm and actually *see* one," I say.

"It's too risky. We still haven't figured out what's going on with the Vondur—"

"I know, I know. All right. Practice on the beach will be fine."

"Same time and place as usual?"

"Works for me."

I give Lilja a final pat. "See you both tonight, then. I'd better go or I'll be late for dinner. And if that happens, given the way this morning went, I'll likely be murdered."

Ari's eyebrows lift. "By who?"

"My mother."

He nods as if that's unsurprising, though I'm not sure whether it's because he's met my mother or because he has a similar relationship with his. "Well, good luck. Try not to die. We'll need your gyrpuff expertise."

"I'll do my best." As I walk past him toward the cave's

entrance, I call over my shoulder, "Take care of my dragon for me!"

"*Your* dragon?" Ari protests, but I'm already halfway out the cave, laughing.

Giddiness has now replaced my exhaustion, and it suddenly feels wonderful to run along the path toward home. Getting to practice with Ari and Lilja almost makes everything worth it.

FOURTEEN

Ari is true to his word. By the time I manage to sneak out of the hut and to the beach, he's set up an elaborate system of fake gyrpuff tracks—marks in the sand, raven feathers to represent gyrpuff feathers, and little rock clusters that we pretend are nests. It feels almost like a scavenger hunt, scouring the beach for the tiniest hint that will lead us to the fake nests, and therefore victory. By the end of the night, we're both covered in sand and laughing so hard that our sides ache.

"Guess I'd better go home," I say reluctantly as the first hints of sunlight peek over the horizon.

"Better get Lilja back," Ari agrees. We both glance at the dragon, who lost interest in our game ages ago and is now rolling around in the surf, ignoring us. Ari and I try attracting Lilja's attention with our gifts, but Lilja acts like she can't feel it and continues chasing waves.

"You are the world's most worthless dragon," Ari says to her. She plops her tail down, spraying water in his direction.

Eventually we get Lilja into the air and back to her cave. Every muscle in my body is now aching from running around all night, but I still have to walk all the way home from the beach.

"Too bad we can't fly her to our front doors," I mumble as we walk.

Ari laughs. "That would definitely cause some gossip in the village."

"Just imagine how jealous the other competitors would be if we did it!"

"Imagine flying her to the first trial. 'Oh, hey, how's it going, everyone? Just brought our own personal dragon along to the competition.'"

I laugh. "I think that should win us the first trial automatically."

"And the second," Ari says. "And the third!"

I stop smiling. "Except we can't both win the third."

I'm being serious, but Ari ignores that and continues the joke. "Lilja can cast the tie-breaking vote."

"Oh yeah? Who do you think she'd pick?"

"Me, obviously."

"Um, wrong. Obviously it would be me."

"No way! I was her first human contact. I was there when she hatched!"

"First doesn't mean best," I say with a smirk. "I'm her favorite human now."

"Yeah right!"

We mock-fight all the way back to my hut, both pretending to be annoyed.

And both of us ignoring the fact that joking about it doesn't make it any less true: at the end of the third trial, only one of us can win.

The next few days pass in a blur of chores in the morning, time with Lilja in the afternoon, and training with Ari at night. As the week draws to a close, I try to put all of that out of my mind and focus on the impending competition. The very first round is coming up faster than I ever would've thought possible, and I'm both eager to get into the arena and dreading it. I try to learn everything I can from Ari about what it will be like, but he isn't very forthcoming.

"So we'll all be in the arena at once?" I ask him. "All the competitors?"

It's the night before the first trial, and we're tucking Lilja into her cave before heading back to the village after a long session of practicing magic on the plants and flowers surrounding the beach, mimicking what we'd do in the Realm.

"That's what Agnar said," Ari replies with a shrug. "He said the first round is going to focus on everything we've covered so far, which is just the basics—tracking prints and identifying plants."

"Right, but what will we actually have to *do*?"

"I don't know, Bryn." Ari has been testy all day, and I suspect his nerves are getting to him. "That's all he said. Really."

"But what kind of magic will we have to perform to prove we know different kinds of plants? Is it like a quiz? Why would we even need to be in the arena for that?"

"I don't *know*, Bryn. All I know is that he said some of the competitors will be eliminated if we fail this round and that we'd need to know everything he's taught us so far."

That seems impossible when I can't say for sure *what* Seeker Agnar has taught them. While Ari seems to be doing his best to relay each of the lessons, getting them secondhand isn't the same as hearing them myself. "Ugh. I can't wait for this to be over."

Ari snorts. "What are you worried about? You're going to be fine."

"How do you know?"

Ari rolls his eyes. "Really, Bryn, how many other competitors do you think have fed a unicorn before? Or flown a dragon?"

"Well . . ."

"And you're like an encyclopedia when it comes to plants, too. I still don't know half as much about them as you do."

"Well . . ."

Lilja snorts, and Ari pats her nose appreciatively. "See, she agrees with me. You're fine."

"Well, so are you. I didn't do any of those things in the Realm by myself."

Ari shrugs again, but the tips of his ears turn pink.

I try to tell myself that he's right, but I'm not so sure. A few days ago, winning this competition felt like the easiest thing in the world, like I could will myself into winning just by wanting it badly enough. But now . . .

Now the pressure is on.

Whether I'm ready or not, it's time to compete.

The day of the first round of competition dawns bright and sunny, with only a slight sea breeze to offer relief from the heat. Summer is truly beginning to make an appearance. So many things in the Realm will be changing right now, as creatures migrate to different habitats due to the changing temperatures, and some plants will flourish under the sunlight while others will wither away for the year—

Focus, Bryn.

There's so much knowledge of the Realm inside my head, and I have no idea if any of it will be useful. I'm going through everything Ari has told me about what Seeker Agnar said in training for the hundredth time, but I still feel like there's something I'm forgetting. Surely there must be something that will trip me up, something I won't be prepared for. . . .

I can't stop picturing Seeker Agnar that first day of training, when he kicked me out of the arena. This will be the first time I've seen him since then. The first time I'll see some of the other competitors, too, as well as the rest of the

Seekers. It's humiliating just to think about. Unlike my family and most of the village, the Seekers and the competitors know what happened. They know that I was deemed unfit, weak, not good enough. They know that I was dismissed before I was even given a chance.

It's embarrassing, but it's also infuriating, and I try to let the rage be the thing that fuels me. I'll show Seeker Agnar he was wrong about me. I'll show the other competitors that they don't have a chance. And I'll show the whole Council of Seekers that I'm the one to watch. The one to pick. The one who will win.

I rush through breakfast so fast that it churns in my stomach. Mama sighs but doesn't scold me, and Papa just winks. "Excited to win the first trial, are we?" he says.

"Definitely," I say with more confidence than I feel.

"We'd better get going." Papa gulps down his own breakfast. "We'll want to get seats in the front row!"

"You really don't have to come." My stomach churns again. "It's only the first round."

"We wouldn't miss it," Papa says, and Elisa claps her hands. Mama even nods in agreement.

Papa tries to insist on escorting me to the arena, but I protest. I don't want them to know I've been kicked out of training, and one of the boys might say something about it when they see me. I make excuses about wanting to study Papa's sketchbook a few more times, and they reluctantly agree to head to the arena without me to get the best seats. The hut is eerily quiet after they leave, more still than it's ever been. I page through the sketchbook, but the beautiful illustrations of dragons and unicorns and icefoxes just make me think of everything I have to lose, and my stomach gets tied in knots.

I give up on studying and grab my boots from in front of the fireplace, preparing to leave. I lace them with tight, careful knots to make sure they won't come undone. I already had Mama tie my hair back into a thick braid last night so that it will stay out of my face.

I'm as ready as I'll ever be.

I leave the quiet hut behind me and head for the arena.

Villagers mill around outside the structure, most making their way inside to take seats as spectators. I don't see any of the Seekers anywhere, though they're probably already inside. I crane my neck to look past the crowd, wanting to catch a glimpse of what might be waiting for us in the arena—

"Bryn!" a familiar voice calls. I spin and spot Ari coming down the path just behind me. He's followed by a tall woman who, after a second, I recognize as his mother. She has wild corkscrew curls just like his, which frame her face and brush her shoulders. Her linen tunic and spangled skirt are both patterned with bright colors that bring out the warmth in her brown skin and the flecks of green in her eyes.

"Hey," I say, walking to meet them.

"I forgot to tell you," Ari says, brushing a stray curl behind his ear, "Seeker Agnar said competitors are supposed to meet around the back of the arena before it starts."

"See, I *knew* you forgot to tell me something."

"You must be Bryn," Ari's mother says, smiling at me. I like her smile—it's warm and bright.

"Yes, Elder Eydis," I say.

Her smile widens. "Ari's told me all about you."

Heat creeps into my cheeks. What exactly has Ari been saying to his mother about me?

"*Mama*," Ari says pointedly. His ears are as red as my cheeks feel.

"All right, all right," she says, laughing at Ari. "I'll go find a seat. Give me a hug for good luck."

"*Mama*," Ari protests again, louder, but she ignores it and wraps him in a massive hug. Ari's whole face flushes to match his ears, and I smirk at him over her shoulder.

"All right," his mother says again, releasing him. "Don't be nervous, Ari. You'll do great!" She turns back to me. "Good luck to you too, Bryn. Show the boys how it's done, eh?" She winks at me and, before I can respond, strides away toward the entrance.

As soon as she's out of earshot, Ari groans, and I laugh. "I like your mama," I say.

"Why, because she couldn't be more embarrassing?"

"No, because she seems nice," I say sincerely. "You should meet *my* mama. Actually, don't. I don't recommend it unless you have a death wish. She can kill people with just her glare."

"I'm pretty sure all parents have that talent," he says.

"You should see mine when I don't do my chores. She isn't so nice then."

"What's her gift?" I ask, suddenly curious.

"She's a healer." His voice gets a little quieter. "She says I get the empathy gift from my papa."

"Oh." Now I feel awkward. Ari doesn't talk about his dad, and it doesn't feel like it's any of my business. "I get my gift from my papa too," I say, just to change the subject. But Ari knows that already, so I add, "My mama is a defender. So is my sister."

"Huh." Suddenly he grins. "With that kind of lineage, I would've thought you'd be better at boundary spells," he teases.

"Shut up." I give his arm a playful shove. "I would've thought *you'd* be better at healing. And smiling. Your mama is much better at smiling than you."

"Whatever. Let's just go before we're late."

We walk together around the side of the arena, not *quite* daring to stay side by side but sort of matching each other's pace. The narrow dirt path around the arena leads to a clearing in the back, where the other competitors have clustered in a loose knot. As with that first day of training, all of them are boys.

"Decided to show up after all, empath?" one of them taunts when he sees Ari. It's Emil, the fourteen-year-old defender. Then his gaze lands on me, and his eyes widen. "You again? I thought Seeker Agnar kicked you out already."

"Yeah, Bryn," sneers an all-too-familiar voice. Johann. "We already told you that girls aren't allowed."

Some of the boys snicker at that, and I ball my hands into fists. "Maybe you should be less concerned with me and more concerned with how you're going to survive in this competition after I beat all of you today."

Johann takes a step toward me, looking like he's about to fight, but Emil grabs his sleeve and tugs him back. "No fighting among competitors, remember?" Emil hisses. "Seeker Agnar said it'd get us thrown out if we tried to fight outside the contest."

Johann glares at him. "She's not a real competitor! She's a *girl*!"

I open my mouth to retort, but before I can speak, everyone's attention turns to the path behind me, where the broad figure of Seeker Agnar has appeared. Ari and I quickly blend into the rest of the group as Seeker Agnar moves closer and stands before us.

Seeker Agnar takes a long look at each of the boys, but his gaze comes to rest on me, and I gulp. He can't throw me out. Not today. He can't, he can't, he can't—

"Are all of you certain you wish to compete?" Seeker Agnar says loudly, his voice ringing across the clearing. "If you have any doubts at all about your fitness or willingness to become a Seeker, do not waste the council's time by participating today."

No one moves. Seeker Agnar's gaze doesn't leave my face.

I bite my tongue and straighten my spine, standing as tall as I can. Ari's eyes dart toward me for a second, but he doesn't turn his head.

"All right," Seeker Agnar says after a moment, "then let us begin." His eyes finally leave mine, flickering across the group. "There are eleven of you assembled here today. Only five will pass this round. From there, only three will proceed to the third and final trial. Each of these trials will give you a task to complete. Those who fail to complete it will be eliminated automatically. If more than five of you succeed today, it will be up to the Council of Seekers to judge your performances and make further eliminations."

I gulp. I knew that judging came into play at some point in the contest, but I was hoping it wouldn't be so soon. The judges might vote to eliminate me right away even if I accomplish the task they give us. I'm sure Seeker Agnar will be happy to get rid of me as soon as he gets the chance.

Which means I don't just have to complete the task successfully. I have to do it better than everybody else, so that they can't possibly vote me out. I can't give Agnar or any of the other Seekers a reason not to pass me.

Of course, there's also the possibility that fewer than five of us will even manage to complete the task, and then it won't matter. But I haven't seen the other boys in training, so I have no real way of knowing how good the competition is. Another disadvantage that the others don't have.

It does give me one advantage, though. Aside from Ari,

none of the other boys know what I'm capable of. They might underestimate me, and I can make that work in my favor.

"As *most* of you know," Seeker Agnar continues, with his emphasis on "most" making it clear that he means everyone except me, "we have been working primarily on identifications during the past few training sessions. Therefore, my fellow Seekers and I have designed a task for you today that will reveal just how well you've been paying attention."

This much, at least, is in line with what Ari told me. I exhale in relief. Identifying plants and animal tracks is something I can do.

But Seeker Agnar isn't finished. He surveys us gravely. "It takes tremendous talent to become a true Seeker. It's not just a matter of being able to recognize a single animal print or identify the right plants. The wilds of the Realm are vast, complex, and always changing. A true Seeker doesn't only recognize pictures of plants the way we've been practicing in training. They must be able to find the real thing, in many different environments that will not make it easy for them. Therefore, the Council of Seekers has devised a task for you today that will truly test your abilities. Today's trial, unlike the future trials, won't focus as much on your magic as on your knowledge. But creative use of your magic may aid you, and the judges will certainly take that into consideration."

Seeker Agnar pauses here, and I get the sense that it's just for dramatic effect. He sure likes his speeches.

"But, sir," one of the boys pipes up, "what *is* the task?"

"Patience," Seeker Agnar says sternly, and the boy gulps.

Seeker Agnar steeples his hands, gazing at each of us again. "Two different magical items have been hidden in this arena. To successfully complete today's task, you must find both. They are in small quantities, so you will want to make sure that you're one of the first to find them before they are gone. You will find that the arena looks *different* today from what you are used to seeing, and tracking these items down is no easy task. You will need all of your knowledge to find them.

"The rules are simple. You may use your gifts if you wish. You may explore the arena as you see fit. You may not, however, enter the stands or interact with any of the spectators or the council before you've completed the task. If you leave the arena during the competition for any reason other than an emergency, you will forfeit your place. You may interact with your fellow competitors if you like; after all, real Seekers rely on one another in the field. But you may *not* attack or fight your fellow competitors in any way, including with magic, and you may *not* use magic to impede the progress of anyone else. Anyone found deliberately fighting or sabotaging another competitor will be automatically eliminated. Are there any questions?"

"What do we do with the two items once we find them?" Tomas asks. He's been so quiet today that I almost forgot he was here. Another competitor to be wary of.

"Present them to the Council of Seekers for inspection.

We will be seated at the judging table at the top of the arena. Any further questions?"

"Does quantity matter?" I ask. Everyone stares at me, and I force myself to speak louder. "Do we only need one of each of these items, or is there a specific number we need?"

"One of each will suffice," Seeker Agnar says, "though in the case of plants, they must be *whole*—roots, stem, and petals must be intact for it to be considered a single item. Half of a crushed stem or root will not count."

"How about quality?" Ari asks quietly. "If one of us has items that are, say, bigger or stronger or have better magical qualities than someone else's, does that matter?"

"Any intact item will be sufficient to pass. But if more than five of you complete the task, the quality of the items you collect will be taken into consideration by the council as we judge."

"So what *are* the two things we have to find?" Johann asks impatiently.

Seeker Agnar smiles; this seems to be the question he was waiting for. "First: snowpetals. Second: a gyrpuff feather."

Murmurs and gasps sound from most of the boys. Ari and I glance at each other. Neither item is particularly rare, and we've already practiced tracking gyrpuffs. How hard can they be to find in the arena?

"Now," Seeker Agnar says, "it is time." He leads each of us to the small doorway in the back wall, which opens directly onto the arena's floor. As we shuffle forward into the space, gasps rise up again, and this time one of them is mine.

I was wrong. This is going to be much, much harder than I thought.

The arena has been transformed.

FIFTEEN

I can hardly believe my eyes.

Where once there was a bare, open space, there is now a sprawling forest, complete with towering trees, thick underbrush, and every plant imaginable. I wouldn't even believe I was still in the arena if not for the stands holding the spectators that wrap around this incredible space, barely visible through gaps in the trees.

"Begin!" Seeker Agnar shouts, but I barely hear him. I don't know where to start. Forests in the Realm are dense, of course, and navigating them is tricky. But there's at least some natural order there—a central forest might contain birch trees and figroses, while an ice forest would contain pines and snowpetals. Even in the thickest of foliage, I always had an idea what I was looking at.

But there's nothing natural about this forest at all. It contains *everything*. Snowy pines are mixed with coastal horsetails and towering poplars. I even see hints of beech ferns that grow in lava fissures in the volcanic regions of the Realm. And all of it is thrown chaotically together, one on top of the other.

This is impossible.

Around me, some of the boys have already taken off running, crashing here and there through the foliage, but I don't move, trying to figure out what I'm looking at. Ari does the same, lingering beside me, his eyes wide. Tomas is hanging around too, studying our surroundings with a critical eye, but most of the other boys disappear into the trees.

"How are we supposed to do this?" Ari says, sounding almost outraged. "If nothing is in its natural habitat, how can we find it?"

"I don't know," I say. My heart is thundering frantically in my ears. *"I don't know."*

Snowpetals. Gyrpuff feathers. Two very small objects that could be anywhere in this massive sprawl of a forest. We could search every inch of it at random, but it would take hours upon hours, and whichever competitors found it would simply be a matter of luck. That can't be what the Seekers intend. There has to be some kind of meaning, something that they want us to do.

Cheers and shouts go up from the spectators as they watch the boys crash around, and my stomach sinks. The whole village is out there. The whole village is going to watch me fail. Most of them are probably rooting for it. And all I can do is stand here stupidly, not knowing what to do. Everyone is going to see. Ari's mama. The Seekers. Elisa—

Elisa, who won't have starflowers anymore because of me.

My papa, who's counting on me to follow in his footsteps.

And my mama, who believes in me even though she thinks I might be setting myself up to fail.

I *cannot* fail.

I straighten my spine, throw my shoulders back, and close my eyes. *One, two, three.* I inhale slowly, counting my breaths until my heart rate slows down. Now I can think.

Okay. Clearly the Seekers want us to know more than just which habitat to look in for a particular item. It's not enough to know that snowpetals grow in the ice forests; they want more. So what else do I know?

I open my eyes. Ari is watching me, and he smiles. "Looks like you figured something out."

I frown. "Why do you care?" Lowering my voice in case anyone overhears, I add, "We're not working together on this, Ari. Not today."

"Maybe we should be," he murmurs. "If we team up, we can make sure to beat the others."

I narrow my eyes. "You just want to team up because you don't know what to do. You want me to give you the answers."

"No," he says. "Actually, I just used my gift, and I figured something out. I know where one of the items is."

I study his face, trying to figure out if he's telling the

truth. His empathy gift doesn't work on plants or objects, so it's not like he can just sense them directly. Even if he could, there's way too much foliage here to pick out individual plants; my nature gift isn't doing me any good. I don't know how he could have figured something out already.

On the other hand, he might be right about teaming up. If each of us goes after one of the items and finds enough to share . . .

"Which item?" I ask, unable to keep the suspicion out of my voice.

"The feathers," he says.

"And you're *sure* you know where they are?"

"I'll make you a deal," he says. "I'll find two feathers. You find the snowpetals and get enough for both of us. That way each of us has to search for only one thing instead of two, so we'll be done before the others."

I wish I had more time to think this through, but the clock is ticking. Tomas is already moving away into the depths of the arena, leaving only Ari and me still standing at the entrance. The one thing I don't have is time.

I guess it can't hurt to go along with his suggestion. If Ari is lying about knowing where the feathers are, then I'll just have to go after them myself—which I'm going to have to do anyway if we don't team up. "All right," I say. "Let's do it."

"Deal." He strides away briskly, but he doesn't step into the forest; instead, he circles around the edge of the arena, disappearing around the curve and out of sight. Interesting . . .

I need to focus. What else do I know about snowpetals?

They cling to snow-covered trees in the glacier region of the Realm. They're some of the few flowering plants that flourish in frigid temperatures, drawing upon the magic of the Realm to actually feed off snow and turn it into fuel. Anywhere there's both consistent snow and magic, there will also be snowpetals. But that's a wide swath of the Realm, and they don't grow in *every* forest. Most of them are found where magic is the strongest. . . .

Oh. Ari already figured it out, and practically told me the answer.

I close my eyes again, but this time I reach for my magic, feeding it through my body and out through my fingertips. The sheer number of plants around me would be overwhelming if I focused on each one of them individually, which is why I didn't try this before. But if I don't focus on them individually, if I let them all blur together into one, a clear picture emerges. Or rather, a *pattern*.

The amount of magic around us ebbs and flows, like a slow-moving river. The northeastern side of the arena, the direction in which Ari disappeared, has a much stronger magical pull than the rest of the space, as most of the magic seems to be flowing there. It's the same direction Tomas disappeared too. They both figured it out before I did. All magical items can be found more abundantly where magic is strongest, so of course we should try to find the pattern within the arena.

"Is that girl just going to stand there all day?" says a loud voice from above me. I open my eyes and turn. The nearest spectators are staring at me.

"What's she even doing down there?" says another. "Doesn't she know this is a *Seeker* competition?"

Heat floods my face. I'm not just going to stand here and let the boys win. I'll show them all what a real Seeker looks like.

I turn around and plunge into the trees.

The underbrush is nearly too thick to walk through, but I let my gift rush out, nudging the life sparks of the plants right in front of me to direct their branches out of my way. They bend to my will, forming a rough path. The ground is relatively even under my feet—this is the arena, after all, not a real forest—so it's actually easy to run once the plants are cleared out. I pass one of the boys, who's cutting his way through the thicket with a knife and watches me openmouthed. After recovering from the shock of seeing me rush past behind a row of shifting plants, he tries to follow, using the path I've created. I quickly direct some of my magic behind me, sealing the path back up once I've passed so that he and anyone else who tries to follow me will be stuck in the brush.

Using my gift this way is exhausting, but I don't have much distance to cover before reaching the northeast corner, and all the magic surrounding me provides extra fuel. I cut the most direct path possible, and within minutes I've arrived in the right location.

Unfortunately, there's still a fairly large section of the forest in front of me, and the magical current feels equally strong throughout. I've narrowed the search down to just this corner, but how am I going to narrow it down further?

There must be something I'm missing.

What else do I know about snowpetals?

They have many uses, since they remain cold to the touch even after they're plucked. They're too bitter to make good food, but they're often eaten by—

By vatnaveras. Who live in lakes.

I cast my magic out wider, searching, searching . . .

There. I didn't imagine it. There's a small body of water somewhere ahead. Freshwater, it seems, just like a lake. Exactly the kind of environment a vatnavera might choose to live in. A cold lake surrounded by snowpetals would almost be guaranteed to have a vatnavera in its depths.

Maybe the Seekers want us to assume that the reverse is true too—where there's a vatnavera, there are also snowpetals.

I creep forward, getting closer and closer to the water. Ahead of me, the foliage has gotten so thick that it practically forms a solid wall, blocking my line of sight. I push my gift forward, shoving the branches out of the way—

Thwap.

Something collides with the back of my knee, and I stumble.

Thwap.

Another tree branch hits me, in my arm this time. I spin around, trying to figure out what's happening. In every direction, the wall of branches and leaves has turned into a writhing mass, all of it moving and shifting. All of it *attacking* me.

I duck as another flying branch aims for my head, but I trip over a coiling tree root that just rose from the ground. A shower of leaves falls into my face, temporarily blinding me, and in the meantime another branch slams into my ankle, knocking me off my feet.

I crawl backward, putting distance between myself and the seemingly murderous plants. What's happening? What did I do wrong?

I can still sense the lake, somewhere ahead of me. And I don't feel any other bodies of water nearby.

Maybe it's not what I'm doing wrong, but what I'm doing right. I'm close to finding the snowpetals, and the arena is trying to make it harder for me to get there.

The foliage went still after I backed away, and everything looks deceptively calm. But I suspect that the minute I try to pass through it, I'll be attacked again.

This makes absolutely no sense. In the Realm, trees don't just come to life and attack you like this. What is it that the Seekers are trying to prove?

I get to my feet and take another look at the jumble of plants surrounding me. So many different kinds, all mixed together.

Maybe that's the point: this isn't the Realm at all, and isn't supposed to be. Everything we have to do here is meant to show the Seekers something.

What do they want me to show them now?

I think back to how I approached the wall the first time. I was moving quickly, using my gift, all things I'd think the Seekers would appreciate—

Except maybe it was the *way* I was using my gift. I was aggressive with the plants, trying to push them out of my way. But that's not what naturalists do. That's not what *Seekers* do.

I call my magic back out—slowly and carefully this time. I gently ease it toward the nearest tree, seeking out its life force. It's not hard to find—a strong, steady pulse, like a heartbeat.

I funnel my gift into the plant, letting it draw on my magic, letting it grow. I do the same to the tree next to it, and the one beside that, and the one beside that . . .

I nurture the forest, and it explodes.

For a split second I think I've made a terrible mistake—as new branches and leaves burst to life in front of me, it looks like I'm about to be buried beneath them. But, just as suddenly, the plants move again. Branches bow out of the way; limbs retreat; leaves disentangle themselves.

A path appears, leading me forward.

I creep closer to the lake, moving much more stealthily this time. Partly because I don't want to anger the forest with any sudden movements, but partly because, if I'm right, I don't want any of the boys to know that this is here. It will be a dead giveaway, if they make the same connection I did. But the lake—more of a pond, really—is small and well hidden, so that only a naturalist would be likely to sense it with magic alone. If I don't give it away, some of the others will never even know this is here.

Creeping through the trees and carefully parting the underbrush, I catch my first glimpse of the water. It's an awfully small pond, so small that I could easily walk a circle around it in less than a minute. For a second I think I've gotten it all wrong—no vatnavera would ever be found in such a tiny body of water.

But this isn't the Realm. Everything in this arena has to be done in miniature, since there's such limited space. This entire arena could be filled with water and it still wouldn't be as large as some of the Realm's smallest lakes. The size isn't the point.

And besides, what a clever way to hint at the presence of a vatnavera. A creature whose size isn't always what you'd expect. Because it can shrink and grow at will.

I pull all of my magic in to circle the pond, trying to get a sense of what's growing here. Grass frozen over with ice, a tangle of juniper trees, lots of weeds and bramble and—

And something with a bright, pulsing magical spark.

No, *two* somethings.

A little clump of snowpetal flowers, dangling on the far edge of the pond.

And the tiny vatnavera that's eating them.

SIXTEEN

The vatnavera hasn't noticed me yet. Its long, coiled body arches up out of the water, reaching for the fluffy white petals of the flowers beside the pond. For a second I can hardly breathe—it looks just like one of Papa's drawings, only smaller, its body no wider than my palm. I can't see how long it is, since the rest of its body disappears into the water, but it hardly matters. The vatnavera can lengthen itself whenever it wants. Which it will probably do, as soon as it sees me. Vatnavera may be friendly toward humans, but they definitely don't like anything that tries to take away their food source. Like, say, the snowpetal flowers it's currently munching on. There's a pretty good chance that it will enlarge and try to scare me away if I come any closer.

Of course, there's also a chance that it will shrink and hide, giving me a chance to snatch up the flowers. And vatnaveras don't typically harm humans, so even if it tries to scare me, it *probably* won't bite me or anything. But it could. And somehow I don't think that charging toward it blindly, with no plan at all, is going to impress the Seekers. I don't know if they can see this little pond from way up in the arena, but I should act as if they can.

I need to come up with a solution, and quick, or the vatnavera is going to eat all the flowers before I can grab a single one. And I need two, one for me and one for Ari.

I approach quietly, coming in from the side so that the vatnavera will be able to see me. The last thing I want to do is startle it. The creature finally senses my presence, turning its head in my direction. Its eyes are small and yellow. Two curling brown horns jut out from its head, and a forked tongue flicks from its mouth.

"Hello there, beautiful vatnavera," I say softly. I give it the smallest of nudges with my magic, letting it sense my gift. Its life spark is cool and humming, like nothing I've ever felt before. Its magic moves like the slow yet powerful current of a chilly glacial river.

The vatnavera stays still, eyeing me warily, a puffy white snowpetal half sticking out of its mouth. I creep carefully forward. If I don't startle it, it just might let me grab some—

"Hey!" a loud voice yells. "Get away from my snowpetals!"

Johann charges out from the brush to my left, heading straight toward the vatnavera.

"No, don't—" I say, but it's too late.

Everything happens fast. One second, Johann is charging

toward the vatnavera and its flowers, reaching out to grab a fistful of the snowpetals. The next second, the vatnavera is shooting upward, its body elongating and enlarging simultaneously in a burst of speed. I blink, and its body is as wide as I am, rising a good five feet out of the water, its tail thrashing. Its head aims for Johann, its massive horns gleaming, its mouth open to reveal rows of newly grown teeth. Johann screams as the suddenly monstrous-looking creature lashes toward him. I reach out with my magic on instinct, wanting to intervene somehow, but it all happens too quickly. In his panic, Johann lunges away from the vatnavera and falls headfirst into the pond. Which is the absolute last place he should go, because the now-massive vatnavera is thrashing around wildly within it.

"Johann!" I yell, but I can't see him through all of the churning, spraying water. The vatnavera is frantic now—it wanted Johann to turn away, not to plunge headfirst into its home.

I do the only thing I can think of and reach for my gift, pushing everything I have toward the lake. I find Johann's life force easily and grab hold, trying to tug him forward. Humans can't be manipulated by sheer magic quite so easily as animals or plants can, but if Johann's smart, he'll cooperate with my magic instead of fighting it. As my gift pulls Johann upward, it simultaneously sinks into the water around him, forming a current to buffer him up. With the very last vestiges of my gift remaining, I try to nudge the vatnavera's life spark in the opposite direction of Johann's, encouraging it to move across the pond.

"Bryn!" a voice shouts. Ari crashes through the trees, his eyes wide.

"Calm it down!" I yell, my voice straining as much as my magic as I try to haul Johann out of the water.

I don't have the energy to explain further, but Ari takes one look at the panicking vatnavera and understands. His hands glow with the yellow warmth of his gift, and within moments the vatnavera's thrashing slows, its body calming. It reacts to the tug of my magic now too, gliding closer to Ari.

Johann resurfaces, gasping, and I lean toward the edge of the pond, offering him a hand up. He shudders for breath, then ignores my hand and hauls himself onto the embankment. The vatnavera, meanwhile, is shrinking back down, calmed both by Ari's gift and Johann's retreat from the pond.

"Are you okay?" I ask Johann.

"'Course I am," he says gruffly. "I did that on purpose. I wanted to tackle that thing and scare it away so I could get the stupid flowers."

"That 'thing' is a vatnavera," I say, "and there's no need to tackle it. It won't hurt you."

"Are you kidding me? Did you see how big it got? It nearly gored me with its horns *and* its teeth! If I didn't have such a strong warrior gift, I couldn't have fended it off."

I roll my eyes. "It wouldn't have done anything to you if you hadn't scared it, and your warrior gift didn't do *anything*."

Johann opens his mouth to argue further, but Ari interrupts. "Bryn," he says quietly, "maybe a little less arguing and a little more winning the competition? Come help me with these."

Johann and I glance down at the snowpetals at Ari's feet. Several of them are in pieces, having been torn by all the movement of the vatnavera or else eaten by it. And Seeker Agnar said they have to be intact.

Only two perfect snowpetals remain.

All three of us reach this conclusion at exactly the same time.

Johann and Ari both lunge forward—Johann reaching for the flowers and Ari trying to block him. It's a fight I'm not sure Ari can win. Johann has a warrior gift, and I suspect he's about to use it on Ari regardless of what the rules say. I have to do something. But I can't grab the flowers myself, not with the boys in the way.

I reach for my gift. But my magic is too drained from the encounter with the forest and pulling Johann from the water. There's nothing but a few sparks left. I'm *empty.*

I can barely summon enough energy to reach out to the plants around me. I seek out the nearest life source, a tiny spark, and draw on it. My magic blooms a little, but it's not nearly enough to do anything. I need more.

I close my eyes and focus on my breathing, the way Ari showed me. The rhythm of magic flows around me, alerting me to all the little sparks of life here. I draw on them one by one, pulling on the grass at my feet and letting its energy feed my own. At the same time, Johann collides with Ari, knocking him to the ground and throwing a punch. Ari fights back, pulling Johann onto the ground too, and within seconds they're a blur of fists and flailing limbs.

Some of my energy restored, I cast around for something, anything I can use to . . .

The snowpetals are bright spots of light, infused with magic that pulses through their life forces. Nearby, the vatnavera's head, considerably smaller than it was the last time I saw it, pops out of the water, watching the boys fight with wide eyes.

Which gives me an idea.

Ari and Johann are between me and snowpetals on land. But not in the water.

I kick off my boots and slip into the pond, the icy water making goose bumps rise on my skin. It's shallow here, coming just under my shoulders. A few feet away from me, the vatnavera has frozen in alarm. I'm an intruder in his home, and he's trying to figure out how best to get me to leave. For a split second, I wish I had Ari's empathy gift so that I could soothe the vatnavera's emotions.

But I'm not an empath. I'm a naturalist. I'm a *good* one. And it's time to prove it.

"Hello," I say quietly, letting my gift brush softly against the vatnavera once more. "I'm not going to hurt you." The vatnavera still looks wary, but he isn't growing in size, so I take that as a good sign and keep talking, letting my magic interact with his as I do. "This is a pretty nice pond you have here. Sorry to disturb it. I just need to walk right over there, okay?"

I step sideways, moving in the direction of the snowpetals while keeping the same amount of distance between myself and the vatnavera. It blinks, uncertain, as I take another step.

"You're doing great," I tell it. "Just let me come right over here. . . ."

The vatnavera blinks again and disappears, shrinking back into the water. I can't see it, but I can sense its energy retreating to the other side of the pond. It's clearly decided I'm not a threat that needs to be scared away, but it also doesn't want to risk being near me. Which is fine, because it's not what I need right now.

My wet clothes weigh me down as I rush the last few steps, reaching the far embankment just below the snowpetals. The puffy white flowers are anchored deep in the earth, and I'm afraid ripping them out might tear the roots too badly. Seeker Agnar said they needed to be intact. So I yank my pocket-knife out and use it to dig up the plant. Its stark white roots stick out among all the dirt, making it easy enough to avoid cutting them as I free them from the earth.

The first intact snowpetal is in my hands when Johann breaks away from Ari and stumbles toward me. "Get away, Bryn!" Johann yells. "Those are mine!"

I don't have time to dig the second snowpetal up properly before Johann gets to it, but trying to yank it up might damage it. I could just take my prize and leave, but then I won't have anything to trade with Ari for the gyrpuff feather. I look at the other snowpetals, just to make sure that there isn't another whole one, but they've all been munched by the vatnavera—

But thinking about the vatnavera gives me another idea.

Just as Johann lunges forward to yank the snowpetal out of the ground, I flood it with my magic. *Please work, please work, please work.* . . .

Usually, when I use my gift on plants, it's in order to make them grow. I've never tried to do the opposite—to make them *shrink*. I don't know if I can do it. But I have to try.

And it works. Instead of strengthening and enlarging the plant's life force, I compress it, making it into a tighter, smaller mass.

Right before Johann's eyes, the snowpetal seems to disappear. His hands, reaching out for it, grasp nothing but air.

It hasn't disappeared, of course. It's just very, very small, too tiny to be seen among all the other plants growing up along the embankment. Like the vatnavera, it's hiding from its enemy. Or in this case, *my* enemy.

"Where'd it go?" Johann spins around, looking this way and that, as if the snowpetal will somehow materialize behind him. When it doesn't, he turns back to me. "What'd you do, Bryn?"

I don't answer; I'm too busy shrinking the snowpetal already in my hand so that it will fit snugly inside my palm, where I can keep it away from Johann.

He lets out a frustrated yell and kicks the dirt, sending it spraying into the water. Red light bursts abruptly around his hands as he calls on his warrior gift, but it won't do him any good. Warrior gifts can't detect the subtleties in life forces. His magic can't tell the difference between a miniaturized snowpetal and a blade of grass.

But naturalist gifts can, and I know exactly where the snowpetal is, even without being able to see it.

Tucking the other snowpetal and my knife into the safety of my pocket, I scramble out of the pond as Johann drops to his knees and runs his hands over the ground, trying to feel the flower. He cries out as a sharp bramble stings his hand. I use the moment of his distraction to swoop down and carefully pluck the snowpetal from the ground. The entire flower is no larger than my fingernail.

As I step away from Johann, I notice something else lying in the grass, right at the edge of the water. A single vatnavera scale, gleaming in the sun.

It's not one of the items we're supposed to be looking for, but a real Seeker would never just leave a magical object lying around. I scoop it up and tuck it into my pocket next to the second snowpetal.

I run up the side of the embankment, leaving Johann to yell angrily at the dirt. Ari is sitting a few feet away, pinching his nose. Blood is smeared along his upper lip. "Are you okay?" I ask.

He shrugs, lowering his hand. "Nothing that won't heal. Did you get it?"

I grin. With a nudge of encouragement from my gift, the snowpetal explodes, growing rapidly back to its original size in the palm of my hand. Ari's eyes widen. "You shrank it? That's so cool!"

"The way you calmed down the vatnavera was pretty cool too," I say, but my cheeks flush with pride. I've never shrunk a plant before. I hope the Seekers were watching. I hope the whole *village* was watching.

I hand Ari the snowpetal, and he gazes at it in wonder. "You got one too, right?" he says.

"Yep. It's in my pocket."

"I have something for you," Ari says, reaching into his own pocket and withdrawing two large black feathers. He drops one of them into my palm.

"How'd you find these so fast?"

"From what you taught me." He grins. "After I narrowed it down to this region, based on the amount of magic here, I looked for rock formations like the cliffs where gyrpuffs would make nests, just like that time we tracked them. Knowing what to look for, the tall rocks weren't hard to find. There weren't any actual gyrpuffs, but there *was* a little cave with some feathers inside."

"Brilliant," I say. The tips of Ari's ears turn red, and I smile. "Ready to win this competition?"

Ari grins. "Let's do it."

"Not so fast," says a loud and increasingly familiar voice from behind us.

Ari and I whirl around. Johann has composed himself and is trudging toward us up the embankment. His hands are glowing bright red with the strength of his warrior gift.

"Only one of us is going to take those snowpetals back to the Seekers," he says. "And it's going to be me."

SEVENTEEN

I don't think so," Ari says. His tone is calm and even, but his jaw is tight. "We got to them first."

Johann sneers at him. "How's your nose, empath?" He raises his hands. "You think I can't make you give them to me?"

I glare at him. "This is against the rules. You can't threaten us."

"What are you going to do about it, little girl? Go crying to the Seekers and tell them I was too *mean* to you? Tell them you couldn't handle competing with the big, bad boys?"

My jaw clenches. "No. I'm going to tell them you're a cheat."

"And so will I," Ari says evenly. "It'll be your word against both of ours."

But Johann just rolls his eyes. "The word of an empath and a girl? I'll take that chance."

I glance at Ari. I'm not sure that either of us can fight Johann directly right now. Ari's still bleeding from their last encounter, and my magic is almost depleted. And besides, neither of us is a warrior.

But Ari doesn't look afraid. He just looks angry. Turning to me and speaking quickly under his breath, he says, "I could use my gift to calm him down, make him less aggressive. But using my gift on another competitor is against the rules. And I don't know if the Seekers can see us right now or not."

I nod. "We'll just have to outsmart him, then."

Thinking fast, I pretend to reach into my pocket and draw something out. I pinch my thumb and forefinger together like I'm holding something very small. Johann didn't see me grow the snowpetal back to its original size. For all he knows, it's still shrunken.

"Here it is," I say boldly, waving my hand around so Johann can't get too close a look. "If you think you can grow it back to size, you can have it."

"Hand it over," Johann growls.

I wind my arm back and make a throwing motion, acting like I'm tossing the snowpetal out into the pond. "Go fetch," I say.

Johann turns, scanning the water, and Ari and I take advantage of his distraction. We run for it.

Johann isn't fooled for long and races after us. My wet clothes weigh me down, and Ari's nose is still bleeding. We're going to need help to outrun Johann.

Quickly I push my gift into the plants surrounding us. I repeat the trick I learned earlier, nurturing the plants, and they clear a path through the woods ahead so that we can run faster. My gift is still depleted from using it so much, but the life forces in all the plants around us give me enough strength to manage it. And Ari helps—he learned the same trick while trying to find the lake, and much to my annoyance, the trees respond to his empathy gift just as well as they do to my nature gift.

I cut straight for the nearest edge of the arena, and within a minute we break free of the woods and reach the stands. Ari points out where the Seekers are sitting near the top of the arena, easily identifiable in their forest-green cloaks, and we race up the stairs toward them.

The Council of Seekers sits in a row: Larus, Freyr, Ludvik, and Agnar. Seeker Larus is the first to speak when we both stop before them, trying to catch our breath. "Have you completed the task?"

"Yes," Ari says, wiping self-consciously at the blood under his nose.

"Both of you?" says Seeker Agnar, his eyebrows rising.

"Yes," I say firmly, reaching into my pocket. Ari and I both produce the snowpetals and feathers. I hand mine to Seeker Larus, and Ari hands his to Seeker Freyr. The Seekers examine them carefully for a moment and exchange glances with each other.

"Congratulations," Seeker Larus says. "Both of you have passed."

"Though of course we must wait until the other competitors have finished before determining if you will move on to the next trial," Seeker Agnar adds.

"Can you tell us how many other competitors have finished so far?" I ask.

The Seekers exchange glances again. "Only one," says Seeker Larus. "You may wait in the arena if you wish to observe more of the competition, or you may go home and find out the results later."

Ari nods, and Seeker Ludvik tilts his head. "What happened to your nose, young man?"

Ari glances at me. This is our opening to tell them about Johann. About how he started the fight with Ari and how he threatened us both. But Johann's words are echoing in my head.

I don't want the Seekers to think I couldn't handle myself, that I let Johann get the best of me, that I have to tattle on him in order to win. Besides, it's not like Ari and I can complain about others cheating when we've been secretly hiding a dragon and flew into the Realm once. From the look in Ari's eyes, he seems to be thinking the same.

"I tripped while climbing the rocks to the get the gyrpuff feathers," Ari says. "Just scraped myself up a little."

Seeker Larus nods and raises his hand. The blue light of his gift glows, and within seconds Ari's nose stops bleeding. "That should do the trick," he says.

"Thank you," Ari stammers.

Seeker Larus looks like he's about to dismiss us, so I

quickly reach into my pocket and withdraw the vatnavera scale. "There's one more thing," I say, holding it out to him. "I know this wasn't on the list of items we were supposed to find, but I happened to grab a vatnavera scale while getting the snowpetals."

Seeker Larus and Seeker Freyr both raise their eyebrows, and Ari gapes at me for a second before collecting himself. Seeker Larus examines the scale. "An excellent find," he says, and the smallest of smiles crosses his face. "Well done."

I grin. "Thank you."

Seeker Larus dismisses us, and Ari and I slip into the stands, finding an empty row near the top.

"Should we try to find our parents?" Ari asks, gazing around the arena.

We probably should—I'm not sure if they've seen anything that's happened and know that I passed or not—but I'm too tired to move. "Let's watch from up here for a minute," I say. "It's a pretty good vantage point."

Ari sits beside me, and we gaze out over the arena. It looks so much smaller from up here. I can easily pick out the set of rock formations in the northeastern section that must be where Ari found the feathers. The pond is impossible to spot, as the trees overhead are too dense, but I'm pretty sure I can tell where it is. I doubt anyone could have seen our fight with Johann there, but other areas are more visible. I can see several boys moving through the trees, though three or four of them are in the wrong section of the arena entirely.

"No wonder they forbade us from going into the stands," Ari says. "It's not just that they didn't want us to get help from spectators. It's that you can see everything way easier up here."

"Imagine if we could've flown on Lilja," I say. "We could've done the whole thing in two seconds!"

Ari laughs. "I don't know about that. Lilja would be such a nuisance—crashing through the trees, eating everything, demanding bilberries. . . ."

"Setting the forest on fire," I add, smiling.

"Our dragon is a piece of work," Ari says, and I laugh. But my laughter fades when I remember that all of this is temporary. Both Ari and I have survived the first trial. We might survive the second.

But in the end, one of us will lose. And then Lilja won't be *our* dragon anymore. Only one of us will ever get to see her again.

I glance sideways at Ari as he looks out over the arena. We made a pretty good team today, with him finding the feathers and calming the vatnavera and me saving Johann and getting the snowpetals. We made a pretty good team in the Realm, too. But someday soon, the teamwork has to end.

What will happen if Ari and I both make it to the top three and we have to compete against each other? What if it had been Ari instead of Johann that I was facing today? Could I have beaten him?

Would I have wanted to?

Of course I would. I *have* to win this competition, and that means beating Ari however I can.

I just thought it would be easier than this.

"Who do you think the other winner is?" Ari asks suddenly, distracting me. "Seeker Larus said there was one more."

"I don't know. I can't tell who's still down there."

"Can anyone else even finish? We got the last two snow-petals beside the pond. The vatnavera ate the rest."

"I bet they hid some in more than one place. They had to have planned for something like that to happen. Like, what if the first person to find the snowpetals took *all* of them and didn't leave any for anyone else, so no one else could pass? The Seekers wouldn't want that."

"Good point," Ari says. "They probably even planned for that vatnavera to eat some of the snowpetals. It's like they were rewarding whoever found them quickly enough to grab them before they were eaten. But that doesn't mean there weren't snowpetals growing somewhere else."

As if to prove his point, at that moment murmurs spread through the crowd, and we quickly turn toward the Seekers. A boy is climbing the steps toward them, clutching a massive snowpetal in his hand.

"Who is it?" I say. "Can't tell from this distance."

"Looks like Emil," Ari says, sounding a bit surprised. I'm a little surprised too. I didn't think Emil had the focus or the dedication to stick through this competition. But he *is* pretty good with his defender gift, from what I've seen, so maybe his magic helped him.

"I haven't seen Johann come out, have you?" Ari asks suddenly. "He was running right behind us. Even if he got caught up in the brambles, he still should've come out by now."

"Unless he went back. Maybe he tried to gather up some of the snowpetals that were shredded. Trying to piece them together, maybe?"

"Or maybe he figured out the same thing we did," Ari says quietly. "Maybe he went looking for a second patch of snowpetals."

I gulp. Johann *did* manage to find the pond on his own. He might be capable of finding the flowers elsewhere. The feathers, too. But it's bad news for Ari and me if Johann passes this round. He won't forget what happened. He'll go into the second trial with an even bigger grudge against us, and that won't end well.

I glance around the arena, but I can't see if Johann's still down there. As the sun slides lower across the sky, more boys come out of the arena, but none of them appear to have passed. One emerges crying and rushes over to his parents without even acknowledging the Seekers. Two more approach the Seekers, but they're empty-handed, and they walk away with their heads hanging. Emil is the only boy we've seen emerge victorious.

Which means four of us, in total, have passed. There's only one spot left for the second trial.

One by one, the boys emerge from the woods defeated. Ari and I begin to keep count. Whoever finished the task before us, plus Emil, plus the two of us, plus the six boys we've now seen emerge empty-handed. That makes ten. There are eleven competitors, so . . .

"Johann's the only one left. If he finds both items, he'll be the final winner," Ari murmurs.

"Maybe he won't find them," I say.

But minutes later, I'm proven wrong.

Johann races out of the forest and up the steps of the arena, the white blur of a snowpetal visible in one of his hands. Ari and I watch intently as he confers with the Seekers for a moment. He hands Seeker Larus something. Then he walks away through the stands.

My stomach sinks. "I think that was it. I think he did it."

Ari nods. "And he was the last competitor. Look."

I follow his gaze back up to the Seekers, who have all gotten to their feet. Simultaneously, each of their hands begins to glow with the light of their gifts.

"This is it," Ari says.

Seeker Larus begins to speak, and several people in the crowd gasp. His voice is booming, echoing across the arena so that everyone can hear.

"How's he doing that?" Ari asks.

"Probably the amplifier potion," I say. "With the right magical ingredients, it can amplify a person's voice. The effects last for only a few minutes, though."

"Attention," Seeker Larus says again. "The first round of the Seeker competition has ended. Five competitors have successfully completed the tasks they were given and will move on to the next trial, which will be held in one week's time."

A hush falls over the arena as we wait.

"The successful competitors are . . ."

I hold my breath. Which is silly, because I already know I'll be one of them. But suddenly I can't help wondering if there's been some kind of mistake, if the council decided not to select me after all, if they're going to disqualify me, if—

"Ari, Petur's son," says Seeker Larus, and Ari exhales. I don't.

"Tomas, Freyr's son." Of course. Tomas is the one competitor we didn't see emerge from the arena, so he must be the one who finished before us. I'm not surprised. He seemed to know what he was doing.

"Emil, Baldur's son," Seeker Larus continues. "Johann, Viktor's son."

My stomach sinks. Did he skip me? Is he going to say my name? Have I somehow lost?

"And Bryn, Jakob's daughter."

The air whooshes out of my lungs, and murmurs go up from the crowd.

I did it. I actually did it.

I'm not only the first girl ever to compete, but I'm the first girl to ever make it to the second round.

I'm not sure how the rest of the village feels about that, but I don't care.

All of my top rivals made it to the second trial too, but I don't care about that either. Not yet.

For once, I am victorious. And I can be victorious again.

This is my competition to win.

EIGHTEEN

After the announcement, Ari and I find our families among the crowd at the entrance of the arena. Ari's mother sweeps him into a hug, and then I lose sight of him as Elisa practically tackles me, jumping up and down. "You won! You won!"

"Only the first round, El," I say, but I can't stop beaming.

"We saw you from the top part," Elisa says, pointing toward the top of the stands. "We saw you running through the forest!"

"Could you see the vatnavera?" I ask.

Elisa's eyes widen. "There was a vatnavera?" she cries. "Was there a unicorn, too?"

Before I can answer her, Mama steps up and gives me a big hug. "Good work," she says, squeezing me tight, and my heart surges. She steps back to examine me, sees that my clothes are drenched, and sighs loudly. Well, it was nice while it lasted.

"My girl!" Papa booms, practically sweeping me off my feet as he hugs me next.

"Too tight, Papa!" I say, laughing. He sets me down, but not before declaring loudly, "That was *my* daughter who won the first trial!"

Several heads turn in our direction, and Mama shushes him, but she's smiling too.

"We're so proud of you, Bryn," Papa says.

"Elisa says you missed the best part," I say. "There was a vatnavera, Papa!"

"Was there really?" He raises his brows. "They usually don't include creatures in the arena until the later trials."

"So there *will* be creatures in the later trials?" I say.

"I shouldn't have told you that," Papa says, laughing. "Forget I said anything."

I grin. "I didn't hear it from you."

"That's right. We've got to stay impartial."

Mama huffs. "As if Seeker Freyr was impartial evaluating his own son."

"I didn't see Tomas finish," I say. "What happened?"

Papa glances at the crowd surrounding us. "Let's discuss this at home, all right?"

But before we can turn to leave, I'm tackled by yet another excited person. This time it's Runa, who's smiling from ear to ear. "You were so great, Bryn!"

"How much did you see?"

"Not much," she admits, "but I saw you racing around in

there with *Ari.*" She gives my shoulder a meaningful nudge.

"Hush," I say. "We just thought it would be easier if we teamed up. It was his idea, actually."

"Sure," Runa says skeptically. "Whatever you say."

"Runa, would you like to join us for dinner tonight?" Mama asks. "We're having a little celebration for Bryn."

"We are?" I ask.

"It's a surprise!" Elisa yells.

"Thanks for the invitation," Runa says in her politest voice, "but I think my mama is expecting me to help with our supper tonight."

"All right, then," Mama says, "we'd better be going. Come on, Elisa."

Runa and I wave goodbye, and I promise to fill her in later on everything that happened during the competition. As I follow my family up the path toward the village, Mama says, "Runa is such a polite young lady," in her fondest tone.

I roll my eyes. Mama always says that about Runa, probably as a pointed hint to Elisa and me about how we're supposed to behave.

Papa isn't paying attention; he's busy waving and smiling at the villagers we pass, who all stop to greet him. Everyone knows Papa well, since he used to be Seeker, and everyone likes him, of course. Though I can't help noticing that most of the people who greet him also look away when they see me and don't offer any congratulations. Hmm. It doesn't seem like the villagers' fondness for Papa extends to the girl who's beating the boys in the Seeker competition. I hope I'm wrong, but I don't think I am. As we walk home, six different people stop to greet us, but not one of them says anything congratulatory to me.

I bet Tomas and Emil and Johann aren't getting the same treatment. They're probably being showered with praise right about now.

But I don't want to let the attitudes of the villagers dampen my good mood. I've won the first of three victories, and I'm going to celebrate it instead of worrying about what the villagers think of me.

As Papa stops to accept congratulations from one of his friends, Seeker Agnar strides out of the arena, heading for the main path back to the village. "I'll be right back," I say hastily to Mama. "I have to ask Seeker Agnar something."

Before she can reply, I race away. "Seeker Agnar!" I call. "Seeker Agnar!"

After my second shout, he stops and turns. "Yes?"

"I wanted to ask you," I say, pausing to catch my breath, "about the Seeker training."

"Yes?" he says again. His expression is not encouraging, but I have nothing to lose by asking, so I keep going.

I try to summon my most polite voice, the one I use when Mama makes me mind my manners. "I was wondering if you'd changed your mind about letting me participate," I say. "Now that I'm one of the five finalists, I'd like to be able to train properly for the next round."

There's a long, terrible pause. "I don't think that would be a good idea," he says, and my heart drops.

"I can handle the training," I say quickly. "I think I proved that today. And it's only fair that I get the same training as the other competitors."

"You did well today," Seeker Agnar acknowledges. "But the competition is only going to get more difficult from this point forward. Being able to find and identify a snowpetal is one thing. Being able to handle potentially deadly magical creatures is quite another. I can't allow young girls in my training class, not when they're likely to be hurt."

"But I—"

"I told you before," he interrupts, his voice rising. "This competition is no place for you."

Anger rises within me, and my polite voice vanishes as I open my mouth again. "The other Seekers said I did well today," I say. "Do they really think this is fair? What if I asked them?"

"Whether or not the rest of the council agrees with my decision is irrelevant," he snaps. "I am the Seeker in charge of the training classes this year, and I will run them as I see fit. I don't allow girls to train, and that's final. Don't ask me again."

He starts to turn away, but a booming voice makes us both freeze. "Agnar!" Papa calls cheerfully, walking up to us.

Oh no. Papa's going to ask him something about my training, I just know it. Even though I asked him not to—

"Jakob," Seeker Agnar says, acknowledging him with a nod.

"Excellent work you've done with the first trial," Papa says, smiling at him. "A great showcase of our competitors' talents."

"Thank you," Seeker Agnar says, a bit stiffly.

Papa places a hand on my shoulder. "This one's not giving you any trouble in training, is she?"

"Papa!" I say indignantly, hoping to stop Seeker Agnar from answering.

Seeker Agnar pauses for a moment, giving me a long look. I can see the moment when he figures it out—that I haven't told Papa the truth. I close my eyes, waiting for him to give me away.

"No trouble at all," Seeker Agnar says.

I open my eyes. Did he just . . . ?

Papa chuckles. "I asked Larus and Ludvik, but they said you're running training all on your own this year, and they didn't know the details. Not that I want to influence any judging, of course. Just curious how my girl's been doing."

"Papa!" I say again, willing him to stop talking.

Seeker Agnar fixes his gaze on me. "She's a very . . . resilient competitor," he says finally.

Papa starts to ask something else, but Seeker Agnar excuses himself and hurries away down the path.

Papa squeezes my shoulder. "I know, I know, I promised I wouldn't say anything. But I'm sure Freyr's been asking after his child as well! Come on. Your mama and sister are waiting for us."

As he guides me down the path, I stare at the retreating form of Seeker Agnar. Why did he lie like that? Why didn't he tell Papa that he kicked me out of training?

There's only one explanation that I can think of—he's ashamed. He doesn't want Papa or anyone else, maybe even the other Seekers, to know that he's not training me. Maybe I should tell Papa myself. He might raise a fuss, tell the other Seekers about it, get someone else to run training. . . .

But it's all too embarrassing. I don't want my papa to have to step in on my behalf. I won the first trial today without formal training, and I can win the next one too. Papa will never have to know. . . .

I try not to think about Seeker Agnar as I enjoy my family's celebration at home. Mama's surprise turns out to be one of my favorite dinners, her creamy potato soup, which is liberally sprinkled with cheese, along with my favorite dessert, a bilberry pie. We all laugh and joke during the meal, and even Mama seems to be in good spirits. I recount parts of my performance in the arena that they couldn't see, and they laugh and cheer in all the right places. I downplay my teamwork with Ari, since they don't know anything about how much time Ari and I have been spending together, but I make it sound like we've teamed up in training a few times and thought it only natural to do it again for this trial. I also downplay the part where Johann fought with Ari and threatened us, since Ari lied to the Seekers about how his nose got bloody and I don't want Papa to say anything about it to his Seeker friends. If Papa knew Johann was cheating, he'd most definitely bring it up with Seeker Larus or Seeker Ludvik, and I don't want them to know.

So instead, I describe it as if Johann were just racing us to get the snowpetals and recount how I tricked him by shrinking the last flower. Papa positively glows at this point. "That's some high-level naturalist magic," he says. "Such a difficult task to perform, especially under pressure!"

"Pressure made it easier," I say. "That way I couldn't overthink it. If I'd had enough time to *think* about whether I could shrink the flowers, I probably couldn't have."

Papa nods. "An important lesson for you to remember, Bryn. Sometimes confidence is all you need. You have good instincts, so make sure you trust them."

"Yes, Papa."

"What about the *unicorns*?" Elisa demands, clanking her fork against her plate. "Were there any unicorns?"

"Sorry, I didn't see any," I say. "Maybe next time. But the vatnavera was so cool! It was cute in its miniature form, snacking on the snowpetal flowers and swimming through the water. . . . It just wanted to be left alone to eat its dinner."

Elisa giggles. "What about when it was big? Was it scary?"

"Not really," I say. "I mean, it did have big horns and teeth, but I knew it didn't really want to hurt us, so I wasn't afraid."

"That boy is lucky you were able to fish him out of the water," Papa says sternly. "The vatnavera might not have intentionally harmed him, but it very well could have thrashed in the water so much that he could have drowned."

"Yeah," I say. "The vatnavera wasn't attacking, but it was definitely scared of him and flailing around."

"How did you calm it down?" Papa asks. "Surely you had to calm it enough to get Viktor's son out of the water?"

"Well, Ari helped with that," I admit. "He used his empathy gift to calm the vatnavera."

Papa takes a sip of his soup, looking contemplative. "That boy may offer you some competition, Bryn. Empathy gifts are powerful magic."

"I know," I say. "Ari would probably make a pretty good Seeker."

"But not as good as you," Papa says, winking at me.

"Well, I *am* the best," I say with a grin.

"And after you win the next round—"

Something large flies through our open window, sailing right over Elisa's head, and slams into a blanket on the clothesline with a thump before thudding to the floor.

"What—" Papa starts, but he doesn't finish the sentence before a second object flies through the window and crashes into the clay water pitcher on the table, breaking it into pieces.

"Get down!" Mama yells, grabbing Elisa. I scramble from my seat and drop to the floor, lying flat with my head below the table. Mama makes sure Elisa is lying down too before she stands again. I can't see what's happening, but Mama's footsteps approach the window even as Papa's heavier steps move away from it, toward the door.

Elisa's eyes are wide. "What's happening, Bryn?" she whispers.

"It's okay," I say, even though I don't know what's going on either. I reach for her hand and give it a squeeze.

The door of the hut creaks open, and Mama says, "Be careful, Jakob."

He doesn't respond for a moment. "It's all right," he says finally. "You can get up now, girls. They're leaving."

Elisa and I both crawl out from under the table and stand. I brush the dirt from my elbows. "What's going on? What happened?"

Mama stands in front of the window. One of her shields, glowing bright purple, is stretched across it, preventing anything else from entering. Papa closes the door to the hut with a *thud*, then walks over to the table and examines the shards of the broken pitcher. From their center, he picks up a large rock.

"Some young boys were throwing these," Papa says, holding up the stone. "They ran as soon as I opened the door."

"Did you see who it was?" I ask, even though I don't have to. I'm pretty sure I know who it was.

"I couldn't say for certain," Papa says carefully, but I'm pretty sure he knows who it was too.

"Why did they throw rocks at our window?" Elisa asks, her gaze roving back and forth from Papa to Mama to me.

Leaving her shield in place, Mama walks over to the clothesline and scoops up a second stone from the floor. "Elisa, why don't you go sit on your bed for a minute? You should make sure your dolls are okay."

Elisa clearly isn't falling for this trick, but she knows Mama's serious tone as well as I do, so she doesn't argue. As soon as Elisa disappears into the sleeping area, Mama turns to Papa and holds up the stone in her hands. "This is large enough to have hurt someone," she says, in a tone so scathing I don't think I've ever heard it from her before.

Papa's expression is grim. "I know."

Dread twists in my stomach, but I force myself to say the words out loud. "It was Johann. Probably with his brother, Aron, or some of his friends. I know it was."

Papa scrubs his hand over his face. "We can't say that for certain, Bryn. And we can't accuse the neighbors unless we know for sure."

"I do know for sure," I insist. "Johann is mad at me and Ari because of what happened today. He almost lost because we got to some snowpetals before he did. He never wanted me to be in this competition to begin with, and now—"

"Bryn." This time it's Mama who speaks, and I turn to face her. "You might be right," she continues, "but we have to consider that there are a lot of people who aren't happy about you being in this competition. It could have been one of the boys who lost the first round. Or boys who aren't old enough to compete yet, who resent the fact that you can. Or boys who have nothing to do with the competition at all, but are acting based on the things they've heard from the adults around them."

I deflate a little. "Are they really . . . ? Do people in the village really hate me that much?"

Papa wraps his arm around my shoulder. "Of course not. Don't worry. There are people who are . . . upset about the idea of a girl competing. People who don't like change. That's all."

But I keep my gaze fixed on Mama, and she doesn't look like she agrees. Her lips press into a tight line.

Mama and I both know that it's so much more than that.

"I still think it was probably Johann," I say. "I bet he wants to scare me. To keep me from competing again."

"You might be right," Papa says, echoing Mama. "I should go pay Viktor a visit, just to see if he knows where his boys have been this evening."

"Jakob—" Mama says, and stops.

"Just a friendly conversation between neighbors," Papa says to her. He releases my shoulder and reaches for his coat. "I'll be back soon."

Mama still doesn't look like she agrees, but she nods. Papa shrugs on his coat, grabs his walking stick, and strides quickly toward the door. He turns to me again. "Don't let this worry you, Bryn. Get some sleep. Champions need their rest." He leaves, and the hut instantly feels emptier without him in it.

Mama walks over to the window, slides her hand easily

through the glowing shield, and tosses the stone into the garden. Then she turns back to me. She looks like she wants to say something, but she doesn't.

"Do you think I should quit?" I say quietly.

Her expression is unreadable. "Is that really what you want?"

"I don't know." I take a deep breath. "You and Papa always told me never to quit. But—but I didn't think that there was a chance somebody could get hurt. What if they come back? What if next time they hurt Elisa or you or Papa?"

Mama reaches for the nearest chair and sits down, so that she's at eye level with me. "It's never wrong to think about your own safety," she says. "If you want to change your mind about competing, there's no shame in that. But you don't have to be afraid. Your papa and I can handle a couple of silly village boys. Don't worry about us."

"But what if it isn't just some stupid boys playing a prank next time? Do some of the villagers really hate me?"

Mama reaches for my hand and pulls me closer. "It's true that there are people in the village who will resent you if you become a Seeker. This isn't something that will simply go away. Not now, and not even if you win. There will always be those in the village who see you as someone who took an opportunity away from their sons, and they won't be happy about that."

"So they *do* hate me."

"Listen," she says. "I don't tell you this to scare you. Whatever you decide to do, your papa and I will support that. But before you decide, you should understand. I had hoped it wouldn't come to this, but I was afraid it might." She takes a breath. "You need to know that winning this competition will affect the way the village sees you for the rest of your life—in some cases for better, but in many for worse. Perhaps this was just some boys playing a prank. Perhaps it wasn't. But either way, this will not be the last time someone will try to scare you, and the next time might be worse. You must be prepared for what could happen."

I swallow hard. "I understand, Mama. I didn't think about any of this before."

She nods. "When you first decided to compete, your papa didn't want to tell you any of this. He didn't want to scare you away from your dreams. And neither do I. But I want you to be prepared."

"But . . . you don't think I should quit?"

"No." She squeezes my hand. "I think that you will make the best Seeker this village has ever seen. And I don't want you to let them scare you away from doing what you love."

"Really?"

Mama smiles. "Really. It's up to you, Bryn. What do *you* want to do?"

I hesitate, trying to give it some thought. But I don't need to think. I already know what I want. "I haven't changed my mind," I say. "I still want to be a Seeker."

Mama pulls me into a hug. "All right, then," she says simply.

She releases me and turns toward the clothesline, where Elisa's eyes are peeking out from between a blanket and one of Mama's aprons. "Elisa," she says, "stop eavesdropping and come finish your dinner."

Elisa's eyes vanish, and Mama turns back to me. "You'd better finish yours, too," she says. "Champions can't compete on empty stomachs."

I smile. "Yes, Mama."

We finish our dinner and have started on the dishes by the time Papa returns to the hut, looking weary.

"How did it go?" Mama asks.

"Viktor was . . . not quite convinced that his boys were responsible," Papa says. "But he was willing to listen, and he shared my concerns about the severity of this . . . incident. He agreed to talk to his boys to find out if they knew who might be involved."

"But they probably won't admit it was them," I say.

Papa nods. "It was the most I could get him to promise. But it's all we can do." He steps closer to me. "Do you want me to speak with the Seekers tomorrow? If I tell them what happened, I know they will take it seriously. Larus and Ludvik, in particular, will be very upset to hear about competitors threatening or intimidating others. They care about fairness in this, and I know they'll listen to what I have to say."

"But what will they do? Will they actually disqualify Johann?"

"Without evidence or his confession, I doubt it. At most, they will impose some kind of penalty."

"I don't want that," I say firmly. "It will only make him angrier. And it might make the other boys angry too, if they think I'm making up stories in order to win. I have to prove to them that I can win fairly, in the arena. It's the only way."

Papa nods. "All right, but let me know if you change your mind."

Mama gestures toward the shards of the broken clay pitcher, which she carefully piled in one corner of the table away from our food. "Jakob, please remove those before someone gets hurt. Bryn . . ." She pauses. "We can get more water from the well later. Right now, just put the bucket away. Elisa, bring your dishes here, please."

We scramble to do our chores, and the rest of the evening passes without incident. Mama and Papa send me to bed early, but I lie awake, and not just because I've got to sneak out to meet Ari. I can't stop picturing those rocks flying through the window.

And I can't stop thinking that there might be something much, much worse in store.

A while later, a loud noise from outside startles me, and my eyes fly open. Papa is still snoring, and neither Mama nor Elisa have stirred, but I'm sure I heard something, somewhere out in the garden.

I rise swiftly from bed and sneak out to the front of the

hut. I glance out the window, but it's too dark to see anything from in here. Carefully, I open the door and peek out.

Ari stands in the garden, his boots crunching against the gravel. I slip outside and rush to him.

"What are you doing? You're going to wake everybody up!"

"I'm sorry," he says quickly. "I just came to let you know that I can't help you train tonight. Don't wait for me."

"What do you mean? Is something wrong?"

He shakes his head. "It's the Vondur. They're back."

"What? Are you sure?"

"I've been keeping an eye on the docks," he says. "A little rowboat just pulled up, with some people wearing dark cloaks inside. I think it's the same one I saw before. I'm going to go back and keep an eye on them."

"I'm coming with you," I say immediately.

"You don't have to."

"It's too dangerous for either of us to go alone. Come on."

We sneak through the village and down to the docks in silence. I consider telling Ari about the rock-throwing incident, but now doesn't feel like the right moment for a conversation. I focus on moving quickly and silently as Ari leads the way up a hill, where we perch behind some overgrown bushes. From here, we have a pretty decent view of the docks and part of the bay.

A flickering light shines from somewhere near the boat— they are probably using a lantern. A few figures seem to be moving, casting shadows back and forth, but they're too far away to make out any identifying features.

"So what's the plan?" I whisper to Ari. "Do you just want to watch them?"

"Let's wait and see if anyone from the village comes down to the boat," he says. "Or if it looks like they're doing anything suspicious. If nothing happens, I've still got some dragon scales in my pockets. I could go down and see if they'll give me information in exchange for them."

"That's way too risky," I say. "We shouldn't let them know we're here."

"Look," Ari says, pointing toward the village. A red light slowly descends along the pathway. As it draws closer to the docks, I can just make out a shadowy figure, but they're too far away to identify.

The figure approaches the boat and stops. There's a pause, and the sound of voices drifts toward us on the wind, but I can't make out anything they're saying.

The figure with the red light climbs into the boat. More voices.

"Should we get closer?" I whisper. "We can't really hear anything."

"I don't think we can get down there without being seen," Ari says. "Look—I think they're done."

The red light moves swiftly back up the path toward the village, and the boat abruptly pulls away from shore, heading into the bay.

"Quick," I say, "let's follow the red light!"

We scramble from the bushes and rush down the hill, but by the time we reach the path into the village, the light is gone. We search the nearby streets, but there's no sign of anyone. At this time of night, the village is sound asleep, and the figure has vanished like a ghost.

"Guess we should head home," Ari says after a few more minutes of searching. "Whoever that was, we lost them."

"We know one thing for sure," I say. "You were right. Someone *is* meeting secretly with the Vondur. That has to be who's in that boat!"

"Not just meeting with them," Ari says. "Trading with them. Why else would they have been carrying Lilja's egg?"

"I wonder what they just traded away," I mutter. We turn down the lane toward my family's hut.

Ari frowns. "I don't know. I wish there were another trading day happening sooner. Then I could go up to the Vondur trading ship and talk to them."

"Do you still think we shouldn't tell the Seekers?"

"For all we know, that person *was* a Seeker," Ari insists. "We still can't rule them out."

"But how are we supposed to stop them on our own?"

Ari looks away. "I don't think we can. We just have to try to figure out who they are, and then we'll definitely report them. Once we have evidence, we can tell the whole village."

We stop at my garden gate. "Well, I guess this was our

training session for the night," I say lightly, trying to release some of the tension we're both feeling. "See you tomorrow."

"See you." He turns.

"Hey, Ari?" I call. He glances back at me. "Be careful, okay? Don't go sneaking around in the dark looking for Vondur by yourself."

"Okay," he says.

But I don't have to be an empath to know that he's lying.

NINETEEN

Everyone is subdued the next morning at breakfast. Mama's shield still covers the window, casting a purple-tinged glow over the whole room. Elisa keeps up her usual stream of chatter, but the rest of us are quiet. I wonder if my parents are picturing more rocks flying through the window. I certainly am.

For once Mama hardly gives me any chores to do, so I ask her if I can head over to Runa's. After everything that's been happening, I need to talk to my best friend.

I find Runa in her family's stable, feeding hay to her horse, Starlight.

"Hey, Bryn," she says. "How's it feel to be a first-trial champion?"

I force myself to smile. "Not as great as I thought, actually."

I quickly describe the rock-throwing incident, and Runa gasps. "You should tell the Seekers!"

"No. If I do that, the boys will just claim that I'm making up stories in order to get them disqualified."

"But the Seekers all know your papa. They have to know that he'd never make up something like that. If it came from him—"

"Yeah, the Seekers might believe him, but I don't know if the rest of the village will. Getting the boys disqualified will just make everyone hate me more. Besides, I don't know for sure that it was Johann. I don't have evidence."

Speaking of evidence reminds me that with everything going on, I haven't even had time to tell her about the Vondur, or about Ari's theories. "And guess what else," I say. "You'll never believe how Ari found Lilja's egg."

Runa listens wide-eyed as I recount the story, from his stealing the egg from someone in a Seeker's cloak to the strange figures we saw at the docks last night.

"You really think it was the Vondur? And that a Seeker is involved?" she asks when I'm finished. She sounds more than a little skeptical.

"I don't know either of those things for sure," I say. "But that's what it seems like."

Runa feeds another stalk of hay to Starlight, considering this. "Why would a Seeker trade dragon eggs to the Vondur? A Seeker's whole job is to protect the Realm."

"Right. I don't get it either."

"You know," she says thoughtfully, "one of my cousins is

a fisherman. He's down at the docks all the time. I could ask him if he's seen anything suspicious lately."

"I don't know," I say. "I don't want to alert whoever this person is that we know about what they're doing. Not yet. They could be dangerous."

Runa brightens. "What if I just visit my cousin for the day and hang out around the docks? Then I could keep a lookout myself. I wouldn't have to tell anyone what I'm doing."

"That seems pretty risky, Runa. What if you get caught?"

"How would I get caught? For all anyone knows, I'm just hanging out with my cousin. Besides, it's *way* less risky than you and Ari sneaking around at night and spying on people."

"Okay, fair point. But just be really, really careful, all right?"

She rolls her eyes. "Oh, please. *You* telling *me* to be careful. That's hilarious."

"I'm serious, Runa."

"So am I. You literally have people throwing rocks at your house. Sitting around at the docks all day is nothing in comparison."

"Okay . . . ," I say, still not convinced. "I guess if you want to visit your cousin, I can't stop you."

"My dearest, dearest cousin, who I just miss *so* much since he started working, and I just couldn't wait to spend more time with him," Runa says in her sweetest, most innocent-sounding voice. Then, in her normal tone, she adds, "That's what I'll say if anyone asks me."

"Okay, that was creepy," I say with a shudder. "You're way too good at that."

"See? I've totally got this."

I laugh. "I don't know why I ever doubted you. Remind me to never get on your bad side."

"What bad side?" Runa asks in her innocent voice again, and we both crack up.

I spend the afternoon training with Lilja and trying not to think about the rock-throwing incident. When Ari arrives, I don't tell him about it. But I do ask to take the night off from our usual training session—what I need more than anything right now is proper sleep. Ari looks confused, but he agrees. I spend the entire night in bed for once, curled up next to Elisa and listening to her breathing.

I don't see Runa again until the next morning. After the rest of the family gets up, I hurry through breakfast and my chores so I can go find her. Mama waves me off with a sigh, and I sprint up to Runa's farm.

"How'd it go at the docks?" I ask as soon as I see her.

"Hello to you too." She steps out of her hut, dragging two water buckets. "I'm on my way to the well. Walk with me."

I offer to take one of the buckets and fall into step beside her. "Hi. But seriously, what happened?"

"Nothing," she says. "It seemed normal. I didn't see anyone suspicious. Except now my cousin thinks *I'm* suspicious."

"You didn't see any Seekers around, did you?"

"I saw Seeker Freyr. He came down and talked to one of the fishermen. But that was all."

I tell her about the person Ari and I sensed in the Realm.

"I think you're right," she says when I'm finished. "It probably is the Vondur, or the same person you saw meeting with them."

"I know. And whoever they are, they probably took something else from the Realm to trade last night."

Runa frowns, biting her lip. "So what are you going to do?"

"I don't know." I sigh. "Maybe once I win the competition, I can tell the Seekers what Ari and I have seen. They'll have to believe me then, whether I have evidence or not."

We reach the well, and Runa lowers her bucket inside. "Speaking of the competition," she says, "has Johann been giving you any more trouble?"

"No. Nothing since the rocks."

"I'd be careful around him. You don't—"

I roll my eyes, cutting her off. "Between you and Mama and Papa, I really don't need anyone else to tell me to be careful. Don't any of you trust that I know what I'm doing?"

Runa raises a skeptical eyebrow.

"Don't give me that look," I protest.

"It's just that we know you, Bryn. You have a . . . tendency to get into trouble."

"I do not!"

"Remember that time Elder Olga chased you out of the bakery with a broom?"

"That's not fair! I wasn't *that* dirty."

"Or the time the bell-ringer dragged you home by the ear for ringing the bells when you weren't supposed to?"

"I was just trying to figure out how the mechanism worked—"

"Or the time you almost drowned when we went sailing with your papa because you thought you saw a sarvalur?"

"I *did* see a sarvalur."

Runa gives me her skeptical look again.

"Okay, okay. Maybe I've gotten in trouble a couple of times. But this is different!"

Runa gives the well's rope a tug, hauling her bucket back to the top. "If you say so."

"No, really. I *want* this, Runa. More than I've ever wanted anything. I'm not going to do something stupid and mess it up. Being a Seeker, it's . . . it's everything for me."

Runa rests her bucket on the lip of the well, tilting her head toward me. "You really *do* want this."

"Of course I do. I've told you that from the beginning."

"I know, it's just . . ." She looks away, tapping the side of her bucket. "It's just that you get so excited about adventures you're going to have, and they don't always turn out the way you thought. And sometimes you get excited about something for a while and then lose interest in it later. When you said you wanted to be a Seeker, I didn't know how seriously you were going to take it."

"What, you thought I'd quit when it got hard?" I put my

hands on my hips. Surely Runa knows me better than that.

"No, that's not what I meant. I know you're stubborn enough to pursue whatever it is you want to do. I just thought maybe you wouldn't want to do it anymore when it turned out to be harder than you thought. Like, maybe you'd change your mind."

"I definitely haven't."

Runa wrinkles her nose. "I can see that. Being a Seeker is all you can talk about now."

"I'm sorry," I say. "It's just that . . . It's just that I feel so much like a dragon sometimes, you know?"

Runa gives me a very confused look. "Um, no?"

"Like—like the way dragons need to fly, because there's something in them that's wild and strong and unafraid. You can't keep them in a cage. I feel like that sometimes. Like the village is a cage, and I need more freedom."

Runa's expression softens. "What's so bad about the village, though?"

"Well, it's not that it's *bad*. Plenty of people like it here, and that's great for them. But not me. It just feels too . . . small. When I was out in the Realm, or when I was flying through the air on Lilja, it just felt like the world is so much bigger, like it's full of endless adventures. When I'm outside the village, I'm free to be whatever I want."

"No limits," Runa says softly, and suddenly she looks sad.

"What's wrong?" I say.

"Nothing. It's just . . . I think I know what you mean.

Sometimes I want to do something more with my healing gift than just help Papa with the occasional wounded sheep. I want to learn how to do more, the way you're learning more about using your gift. I could make medicines and help people who are sick. But every time I ask an adult healer questions, they tell me I don't need to know. They tell me that girls don't become doctors."

I drop my bucket. "Runa! Why didn't you tell me? This whole time, you've been letting me go on and on about my own dream, and you never said a thing about yours."

She shrugs. "What's the point? It'll never happen."

"Of course it will! Haven't you been listening to me? You have to *make* it happen. When they tell you that you can't learn new things, you learn them anyway. When they tell you that you can't train your magic, you train anyway. That's what I've been doing, and it's working. It *will* work. And if I can do it, so can you."

"I don't think it's that simple."

"Yes, it is! If girls can be Seekers, why can't they be doctors? I already know you're the best young healer in the village. Anyone who's seen what you can do will admit to that."

"But there's no competition to become a doctor, Bryn. There's only *one* doctor in the village, not five like there are Seekers, and the only way it will happen is if he agrees to train me as an apprentice. And he'd never take on a female apprentice."

"Have you asked him?"

"No."

"Well, there's your first step."

"*Bryn*. You're not listening. I don't need to ask him, because I already know the answer."

I shake my head. "You need to be more stubborn. Refuse to take no for an answer. If he doesn't think you can do it, show him that you can. If there's no competition, make one of your own. Challenge any of the boys and prove that you're a more skilled healer than they are. Once he sees what you can do, he'd have to be a fool not to take you as an apprentice."

Runa shakes her head. She hauls her bucket from the well, water running down its sides and muddying the dirt at her feet. "Bryn, I'm really glad that your dream is coming true for you. I know you're going to make a great Seeker. But let's face it—a girl becoming a Seeker is kind of a miracle. And I don't think we're going to get to see more than one miracle."

I open my mouth to argue, but she shakes her head again, cutting me off. "Can we not fight about this anymore, please?"

"All right," I agree reluctantly. I lower the second bucket into the well, and when I've finished drawing water, we head back toward Runa's farm. "What do you want to talk about instead?"

Runa smiles. "How about you and *Ari*?" She's started putting this weird emphasis on his name every time she says it, like it's something special. For some reason she keeps insisting that I like him, which obviously I do not.

"Seriously, it's nothing. We're friends now, I guess. But we're really just training each other for the competition. Once we get to the third trial, our friendship has to end."

She shakes her head. "I don't think that's how friendship works."

We reach the main path. "Guess I'd better head back," I say, nodding toward my family's hut in the distance. Runa's farm is in the opposite direction.

"I'll try to go down to the docks again," she says. "I'll let you know if I see anything suspicious."

"Be careful. And . . . just think about the other thing I said, okay? About the doctor."

Runa sighs. "Bye, Bryn."

When I return home, Mama sends me to the fishmonger's to pick up today's catch. The fishmonger's is my least favorite place in the village—I hate both the smell and the sight of all of those dead fish—but I'm glad to have an excuse to get out of the hut and run.

Just as I arrive at the village square, I sense a commotion down by the bakery and turn to look. A couple other villagers are rushing across the street and ducking away behind the blacksmith's, putting as much distance between themselves and the bakery as possible.

There's only one person standing outside the bakery.

A Vondur.

I've never seen one in person before, but the dark cloaks they wear are unmistakable—made of heavy black wool and trimmed in red, with a crimson symbol threaded over the heart. A cloak like that is only ever worn by dark magicians from the mainland.

This particular Vondur is unremarkable in most other ways, though. He's stocky and middle-aged, and wears both his hair and beard short the way mainlanders do. He leans casually against the side of the bakery, glancing around as if he's waiting for someone. Or looking for something.

I duck behind the nearest shop, out of his line of sight. What could he be doing here, out in the open? It's not time for the next trading day yet.

I'm not the only one wondering—a few women standing behind the shop next door are peering out and discussing the Vondur in low voices.

". . . saw the ship dock this morning," one of them says. "They were just here, what, a week ago?"

"Seems like it," says the other. "I heard the council had given them permission to come back, but I just didn't believe it could be true. . . ."

"What more can they possibly have to trade?" the first woman asks, shaking her head.

"It's not what they bring, it's what they *want* that concerns me," the other says. "It's never good when the Vondur show up so frequently."

"What do you mean?"

"The way I see it, either the Vondur are trying to trade for something they're not getting and they keep coming back to put pressure on whoever won't give it to them, or they *are* getting something, something they want badly enough that they've gotten greedy and are docking as often as possible to get more of it."

The first woman gasps. "Surely you don't think someone might be . . ." She lowers her voice. "Surely you don't think anyone is trading things from the Realm?"

"Of course not." She hesitates. "But they've wanted to conquer this island and plunder it ever since the day they first discovered it. Their magic is no match for the Seekers, but if that should ever change . . ." She shudders.

Their conversation veers into a discussion of how much some goods cost from other mainland traders, but my mind spins wildly with everything they've said. Could the Vondur be trying to pressure someone into trading with them? Or are they getting something that they desperately want?

Both options are terrible, for a single reason: the only thing the Vondur want that badly is creatures from the Realm.

Ari and I were right; that mysterious figure we saw *must* be trading with them.

My first instinct is to tell Papa and the Seekers. But I'm getting a sinking feeling in my chest that Ari was right not to trust the Seekers. Because why else would they have allowed the Vondur to return so soon unless at least one of them is in on it with them?

And I still don't think I can tell Papa, because I don't have any solid evidence to go on. Lilja is evidence herself, of course—but she's evidence against *me*, too. I can't tell the Seekers about her without also incriminating myself. If the Seekers find out that I've known about Lilja all this time and kept her hidden—if they find out Ari and I secretly went into the Realm . . .

There's no way they'll let me become a Seeker then. They'll kick me out of the competition for sure.

I'm torn. On the one hand, a Seeker's true duty is to protect the Realm, and that means telling the other Seekers if I suspect someone might be harming the Realm's creatures or trading its secrets away to the Vondur. But on the other, I don't have much evidence, and I might be incriminating myself for nothing, and then I'll lose my one shot at becoming a Seeker. I'll never be able to get starflowers for Elisa, never be able to help my family, never be able to enter the Realm. I'll never see a single magical creature ever again.

It's too much to risk losing, too much to throw away on suspicion alone. If I go to Papa or the Seekers, I have to be absolutely, one hundred percent sure.

I don't have evidence yet. But we have to find some.

TWENTY

That afternoon, when Ari meets me at Lilja's cave after training as usual, I tell him about Runa's report from the docks and the Vondur I saw in the village.

"We definitely need to stay out of the Realm tonight," Ari says. "If the Vondur are here, whoever is trading with them might be sneaking around again."

"But shouldn't that mean we go into the Realm again in order to see who it is and catch them?"

Ari shakes his head. "Too risky. If it was just us, I'd say yes, but with Lilja . . . We can't risk whoever it is finding her. Not when they already tried to trade her away to the Vondur once."

"Yeah, I guess you're right."

"We'll just have to train on the beach."

"What are we doing? What did Seeker Agnar teach you today?"

He smiles, pausing for maximum dramatic effect. Lilja

snorts behind me, her breath ruffling my hair and echoing my sentiments. "Just tell me already," I say.

"Seeker Agnar told us what the second trial is going to focus on."

I straighten up. "Go on."

"He said it's going to be all about spellwork this time, focusing mostly on defensive, boundary, and healing spells."

"I *knew* it," I say, jumping in excitement. "I guessed the next round would focus on magic!"

"I don't know why you're so happy about it," he says dryly. "It's bad news for us, seeing as how neither of us is a healer or a defender."

"True," I say, deflating a little. "Neither of those are spells I know yet."

Ari nods. "I think the first round was definitely better suited to naturalist and empathy gifts, and I suppose warrior gifts too. Now it's our turn to be the ones out of our elements."

"And Tomas and Emil will be in theirs," I say darkly. "At least Johann won't know what he's doing any more than we do."

Ari waves one hand dismissively. "I don't think Johann stands a chance at winning anyway. It's the other two I'm worried about."

"Good point. I'm not so sure about Emil. He's a strong defender, but I don't think he's studious enough to learn the healing spells properly. Tomas, on the other hand . . ."

"Is already a healer," Ari finishes. "And might already know some boundary spells, since his father's a Seeker. How about you? Did your papa ever teach you any of this?"

"Not really," I admit. "My interests were the magical creatures, mostly. And naturalist magic."

"So neither of us knows what we're doing. Great."

"I take it you've never learned any boundary or healing spells either?"

"Nope." He smiles wryly. "Empathy gifts aren't much good for any of that. Mama tried to teach me some healing spells a few times, but she gave up because I was hopeless."

"You'd think empaths would be good at healing," I counter. "Can't you sense pain? So you'd be good at identifying the problem."

"A little too good at it. When I focus on someone with my gift, their pain feels as real to me as if it's my own, and that makes it difficult to concentrate on doing spells."

"Oh." I pause. "Are all emotions like that for you? I mean, do you sense other people's emotions as if they're your own?"

"If I focus enough on them, yes," he says. "It's like I can see it in their life force, so I know it's not originating with *me*, yet I can feel it as strongly as if it were."

"Huh," I say. "That would be kind of awful when people are sad or in pain."

"You have no idea," he mutters. "But when people are happy, it isn't so bad. And anyway, I can pull my gift away from someone if they're hurting me too much. I didn't have as much control when I was younger, but I'm better at making sure I don't get overwhelmed now."

"Good. Maybe you'll be better at healing spells now."

"Maybe," he says doubtfully. "I don't know if Mama will have time to teach me much, though. She's busy at the bakery at night and asleep during the day."

"Well, I'm sure you'll learn about it at training," I say, ignoring the pang of sadness his words just gave me. I can't imagine what it's like for him to not even get to see his mama very much, especially when he doesn't have any other family. "Then you can pass it on to me."

"I'll do my best," he says. "But for now, how do you want to practice this?"

"We could try putting boundary spells of our own around this cave and the beach," I say. "Even if the Seekers' spells keep Lilja from getting near the village, I don't know exactly where the boundary is, and she might be able to wander far enough that someone can see her. We should put up proper spells around the beach so we can be sure she's safe and hidden. We've been risking a lot, giving her so much free rein."

"Agreed," Ari says, nodding. "And Seeker Agnar *did* talk about boundary spells a little in today's lesson, though we didn't get very far. Mostly he just reviewed our performances during the competition."

"Oh?" I say, raising my brows. "What did he say to Johann?"

Ari laughs. "That he took too long to complete the task, being the last one out. Johann glared at me the whole time."

"I'll bet. And the others?"

"He said the opposite to Tomas: that he ought to have taken more time to explore, and that he could've gotten some vatnavera scales like you did if he hadn't been so hasty to grab the snowpetals and ignored what else was present."

"Wait, did Agnar really mention me like that?"

"Well, no, he didn't mention you by name. He just pointed out that 'other competitors' got vatnavera scales, and that Tomas ought to have done the same. But as far as I know, you're the only one who did that, so 'other competitors' just meant you."

"Ah. I knew he wouldn't actually praise me or anything."

"Right. He's not much for praise, actually. Spends most of the training sessions criticizing us. He lectured Emil for bringing in items that were of lesser quality than what the rest of us got."

"And you?"

Ari hesitates. "He told me I relied on you too much."

"Oh," I say awkwardly. "I guess he wasn't a fan of us teaming up?"

"Guess not. You missed this because you'd already gone with your family, but after the competition ended, Seeker Ludvik congratulated me and said the way you and I teamed up was, and I'm quoting directly here, 'ingenious.' So not *all* of the Seekers disapproved. But Agnar definitely did. He said . . ."

"What?" I ask when Ari trails off. "What did he say?"

"I don't know . . . He made it sound like you were dragging me down or something. Said I wasn't reaching my 'full potential.'"

I cross my arms over my chest. "Why, because you're not doing stuff yourself? Or just because I'm a girl and therefore inferior to the rest of you and not worth your time?"

Ari shakes his head hard, sending his curls flying. "I don't know. I'm not really sure what he meant. But I don't think he was happy that you passed the first trial."

"Of course not," I fume. "He's embarrassed to have kicked me out of training now that he's seen what I can do *without* training. He doesn't like that I'm proving him wrong. He's hoping that I'll fail just to save face."

"Probably," Ari says. "Anyway, that's about all he said. He did talk about boundary spells for a couple of minutes at the end."

"What did he say?"

"Mostly he just talked about how those of us who aren't defenders will find them challenging, since we can't just pop up a shield like they can, but that we can all find our own way to make them work. He talked about how warriors can move objects to create physical boundaries and how naturalists can use the elements surrounding them. Didn't offer much advice for healers or empaths, though."

"Hmm," I say. "Guess we're going to have to figure it out on our own. I could ask my mama and sister for help, maybe. They're both defenders."

Ari brightens. "That's a great idea!"

I shake my head. "But Elisa is six years old and not so good at explaining abstract things like how her gift works yet. And my mama is . . . Well. She's Mama."

"Meaning . . . ?"

"Meaning she's intimidating, and I'm not sure how much she really wants me to become a Seeker anyway, and I really don't want to have to ask her for help."

"Oh."

"I could ask Papa, though," I say, brightening at the thought. "He might have more useful advice for me anyway. A defender would just talk about how easy it is to make shields or whatever, but Papa will understand how my gift actually works, and he'll know the secret to making boundary spells as a naturalist."

"Right," Ari says. "Good idea." But he sounds kind of sad when he says it, and it takes me a second to figure out why. Ari can't ask anyone for help with his empathy gift the way I can ask Papa. However an empath is supposed to do a boundary spell, Ari will have to figure it out on his own.

The thought makes me sadder than it probably should—I need to be better at these spells than Ari so that he doesn't beat me during the next trial, after all. But it just doesn't seem fair that there isn't a single person in the village he can ask for help with his gift the way the rest of us can.

I may not be an empath, but I do know what that feeling is like, of not having an advantage that everyone else in the group has because you're different from them. It's a feeling I'm becoming increasingly familiar with, and I wish Ari didn't have to be so familiar with it too.

"All right," Ari says, "here's what I'm thinking we should do. Tomorrow, I'll try to learn more from Agnar in training about how boundary spells work. And you can talk to your family about it and hopefully get some information from them. Then tomorrow night we can set up the spells around the beach."

"Sounds like a plan," I say. "Then what do you want to do tonight?"

He hesitates. "I was thinking I'd go down to the docks and see if the Vondur will let me trade with them. I still have some dragon scales. Maybe I can get some information."

"I'll go with you," I say immediately.

"I don't think that's a good idea. It'll seem suspicious enough if one kid somehow has access to Realm items they're not supposed to have. If both of us go, it'll make it worse."

"Okay, but I'm at least going down to the docks with you to make sure you don't get murdered or something."

"Deal."

Lilja snorts from behind us, as if to tell us how stupid we're being, but we ignore her. Finally, we're going to figure out what's going on with the Vondur.

And it's only a little, tiny bit dangerous. Probably.

TWENTY-ONE

When I sneak out of my hut that night, Ari is already waiting outside the garden. Together, we creep into the village and down the path to the docks, where the main Vondur ship now sits, its red flags whipping in the breeze.

"Sure you're up for this?" I ask him.

"It's fine, Bryn. I'm an empath, remember? I can read a room. If they seem too suspicious or like they're going to murder me, I'll get out of there."

"Right," I say skeptically. "Well, good luck. Don't die."

"Not planning on it."

"If you're not back here in fifteen minutes, I'm going for help."

"Okay. See you in less than fifteen minutes, then."

He strides away toward the ship, and I hide in the shadows cast by the fishmonger's shop, watching.

There are a couple of Vondur men sitting in the tent they pitched on the walkway, displaying a few wares from the mainland. Ari walks up to them, but I can't hear what they're saying—I'm too far away.

Ari gestures toward their wares, and one of the Vondur says something in response. Ari reaches into his pocket and withdraws something so small I can't see it from here. A dragon scale, most likely.

This definitely seems to have caught their attention; both men stand up and inspect the item closely. There's a long, agonizing minute of conversation. Then two. Then three.

How long has it been? More than fifteen minutes? I should've been counting—

But they're done. Ari backs away from the tent, gives the men a goodbye salute that's common among mainlanders, and then walks briskly up the lane. As soon as he's out of sight of the Vondur tent, he ducks toward the fishmonger's shop. I double around it, and we meet in the front of the building, where we can't be seen.

"What happened?" I ask breathlessly.

"We were right. Someone *is* trading with them. But they wouldn't tell me who. They seemed excited about the scales, and they asked me if I could bring them something 'more valuable.' I'm guessing they mean a living creature."

"And what did you say?"

"I pretended like I was interested, but I said it was risky, because the council would be upset if they found out I'd given them anything. And then one of them said, 'We've got other sources. We'll give our gold to them if you don't want the risk.'"

I gasp. "Then what?"

"Then I said, 'No other source could give you something from the Realm except the Seekers.'"

"And what did they say?"

"They kind of exchanged glances, like they knew something I didn't, and their emotions were . . . secretive but also amused. Bryn, I definitely think their source is one of the Seekers."

"No way. We've been over this. Most of them have been Seekers for at least a decade. Why would they suddenly stop protecting the Realm and trade with the Vondur for gold?"

Ari doesn't answer, but he looks like he's thinking about it. "Who did your friend Runa say she saw at the docks the other day? Seeker Freyr?"

"Yes. She said he just talked to a fisherman, though. That could be nothing."

"Yeah, maybe." Ari sighs. "Let's get out of here before someone spots us. We can talk it through some more tomorrow."

"Okay. And we're going to do boundary spells on the beach tomorrow night, right?"

"Right. Don't forget to ask your family about them."

"I won't."

We've reached the main path branching into the village.

From here, our homes are in opposite directions. "See you tomorrow," I say. "Promise you'll stay out of trouble until then, okay? No spying on the Vondur without me."

Ari smiles. "See you tomorrow, Bryn."

It does not escape my notice that he didn't promise anything.

The next morning, I catch Papa in the garden. I'm still reluctant to ask Mama or Elisa about boundary spells, so I've decided to start with him. "Hey, Papa?" I ask.

"Yes, Bryn?"

"I had a question for you. About magic."

Papa smiles and settles on the garden bench, leaning his cane against its side. "Go ahead."

"We learned about basic boundary spells in training yesterday, and I was wondering . . . Well, I was wondering how to cast boundary spells. Like, say you wanted to prevent dragons from coming close to the village. How would you do that?"

"Are you sure I should be telling you this, Bryn? Shouldn't you ask Seeker Agnar in training?"

"I have," I lie. "But I need a naturalist's perspective. And I'm not asking you as a former Seeker, just as a naturalist. That's not an unfair advantage, is it?"

Papa considers this for a moment. "Well, different Seekers set different spells, depending on their personal gifts. Surely Seeker Agnar explained that?"

"Right," I say. "But that's what I wanted to ask you—as a naturalist, how would *you* set a boundary spell?"

"Well," Papa says, stroking his beard, "as naturalists, boundary spells aren't really our strongest suits. Defenders are the Seekers who most often set and maintain those kinds of spells. But the other Seekers *do* need to know how to set the spells themselves, in case of emergency or in case a defender is unavailable. For all types of boundary spells, naturalists usually draw on natural elements as much as possible."

"Like what?"

"Take temperature, for instance. A fire can't exist without heat, and dragons won't stray into territory that they find too cold. You could create a natural, fireproof barrier just by using cold winds or ice. Both are readily available in parts of the Realm."

It's a good suggestion, but neither of those things are available near Lilja's hiding place. "What else could you use? What about water?"

He nods. "Yes, water would certainly work."

"But how?"

Papa smiles. "You know the answer to that, Bryn. Magic is about will."

"Right, but how do I picture something complex like that? Like a water spell triggered by the presence of a dragon? What if I wanted it to prevent dragon fire?"

"Take it one element at a time," Papa says. "First, picture the water. Where would you want it to come from? A nearby river? The ground? The air? How much water would you use? How will it come together? You must think very carefully about these details and plan them in advance so that you can picture it as clearly as possible while setting the spell. Then you move on to the rest of it. Picture the water surging up when there is fire, and—this is the important bit—picture it *not* moving when fire isn't present. Then, as you picture the flames, imagine what you want the water to do. Imagine multiple scenarios, to ensure that the spell will work correctly in any situation."

I frown. "Sounds complicated."

"Spells at this level are complex," Papa agrees, "but it's no less intuitive than any other use of your gift. Just like when you were five years old and you used to make plants in the garden grow. You simply sensed the life force of the plants and wanted to strengthen them, and you did."

I wish I could practice the spell with him, but there's no way I can ask that without it being suspicious. He thinks I'm in training for this, after all. "Okay," I say instead. "Thanks, Papa."

I feel better after this conversation, but I'm not still not sure how exactly I want to go about setting a spell up. And even if I figure out how to do it for Lilja, I have no idea what kinds of scenarios the Seekers will cook up for us in the next round. What if there's a situation where there is no water or fire for me to draw from? I need to figure out something foolproof, something that works at all times.

After Papa leaves, I sit on the garden bench for a little while, playing with my magic. The life forces of the plants around me hum happily in response to the touch of my gift, but my magic is completely unreceptive when I try to imagine making borders or shields the way defenders do. If magic is about will, like Papa says, why can't I will it to do what I want?

I let out a sharp sigh of frustration, and Elisa wanders over, abandoning the dirt house she was building for her dolls in the corner of the garden.

"What's wrong?" she asks.

"You'd better clean that up before Mama sees you playing in the dirt."

"Is it your gift?" she asks, watching the green light of my magic swirl across my fingers.

"Sort of," I say. "I'm supposed to be practicing boundary spells for the Seeker competition."

"Oh. That's easy."

"For you, maybe. You're a defender. Shields are what you do. But naturalists can't make them."

Elisa shrugs. "Can't you make a shield with the plants or something?"

"I guess I could. Or I could move the earth around. But what happens if there aren't any plants in the arena during the competition? What if the floor is stone instead of soil? I know I can probably make a physical border somehow, but that isn't enough. I need to be able to make a boundary even if they don't give me anything to work with. But what is a naturalist supposed to do when there's no nature?"

Elisa tugs at a loose thread on her sweater. "There's *always* nature around, silly."

"What?"

"There's always dirt. There's always air. Even inside the hut."

I blink. "El, you're a genius."

She grins. "I am?"

"Of course. Why didn't I think of that? The one thing that will always be present in the arena is *air*." It's a hard element to work with, not as easy as sensing the life force of a living being, but it's something.

"Elisa," I say, "when you make a shield appear out of the air, how do you do it? Like, tell me step by step."

Elisa raises her hands. "I call my gift first," she says, the sparks of violet dancing across the tips of her fingers. "Then I close my eyes." She closes her eyes, continuing the demonstration.

"And then?" I prompt.

"Then the magic goes *whoosh* and all the little purple sparks go where I want them to go, and they make the same shape in the air that I pictured in my head. Then I open my eyes, and . . ."

As she speaks, purple magic shimmers through the air. A solid, square shield of violet, a foot in length and only half an inch deep, hovers in the air between the two of us, right at Elisa's eye level.

"And what do you do when you want to move it around?" I ask. "Just tell the sparks where to go?"

"Yep," she says. She turns abruptly, looking toward the corner of the garden where she was playing earlier. Just as suddenly, the shield whizzes over the top of her head, drops down into the garden, and slices through the top of the pile of dirt Elisa had built, sending pieces of earth flying. Before I can blink, the shield vanishes into thin air.

"See?" Elisa says, turning back to me. "Not so hard."

"Right," I say, wiping a speck of dirt from my cheek. I'm not sure exactly what "the magic goes *whoosh*" is supposed to mean, but the rest of her instructions seem pretty straightforward. The visualization seems like the key part, and that's in line with what Papa told me too. Magic does what you picture it doing. What you *will* it to do.

"Does that help?" Elisa asks, picking a clump of dirt from the end of one of her braids.

"I think so," I say. "Do you think you could show me—"

Elisa seems to be reaching for her magic again, the sparks dancing across her fingers, but suddenly she coughs, and the light of her gift vanishes. She coughs again, a deep, rattling sound from her chest, and opens her mouth to gasp for air.

Oops. I forgot that using her magic can trigger Elisa's cough. "Do you need starfl—" I start to ask, but before I can finish she doubles over, her whole body racked with coughs. I leap up from the bench, turning toward the house to get the starflower paste, but the door of the hut flies open and Mama rushes out, the jar already in her hand. Mama quickly tends to Elisa, rubbing the paste across her chest and urging her to take deep breaths.

All I can do is stand there helplessly until the coughing fit subsides. When it's over, Mama puts the lid back on the jar of medicine, but not before I see that it's almost empty.

"That's enough playing outside for now," Mama says to Elisa. "This air is bad for the lungs. Come help me in the kitchen. I'll show you how to make your favorite rice pudding." They head inside, leaving me in the garden alone.

I sit back down on the bench, trying boundary spells again with renewed vigor. If winning this competition is the one thing I can do to help Elisa, then I'm going to do it. I *will* figure this out.

Manipulating the air around me seems like a step in the right direction, but it's harder than I thought it would be. Air has never been one of my favorite elements, since the slightest shift in the wind while I'm attempting to guide it can ruin a spell.

An hour of practice later, it's almost time for me to go check in on Lilja, but I still haven't managed to create anything resembling a solid shield, let alone a full boundary tough enough to deter a dragon. But I can't quit. There's only one thing left to do.

I just really, really don't want to do it.

"Mama?" I say, entering the hut with great reluctance. Elisa must be in the back of the hut out of sight; Mama is alone in the kitchen, hanging laundry along the line.

"Yes?" she says without looking up.

"What's the secret to creating boundary spells?"

Mama pauses for a moment before turning around. "You're asking me?" she says, brows raised in surprise.

"Well, you're a defender, aren't you?"

Mama laughs. "Of course. You've seen me use my gift."

"Yes," I say, "but I need to know how it works. I need to figure out how, as a naturalist, to make boundary spells. It's part of the competition."

"Of course," Mama says, nodding. "Seekers are responsible for the spells that prevent dragons from carrying off our livestock or setting fire to the village, that keep sea wolves from stealing our fish, that keep every part of the Realm exactly where it needs to be."

"Right," I say. "Papa's told me that before. I'm just confused about how to do it, since I can't make shields the way defenders can."

Mama smiles. "I'll tell you the same thing I told your papa, when he asked me that question: magic doesn't come from nothing."

"What?" I'm not sure which confuses me more: the second part of her response, or the fact that my papa, who always seems to know everything about magic, once asked Mama about hers.

Mama lowers herself into the nearest chair, leaning forward so that we're eye level with each other. "When you see a defender make a shield, it looks like it comes from nowhere, doesn't it? One minute there is no shield, the next it appears."

"Right . . ."

"But that's only how it *looks*. Magic doesn't come from nothing. Naturalists and healers—and empaths, I suppose— all draw upon their own life force—their own *gifts*—and use them to interact with the life forces of others. Warriors use their gifts to interact with the objects around them, rather than living beings. But what is it that defenders do?"

My brow creases in confusion. "Create shields?"

Mama shakes her head. "Not create. *Shape*. We are not creating the magic that forms the shield. We are drawing it from within ourselves and shaping it in the way we desire. We do not make magic from nothing."

"Oh," I say. I guess that makes sense, although I never thought about it before. "But naturalists can't do that."

"Not in the same way," Mama says, smiling. "But you shape your magic all the time. When you decide which plant to let it flow into, or which creature, or when you tell it what you need it to do, you are shaping the world around you. The only difference is this: you need anchors."

"Anchors? Like on boats?"

"No. Anchors to help shape your magic. Us defenders, we do not use anchors to shape our gifts. That is what makes our ability so different from the rest. But naturalists do. When you set out to make a boundary, you must anchor your magic in the things around you—the earth, the trees, the plants, whatever it is that you naturalists use. If your gift is anchored properly in the natural world, it will respond more easily to whatever shape you wish to make. Do you understand?"

"I—I think so?"

"When a defender makes a shield, they draw upon their gift and shape the magic into a shield. When a naturalist makes a shield, they draw upon their gift, anchor that gift in the living things around them, and *then* use those things to shape the magic. Try it, and you will see."

"Okay," I say skeptically. "I'll try."

Mama rises from her chair and pats my shoulder. "You can do it, Bryn. You're the daughter of a defender and an even stronger naturalist than your father, and even he got there eventually."

"Really? He struggled with this too?"

Mama winks. "Don't let him fool you. He didn't always find magic so easy. Luckily he had me to teach him a thing or two."

She gives my shoulder a squeeze, and I smile. "Thanks, Mama."

"Go on," she says, waving me toward the door. "Go out there and practice. You have work to do."

I grin. "Yes, Mama."

TWENTY-TWO

I practically race out of the hut earlier than usual that night, eager to try putting up the boundary spells for Lilja again. I've been practicing all afternoon—except when Lilja insisted I pay attention to her, so I had to feed her bilberries instead—and I think I might have finally figured it out.

Mama was completely right about the anchors. Before, I was trying to move the air without really realizing that was what I was doing. Of course it didn't work—the wind was shifting too much to hold magic properly. But once I sink my magic into the living things around me—the grass and trees and earth—then I can draw upon it and direct it more easily, making it actually possible to shape the air currents into what I want. I practice with the water, too, which makes an even more effective boundary. Being skilled at both will come in handy for the competition, not to mention ensure that the boundaries I set to keep Lilja away from the village will be sturdy.

When I meet Ari at the cave, he recaps everything he learned in training that we didn't have time to discuss earlier in the afternoon. As we predicted, Seeker Agnar spent more time on boundary spells.

"Agnar told us that there are spells all around the bay to protect the village, the farms, the docks, all that," Ari begins. "Then there are the spells in the Realm itself that help keep creatures from leaving their territory, so they can't prey on other creatures when they're not supposed to or go to an area that's not safe for them."

I know all of this already, but I don't interrupt him. I want to make sure I hear *everything* Agnar had to say, even if I've probably heard it before. I need to know what my competitors know.

"So, since neither of us is a defender, we have to find other ways to create a shield or a barrier, one that Lilja won't want to cross," Ari continues.

"Temperature," I say instantly, thinking of Papa's suggestion. "Dragons don't like the cold."

"That could work," Ari says, "but there isn't ice or anything to draw from out here. Anyway, that doesn't help *me* much."

"Oh. Right." I bite my lip. I shouldn't try to help him— after all, only one of us can win, and it's got to be me. But it does seem unfair that he doesn't have anyone to help him with his gift the way my family helped me today.

So, against my better judgment, I say, "Well, there's got

to be something you can do. If you can't change anything around Lilja, then how about Lilja herself?"

Ari's head snaps up. "You're right," he says. "My gift works best with emotions. Maybe I could try to change her emotions—like, so that she'll feel a little scared every time she gets too close to the village, to stop her from heading in that direction."

My eyes widen. "Will that work?"

Ari shrugs again. "I can't create an emotion out of nothing—maybe empaths are supposed to have that ability, but I've never figured it out. I can adjust what's already there, though. Make her feel some things more than others."

"Okay," I say, a plan starting to take shape in my head. "So how about this. I'll try to figure out how to make a physical boundary around this area, and you focus on making an emotional one. Between the two of us, surely one of them will work."

Ari nods. "All right. But what are you going to do?"

I glance out at the waves beyond the shoreline. "Leave it to me."

Ari nods and turns to Lilja, who has been trying to get our attention during this conversation by huffing dramatically and scraping the rocky beach with her claws. I leave Ari to it and face the sea.

Magic is about will, Papa's voice says in my head. I just have to *will* it to work.

I take a deep breath and close my eyes.

My gift rushes through my veins and pools easily into my hands when I summon it. Extending my reach, I can sense everything around me—the bright, dual sparks of Ari and Lilja behind me, the shimmering blur of overlapping life-forms that is the forest to the east, and the steady hum of the sea stretched before me, brimming with life.

I reach for the anchor points I find all around—the sparks in the trees, in the grass, in the sea. Keeping my eyes closed, I picture what I want. I imagine Lilja walking in the direction we don't want her to go—toward the village—and then imagine waves cresting up from the sea, water spooling into ribbons that rise and rush onto shore, crashing forward into a solid wall of water twice as high and wide as Lilja. I imagine Lilja turning back, causing the wall to break apart, the water swirling back to the sea. I imagine it over and over again, to make sure I get it right. Then I picture Lilja trying to *fly* in that direction rather than walk, the water blocking her at every turn and height.

As I picture it, my magic seeps through my hands and out into the world. It sinks into the sea, the trees, the earth. It rests beneath the surface of things, like a fisherman's net waiting to be raised, a trap ready to be sprung. I go over the images again and again, making sure I get them right.

"Well?" Ari asks when I finally open my eyes. "Do you think it worked?"

"Yes," I say. "At least I think so. It feels sturdy enough."

"I think mine worked too." His eyes are shining. He loves

figuring magic out—he always gets excited when he masters something. It must be hard, figuring out how to use his gift without anyone to teach him, but he's always so happy when he learns things on his own.

"Should we test it?"

"Hold on," Ari says, a puzzled look crossing his face. He's watching Lilja closely. She's stopped digging and is now sniffing around her own claws. "I think something's wrong with Lilja."

I snap my focus to her immediately and could kick myself for not noticing it sooner. He's completely right. Lilja is sniffing at her foot the way dragons do when they have an injury. And she's giving all of her attention to one particular claw, as if there's something wrong with it.

Ari and I race toward Lilja at once, diving down to get a better look. "You think she hurt it in the sand?" I ask. It's rocky enough that she could've cut herself.

"Most likely," Ari says. He brings his hands closer, using his gift to illuminate her. "Look—is that blood?"

I see it too—a spot of red near the tender place where her claw disappears into the skin of her foot, one of the few soft places where she has no scales for protection. "Oh no," I say. "That's definitely blood. We have to heal her."

"How?" Ari asks. It's possibly the first time I've ever heard him sound a little panicked. "Neither of us knows anything about healing, and Agnar hasn't covered that in training yet."

"It's just a tiny spot of blood," I say. "How bad can it be?"

"Neither of us knows how to handle an open wound, Bryn. And what if it gets infected?"

"You're worrying too much."

Ari takes a deep breath. "I know, but . . . We can't take her to the Seekers. We can't. Anything that needs to be healed, we have to handle it ourselves. And we don't know what we're doing." He sounds calmer now, more rational, but worry still creases his face.

My mind races, trying to come up with a plan. It *is* a tiny injury, but . . . But the idea of experimenting with healing magic on Lilja makes me very, very nervous. There's way too much possibility that something will go wrong, that we might hurt her more accidentally.

Lilja looks at us with wide, trusting eyes, and I know we have to do something to help her. The wound must be painful, from the way she's acting, so it can't wait to be treated. We don't have time to learn the spells we need. And we still can't go to the Seekers.

There's only one possible solution.

"I'll get Runa," I say. "She has healing magic. She'll know what to do."

Ari frowns. "Are you sure?"

"She's a great healer," I say, feeling defensive at the sound of his doubt.

"I'm sure she is, but it's not like she's ever healed a dragon before."

I shrug. "She knows how to stitch up open wounds. Besides, she's more likely to be able to heal this than either of us, and I can't think of a better option."

Ari pauses for a moment but is clearly unable to come up with anything either. "How fast can she get here?" he says finally.

"You stay with Lilja. Try to keep her calm and get her to focus on something else. I'll run to Runa's and be back as fast as I can."

"Okay," he says. "Be careful. Don't let her parents catch you."

"I won't." But a little knot of fear slips inside my chest. I leap to my feet and take off across the rocky shore.

The night air is muggy and thick, and I have to stop twice to catch my breath before I reach Runa's hut. I sneak around to the back door, knowing that's the closest entrance to the place where Runa sleeps. Still, her parents won't be far away—I'll have to be very, very quiet.

The back door creaks as I ease it open, holding my breath. I tiptoe across the cool dirt floor, trying to make out the shape of things in the dark. I don't know her hut as well as my own, of course, so it's much harder to sneak around without being able to see. I dare to use a tiny spark of my gift for light and finally manage to orient myself. There, close to the hearth, is Runa's tiny bed. And across the room, sound asleep, are her parents.

I hardly dare to breathe as I shuffle to Runa's side and

nudge her gently awake. *Please don't be a heavy sleeper, Runa.*

Her eyes flutter open, and she jumps, seeing a stranger looming over her.

"Shh!" I whisper as loudly as I dare. "It's me!"

Runa freezes, her eyes wide. "Bryn?" she whispers.

I lift one finger to my lips and gesture silently for her to follow me.

Runa shakes her head rapidly, then points to the corner where her parents are asleep.

But I wave her forward insistently, gesturing toward the back door. After a moment, Runa glances guiltily toward her parents one more time before slipping out of bed. She stuffs her feet into a pair of boots sitting beside the hearth and follows me out of the hut and into the night.

"What's going on?" she whispers as soon as we've cleared the back garden.

"It's Lilja," I say. "She's bleeding. She hurt her foot somehow. Ari and I don't know healing spells yet, so we don't know what to do, and we don't want to risk experimenting on her. We need you to heal her."

Runa glares at me. "Aren't you two supposed to be the Seekers? Taking care of dragons is going to be *your* job, and now you're trying to get *me* in trouble. If my parents find out—"

"Please, Runa," I say. "We don't know what else to do. It's to help Lilja. I wouldn't ask otherwise."

Runa sighs. "All right, all right. For Lilja."

"Thank you! You're the bestest friend ever."

Runa heaves an even bigger, more dramatic sigh. "Don't I know it."

Without another word, we run through the darkness toward the beach.

TWENTY-THREE

E ven Runa is winded by the time we reach the beach. "I can't believe you brought me all the way out here in the middle of the night," she huffs.

But when Lilja comes into view, Runa freezes. *"Oh."*

I can't help but smile. "She's beautiful, isn't she?"

"She's *gorgeous*," Runa says breathlessly. "I've never seen one so close before. And she's so big! I thought you said she was a baby."

"She's still growing." I feel almost proud saying it, like Lilja's my own child or something.

Ari waves frantically, reminding us of our purpose, and we rush quickly forward.

Runa looks a little reluctant to approach Lilja, but I reassure her. "She won't hurt you. She likes people. Say hello to Runa, Lil."

Lilja eyes Runa curiously, tilting her snout in Runa's direction and taking a big sniff, but she's less energetic than she'd normally be, I'm guessing. She's lying in the sand with her injured foot splayed out beside Ari, who's hardly taken his eyes off it. "Hurry," he says sharply.

"Hi, Lilja," Runa says. Blue light dances across her hands as she calls upon her gift. "I'm just going to take a look here, okay?"

Runa and I both kneel beside Lilja's foot, across from Ari, and Runa leans in to examine it. "Look, I think there's a splinter at the bed of her claw. The skin must be very tender there."

Now that she points it out, I can see it too—a sliver of wood embedded in her skin. She must've gotten it from the driftwood on the beach or something.

"Can you help her?" Ari asks.

Runa nods. "I think so. I mean, obviously I've never healed a dragon before, but it should be easy. The wound doesn't look that deep. I just need to remove the splinter and seal it up."

Ari and I watch mutely as Runa works. "Here we go," she murmurs, bending low over the wound. The sparks of healing magic fly from Runa's fingertips to the base of Lilja's claw. I try to observe what she's doing, but it's all happening too fast. Ari's hands are glowing with his gift too, as he uses it to keep Lilja calm. I feel like the most useless person in the world. All I can do is sit and watch Runa work.

The piece of wood rises from Lilja's skin, buoyed by

Runa's gift, and falls into the sand. "I need some more light," Runa murmurs. "Bryn, could you . . . ?"

"Of course," I say quickly, eager to do something to help. I let my gift flood into my palms, the green light springing up around my fingers, and hold my hands out over Lilja's claw, illuminating the area as Runa tends to it. The lights of our three gifts—green for nature, blue for healing, yellow for empathy—cast skittering shadows across the sand as we all hold our breath.

Well, all of us but Lilja, who lets out a roar, raises her head, and shoots a plume of fire up into the sky. Ari jumps, but Runa holds steady, never looking up from her work. The flames stretch a few feet above our heads before hitting one of the boundary spells I just set, which promptly releases a jet of water to put the fire out. A fine mist of droplets sprays down on the three of us, and I duck my head as the flames are extinguished.

"Well," Ari says, "at least we know your boundary spell worked."

"Good thing," I mutter. "What happened to keeping her calm?"

"*You* try keeping an injured dragon calm for five minutes."

"Done," Runa announces loudly before I can retort. "She's all patched up."

"You're sure?" I ask as Ari leans forward for a closer look. "She's all healed?"

"Yep." Runa grins.

"Thank you," I say, giving her a quick hug. "I owe you one."

She smirks. "You owe me more than one. I can't believe you brought me all the way out here for a *splinter.*"

"It looked more serious at the time," I say defensively. "There was blood and everything."

Lilja, who has apparently had enough of three humans crowding around her foot, spins away from us, spraying rocks everywhere, and trots briskly out to the sea.

"Not even a thank-you," I joke. "We need to teach that dragon some manners."

I glance over at Ari, who's staring after Lilja with an odd expression on his face. "Someone else could use some manners too," I say loudly. "I don't think the two of you have been properly introduced."

Ari snorts. "It's a small village, Bryn. We've met before."

"Barely," I say. "Anyway, you just helped heal a dragon together, so you ought to say hello to each other properly."

Runa rolls her eyes. "You're starting to sound like your mama."

I open my mouth to retort, but Ari cuts me off, finally addressing Runa. "So how'd you do it?" he asks. "How does healing magic work?"

"What do you mean? I'm a healer. It's my gift."

"I *know*, but . . . We're going to have to be able to do passable healing spells, even small ones, to win this next round of the Seeker competition. But how do we learn that? What do healers actually *do*?"

"Why do you even need to know that?" Runa asks. "Two of the current Seekers are already healers. If you come across an injured creature in the Realm, you can just get one of the other Seekers to help. I don't get why they make you learn all these different types of magic."

"That's true," I say, "but think of it like this. Say I'm wandering the lava fields by myself and I come across a severely injured dragon that needs immediate help. By the time I track down one of the other Seekers and direct them to the injured creature, it might be too late to save the dragon. But if I know a few basic healing spells—like how to stop a wound from bleeding—then I can at least keep the creature alive long enough for a proper healer to get there and finish the job.

"I don't think the council is really looking for healers this year, since they have two already. They don't need a specialist. But they *do* want to make sure that we have a passing knowledge of the spellwork, in case we ever need to handle a problem on our own. It's the same with boundary spells—Seekers with defender gifts will do the most complicated ones, but all Seekers need to know the basics."

"I get it," Runa says. "So you have to figure out how to heal without a healing gift."

I nod. "Exactly."

Runa bites her lip, considering this. "Healing isn't all that different from either of your gifts, I suppose. The first thing you do is locate the life source of the injured creature or person and let your gift interact with theirs. You sort of . . . direct their gift to do what you need it to do."

"I don't get it," Ari says, but I nod.

"It's like what Mama was telling me about anchors," I explain. "She said that naturalists and empaths and healers all have to anchor their magic to living things to do different spells. That was the secret to figuring out how to do a boundary spell with my gift. So you use their life source as an anchor, and then you shape it to fix the problem."

"Yeah, basically," Runa says.

"But wait," Ari chimes in. "Do you use *their* life force to heal, or yours? When you lifted that wood from Lilja's foot, it was *your* gift surrounding it and lifting it up. And wouldn't an injured person or creature have a weak life source anyway? Isn't that difficult to draw from?"

Runa grins. "Now you're asking the right questions," she says. "Healing is all about restoring balance. Every life source has an appropriate level of energy. Healing is basically lending some of your energy to the wounded to help restore theirs. If you don't lend enough, you can't heal; if you lend too much, the balance gets out of whack."

"That's like the nature gift," I say. "Tending to things and helping them grow is all about balance."

Runa nods. "So what I just did for Lilja, for instance—I didn't need to lend her very much of my gift, because her life source wasn't that depleted by a tiny splinter. If I had given her a lot of energy, it would have been way more than she needed. Instead of funneling my magic into hers, I used it to lift the wood out myself. But if she were severely injured and her energy was drained, I would have focused on improving that first, by giving my energy directly to her."

"But if that were the case, wouldn't you still want to use your own energy to lift out the wood, so it doesn't cost her any?" Ari asks.

"You could, if you have enough," Runa says. "But remember, you've got to keep your own balance in mind too. If I give a lot of energy to an injured creature, then I might not have enough left to tend to the wound itself. So instead I would guide their newly energized life spark to do it, which wouldn't tire me out as fast. It all depends on how everything is balanced."

"We really need to practice this," I say. "But it's not like there are a lot of injured creatures around."

Runa grins. "Honestly, Bryn, I'm ashamed of you. What kind of naturalist doesn't notice the nature around her?"

It takes me a second too long to catch on. "Oh! You think I should practice on plants? But how do you heal *plants*?"

Runa shrugs. "They have their own energy, don't they? And you can improve their health. What if you tear a petal off a flower and then try to reattach it, or break a blade of grass in two and then try to sew it back together, the same way you'd stitch a wound? It's different from healing a person or a creature, obviously, but it's something to get you started."

Ari's shoulders droop, and it takes me a second longer than it should to realize the problem. "But that won't work for Ari," I say. "Empaths don't really work with plants. How can he practice?"

Runa considers this. "Why don't you start by seeking out living creatures nearby, and then try to practice balancing their energies? Look for birds or fish or insects or something, I don't know. Practice transferring energy back and forth and sensing whether they have too much or not enough of their own. That's the first step of becoming a healer. The actual stitching of wounds and stuff is all just visualization anyway. The balance is the hard part."

Ari shrugs. "Guess it's worth a shot."

With Runa's help, Ari and I spend an hour or two practicing. Once I think about it in terms of a naturalist spell, healing makes a lot more sense. Nurturing the life sources of living beings is already my specialty; figuring out how to use that interaction to heal is hard, but not impossible. Ari seems to be getting the hang of it too; he practices balancing the energies of some of the crabs that scuttle along the beach. Lilja, meanwhile, seems to have completely recovered from her injury and is now rolling around in the surf, bathing herself with seawater and occasionally splashing us with it.

Successfully stitching together the sixth flower petal in a row, I can't help but feel elated just thinking about how impossible this would've seemed earlier today. This morning I was convinced that I couldn't do boundary or healing spells properly; now I can do both. Papa helped me a little, but I never would've guessed how much everyone else would help too. It was Elisa who told me I could use air for boundary spells, it was Mama who explained about anchoring my magic, and it was Runa who taught me healing. Without the three of them, I'd never be able to pass the second trial.

Finally, Runa calls an end to the practice. "I'd better get home before my parents find out I'm gone," she says.

"It won't be dawn for ages," I say, glancing up at the sky. "You've got time."

"My papa always gets up before dawn," Runa says. "He says farmers don't sleep. Anyway, I'm not sure I can even stay awake much longer."

"Do you want me to walk back with you?"

"Nah, I know the way," she says. "Stay here and practice some more."

"Are you telling me I need it?" I joke.

"Most definitely," she says, smiling. "You too, Ari."

To my surprise, he laughs. "You should take over our training from Seeker Agnar. You're a better teacher than him."

Runa grins. "One of my many talents." She waves goodbye to Lilja, then turns back to us. "Stay out of trouble, you two."

"No promises," I say.

Runa heads up the path toward home, and then Ari and I turn to each other.

"We've still got a few hours," he says. "You want to just sit out here for a bit?"

"Sure."

We sit down on the beach, and Lilja comes bounding out of the surf and nearly tackles both of us, flinging water everywhere.

"Dumb dragon," Ari mutters, wiping water from his face.

"Don't insult my dragon," I say. "She's had a rough night."

"*Your* dragon?" Ari protests, but I ignore him.

"I wish we *could* go into the Realm. I already miss it," I say.

"Yeah. Can you imagine what it's like during the day?"

"It must be incredible. I can't wait to see it like that."

"Not going to happen, since you're going to lose and *I'm* going to win," he teases.

"You wish," I say, with less bite than usual. "I just meant, it's a shame we can't fly Lilja into the Realm."

"Yeah, but there's no way. Just look at how noisy she is. Whoever it is sneaking around in there would catch us."

"Yeah." I sigh.

We're silent for a minute until Ari says, "Thanks for getting Runa tonight. That was really smart thinking. And I had no idea she was so good at healing."

"You're welcome." I can't help but roll my eyes. "You boys, always thinking girls can't do anything."

"I didn't say that!" Ari protests.

"No, but you were thinking it. If you'd paid any attention to Runa's magical abilities at all in the past, you'd know she's the best young healer in the village. If she were in the competition, Tomas wouldn't stand a chance."

"Why isn't she competing, then?"

"I tried to talk her into it, but she doesn't want to be a Seeker. She wants to be a doctor. Anyway, it's better for us that she doesn't."

"True," Ari says. "Better for us that she's on our side."

It's weird how he says "our side" as if the two of us can remain some kind of team. But I let it go. "She's like our secret weapon."

"Well, and Lilja."

"We have more than one secret weapon." I grin.

"Yeah," Ari says. He pauses. "And we have each other, too."

I have to swallow past the lump forming in my throat and can't respond. Because he's right, and also wrong.

We have each other for now, but it can't last much longer.

TWENTY-FOUR

The rest of the week passes in a blur. I spend most of my time practicing spellwork for the next round of the competition. Ari and I both get better at healing and boundary spells, to the point that I'm sure we can handle whatever the second trial will throw at us. Who knows if we're good enough to beat the other competitors, though. Neither of us will ever be as good at these spells as a healer or a defender, which means there's a chance that Tomas and Emil might pose real threats. Only three of us can pass to the next round.

These are the thoughts that have me picking at my breakfast the morning of the second trial, while Elisa chatters with Mama about one of the other village girls. Papa notices me listlessly prodding the food on my plate and leans closer to me. "Everything all right, Bryn?"

"Fine," I say, sticking a small bite of fish into my mouth and pretending to chew.

"Not nervous about the competition, are you?" Papa says knowingly. "Surely the village's next Seeker has nothing at all to be nervous about."

"Definitely not," I say.

"Not that there's anything wrong with getting a little nervous," Papa says with a small smile. He lowers his voice conspiratorially. "I certainly did during my competition."

I look up. "You did?"

Papa laughs. "I vomited in the bushes before the third trial, I was so nervous."

"I didn't know that."

"Didn't stop me from winning, though, did it?" Papa says with a wink. "Nerves are normal. But don't let them prevent you from doing your best. If you can do that, I have no doubt you'll win today, and in the final trial too."

I smile. "I'm planning on it."

Papa grins back. "That's my girl. Now, eat your breakfast before it gets cold. Champions need to keep their strength up."

I gulp down the rest of my meal with renewed vigor. Papa's right, of course. There's nothing I need to be nervous about. I've done all I can do to prepare.

Together, my family and I head for the arena.

The crowd outside is smaller today than it was for the first round. Probably because there are fewer competitors, so fewer families are attending. And some people will wait until the final trial anyway—that's when the whole village will come out to see who is chosen as Seeker. I spot Elder Viktor and Aron walking inside, though, and my stomach twists. That means Johann is already here.

"Are you ready?" Papa asks, clearly thinking the same thing.

"I'll walk to the back entrance with Ari," I say.

Papa, Mama, and Elisa all give me a hug and wish me luck. I wave them into the arena and wait for Ari. He arrives moments later, along with his mama, who greets me warmly before entering the arena.

As we walk toward the back entrance, it occurs to me that I'm about to come face-to-face with Johann for the first time since the rock incident. Despite myself, I shudder at the thought.

"Are you okay?" Ari asks. "Not trying to pry, but your emotions just went all . . ." He trails off.

Which is when I realize that I never told Ari that Johann threw rocks into our hut. Which is dumb, because Johann is probably just as mad at Ari for what happened during the first trial as he is at me. Meaning that if he hasn't retaliated against Ari yet, he might try today.

"You should know something," I say. "Someone threw rocks through our window the night after the first trial."

Ari freezes. "What?"

"Nobody was hurt. They just broke a pitcher. But it could have been worse."

"Johann," Ari says instantly. "Because of what happened during the trial."

"I think so. Papa saw some boys running away and

couldn't identify them, but I'm pretty sure it was him. Probably with his brother or one of his friends. And I'd bet he used his warrior gift to throw those rocks."

"Are you going to tell the Seekers?"

"No. I think that will just make it worse."

Ari nods. "I'm so sorry, Bryn."

"Don't. I don't want to be pitied. I just want to compete. And I thought you should know, because he might try to get revenge on you, too. He's probably got something planned for today."

Ari nods again. "Well, at least we know Johann will lose, and he'll leave us alone once he's out of the competition."

I look down at my feet. "My mama doesn't think so. She thinks that it's only going to get worse if I win, because Johann won't be the only one who's upset."

Ari kicks a stone in the path, sending it skittering into the grass. "*If* you win?" he says finally. "I don't think I've ever heard you say that before."

I shrug. "Guess I'm not feeling very competitive today."

"You'd better start, then. How am *I* supposed to be competitive when my biggest rival isn't baiting me?" He gives me a teasing smile, and I slowly smile back.

"Your biggest rival, huh? I don't think I've ever heard you admit *that* before."

Ari gives a lazy shrug. "Guess I have to start, since it's all anyone will be saying once we both win today and get into the top three."

"True. After I defeat all four of you today, everyone will know I'm the one to beat," I say, grinning wider.

"That's more like it."

Johann and Emil are already waiting when we reach the back entrance, talking and laughing among themselves. They glance our way a couple of times and snigger, but Ari and I keep our distance, pretending not to see them. Tomas arrives a moment after us, his expression as stoic and unreadable as always. He gives Ari a slight nod of acknowledgment, but his gaze slides right over me and lands on Johann and Emil, who both earn a slight sneer before he turns away, leaning against the stone of the arena wall as if he doesn't care about anything. I glance at Ari.

"So you're in Tomas's good graces now?" I say.

Ari shrugs. "We both pretty much keep to ourselves during training sessions, and he seems to like that. He doesn't have much patience with Johann or Emil. I'm pretty sure he thinks they're idiots."

"That's because they *are* idiots," I say quietly, and Ari snorts.

I almost expect Johann to say something taunting to me, or to make a veiled remark about the rock incident, but he doesn't acknowledge me any more than Tomas did. Maybe I'm wrong and he had nothing to do with it. Maybe his father really did talk to him about it, like he promised Papa he would. Or maybe Johann is just saving up his nasty remarks for the arena.

Emil, though, looks a little shakier today than he did before the first round. Probably the nerves getting to him. Though Emil and Tomas ought to be the most confident out of any of us, really, since it's their magical specialties that this trial is focused on. . . .

The swish of a Seeker's cloak causes all five of us to look up, only to see Seeker Ludvik rather than Seeker Agnar making his way up the path.

"Good morning, future Seekers," he says, smiling brightly and clapping his hands together. "Gather 'round, please."

We form a loose half circle around him, though Ari and I keep our distance from the others. Ari places himself directly between me and Emil, and there's a big gap on my other side that Tomas, who's closest, makes no effort to fill.

"Seeker Agnar has asked me to prep you all today," Seeker Ludvik says, "since I used my own gift quite a bit in preparing today's challenge for you all. The rules of this trial will be the same as the previous one. You will all be given a task to complete, and you will report to the council's table as soon as you are finished. Three of the five of you will advance to the next round. If more than three of you complete the task successfully, it will be up to the judges' discretion to select which competitors advance. In that case, the speed with which you complete the task, the quality of your spellwork and overall performance, and the knowledge and competency you display will all be factors in our decision."

He pauses, gazing around the circle at each of us. "Today's

task will be different from the previous one, however, because for this round we are less interested in your abilities to seek out plants and track creatures, which you all demonstrated wonderfully before. This time, we are interested in your spellwork, and particularly the defense, boundary, and healing spells that you haven't yet had the chance to perform for us. Each of these spells is vital for Seekers to use in our everyday work, so it is important that each of you, regardless of your particular gift, is able to display competency and familiarity with these tasks.

"Having said that, the judges will, of course, take your natural gift into account. While someone with a healing gift who performs healing spells well is admirable, we will be much more impressed by, say, a warrior who can achieve the same result with creative use of their gift. The way in which you complete the task is just as important as the completion of the task itself. Does everyone understand?"

We all nod, though Emil has begun tapping his fingers nervously against his side. Maybe he was counting on his natural abilities as a defender to get him through this round.

"All right, then," Ludvik says cheerfully. "Formalities aside, let's move on to the fun part, shall we? I can't wait to show you what I've been working on."

He claps his hands again, but this time the bright purple sparks of his magic fly forward. We all take instinctive steps back as a shimmering shield of sparks forms in the center of the circle.

Only it isn't a shield at all, or at least not one I've ever seen. It's flowing rapidly through the air, forming some kind of shape. . . .

"The healing spells for today's competition are a bit of a challenge," Ludvik says. "Obviously we didn't want to hurt a real creature in order to test your abilities; nor did we want to risk the possibility of someone misperforming a spell and causing further harm. We needed a way to simulate the creatures of the Realm. Luckily, there's a little trick that I've been working on. . . ."

As Ludvik speaks, the sparks of his defender gift continue to move, taking on a more recognizable shape—a head with a beak, a long slender body, feathered wings and tail . . .

A phoenix.

Emil gasps at the sight, and both Johann and Ari are wide-eyed. Tomas is pretending to look unimpressed but doesn't quite manage it.

I've never seen a defender use their gift like this before, and I don't think the others have either. Of course, I've seen defenders make shields of varying sizes and shapes, so I suppose it makes sense that something like this is possible. But the intricacy and level of detail required to take this kind of shape . . . It's some of the most impressive magic I've ever seen.

Ludvik smiles, pleased by our reactions. "There are five simulations just like this one waiting for each of you in the arena," he says. "But I have deliberately given each of them a misshapen element—perhaps a phoenix that's missing its beak or a dragon with a broken claw. Your first task will be to use your gift to interact with these pretend creatures and, combining your energy with theirs, 'heal' the misshapen element and mold it into the right shape. While this task isn't *quite* the same as performing an actual healing, it does mimic all of the skills you will need and visually demonstrates your abilities for us, so I think it will do the job quite nicely."

"The first task?" Tomas asks quietly. "How many tasks will there be?"

"An excellent question," Ludvik says. He waves his hand, and the shimmering phoenix in the air disappears in a shower of violet sparks. "After you have healed one of the five creatures, you will enter a tunnel that will lead you to a second section of the arena, where there will be *real* creatures of the Realm waiting for you. In fact, there are five creatures, one for each of you. Your second task is to create a boundary spell that will keep one particular creature safely contained. There is a physical barrier surrounding the enclosure to protect the audience in the stands, but you must create a magical one as if there is no physical barrier at all. At the end of the competition, we will test the solidity of the one you create. Anyone whose barrier does not hold will fail this round. Anyone who did not correctly heal their fictional creature will also fail the round."

Ari clears his throat. "So once we've created our barrier, we report to the council to let you know we're finished?"

"Precisely," Seeker Ludvik says. "Are there any more questions?"

The five of us exchange glances, but no one speaks.

"Excellent," Seeker Ludvik says. "I wish all of you the very best. I'm sure you'll do marvelously." He strides forward, breaking the circle, and opens the back door to the arena.

He gazes down at the five of us. "Let the second trial of the Seeker competition begin."

TWENTY-FIVE

The arena isn't as dramatically altered this time, but that only makes me more nervous.

We step into an open semicircle that takes up maybe a third of the arena's space. Beyond it are tall, darkly colored walls that arch into a large tunnel. The tunnel is dark, and nothing within or beyond it is visible. We can't see over the walls, either, so we have no clue what might be waiting for us on the other side. At least with the forest I understood what kinds of things I might expect to find, but this tunnel seems more sinister somehow, a yawning chasm leading to something unknown.

I take a deep breath, forcing myself to stop worrying about it. I have to complete the healing part of the competition first anyway. The tunnel, and whatever lies beyond it, must wait.

As soon as all five competitors have filed into the arena, the door bangs shut behind us, and the audience cheers. I glance around, looking for my parents, but they must be on the other side of the arena, beyond the walls.

Violet sparks burst into life in front of us, and I straighten my spine. The test has begun.

Five bright, shimmering creatures form in the air. Just like with the phoenix Seeker Ludvik used to demonstrate, the magic takes a while to form. It seems that each of the creatures is different, though, and some are much larger than the others—

The one in front of Ari sprouts what looks like a horn, and I'm guessing it's a unicorn. On my other side, the sparks closest to Tomas shape themselves into something small, four-legged, and furred—probably an icefox. On the other side of the circle, near Emil and Johann, the twisting coil of a vatnavera rises up, next to something small and beaked that's most likely a gyrpuff.

And in front of *me*, the shape is growing larger and larger, and larger still—

It's a dragon.

I smile.

This imaginary dragon is larger than Lilja, but not as big as most fully grown dragons, probably because there simply isn't enough space for the illusion to take on that much mass, or because it requires too much energy for Seeker Ludvik to maintain. Regardless, it's close enough in size to Lilja that I should be able to tell what its energy should feel like.

I reach for my gift, bringing the sparks of magic to life on my fingertips, and close my eyes. The magic rushes forward, seeking out Ludvik's. The energy is all wrong for a dragon—because, of course, it isn't one. It's simply a shield given shape. But it's a spark of magical energy nonetheless, so it's a close enough substitute for the life spark of a real being. I gently probe it with my gift, getting a sense of where the energy ebbs and flows and how strong it is.

There's definitely something wrong with one of the dragon's wings, which is hanging lower than the other. There's less energy surrounding it than the other wing, or any of the dragons' limbs. In fact, it seems to be *draining*, with energy flowing away from it. Like . . . like blood flowing from a wound.

Once I make the connection, it's easy enough to locate the fake "wound" the energy is leaking from and, using the tricks Runa taught me, bind it up with a quick infusion of magic. The energy stops flowing away from the wing, and I balance out its life source carefully, making the injured wing match the other.

There's just one problem—this is taking a *lot* of energy. I don't know how Seeker Ludvik is managing to maintain this, but just trying to fill up its wing is draining me. I pull in any loose strands of my gift that are hovering around, trying to be as precise as possible and make every bit of my energy count.

Almost there . . . Just a need a little bit more . . . more . . . more . . .

There.

I open my eyes in time to see the fake dragon stretch

both wings, bow its head toward me, and disappear in a shower of sparks.

I exhale in relief and dab at the sweat that's broken out along my hairline. That took a lot of concentration, and now I feel completely empty. I reach for my gift, but there's hardly anything left.

First task down, one more to go.

Beside me, Ari's eyes are closed as he concentrates, yellow magic swirling around his fingers. On my other side, both Tomas and his icefox are gone. He must already be in the tunnel. I leap into action, not bothering to check if Emil or Johann has completed their task. I run straight into the tunnel, allowing the blackness to swallow me up.

The air in here is cold, and I wrap my arms around my chest as I run. Ahead, a small pinprick of light is visible. The other side of the arena.

The tunnel turns out to be short, and I'm barely even winded as I reach a door at the end with a wide opening set in the top to allow light to pass through. I open the door and emerge from the tunnel's depths into the second section of the arena. There are more walls here, between the edge of the arena and the stands, and also a series of five enclosures lined up along the back wall—

And there are five firecats prowling in front of me.

The task is obvious and terrifying all at once. Five firecats, five enclosures, five competitors. Each of us has to herd one of the firecats into an enclosure, then set a boundary spell to keep it there. The enclosures have only three walls, so we'll have to create the fourth using magic, one that it can't break or leap over or burn down.

Unfortunately, the firecats don't seem at all happy about this situation.

To my right, two firecats are prowling along the edge of the walled arena, looking for a way out. A third is shooting fireballs at the walls, trying to tear them down.

To my left, Tomas is halfway to one of the enclosures, his head bowed, blue sparks of magic dancing between him and the fourth firecat, who is growling in warning and spouting huge flames on his back.

There is one more firecat in the arena, and it's standing right in front of me.

It whirls around as soon as it senses me, eyes wide, flames flaring up along its paws, back, and tail. Both its size and the crest of fire along its spine tell me it's a male, though it's probably a young one, since it's on the small side, a little under two feet tall on all fours. Not that it matters, since it could kill me either way.

But firecats don't harm humans unless provoked. They guard their territory fiercely, though, and can be deadly if mishandled.

And this one, like his friends, does not look happy about having been taken out of the Realm and placed in a small enclosure.

The firecat watches me without blinking, its claws digging into the dirt beneath its feet.

At this moment, there are two things it could choose to do if it decides I'm a threat. One is to run away, which is generally a firecat's first course of action, since they can run faster than the human eye can see. But in such a small enclosure, it has to know already that running won't do it any good. There's no place to go.

The second option is to use its flames to conjure up a deadly fireball and launch it toward its enemy. Which, at the moment, is me.

If I were a defender, I could use my gift to make a shield to protect me from the fire. If I were a warrior, I could use my gift to redirect any flaming fireball the cat decides to send my way. If I were an empath, I could use my gift to calm it down and make sure it doesn't feel aggressive.

But I'm a naturalist. And interacting with magical creatures is where *we* shine the most.

Which means this should be easy. Unfortunately, I barely have any magic left. And this is going to take a lot more energy.

I sink a few tendrils of my gift into the ground, seeking any source that I can draw upon . . . anything at all . . .

Nothing.

I try again.

Nothing.

The firecat is still prowling in front of me, and I don't have much time. But I can't find any energy. Not a single leaf or an ant or *anything*.

The Seekers must have done this on purpose. There's no other explanation. Somehow they removed all of the life sources from this arena and planned for Seeker Ludvik's first challenge to drain us.

Aside from the other competitors and spectators, whom I'm not allowed to interact with, there's only one source of energy left in this arena:

The angry firecat in front of me.

I drop to the ground, sitting with my legs crossed so that I become a smaller, less threatening presence. At the same time, I reach for what remains of my gift and pull it out quickly, letting it flow into the air and head toward the firecat. His energy is hot and bright and churning, and I allow my gift to just barely touch his, finding the pattern in the flow and moving along with it. I don't use my gift to try to smother his essence or pull at his energy; I simply let mine float alongside his, companionably, the way a flower might bloom beneath a mighty tree.

The flames alongside the firecat's spine lower and eventually die out, with only a few sparks remaining. His paws and tail are still alight, but he lowers his tail to the ground and takes a slow step toward me, more curious than aggressive.

"Hello there," I say quietly, watching him approach. "You're a beautiful creature, aren't you? And it's not fair that you're stuck in this awful cage right now."

The cat tilts his head to the side, ears perked.

I laugh. "You just want some food, don't you? And you

want to go home. Well, I can help you with that. But I need you to stay calm while I work, okay? And you need to let me borrow just a teeny-tiny bit of your energy."

The firecat doesn't move, and I wish Ari were here to tell me if he's calm enough or not. But I'm not a naturalist for nothing, and I can tell that neither his energy nor his flames are spiking up the way they would be if he were considering, say, making me into a snack.

I reach for a little spark of his energy and let it flow into mine. He doesn't react.

I try it again, with a large spark. This time, he sort of startles, like he's realizing what I'm doing, and I quickly let go. "Easy," I say. "We're just working together, okay? You're going to lend me a little tiny bit of magic. . . ."

The firecat is not remotely happy about this. As I reach for another spark, he shies away from me, both physically and magically—he takes a step back, and his life source pulls away from my gift.

"Okay, okay," I say. "I went too fast. I'm sorry. Let's try that again."

Drawing on my gift *hurts* at this point, there's so little left. But I try it again, just letting my gift flow alongside the firecat for a moment, not doing anything. Then I pull a tiny spark from him. And another. And another. If I try for anything larger than that, the firecat shies away.

I'm just going to have to do this one spark at a time.

I keep going, talking in a soothing voice to the firecat

while mixing my magic with his and drawing on the tiniest possible ounces of his magic. At this rate, it would take *hours* to fully replenish my gift. But I don't need full. I just need enough to guide him into the enclosure.

Another spark, and another, and another . . .

Finally, I feel like I have enough control over my gift again to give the firecat a nudge. But I've learned my lesson about moving too fast, so I just let my gift ease over him for a moment without giving him any directions, keeping him relaxed in my presence.

I use this moment of calm to sneak a peek at Tomas. Unfortunately, he's doing well. His firecat is pacing nonchalantly in front of him while blue magic dances through the air. I don't know how Tomas is keeping him calm, but I have to admit he knows his technique—he's sitting with his head bowed just like me, to seem less threatening. He does seem to be struggling with getting the firecat to move in the right direction, though. It's taken him several minutes just to move a few feet closer to the nearest enclosure.

But thanks to Lilja, I already have plenty of experience guiding wild creatures. I rise slowly, keeping my head low, and when the firecat doesn't react, I give him a nudge with my gift, pointing him in the direction of the nearest enclosure.

"Come on, buddy," I say. "We're friends now, right?"

The firecat tilts his head questioningly at me, his tail swishing.

"I know the last thing you want to do right now is move into a smaller space," I continue. "But it's only temporary, and it would *really* help me out, okay?"

"Would you shut *up* over there?" Tomas shouts, and I jump in surprise. And so does my firecat, his flames suddenly whooshing higher on his back, his hackles rising.

"Shh, it's okay," I say quickly to the firecat, reaching out again with my gift in an attempt to be soothing.

But Tomas isn't finished. "You're breaking my concentration, Bryn," he yells, even though his firecat is perfectly calm.

He's trying to sabotage me.

"There will be plenty of distractions in the Realm," I call back, trying to maintain a cheerful tone for the sake of the agitated firecat in front of me. "A real Seeker could work through them."

"A real Seeker wouldn't talk to a firecat like it's her pet kitten," Tomas sneers. "It can't understand you, you know."

"It can understand my tone," I call back, still in my most cheerful voice.

Abruptly, Tomas turns and walks toward me. His own firecat watches placidly, making no attempt to move thanks to whatever spell Tomas has cast.

My firecat, however, spins toward Tomas, the flames along its crest rising higher in warning. It doesn't like this new intruder, not at all.

"Stay back," I say. "What are you doing?"

Tomas stops right in front of me and lowers his voice. In the softest of whispers, so low that no one in the arena could possibly hear but me, he says, "You should've stayed home, Bryn. I thought Johann's rocks would be enough to scare you away, but I guess he's too stupid to even do that properly."

I take a step back from him, all thoughts of the firecat forgotten. "The rocks were *your* idea?"

"You didn't think he was smart enough to come up with that on his own, did you?" Tomas rolls his eyes.

I remember how close one of those rocks came to Elisa's head, and my fists clench. "Why are you telling me this?"

Tomas shrugs, almost lazily. "You might want to check on your firecat, Bryn. He seems to be a *bit* upset."

I spin around. My firecat can clearly sense my anger. His crest of fire is rising still higher. Heat rolls off him in waves.

Grinning, Tomas turns and strolls away, back to his own firecat.

While mine bares his teeth and takes a menacing step toward me.

TWENTY-SIX

N ice kitty," I mutter under my breath, reaching for my gift as the angry firecat advances. "Nice firecat. We're friends, remember?"

The firecat doesn't react, and I grit my teeth. Tomas made me angry on purpose. I have to get myself, and my firecat, back under control and win this competition.

But just as I reach out with my gift to soothe it, the sound of footsteps reverberates from the tunnel.

Ari bursts through the door, followed closely by Johann, who seems to have been chasing him. Ari skids to a stop when he sees the firecats, but Johann doesn't. He almost barrels straight into one of them, which lets out a loud, threatening growl.

Across the arena, all four of the other firecats respond with a similar growl. All of them are agitated now.

Instinctively, I look at Ari, only to find him looking back at me.

"I'll calm them down if you guide them?" he asks.

At this point, I could use his empathy gift more than anything. I nod in agreement, and we both get to work.

Sparks of yellow dance across Ari's fingers as he sends his gift out, targeting both my firecat and one of the ones to our right that seems less agitated than the others. I copy him, mixing my gift in with the life spark of both cats, moving alongside their energy, letting them get used to the feel of it. I'm still running low on magic, but I might have *just* enough left. . . .

Whatever Ari's doing with his empathy gift is working much faster than anything I could ever do. The flames along the cats' spines start getting lower and lower before dying out completely.

"Careful," I say to Ari as the firecats' energy starts to feel almost droopy. "We don't want them to go to sleep yet!"

"Right, sorry," he says, dialing his energy back a little.

Now that the firecats are calm, it's my turn to act. I nudge each one with my gift, guiding them toward the enclosures. "Come on, guys," I say cheerfully. "Don't you want to take a nap now? Don't these little rooms look like the *perfect* places to sleep?"

I walk toward the nearest enclosures, and the two firecats follow. When I get close to the enclosures, I stop one of the cats and beckon the other into the nearest space. It'll be easier to direct only one at a time for this part.

Unfortunately, now that the firecat sees where I want

him to go, he's much more reluctant to move. "Come on," I coax, "just a few more steps. . . ."

Finally, the firecat moves forward and enters the enclosure. He looks around warily, but Ari raises his hands and casts more magic. In seconds, the cat's wariness turns to drowsiness, and he curls up in the middle of the space, looking ready for a nap.

We repeat the process with the second firecat, moving him into the enclosure next to the first. When he, too, curls up inside, Ari and I grin at each other. "Nice work," I say.

"You too. Ready to cast a boundary spell?"

"Just a minute," I say. "I'm really running low." Now that the firecat is in his enclosure, I can risk drawing a bit more from him to replenish my gift. "How'd you get past the healing without using up all your gift?" I ask Ari.

"Patience," he says, with a slight smirk. "I did it more slowly than you did."

I glare at him. "Ready now," I say, pulling my gift away from the firecat. I step toward the first enclosure to cast the spell that will keep the firecat from leaving it, and Ari steps toward the second—

A scream reverberates through the arena, and both of us whip around. We were so busy that I forgot about Tomas and Johann. Tomas is still guiding his firecat into an enclosure, but while we've been preoccupied, Johann has been getting himself into trouble.

The red glow of his warrior magic silhouettes his figure, surrounded by flames. The two remaining firecats near him are clearly upset, their crests flaming, their backs arched. Even as I watch, one of them shoots a fireball in Johann's direction, and he lets out another scream. Luckily, his magic catches it and sends the flames careening to the ground near the tunnel entrance, where they soon extinguish.

But diverting the firecat's flames only makes it angrier, and as soon as it gathers enough fire, it shoots another ball of flame in Johann's direction. He's expending a ton of energy just trying to avoid the flames, and he can't possibly guide the firecat into an enclosure while it is attacking him. As much as I should enjoy seeing Johann fail, I'm worried about the firecat. I hope it isn't too scared and that Johann hasn't done anything to hurt it. Have the Seekers been monitoring the situation? Would they step in if a creature were being abused by a competitor? Surely they would.

Johann dodges another ball of flames, and Ari turns to me. "We should—"

BOOM.

I'm knocked to the ground by a blast of heat and throw my arms over my head. The explosion rings in my ears, and for a moment I can't hear anything. I open my eyes and blink at the wall of fire racing through the center of the arena, scorching everything in its path.

Was this supposed to happen? Did Johann's firecat manage to release *this* much flame? Or has something gone wrong?

I scramble to my feet, checking that no part of me is on

fire, and spin around, assessing my surroundings. The ringing hasn't faded from my ears, and the shouts and cries of the
spectators in the arena are only a distant hum. But I've been
lucky—I'm far enough away from the blast that I don't seem
to be hurt. But what about—

"Ari?" I yell. "Ari!"

Someone coughs, and I spin around. Ari is behind me
at the firecat enclosures, his gift swirling wildly around his
fingertips. Both of the firecats we were trying to tame are
now more agitated than ever, their energy spiking all over the
place, and it seems to be taking all of Ari's strength to keep
them from firing more flames into the arena. I race toward
them, coughing as smoke fills the air.

"Have you got them?" I call, reaching out with my gift.

"Barely," he shouts back.

"I'm going to try to put out the flames before someone gets hurt. Make sure they don't attack me from behind,
okay?"

"I'll try!"

I turn back to the center of the arena, reaching for my
gift. I can't see any of the other competitors through the
smoke and flame, or any of the other firecats, either. I'll just
have to hope they stay out of my way.

I was already planning to use water to make my boundary spell—it's the one thing firecats hate. I use the energy of
the firecats behind me to anchor my magic just like Mama
taught me, then reach for the particles in the air the way Elisa

suggested. I try to picture the spell I want as clearly as I can, imagining a spray of water dousing the flames. My magic is so low, but I don't dare draw on any of the firecats in case it makes them more upset. I grit my teeth and dig deep inside myself for my gift, using as much of it as I can spare.

The green light of my magic races toward the flames, and water bursts from the air. The flames directly in front of me are drenched, and some of them are extinguished. But the air is dry and full of smoke, and my magic is too low, and it isn't nearly enough. I can't put them all out by myself.

I take a deep breath and cast my magic toward the fire. Naturalist gifts are supposed to be good with fire, though I've never tried it myself. Maybe I can—

Something is wrong. The energy of the fire doesn't feel natural at all. An undercurrent runs through it, something dark and thick and heavy. An energy that shouldn't be there.

I've only felt something like this once before: the mystery figure in the Realm. The one Ari said was a Vondur.

But I don't have time to think about what that means. The energy is fighting me, resisting the flow of my gift, and I can't connect with it the way I should be able to. I try to take a deep breath, but smoke sticks in my throat, and I cough. There's not enough moisture in the air, not enough anywhere—

A jet of water arcs through the air, streaming toward the flames. It's followed by another, and another, and another.

The Seekers have arrived.

Purple shields burst into life, encircling what's left of the flames and creating a barrier between the crowds in the stands and the arena floor. Sparks fly across Seeker Ludvik's hands as he casts them. Following him through the arena doors are Seeker Freyr and Seeker Agnar.

And leading the way through the smoke, casting water onto the flames as they go, are Seeker Larus and—

"Papa!"

He turns and rushes toward me, limping, his cane nowhere in sight. I'm guessing he forgot it in the stands in his rush to get down here. "Bryn!" he shouts, wrapping me up in a hug. "Are you all right?"

"I'm fine," I say. "But we need to find all the firecats and make sure they're okay. And Ari—"

I glance back toward the enclosures, where Ari is still standing over two of the firecats. Who are now, incredibly, both curled up on the floor of the arena like they're about to take a casual nap.

"Actually," I say, "I don't think Ari needs any help. But Johann does, and I don't know where Tomas and his firecat went. . . ."

"Tomas is in one of the tunnels," Papa says. "We could see from the stands—he managed to duck into one after the explosion."

"And Emil?"

"Never left the other half of the arena," Papa says. "But I didn't see the other boy—there was a lot of smoke up there."

"Contestants!" shouts a booming voice. Papa, Ari, and I both turn toward Seeker Larus, who is now standing in the center of the arena, having doused the flames. "Report to Seeker Freyr immediately if you have any injuries. If not, follow Seeker Agnar out of the arena." He turns to Seeker Ludvik, who is still holding up his shields, and they exchange a few words too soft for me to hear. Then Seeker Larus raises his voice again. "We ask all spectators to remain in their seats for a few more moments. You are all safe—the flames have been doused, and Seeker Ludvik's shields will protect you."

Papa takes a step toward Seeker Larus, who nods at him and adds quietly, "Jakob, if you wouldn't mind helping me with the remaining firecats?"

"Of course." Papa gives me another quick hug. "Out of the arena, Bryn," he says. "I'll see you in a few minutes."

He and Seeker Larus stride purposefully away, and I walk over to Ari, who appears to have constructed some kind of boundary spell around the two sleeping firecats.

"Did you feel it?" I whisper to him. "The magic in the flames?"

He nods once. "It wasn't the firecats that caused the explosion, was it?"

"No," I whisper back. "The Vondur were here. And we have to tell the Seekers."

"But—"

"I know. I know you think one of them might be involved. Maybe you're right. But there's no harm in describing what we felt—we can pretend we don't know what it means, but then at least any Seekers who *aren't* working for the Vondur will know what happened and be on high alert. This is bigger than us now, Ari. That fire could've killed someone."

"I know," he says. "You're right."

Together we walk to the side of the arena, where Seeker Agnar waits for us at the door. Beside him, Tomas is talking to his father, Seeker Freyr, who is also tending to what looks like a burn on Johann's arm. The sparks of Seeker Freyr's healing gift dance around his fingertips.

Seeker Agnar grunts an acknowledgment at us as we pass. Outside the arena, Emil is leaning against the wall. His face is streaked with tears, and he wipes his cheek with the end of his sleeve.

Tomas steps outside next, followed by Seeker Agnar. Tomas scowls at all of us. There's a streak of ash on his forehead, but otherwise he seems fine. After a moment, Seeker Freyr and Johann walk outside as well. Johann is carefully examining his arm as if there's still something wrong with it, even though the skin now looks fully healed.

The two Seekers stand beside each other, and we wait for them to speak.

Clearly, that explosion wasn't supposed to be part of the trial. So what's going to happen now? Will we redo the second trial? Will all of us move on to the third?

It's Seeker Freyr who speaks first. "We would like to thank all of you for remaining calm during today's difficult circumstances." He casts a significant look at Emil, who's still sniffling, and Johann, whose screams in the arena were the opposite of calm, before continuing. "Obviously we did not expect *quite* that level of reaction from the firecats we selected for today's trial."

Ari and I look at each other. Does Seeker Freyr not know that it wasn't the firecats who started the fire? Or is he the one working with the Vondur? Is he trying to cover it up?

"That being said," Seeker Agnar interjects, "you all knew what you signed up for. Being a Seeker and working with magical creatures is dangerous work, and these trials are not without some level of risk."

Seeker Freyr adds, "The council's policy, in situations like this, is to select which three contestants will advance to the next trial based on your performance before and during the, er, emergency situation."

Johann looks up. "But, Seeker, shouldn't we just do the second trial over again? Nobody got to finish."

Seeker Freyr shakes his head. "It is important that we appoint a fifth Seeker as soon as possible. Five is nature's number, the number of the gifts, and having five Seekers is essential for maintaining the balance of magic in the Realm. And, as you saw today, it is also beneficial to have five Seekers to deal with any emergency situations that may arise. We do not wish to delay much longer."

Something shifts in Seeker Agnar's expression, and he glances around at all of us. "We believe we've seen more than enough of your skills today to determine who can advance to the next trial. We would like the five of you to wait here. The council will vote on which of you will advance, and then we will make the announcement."

The Seekers return to the arena, and the five of us wait in tense silence.

It feels like ten years pass as we stand around, staring at each other.

"What's taking so long?" Johann says finally. "How long can it take to hold a vote?"

For some reason, Tomas glances over at me, but he doesn't say anything.

"This isn't fair," Emil says. "I didn't even get a chance to work with the firecats before the explosion happened. What did you all *do*, anyway?"

"Nothing," Johann snaps. "It wasn't one of the firecats I was working with. I was facing them, and the explosion happened behind me."

Tomas frowns. "Wait, if it wasn't one of yours, which one was it?"

Ari and I glance at each other, but we don't say anything.

Johann misinterprets our expressions and sneers at us. "Must've been *theirs*," he says meaningfully to Tomas. "Guess this is what happens when you let a girl and an empath near dangerous animals."

But Tomas is still frowning, gazing at us. He saw me only minutes before the explosion happened. He did agitate my firecat, but I don't doubt he was still keeping a close watch on us. He knows that we had them under control.

He looks like he's about to say something else, but the sound of the arena door opening interrupts him.

Seeker Agnar beckons us forward, and we file back into the arena.

The crowd in the stands is restless, but they let out a cheer as we emerge and line up in the center of the scorched arena floor, facing the council's table. Seeker Agnar hastens up the stairs to join the other three Seekers.

In front of us, the firecats have all been herded into their enclosures, and Seeker Ludvik's thick purple shields are keeping them in place. I glance around for Papa, but I don't see him—he must have rejoined Mama and Elisa in the crowd.

Finally, Seeker Larus's voice booms throughout the arena once more. "Ladies and gentlemen. The time has come to announce the decision of the council. Though none of the competitors were able to finish today's challenge due to extenuating circumstances, we have decided to select three of them to advance to the next round, based on the skill they showed us today. The council has voted, and we will now announce our selections for the third and final round of competition."

Cheers rise up from the crowd, and my heart pounds. I'm pretty sure I know who they've chosen. Surely not Emil, who was behind the rest of us even before the explosion. And surely not Johann, with the way he was mishandling his firecat . . . right? But there's a chance they could select any-one. I'd bet that Seeker Agnar voted for Johann over me, just to save face. And I have no way of knowing how the other Seekers will vote. I forced my way into the second trial just by being one of the only five to complete the tasks, but this time the Seekers can vote me out if they choose.

"Our first selection," Seeker Larus booms, "is Tomas, Freyr's son."

Cheers rise from the crowd. When they die down, Seeker Larus continues, "Tomas demonstrated the greatest aptitude for healing out of all of the contestants today, which of course we would expect from a healer. But he also demonstrated an ability to work well with his firecat and was in the process of completing a boundary spell before being interrupted. We believe he may have finished first, had the trial continued, and therefore deserves a spot in the third trial."

"I bet we would've beat him," Ari mutters to me under his breath. "He's been struggling with boundary spells in training. He's slow at them."

"Our next selection also demonstrated aptitude for both defensive and healing spells and worked admirably well with calming two of the firecats even during extremely stress-ful circumstances," Seeker Larus continues. "He not only demonstrated skill with his own gift but also a creative abil-ity to master other types of spellwork. Therefore, our second selection is Ari, Petur's son."

The crowd applauds, and Ari visibly deflates in relief. I

should probably be polite and congratulate him, but my heart is in my throat.

It's got to be either me or Johann who's being eliminated. There's no way they passed Emil, when he never even finished the healing spell.

"Our third selection," Larus continues, "also successfully completed a healing spell and demonstrated a skilled gift following the explosion. Therefore, our third selection . . . is Johann, Viktor's son."

The sound of the crowd is a roar in my ears. I don't move. I don't blink. I don't breathe.

I *lost*.

Ari is murmuring something in my ear, but it takes me a minute to focus on the words.

"—all wrong. It should've been you. I *know* it should've been."

He's right. I was doing much better with the firecats than Johann. That's just a fact. And I helped put the fire out after the explosion—or at least tried to, anyway. If the explosion hadn't happened, Ari and I would've completed our boundary spells and probably been the first ones to finish the trial. Anyone who was paying attention would know that I should've passed.

But the Seekers voted against me anyway.

Ari's still talking, but I shrug him off. It suddenly feels like everyone in the crowd is staring at me, witnessing my failure. I have to get out of here.

"Bryn, wait!" Ari races after me as I stride past him, heading for the door.

"Congratulations," I mutter to him. "Good luck in the third trial."

"*Wait.*" The urgency in his voice is enough to slow me down.

"What? What could *possibly* matter to me now, Ari?"

"The Vondur," he says, and I stop in my tracks. "Remember what Seeker Freyr said, about the explosion being caused by firecats? I don't think they know. We have to tell them what happened. That was *your* idea, remember?"

I turn to face him. "And you really think they'll listen to us? Apparently the Seekers think so little of me that they ranked me below *Johann*. Why would they care about anything I have to say?"

"Because I'm going to go with you. And we'll tell them to ask the others, too—Tomas knows that it wasn't a firecat, at the very least. He knows something's wrong, and I think the Seekers suspect that too."

I kick a stone on the arena floor, watching it skip. "Go without me. I don't want to talk to them right now. I don't want to see the look on Seeker Agnar's stupid smug face."

Ari shakes his head at me. "Who are you, and what happened to Bryn? The Bryn *I* know would never stop fighting to make the Seekers give her another chance. She'd march right up to the council and *demand* to be let into the third trial, and she wouldn't let anyone get in her way."

"She's tired," I say. "She wants to go home." But I straighten up a little. Could he be right? Could there be a chance I could convince the Seekers to let me stay in the competition? If there's any chance at all, I have to take it.

Ari senses the shift in my mood instantly, and he grins. "Come on."

We change direction, walking toward the steps leading up to the council's table. "Did you just use your weird empath abilities on me?" I grumble.

"Nope. This is all you."

I narrow my eyes at him. "I don't believe you. I saw you put some scared, angry firecats to *sleep* earlier."

Ari grins. "I *might* have been a little overzealous in calming them down. You know, since I feared for my life and everything."

"Oh, come on, it's just a little firecat. What harm could it do?" I tease.

Ari rolls his eyes. "Only you would say that."

We reach the council's table, where the four Seekers appear to be in deep discussion about something. They all look startled when Ari and I approach.

Ari fidgets with his cloak, suddenly looking nervous, so I speak first. "We need to talk to you about what happened. About the explosion."

Seeker Agnar cuts over me immediately. "If this is an attempt to get back into the competition—"

"It wasn't the firecats that caused it," Ari jumps in.

Seeker Ludvik straightens, looking more attentive, and Seeker Larus frowns. "What do you mean?"

"None of the firecats caused it," Ari continues. "Both of ours were under control, and so was Tomas's. Johann was struggling with the other two, but he was facing them at the time, and he said the explosion happened *behind* him. You can ask him. Ask Tomas. They'll tell you."

The Seekers exchange glances. "And if it wasn't a firecat . . . ?" Seeker Ludvik asks.

"We don't know exactly," I say, "but . . ." I have to tread very carefully here, to pretend that I know less than I do. They don't know that Ari and I went into the Realm once and sensed Vondur magic there. "I tried to put that fire out, and there was energy in it that wasn't like anything I've ever felt before. That wasn't ordinary fire. And it wasn't someone else's gift, either. It was . . . a dark kind of magic. Heavy feeling, kind of twisty and . . . and slow, without very much energy. It was . . . *wrong*."

A shadow has fallen across Seeker Larus's face. "And you felt this too?" he asks Ari, his voice sharp.

"Yes, Seeker. It's just like Bryn said. There was another energy, and it didn't feel right."

No one speaks for a long moment.

"Thank you for bringing this to our attention," Seeker Larus says. "We will investigate the matter further."

It's clearly a dismissal, but I step forward. "There's one more thing." I take a deep breath, shoring up my courage.

"I'd like to formally petition the council to be allowed to compete in the third trial."

"No," Seeker Agnar says immediately. "We have already made our selections, and it would be unfair to the others to—"

"I'm not asking you to kick any of the others out. I'm asking you to let four of us compete in the next round. You know this wasn't really a good demonstration of our skills, and none of us got the chance to finish. But if we had, I know I would've finished sooner than Johann. Maybe sooner than Tomas, too. I completed my healing spell, I was handling my firecat, and all I had left to do was the boundary around the enclosure."

"We're aware of your performance," Seeker Agnar says. "We already held our vote."

"And how could you have voted for Johann?" I stare directly at Seeker Agnar. "With how poorly he was handling his firecat? And he was slower than me at the healing. And when the explosion happened, only one of us managed to put out any of the flames. Only one of us noticed that strange magical energy and brought it to your attention. If you're going to give Johann a spot in the third trial, then I've earned one too."

Seeker Ludvik is smiling at me. Seeker Agnar's jaw clenches. Seeker Freyr is unmoved.

And Seeker Larus rises to his feet. "We do not allow contestants to question the decisions of the council," he says firmly, but I sense that there's something else coming. "However, you do raise some fair points. In fact, when it came down to our vote, there was a tie—two Seekers voted to put you through, and two voted for Johann."

This doesn't surprise me. I can see how it happened—they all agreed to let Ari and Tomas through, but then only two of them were willing to vote for me. I'm sure it was Agnar who voted against me and probably Freyr, too—I bet he wants his son Tomas to win, and he'd rather put through a competitor like Johann, who doesn't pose much of a challenge.

"If it was a tie," I say carefully, "then why did you select Johann and not me?"

No one answers, and we all know what their silence means.

Finally, Seeker Larus speaks. "I'm sorry. But as a council, we have rules we must adhere to—and one of them is the result of a vote. Our decision stands."

For a moment I swear my heart stops beating, and I forget how to breathe entirely.

I've been eliminated from the competition.

It's over.

TWENTY-SEVEN

I'm sorry, Bryn," Ari says again as we leave the arena.

I shake my head, not entirely trusting myself to speak. "Just do me a favor and beat Tomas and Johann in the next round, okay?"

Before he can reply, his mama rushes up, congratulating him, and I slip away through the crowd.

I find Mama and Papa, who are talking in hushed voices.

"It's outrageous," Mama says as I approach. "We all saw it—" She breaks off when she sees me.

Wordlessly, Papa envelops me in a hug. "You did well, Bryn," he says. "You should be proud of your performance today."

"But I lost."

Mama huffs. "That Johann boy almost got himself killed. We all know who really won." She sweeps me up in a hug herself after Papa releases me. "Are you all right? Did you hurt yourself in the fire? Inhale too much smoke?"

"I'm fine, Mama."

She looks me up and down, checking for injuries despite my protests. When she's finally finished her investigation, she says, "It's an injustice, that's what it is. We all know what really happened."

"They told me it was a tie vote," I say. "Between me and Johann. And they picked him."

"Cowards," Mama says, so loudly that Papa glances around to see if anyone's in earshot. "They didn't want to cause an uproar by selecting you over one of the boys."

"Where's Elisa?" I ask.

Mama and Papa exchange glances. "She wasn't feeling well," Mama says. "One of the neighbors offered to take her home so your papa and I wouldn't miss seeing you compete."

"Is she okay?"

"It's her cough," Papa says. "She'll be fine."

But worry lines crinkle his brow, and I don't believe him.

I've failed completely. I don't know how we'll get more starflowers now. I had one chance to help Elisa, and now it's gone.

My only solace is thinking about Lilja. She'll have to return to the Realm someday, of course, but until then I can still see her. She's my dragon now as much as Ari's, and I'm sure he wouldn't mind. . . .

Mama and Papa chatter away during the walk home and the entire rest of the evening, clearly trying to get my mind off the competition, but it doesn't help. I excuse myself from dinner early and lie in bed, staring at the ceiling. I don't have the energy to sneak out, to try to see Ari or Lilja. It takes too much effort to do anything.

I'll never get to be a Seeker now, and I don't know what to do.

The next day, I try to distract myself as much as possible. I spend the morning running errands for Mama and playing with Elisa in the kitchen. Elisa's fascination with unicorns has morphed into a fascination with firecats now, and I spend several minutes explaining that no, her dolls cannot ride on the backs of firecats because they don't actually allow human riders and also they're covered in flames, but I somehow lose that argument. So we end up racing the dolls around the room as we pretend they're riding firecats like horses, making Elisa giggle and causing Mama to send us out into the garden so we won't "be underfoot."

It's almost noon as we sprint through the garden, and I race to beat Elisa over the finish line, which is Papa's patch of tomato plants. Skidding through the dirt, I slide past the plants so fast I nearly collide with the gate. "I win again!" I yell triumphantly.

No response. I spin around, clutching one of Elisa's dolls in my hand. She's halfway across the garden, doubled over.

I race toward her as her coughs get louder. "Elisa, are you okay?"

She can't answer. She's coughing too hard. Her doll has fallen into the dirt.

"Mama!" I yell, racing for the hut. I fling the door open and reach for the starflower paste, even as I shout for Mama, who instantly figures out what's happening. We race back to Elisa together, and I hold the jar while Mama scrapes the medicine out. When the coughs don't ease right away, she scoops out another handful.

The jar is empty now.

Elisa's coughs subside, but just barely. Her breaths are still wheezy and hoarse.

"Just breathe, baby," Mama says, rubbing circles across her back. "There you go."

I glance into the empty jar again. We are officially out.

And Elisa's next coughing fit could happen at any time.

Mama follows my gaze to the empty jar. "Bryn," she says with forced lightness, "why don't you run to the herbalist and trade for some more starflowers, okay?"

"What am I going to trade?" I ask quietly.

Mama doesn't answer right away. She rubs Elisa's back more briskly. "I'm sure I can find something. Come inside for a moment."

Mama leads Elisa inside and settles her onto our bed to rest. I trail after them, setting the useless jar on the table and handing Elisa both of her dolls.

Mama rummages in the dresser beside her bed, pulls something out, and hands it to me. "See if you can trade this," she says.

I look at the object in my hand and gasp. It's the necklace of icefox crystals Papa made for Mama many years ago. He found every one of these crystals in the Realm himself and handpicked them for the necklace. He gave it to her as a wedding gift.

"Mama," I say quietly, "are you sure you want . . . ?"

I can't read her expression. She places a soft hand on my shoulder. "You should be able to get a fair number of starflowers for it," she says. "Don't let the herbalist undersell you, all right?"

Always practical, even when trading away her most prized possession. "I . . ."

"Hurry, Bryn," she says firmly.

I turn and run from the hut, slipping the necklace into my pocket.

But I don't go to the herbalist.

I run past Runa's farm and out to the beach faster than I've ever run before. I'll bring home starflowers, but I won't do it by trading away Mama's necklace. All I have to do is find some in the Realm. I know they're rare, but Papa's told me where they tend to grow, and I bet I could find them in the northern forests.

There's just one problem: it's the middle of the day. Seeker Agnar will be headed for the training session in the arena, but the other three Seekers will all be working in the Realm right now. Any one of them could catch us.

The Realm's a big place. They could be in a completely different territory. There's no reason to expect them to be in the same forest.

But Lilja isn't exactly easy to hide, and one of the Seekers or their dragons could easily sense her presence or see her flying overhead. Not to mention that the mystery person using Vondur magic could be there again.

It doesn't matter. I don't have a choice. I can get way more starflowers by going into the Realm than by trading Mama's necklace, and this way she won't have to lose it. It should be a quick, easy trip.

I just have to hope we don't get caught.

Lilja is asleep when I reach the cave and looks confused to see me. She blinks sleepily, and her tail gives a few half-hearted thumps against the rocky floor.

"Sorry, Lil, I know I'm a bit early," I say. "But we're going to go on a fun trip, okay? And you'll get to fly *fast*."

Lilja's energy rises up to meet mine, like she senses that something's wrong and is trying to figure out what it is. I wind my gift through her life source in what I hope is a reassuring manner. "Come on, let's go for a flight!"

A few bilberry bribes later, I manage to get Lilja out of the cave and into the air. I let her fly much higher than normal, hoping it will keep us out of sight as she passes over the mountains and into the Realm.

The daylight has completely transformed the Realm from the last time I was here. Miles and miles of lush greenery spread out below us, interspersed with mountain peaks and the shimmery gleam of crystal-blue lakes and rivers. The dark line of the lava fields cuts a diagonal gash through the greenery, while to the far north, the snowcapped peaks and glaciers turn everything white. It's a riot of color that's been invisible to us at night, with only the moon and stars to illuminate the darkness.

It's so jarring that it takes me a moment to recognize the correct forest and send Lilja in that direction. I have to make her fly lower in order to get a better look, and my heart pounds in my chest at the risk. But there are no other dragons in the sky and no sign of where the Seekers might be.

As long as they're not in the forest . . .

As long as they don't see us . . .

I steer Lilja toward the clearing she landed in before, causing a stir from the many birds chirping loudly in the trees. The ground is an unfamiliar field of green grasses mixed with flowers of all colors, and that's when I realize the new problem.

Starflowers only bloom at night.

Finding them during the day is going to be much harder.

Lilja looks at me with that confused head tilt again, probably wondering what we're doing.

"It's all right," I tell her. "I just need to find some flowers and then we can go, okay?"

I hardly dare to breathe as I make my way through the forest, casting out my gift for any hint of starflower magic. If I can just find the right spot, then I can identify the flowers themselves even if they're not blooming. They may not look like much, but I'll know what they are. . . .

Lilja crashes through the underbrush, making enough noise to wake the dead, but I don't dare leave her behind in the clearing. She might run off if she senses other dragons nearby, or one of the Seekers might find her, or she might get lost and I'll have to track her down, or . . .

The trees finally part again, and I stop. This is it. I can feel it.

We travel alongside a stream for a few minutes, following the faint echo I can feel in the air. I'd know the feeling anywhere.

We come to a little hollow beside the stream, and there, tucked away under the trees, are nearly two dozen tiny plants.

The starflowers don't look like much now, just thin green stems with tiny furled buds on top. But they're the right flowers, I know. I can sense their essence with my gift.

Lilja is intrigued by the river and the promise of fish, so I let her hunt in the water a little as I get to work digging up as many starflowers as I can carry. The sun beats down overhead, and I scrape through the dirt with nothing but my pocketknife and frantic speed, pulling up entire flowers and stuffing them into my pockets.

What feels like hours later, I'm covered head to toe in dirt and have a dozen starflowers weighing down my pockets. Strands of hair have come loose from my braid, and I brush them aside as I sheathe my pocketknife and whistle for Lilja. She bounds up a moment later, splashing through the water and drenching me.

"Good dragon," I say, patting her nose and giving her a bilberry. "All right, let's go."

Lilja doesn't have enough room to take off in this small clearing, so we trudge back through the forest into the larger space before launching into the air. Again, I direct her to fly higher than usual. By the time we leave the Realm and arrive at the caves, I'm feeling light-headed from either exhaustion or the thin air or both.

That's probably why I don't sense them at first.

Lilja figures it out before I do—moments after landing on the ledge outside her cave, her whole body suddenly stiffens, the spines on her back rising in alert.

I reach for my gift on instinct and immediately feel it too.

There are three life forces inside Lilja's cave. Two of them are human. And one of them is a dragon.

We have to run, now, before they sense us—

"Bryn!" A familiar voice booms loudly from the cave.

The same voice that echoes across the arena to announce the winners of the competition.

Seeker Larus's voice.

We could still fly away, but it wouldn't matter. They know we're here.

We're caught.

TWENTY-EIGHT

Bryn," says Seeker Larus again in a terrible, terrible voice. "Step away from that dragon at once."

Beside Seeker Larus stands Seeker Agnar, his arms folded across his chest and his expression sterner than I've ever seen before. Behind them, something moves in the shadows of the cave—I can't see it, but I can tell it's another dragon.

"I . . . I can explain," I say, not knowing how else to respond. How much do they know? How did they find this place?

"I would certainly hope so," says Seeker Larus firmly. "I'm sure you can imagine how shocked we were to discover that a village citizen—and one of our former competitors, no less—has been illegally hiding a dragon outside of the Realm."

I gulp. At this point, there's pretty much nothing I can say to save myself. I've been caught red-handed with Lilja. But I still need to speak very, very carefully. I need to find out if they know about Ari and about our trip into the Realm. If not, maybe there's still hope for a lesser punishment. . . .

"I . . . ," I start, and stop again.

Seeker Agnar takes advantage of my stumble. "We were told that you were hiding a dragon in this cave, and what do find here but you and a dragon?"

They were *told*?

It takes me a minute to puzzle this out. My first assumption was that they must've seen me and Lilja in the Realm just now. But that can't be, because then they wouldn't have known the location of the cave. They were lying in wait here. In fact, if I'd stuck with my normal routine, I would've been here sooner.

Someone told them that I would be here.

But no one knows about this place except Runa and Ari. So who would tell them?

"Bryn," says Seeker Larus again. "You are Seeker Jakob's daughter and one of the competitors, so I trust I don't have to explain how serious this is. Magical creatures belong in the Realm, where they can be both free and safe. To hide a dragon outside the Realm is to risk letting it be harmed, not to mention the risk it poses to others. What if this dragon had entered the village? What if it had wandered onto a farm and helped itself to the livestock? What if it had become injured or—"

"As a *former* competitor," Seeker Agnar cuts in, "you really ought to know better."

Heat floods my face, but I can't tell if it's shame or anger or both. "And how would I know anything," I snap back, "when I haven't been allowed to train?"

Antagonizing him right now is absolutely the worst thing to do, and as soon as I say it I wish I could take the words back. Seeker Agnar looks livid. Seeker Larus doesn't, though. In fact, his expression is . . . sympathetic? Whatever it is, it's gone in an instant, so maybe I just imagined it.

"Why?" Seeker Larus asks. His voice is almost quiet. "Why didn't you tell us about this dragon? Why did you hide her?"

All at once, a horrible sickening feeling tightens in my stomach. I didn't tell them because Ari and I suspect that one of them is trading with the Vondur, and we still don't know if that's true. I can't say anything about that. And I can't even explain how Ari got Lilja's egg without incriminating him, and it doesn't sound like they know he was involved.

I won't be the one to tell them about Ari if they don't already know. At least one of us has to become a Seeker. It can't be me now, so it has to be him. One of us needs to be able to take care of Lilja.

So I lie. "I thought it would help me win the competition," I say quietly. Maybe, if that really was sympathy on Seeker Larus's face, maybe . . . "I thought it was only fair, since everybody else got to train. I needed a way to learn too."

"So you stole a dragon from the Realm?" Seeker Agnar

says. Where Larus and I have gotten quieter, his voice has only gotten louder.

"I didn't steal her," I say. "I found her egg . . . on the beach. I didn't know how it got here, but I wanted to protect it. I was going to turn it in, honestly I was, but then it hatched and . . . and I thought maybe if I kept her for a while, just for a few weeks during training . . ."

"You cheated," Seeker Agnar fumes. "And where were you just now? Did you fly this dragon into the Realm?"

I bite my lip and tell another lie. "Of course not. I know only Seekers can enter the Realm. Besides, I knew if I did that we'd be seen."

Seeker Agnar starts to say something else, but Seeker Larus holds up a hand, cutting him off. "The welfare of our island's creatures is a Seeker's first and foremost responsibility, Bryn," Seeker Larus says sternly. "Your behavior was selfish and could have caused harm to come to this dragon. While I am inclined to agree that you deserved a fair shot at training with your fellow competitors, that doesn't give you an excuse to break our most important rules and endanger a magical creature in the process. If you were still participating in the competition, this alone would disqualify you."

Heat floods my face again, and this time it's definitely shame. "I'm sorry," I say. "I never meant for anything to happen to her. I thought I was keeping her safe."

"This dragon belongs in the Realm, with its family,"

Seeker Larus says, more gently. "She must be taken there, Bryn."

"Wait." I glance back at Lilja, who is glaring at the Seekers, her spines half raised warily. "You're going to take her there now?"

"Immediately," Seeker Larus says.

"But—"

But that means I will never see her again.

It's all over. I can't become a Seeker. I can't ever fly into the Realm. Lilja will be reunited with her fellow dragons, but I won't get to see it.

"Say your goodbyes," Seeker Larus says softly.

I reach out for her, wrapping my arms around her leg and giving her the closest thing to a hug I can manage. "You're such a good dragon, Lil," I whisper against her scales. "The best dragon ever."

I reach into my pocket, produce my last handful of bilberries, and present them to her.

Lilja knows something's wrong; she can sense it in my gift. She studies me carefully for a moment before lowering her head and swiping the berries from my palm.

"Don't worry, Lil," I say. "You'll like the Realm. It's nice there, and you'll make lots of new dragon friends." Sniffling, I give her another hug. "Don't forget about me," I whisper into her scales.

Her gift twines around mine, her heartbeat thudding in my ears. I memorize the feel and sound of her as Seeker Larus leads me down to the beach, away from my dragon.

Blinking back tears, I can't do anything but watch as Seeker Agnar climbs onto Lilja's back.

She flies high into the air and over the mountains, where the sun shines down on the Realm.

I watch through the blur of tears until even her shadow has disappeared from view.

TWENTY-NINE

It doesn't make any sense.

I have plenty of time during the long, cold walk home to turn everything over in my head, but I can't figure it out.

Someone told the Seekers that Lilja and I would be in the cave in the afternoon. Someone told them I'd been hiding a dragon. But who?

Only Ari, Runa, and I knew about Lilja. Runa would never have said anything—and even if she did accidentally let something slip, she would have warned me. Besides, she'd never even been all the way up to the cave. She didn't know which cave, specifically, was the one where Lilja was hiding. But the Seekers did.

And Ari never would've said anything. I don't think he'd betray me like that, and anyway, he loves Lilja too much. He's lost access to her now too, unless he wins the third trial.

Who else would have known exactly where and when the Seekers could find us?

I kick a pebble down the path, watching it disappear into the trees. Maybe it was the person who almost caught us in the Realm. Maybe they knew more than we thought. Maybe . . .

Maybe they're a Seeker?

My mind is racing so fast that I can't think straight about anything anymore. I don't want to go home, don't want to tell my family what's happened, but I need to talk to someone who can help me sort this out.

Without thinking twice, I race down the path and head for Runa's.

I find her in the garden, pulling up weeds. She takes one look at my face and drops the clump of roots in her hand. "Bryn, what's wrong?"

"They took Lilja," I wheeze. "They took her!"

"What? Who took her?"

"They knew! The Seekers *knew*."

"Whoa, slow down," Runa says, stepping closer. "Take a few deep breaths, then start from the beginning."

I do. After I've told her everything, Runa gasps. "I can't believe it. How'd they find out? You have to go back to the Seekers and tell them the whole story. They'll change their minds! Besides, it was Ari who found Lilja and hid her in the first place. Not you."

"But we both knew about her," I say bitterly. "If I tell them about Ari, they'd just disqualify him. And right now, it's either him or Tomas or Johann who will be Seeker. It should be him."

"It isn't fair," she says. "It isn't fair. He's the one who found Lilja. He broke the same rules."

"What else can I do?" I sink to my knees in the dirt, finding comfort in the life sparks of the plants all around me. I nudge them with my gift, tugging little bits of their energy into mine. It makes me feel stronger somehow.

"There has to be something," Runa says. "This is your dream, Bryn. You can't just *quit*."

"I've tried everything. I practically begged them to let me stay in the competition yesterday, and they wouldn't. And now they've taken Lilja, too."

She shakes her head. "The Bryn I know always finds a solution. When Seeker Agnar kicked you out of training, you found a better way."

"And look where that got me."

"What it got you was an awesome dragon and the skills you needed to win," Runa argues. "Maybe you just need to talk to the Seekers again. If you can explain to them that you didn't let any harm come to anyone, that you were only making up for the lack of training . . . If they see you compete in the final round, I know you'd win. If they'd just give you the chance—"

"There aren't any more chances," I say, louder than I intended, and Runa jumps. More quietly, I add, "It's over, Runa. This isn't something we can fix."

Runa drops to the ground beside me and wraps an arm around my shoulders. "It'll be okay. I know it will. Somehow it will work out."

I sniff and drop my head on her shoulders. "I was supposed to win. I *knew* I was meant to be a Seeker."

"I know," Runa murmurs.

"All that work. Everything you did to help me. Passing the first trial. All of it was for nothing."

"Not nothing," she says fiercely. "You showed everybody in this village that a girl can compete to be a Seeker. I bet there are other girls in the village who will compete next time, because you proved to them that it was possible."

I sit up with a sniff and look at her. "You're getting dirt on your dress," I say. Unlike me, Runa actually cares about keeping her clothes clean.

She laughs. "I think it'll survive, just this once."

"Can I stay here for a while? I don't want to go home."

"Of course," she says. "But fair warning, Mama's making me weed this whole garden. If you stay, you'll be put to work."

"That's okay. I don't mind."

Runa stands and brushes the dirt from her dress, then offers me a hand up. "I admit I might have an ulterior motive," she says with a grin. "If you use your gift on these weeds, this will go a *lot* faster."

"I think I can make that happen." I manage a small smile in return. "I'm pretty sure I owe you one."

Runa grins. "I'm pretty sure you owe me *way* more than one," she says, "but this is a good place to start."

Papa is waiting for me when I get home.

He sits on the garden bench and watches silently as I open the gate and walk toward him.

"Seeker Larus was here," he says finally.

In a way, it's a relief that I don't have to tell him myself. That I don't have to watch the horrible moment when the news sinks in. But on the other hand, I have no idea what Seeker Larus said or how bad he made it sound. And of course, he doesn't know about Ari.

"It's not what you think," I say.

His eyebrows rise. "And what do I think?"

"You think I was careless and I broke the rules and I lied to you and I cheated to win the competition."

Papa doesn't react for a moment. "And did you?"

"No. Well, I did some of it. But it wasn't like that. It was Ari who started it."

"Ari?"

I tell Papa *almost* everything. How Ari was the one who found Lilja, how he offered to help me after Seeker Agnar kicked me out of training, how he said he needed someone to help look after her. I admit to sneaking out at night and training with Ari in secret.

But I do not tell him about how Ari got Lilja's egg or our

suspicions about the Vondur and one of the Seekers. If I tell him, he'll go straight to Seeker Larus, and I still don't think it's safe to do that until we know for sure who stole Lilja's egg in the first place.

Papa doesn't say anything for a long time. "Why didn't you tell me, Bryn? When Seeker Agnar told you that you couldn't train, when Ari told you about the dragon, why didn't you come to me for help? Why did you lie?"

"I don't know," I say. "I was embarrassed, I guess. I hated how I was being singled out like that, how I was the only one who wasn't allowed to train. I didn't want to admit what happened. And then when Ari showed up with this dragon, it just . . . It just seemed like the perfect solution to everything. It only seemed fair, that I could have a way to train just like the boys did. And we both took really good care of Lilja. I promise we did. We found the cave for her and put up boundary spells and made sure that she was safe and that she wouldn't wander too far. We weren't being reckless, honestly."

"You were," Papa says gravely. "For two twelve-year-olds who haven't completed training to handle a dragon on their own is incredibly dangerous, Bryn. You could have been hurt."

"She's just a *baby*," I say. "And she's friendly, and—"

"And none of that matters," he says sternly. "Anything can happen when working with magical creatures, even those that you trust. I thought I taught you better than that."

"I'm sorry," I say. "I just thought . . . I thought that I'd become a Seeker and that none of it would matter."

Papa exhales heavily. "Go inside," he says finally. "Your mother and I will discuss your punishment."

"Do Mama and Elisa know?"

"They know what Seeker Larus told us," Papa says. "But I will tell your mother about Ari."

"Don't turn him in to the Seekers, please."

Papa looks surprised. "Why not? He broke the same rules you did."

"I know. But if he gets disqualified, then neither one of us can look after Lilja. Someone needs to check on her in the Realm and make sure she's okay. If I can't win, then it ought to be Ari."

"By all rights, both of you should be disqualified," Papa says.

"I know."

Papa is quiet for several agonizing seconds. "I will admit," he says, "that I didn't know about Seeker Agnar keeping you from training. That was wrong, and it was unfair. But that doesn't make it okay for you to decide that some of the rules don't apply to you, Bryn."

"I know," I say again.

"Go on, then."

I run inside and flop down on my bed without looking at

Mama or Elisa. I can't bear that right now. I bury my face in the pillow and stay that way.

Later, Mama and Elisa enter, and Mama tucks my sister into the bed beside me. I don't stir, and they leave me alone.

But as soon as Mama's gone, Elisa taps my shoulder. "Bryn? Are you awake?"

"No," I say.

"I'm sorry about your dragon," she whispers.

"Me too."

"Are you sad now?"

"Yes."

Elisa is quiet for a second. "Next time we play dolls, yours can have the pink unicorn if she wants."

I roll over to face her and give her hand a squeeze. "Thanks, El."

She falls asleep first, her hand still tucked into mine. I close my eyes and try not to think about anything.

In the morning, Mama forces me out of bed, and I help her make breakfast. She's surprisingly quiet. We work in companionable silence until Elisa wakes up and fills the kitchen with her chatter. It could almost be a normal morning as we eat breakfast, except for the fact that everyone keeps darting glances at me when they think I'm not looking, and neither Mama nor Papa ever really looks me in the eye.

By the time breakfast is over, I can't stand the quiet

anymore, so I bring it up myself. "How much trouble am I in?"

It's Mama who answers. "You are grounded indefinitely and are not to leave this hut until I say otherwise."

"But can I—"

"But nothing. You've been lying and sneaking out, and you can consider yourself lucky if I don't make you stay in this hut until you're thirty-five."

I open my mouth, but Papa shakes his head. "Listen to your mother, Bryn."

"Fine." I sigh.

Mama is as good as her word. She keeps me busy inside all day with chores, and I never get the chance to go out. She never even lets me go to the well for water—she goes herself instead, assigning me something to do in the hut in the meantime.

All I really want to do right now is talk to Ari. I want to say I'm sorry for losing our dragon and to wish him luck in the third trial. And I want to know if he's learned anything more about the Vondur, or the Seekers, or how they found out about Lilja. But the only way I can think of to see him is to sneak out of the house again.

Unfortunately, my parents are way ahead of me on that one. After Mama has tucked me and Elisa into bed, Papa drags his chair in front of the hut's door and falls asleep in front of it, effectively barring anyone from leaving until morning.

"Go to sleep, Bryn," he says when he sees me watching him, and I do.

The rest of the week passes the same way. I don't get to go anywhere. I don't get to see Ari, or Runa, or Lilja.

I will never see Lilja again.

And I will never be a Seeker.

THIRTY

The morning of the third trial, I help Mama make breakfast, and she ushers Elisa into the kitchen.

"Hurry up, now," Mama says when Elisa starts playing with her spoon. "We have a competition to get to."

I nearly spit out my oatmeal in surprise. "What?"

"Your mama thinks it's best," Papa says softly, "if we attend the final trial today."

"Why? I won't be competing."

Mama looks at me, *really* looks at me, for the first time all morning. "The rest of the village will be there," she says finally. "We're not going to hide in our hut like we're ashamed. They're the ones who should be ashamed, doing everything they can to force you out of this competition and favoring the boys with half your skill. No. We're going to walk into that arena with our heads high, and we're going to congratulate the winner, and we're going to make all of them remember how they treated you."

Before I can speak, Mama adds, "Well, your father and your sister and I will. You will be staying here. You're still grounded."

"But you just said—"

"No arguing. Finish your breakfast."

I sigh. I didn't really want to go to the competition anyway, I guess. I think Ari stands a better chance of winning than Tomas or Johann, but even so, I can't stomach the thought that one of them might become the next Seeker. And I *know* I can't bear the stares of all the villagers.

Mama makes me do all of the breakfast dishes while everyone else gets dressed. She bundles Elisa into her coat and rushes her out the door.

Papa gives me a hug before he leaves. "Don't worry. It will all work out."

I nod, unconvinced, and he leaves.

By the time I finish the dishes, the village bells are ringing loudly, signaling the start of the final trial. I'm probably the only person not in attendance. Ari and Tomas and Johann are probably walking into the arena right this second. . . .

To distract myself from the thought, I start tidying up the hut. My coat is still lying in a crumpled heap under the bed, where I flung it the other day; I couldn't stand to look at it knowing I wasn't going to go outside anytime soon. I pick it up, preparing to hang it on the clothesline—

And a starflower falls out of the pocket.

Of course. With everything that happened, I never did

tell Mama that I got some starflowers for Elisa. We're completely out of starflower paste, and Elisa might have a coughing fit at any time. I should grind these up and get them to her right away, just in case. I know Mama said not to leave the hut, but in this instance, I think she'd approve. After all, Elisa had to leave during the previous trial because of her fits. If she has another one, and no one has any paste with them to help . . .

Quickly I gather up the starflowers and get to work. I've watched Mama grind them up a hundred times, so I know exactly what to do. I add water to Mama's prescribed mixture of chamomile, onion, and thyme oil, then stir with the ground starflower leaves until it's all mixed together. I dump the finished paste into the jar and screw the lid on tightly.

Without bothering to clean up my mess, I throw my coat over my shoulders, tuck the jar into my coat pocket, and run toward the arena.

The village is completely deserted and eerily silent as I pass through it, but the sounds of the crowd can be heard as I make my way down to the arena. I doubt the trial has started yet, but I try not to think about it.

I crest the top of a hill and stop to catch my breath. The arena is in view, just down the path. To my right, the sea glimmers in the sunshine. The wind has picked up, tossing the waves and the sails of the boats—

The boats?

There shouldn't be anyone out on the water today. Everyone is in the arena. All of the ships should be docked in the harbor on the other side of the village. Why would there be so many here, so close to the shore?

I crane my neck and squint, trying to get a better look. Two ships have pulled ashore, and two more are pulling up behind them. Red flags fly proudly above their masts.

The Vondur flag.

My blood runs cold. I leave the path and race down the side of the hill, darting behind some bushes to get a closer look. What could they possibly be—

Two figures are walking down the beach, away from the ships. My view was blocked by the arena before, but now I can see what they're doing. Their arms are wrapped around heavy iron chains.

And at the other end of the chains is a dragon.

I creep behind the rocks at the top of the hill, trying to get a closer look.

The dragon is only a baby—in fact, it looks like it's about the same size as Lilja. But it's skinny, and its scales are a deep crimson red, and the crests along its spine are ashy black. A heavy iron shackle is clamped around its neck, connecting it to the chains that the Vondur are hauling forward. It limps a little on its back leg, like it's wounded. As I watch, the dragon makes a high, pitiful sound, like a desperate cry for help, and my heart leaps into my throat.

It must not be old enough to breathe fire yet, or these Vondur never would've been able to chain it like this. But how did they get this dragon? And what are they doing with it now?

It doesn't matter. Whatever it is, it can't be good. I have to warn the Seekers. I have to warn *everyone*.

I scramble to my feet and rush forward, keeping myself hunched low behind the rocks so that they won't see me from the shore. The path to the arena winds around here, so as soon as I get past the next bend they won't be able to see me—

No. I'm too late. An entire row of soldiers, carrying Vondur-style spears and even silver swords, are blocking the entrance to the arena. An uproar rises from inside—whatever's happening, everyone in the village already knows. But no one is emerging. No one is coming out to fight the Vondur, to force them away.

My heart skips several beats, and my body goes cold like I've dropped into a glacial lake. No one is going to come out of the arena, because they can't.

The Vondur have trapped them inside.

Somehow they must have known about the competition today. Somehow they knew that everyone in the village would be in the arena, that they could easily trap them all in the same place.

There's only one reason the Vondur would do this. For years, there's been only one thing about our island that truly interests them.

They've come to conquer the Wild Realm.

I look up, scanning the sky, and see exactly what I feared. The thin red dragon is now charging through the main entrance of the arena. I can't see if there are any riders on its back at this distance, but I'm sure there are. I'm sure their soldiers are going to fight the Seekers while they're trapped in the arena. And once they're out of the way, there will be no one to stop the Vondur from entering the Realm.

Except me.

I have to do something, and I have to do it fast. But what? I can't fight off an army of Vondur soldiers alone, especially when they have a dragon and I don't. Maybe if I had Lilja, but she's somewhere in the Realm now, on the other side of the mountains.

Unless . . .

I have no doubt that the Seekers have already created new boundary spells to keep Lilja from returning to the cave, but they don't prevent the dragons from flying out over the ocean to fish. And dragons can be creatures of habit. Lilja will want to hunt in the same place she always has, at least until she gets more used to the Realm. As soon as the Seekers released her there, she probably tried to find her way back to the beach, or went hunting for fish in the water.

Which means there's a chance—a tiny, infinitesimal chance—that she's still there, or at least nearby.

It's the only chance I have.

I run, no longer caring if the Vondur see me as I race back over the hill and into the deserted village. Lilja's beach is far from here, on the other side of the bay, and I don't know how I'm going to make it. Past Johann and his family's hut, past our own hut, past Runa's farm, through the woods . . .

I make it to the beach in record time. I don't spy any dragons overhead, but that doesn't mean they aren't nearby. I need to get as close to the Realm as I can, so that she can hear me. Which means climbing.

I make my way up to Lilja's cave first, then find another handhold and continue moving above it, scaling the side of the cliff. The waves crash far below me, and I don't dare look down.

Finally, I can climb no farther. There are no more ledges or handholds, just a smooth sheet of rock above me. I can't go up, and I'm not even sure I can find my way back down. This plan had better work, because there's nowhere else to go.

I throw my head back, suck in air, and whistle as loudly as I can. Three sharp, piercing notes. The same ones that Ari taught her, the signal she's responded to ever since.

I hold my breath, listening for the beat of a dragon's wings, but there's nothing. I try again, whistling as loud as I can. Again, again, again. My lungs start to heave. My hands are still slick and sticky with starflower paste, and I'm losing my grip on the rocks.

With the last of my breath, I yell. "Lilja! Lilja, I'm here!"

My voice echoes, bouncing around the rocks.

And a shadow appears on the horizon.

Lilja charges right toward me, the sunlight glimmering

off her silver scales, more beautiful than she has ever been. Her eyes are wide with excitement, and she drives straight toward me—

And pulls up short, her wings flapping frantically, as a violet shield shimmers in the air above me, preventing her from getting closer. A new boundary spell. The Seekers have sealed this area off. They probably did it as soon as they found out I'd been hiding Lilja here.

I don't have the defender gift, and I am not a Seeker. I have never undone another person's spell before, let alone someone as powerful as a Seeker. But none of that matters. I am strong, and I am desperate, and that's enough.

My gift reacts almost without thought, spilling from my fingertips, filling the air with a bright-green glow. The force of my energy slams into the shield, again and again. I'm not thinking about spellwork or strategy. I'm not thinking about anything except what I need—to get to my dragon.

Magic is about will.

And right now my will is stronger than anything.

The shield crumbles under the force of my gift, bursting into sparks of purple, and Lilja lets out a roar and surges forward, dropping rapidly through the air toward me.

My left hand slips from the rock, and I can't hold on any longer. There's no time to position myself, no time for anything. I press my feet against the rock and push off with all of my might, leaping into the air.

I fall.

And fall.

And fall.

Lilja dives as fast as she can, nearly hitting me with one of her wings, but she isn't going to make it. She can't catch me in time—

She lunges forward, stretching as far as possible, and I slam into her neck.

I scramble for purchase, gripping the nearest spike and clinging to it for dear life as Lilja rises, the beat of her wings thudding in my ears. I reach for my magic and steer her with my gift, showing her where to go.

As I wrap myself tightly around her neck, Lilja soars higher and higher, flying across the bay and toward the arena.

Thirty-One

The arena is in utter chaos.

Shimmering violet shields wrap around the stands—
it looks like Seeker Ludvik put them up to protect the
villagers. In the center of the arena floor, a beautiful golden dragon
roars—it must've been brought in for the competition. A figure
sits on its back, but from this distance I can't see who it is. The
chained red dragon is roaring back at it, its rider clearly leading
the charge.

Scurrying below the dragons like ants are the Vondur soldiers, shouting and wielding their weapons. Lines of soldiers
block both the main entrance and the back door of the arena,
keeping any of the villagers from leaving. But the shield protecting them is also trapping them in place, preventing anyone
from fighting back.

As Lilja storms into the arena and lands, both the golden and
red dragons turn sharply in our direction. The nearest Vondur

soldier raises a spear toward Lilja, but she roars and twists away from him, her tail sideswiping at least two other soldiers and sending them sprawling.

"About time you showed up," yells a familiar voice.

The figure on the back of the golden dragon is Ari. The yellow light of his gift swirls around his hands, which grip the back of the dragon tightly.

"I was a bit busy finding a dragon," I yell back.

I move Lilja closer to Ari and the golden dragon as the Vondur gather around us. They raise their spears, but Lilja and her golden friend roar, sending the men sprawling with swipes of their claws. Ari and I are both channeling our gifts, using them to strengthen the dragons' energies and keep them alert.

"Look out!" Ari shouts, and I turn to see a Vondur swordsman stepping closer. I give Lilja a prod with my gift, helping her turn, and she snarls at him, sending him running. A spear flies through the air, aimed at Ari, but Lilja snatches it in her jaws and snaps it in two with one clean bite. Three more Vondur advance toward her, but Lilja exhales a burst of flame, cutting them off. How long has she known *that* trick?

Within moments, the Vondur retreat toward the red dragon as whoever is on its back shouts orders. I don't think they're giving up, though—not by a long shot. Lilja's arrival surprised them, but now they're regrouping.

"Where are the Seekers?" I ask Ari, nudging Lilja closer to him so we can talk without being overheard. He points toward the council table, and I finally notice the smaller battle raging there. Seeker Ludvik is using his gift to shield the spectators, and it's clearly taking all of his magic to do so—he stands still, gift swirling through the air, unable to do anything about the Vondur. Seeker Larus stands in front, protecting Seeker Ludvik from the three Vondur soldiers advancing toward them. But Seeker Larus is a healer, not a warrior, and I don't know how long he'll be able to fend off the Vondur. Ari and I could help, but we'll have to fight our way through a sea of soldiers to get there.

"Where are the others?" I ask Ari. "Where's Agnar?" He's the one with the warrior gift; he should be helping.

"You didn't see?" Ari asks. He points across the arena, in the direction of the red dragon.

For a second, I'm not sure what he's talking about. But I can feel it now—the gift that's swirling all around the red dragon. Not dark and heavy like the Vondur magic. A warrior gift, the strongest one I've ever sensed.

I look again at the figure on the red dragon's back, and suddenly it all makes a horrible kind of sense.

It's Seeker Agnar.

He isn't fighting the Vondur. He isn't doing anything to stop them.

He's *helping* them.

He's the traitor.

This is how the Vondur knew that today would be the best day to invade, because they could trap everyone in the arena. This is how they got the red dragon. It's how they got into the Realm. It's how they sabotaged the second trial with that explosion.

Agnar told the Vondur everything they needed to know. He let them into the Realm. He used one of their spells at the second trial. He tried to trade them Lilja's egg and who knows how many other magical creatures or items from the Realm.

He's been helping them all along.

I look at Ari. "What are we going to do?"

Agnar didn't become a Seeker for nothing—his magic is strong. And Seeker Larus and Seeker Ludvik are barely holding off the Vondur soldiers, and Seeker Freyr is nowhere to be seen, and it's just Ari and me, in the center of the arena floor. What can we do, against him? We're not Seekers.

Abruptly, the line of Vondur in front of us shifts, allowing the red dragon to move closer to Ari and me, with Agnar on its back. Whatever they're planning, it's happening now.

Lilja lets out a sudden cry, more of a whimper than a roar, and I reach for her with my gift immediately.

Agnar's magic is spreading toward her.

"No!" I yell, and I push back without thinking. My gift bursts from my fingertips, its green sparks surrounding Lilja, forcing Agnar's magic away from her. It's not a spell; there's nothing organized or deliberate about it. But the force of my reaction—and the suddenness of it—is enough to force Agnar's dragon back a step, and his magic moves back with him.

"Get out of the way, girl," Agnar says. "The time for playing games is over."

But it's too late. I saw him back away, and I felt his magic do it too.

He's been trying to convince me ever since that first day in training that my magic isn't good enough, that *I'm* not good enough.

But now my gift is coursing into my fingertips, and my dragon is by my side. I have flown over mountains and tamed firecats and found starflowers. I have learned powerful spells and trained a dragon and survived two trials. I am a naturalist and a defender, a healer and an empath and a warrior.

I am a Seeker, and I have a dragon, and I won't let them take the Wild Realm without a fight.

I lift my chin, straighten my spine, and stare Agnar down.

The green sparks of my gift burst from my fingers. Lilja senses my intention and lets out another roar—but this time it's accompanied by a jet of fire. Agnar and the closest Vondur are forced back as Lilja spouts a wall of flames.

Agnar gives some kind of signal to the Vondur standing below him, and the soldiers swarm forward at once. But they're not divided now—all of them charge toward Ari and the golden dragon. Meanwhile, Agnar and the red one charge toward me and Lilja. She stands her ground, claws digging into the earth, and I act completely on instinct. I reach out with my gift for the red dragon's life source.

The spark is all wrapped up with the angry red streaks

of Agnar's gift, and the dragon seems too tired and small to fight him off. I let my gift bleed into his, so the dragon will sense my intentions. Agnar realizes what I'm doing at the last minute and pours more of his own gift toward the dragon, but I'm faster.

"I'm not going to hurt you," I whisper. "I'm your friend. But they aren't."

The red dragon lets out a frightened roar, and Agnar's magic surges, but my gift is now a barricade, keeping him at bay.

"Don't be afraid," I whisper, feeding it more of my gift. I wish Ari could help me with its emotions, but he's a bit busy at the moment fighting the Vondur army—I catch flashes of gold out of the corner of my eye as his dragon spins and whirls, fending off the enemy from all sides.

Agnar shouts something, and three of the Vondur soldiers break away from the fight with the golden dragon and advance toward the red one, who is slipping out of Agnar's control. The red dragon lets out a burst of fire, forcing two of the men back. But the third is circling near the dragon's tail and raises his spear, preparing to strike. On instinct, I reach for the man's life spark and give it a tug. The energy starts to drain from him, and he lowers his spear, backing away from the dragon in confusion. I stop drawing on his energy before I do serious harm and instead focus on Agnar and the other Vondur he called over, who are trying to approach me. But Lilja is doing a fine job of keeping them away with her flames and doesn't need any help from me.

I reach for the red dragon again. Agnar has a good hold, but he's not a naturalist, and when it comes to living beings, his gift is not as strong as mine. I flood the red dragon with more magic, drawing strength from all the other life sources around me, and Agnar's hold on it breaks. The dragon lurches and rolls its back, knocking Agnar to the ground. He lands hard and doesn't get back up. The dragon jabs at the nearest Vondur with its claws, sending him stumbling to the ground.

I funnel all of my strength into it, feeling its energy surge and grow, and the dragon lets out another fierce roar. A jet of flames bursts from its mouth, sending the other Vondur running.

All three of the dragons in the arena are now under Ari's and my control. The Vondur have only spears to fight with and no escape route. They're realizing it too—some of the ones who were fighting Ari are retreating across the arena. Others are lying on the ground, injured or maybe even killed by the golden dragon.

My gift should be depleted by now after so much use, but connected to the magic of both Lilja and the red dragon, it only grows stronger. Its pulse thrums in my ears.

I glance at Ari. "I'll get Larus and Ludvik, if you want to take care of the rest of these guys?"

Ari nods, his curls flying wildly, and directs the golden dragon to charge toward the Vondur again.

I direct Lilja across the arena, toward the council table where Seeker Larus and Seeker Ludvik are still standing against the Vondur soldiers. As we draw nearer to this end of the arena, I finally catch sight of Seeker Freyr—he's crouched behind some kind of enclosure, which was brought in for the third trial. At first I think he's being cowardly, but there's a figure lying at his feet, and the blue sparks of healing magic fly through the air. It's Tomas. He must have been injured at some point, and his father is trying to heal him. Behind them, I barely catch sight of Johann, peering out at the fight with wide eyes.

I stop Lilja immediately in front of the Vondur in the stands. "Hello," I call out to the Vondur. "This is my dragon, Lilja, and if you don't run right now, she's going to eat you."

Right on cue, Lilja snaps her jaws and growls.

Half of the soldiers run, scurrying down the steps and fleeing toward the exits. Behind me, the golden dragon roars, and I suspect Ari is leading the charge against some of the Vondur remaining in the arena.

But I keep my focus on the ones trapping the Seekers. Those that remain are aiming their spears at me and Lilja.

Reaching for my gift, I pull water from the air until I have enough to form a wave. The blast rips through the soldiers and sends most of them sprawling. That's all the assistance Seeker Larus needs. He leaps to the top of the arena, pulling a glass vial from the pocket of his tunic. He drinks its contents, and within moments his voice booms over the whole space.

"The dragons of the Wild Realm will defend their

home," he declares, his voice echoing. His words are punctuated by wingbeats and roars from the red and gold dragon, still fighting the last remaining Vondur. "They have surrounded the arena. If you try to fight, you will lose."

There is a pause, and then he continues. "I will give you sixty seconds to exit the arena, return to your ships, and leave this island immediately. If you go now and never return, you may leave with your lives. This is your final warning."

I turn to watch the Vondur react. Ari has brought the golden dragon to a halt; he's positioned near the main entrance, where it looks like he was threatening the Vondur guarding it, and many of them have already fled. In the silence that follows Seeker Larus's announcement, most of the rest turn and flee. The crowd of villagers erupts into cheers as the Vondur run.

I nudge Lilja into the air, rising above the arena. Beside me, Ari and the golden dragon rise too. Together, we watch as the fleeing figures of the Vondur race for their ships. We cheer as they set sail toward the horizon.

Returning Lilja to the floor of the arena, I find that the Seekers have subdued the remaining Vondur, trapping all of them behind Seeker Ludvik's boundary spells. Seeker Larus is now coaxing the red dragon into the enclosure along the arena's far wall, where it can be contained safely until it can be returned to the Realm. Seeker Larus's healing gift is already going to work on the dragon's wounds. Meanwhile, Seeker Freyr is helping Tomas get to his feet—he now looks dazed but otherwise unharmed, so I guess the healing worked. Johann is nowhere to be seen—he's probably fled into the stands.

Ari and I leap off our dragons' backs and approach the Seekers. Seeker Larus emerges from the red dragon's enclosure. "Ludvik, release the protection spell on the villagers and allow them to leave—but make sure they do so in a calm and orderly fashion. Freyr, make sure there is no one else who requires healing."

Larus then turns to Ari and me. "Are both of you all right?"

"Yes," I say, and Ari nods.

"Very well," Seeker Larus says. "Ari, you seem to be doing fine on Gulldrik, so, if you would, fly her around the coast and make sure that all of the Vondur have departed. If you find any more on the island, use a boundary spell to hold them and then report back to the arena."

"Yes, Seeker," Ari says quickly. At his urging, the golden dragon whips out its wings and launches into the air once more.

"Bryn," Larus continues, "please continue keeping your dragon under control and be prepared to assist me as I confront Agnar."

I can't help but grin. He's giving me something do just like I'm one of the Seekers, and he called Lilja *my* dragon. "Yes, Seeker," I say.

Seeker Larus crosses the arena floor to where Agnar lies, clearly injured after being thrown off the red dragon's back.

Lilja and I follow Seeker Larus, whose healing gift swirls around Agnar. After a moment Agnar sits up, and he and Larus stare at each other for a long time without speaking.

Finally, Seeker Larus asks the same question I've been wondering: "Why?"

"I've told you before, Larus," snarls Agnar. "We're sitting on a gold mine here. Do you know how much the rest of the world would pay for these creatures? For their magic?"

Seeker Larus's jaw tightens. "The treasures of the Realm will no longer exist if the balance of its magic is disturbed. You should know this, Agnar. We cannot take more than the Realm can give."

"There is more than enough," Agnar growls. "It is *wasteful* to leave it all there."

"It does not belong to us," Seeker Larus says sternly. "When we trade the gifts of the Realm, we do so in moderation, never taking more than we need. We certainly do not allow this island to be pillaged by those who do not understand its value or its balance. And *especially* not by those who use their magic to harm other creatures. We do not sell dragons so that they can be slaughtered."

"I've been teaching them," Agnar says. "The Vondur slaughter dragons because they do not know how else to use them. But I've been teaching them. They trained the dragon that I gave them to fly, and learned to ride it. They will not kill the dragons if we simply *teach* them, Larus. You guard your precious secrets too closely."

Seeker Larus raises his voice. "You do not guard the Realm closely enough!"

"They hurt that dragon," I say quietly, and both Agnar and Seeker Larus turn to face me. Louder, I add, "That red dragon was underfed and wounded. It was in *chains*. Is that what you've been teaching them?"

"They don't trust dragons enough yet," Agnar says. "The Vondur see them as deadly creatures who will try to kill them. They thought they needed the chains to control it. But they can learn otherwise. With more time, I could show them—"

"You will show them nothing," says Seeker Larus. "You have betrayed the creatures of the Realm, for no more than the promise of Vondur gold. These dragons deserve to live in peace, undisturbed by humans who would abuse them or slaughter them for their magic. We guard the knowledge of how to train dragons because there are too many humans who cannot be trusted with it. Unfortunately, that now includes you."

"You know me, Larus," says Agnar. "I have dedicated years of service to the Realm. I am not your enemy."

"No," says Seeker Larus, "you are not. But you have broken every promise you made when you became a Seeker and betrayed the trust of this village. Therefore, the people of the village must decide what to do with you."

Agnar spits on the ground. "The villagers understand nothing. They've never even *seen* the Realm."

"They have never seen it," Seeker Larus says, "because they do not dare. They treat it with more reverence than you."

Agnar starts to respond, but Seeker Larus cuts him off. "And the explosion at the second trial? The use of Vondur magic? That was you as well? You could have killed the children."

"I had it under control," Agnar snaps. "It was only meant to disrupt the end of the trial. I hoped I could convince you to retake the second trial, or at least delay the third."

"Why?"

"I couldn't let you appoint another Seeker. Three of you are hard enough to fight, and I didn't want a fourth to deal with." He glares directly at me. "At first I wanted to bring the Vondur over before the trials. But we needed a dragon for the plan to work, to fly us into the Realm. And the first egg I took from the Realm was stolen by *her*. We got the red dragon eventually, but it wasn't ready. I needed to delay the trials as much as possible. But you insisted on taking a vote and advancing the competition, so we had no choice but to arrive today, before the trials could finish."

"No choice?" Seeker Larus says. He shakes his head sadly. "You had plenty of choices."

Agnar opens his mouth again, but Seeker Larus turns away from him. His gift sparks around his fingers, and I sense a boundary spell of some kind surrounding Agnar. Seeker Larus looks at me.

"Thank you for your assistance," he says. "I trust you will return your dragon to the Realm?"

"Yes," I say, but I can't help sighing. For a second, Seeker Larus smiles. Then he strides away, joining Seeker Freyr and Seeker Ludvik and conferring quietly with them.

Dragon wings beat overhead, and both Lilja and I glance up to see the golden dragon land once again in the arena, Ari on its back. He slides gracefully to the ground and walks up to us.

Lilja practically flattens him as she nudges him with her nose in an excited greeting, and Ari gently rubs her scales. "Hey, Lil," he says quietly.

Then he turns to me. "Hey, Bryn."

"Long time no see," I answer, grinning.

Ari glances over at where Agnar sits, trapped by the boundary spell. "I can't believe it. We spent all this time trying to find the traitor, and he was right in front of us."

"Yeah," I say. "He was the person you saw trading away Lilja's egg, and the one who let the Vondur into the Realm that night, when we almost got caught. This is what they were planning. He's probably the one who told the other Seekers about me and Lilja, the day they caught us."

"No," Ari says abruptly. "That was Tomas."

My jaw clenches. "How do you know?"

"He was taunting me this morning as we went into the arena. He said something like, 'I got your dragon taken away. Shame they didn't catch you, too.'"

"But how did he know about Lilja?"

"I asked him, and he said he knew that you must be hiding something, that you were too well trained not to be cheating. There was one day when he was late for training; I think he must have followed you out to Lilja's cave and spied on you. Then he told his father, and his father told the other Seekers. He didn't see me with the dragon, so he couldn't prove that I knew about her too, but I think he suspected."

"But why did he do it after I'd already lost the second trial? Why bother turning me in?"

"He was probably hoping I'd be there too, and then I'd be disqualified."

"I should have reported him to the Seekers sooner. As soon as he told me that the rock throwing was his idea, I should've . . . I think I was too embarrassed."

"*I* should've reported it," Ari says. "After you told me about it, I should've said something. And I'm sorry about . . . about you getting caught with Lilja. When I asked you for help with her, I never meant for you to get in trouble. You should be the Seeker, really. You were amazing today, with how you handled those dragons and saved everyone."

"Well," I say, heat rising in my cheeks, "I couldn't have done any of that if I'd been trapped in the arena with everyone else, so I guess it's a good thing I didn't pass the second trial *and* got caught cheating."

Ari gives a hesitant laugh. "In that case, you're welcome."

"And *you're* welcome for saving you from the Vondur."

"Um, don't you mean *I* saved *you* from the Vondur?"

"You *did* look pretty cool on that golden dragon," I say. "But you learned it all from me, of course."

"No way! I knew Lilja first. *You* learned everything about dragons from *me*."

Ari grins, and I smile back, and for the first time since the Seekers caught me with Lilja, it feels like things might actually be all right.

THIRTY-TWO

The rest of the day passes in a blur. Seeker Ludvik questions me about how I broke the boundary spells to free Lilja from the Realm, then rushes off to restore them properly. Seeker Larus interrogates the Vondur and Agnar about their plan, and everyone else is quickly ordered out of the arena.

With Ari once more on the golden dragon and myself on Lilja, we fly to Dragon's Point. It's here, on an outcropping of rock just outside the Realm, that I have to say goodbye to Lilja again.

"Say hi to your new dragon friends for me," I say.

Lilja blinks and nudges me with the end of her nose.

"Go on, now," I say. "I'll see you soon."

It's a lie, of course, but I don't want to tell her the truth. I turn away quickly and give her a tap with my gift, sending her into the air. I can't bear another long, tearful farewell.

Ari, who has already sent the golden dragon on its way,

doesn't say goodbye to Lilja. He doesn't need to. I don't know what exactly the Seekers plan to do, what with the third trial never taking place, but I'm sure he will be selected as the next Seeker eventually. I can hardly look at him as the two of us make our way down the rocky slope toward the village, our dragons soaring into the Realm behind us.

It's nearly dusk when we return to the arena and ask Seeker Larus if there's anything else we can do to help.

"I want to thank you both for your assistance today," he says. "I don't know what might have happened if the two of you hadn't demonstrated such bravery and skill."

Ari ducks his head, embarrassed. "It was mostly Bryn."

"Seeker Larus?" I ask. "What's going to happen to the Vondur we captured? And Agnar?"

"We would like to get more information from them about how this happened and what they were planning," Seeker Larus says. "Then I expect we will release all of them back to the mainland. We have neither the means nor the desire to hold them here."

"But what if they try to come back?"

"Without a dragon to help them into the Realm, it would be a futile effort," Seeker Larus says. "Still, there are more protections that we can put in place to better secure the Realm. It's something we have discussed before, but we didn't realize how urgent the need really was."

I nod. "And I guess you'll need to finish selecting a new Seeker to help you with that."

Seeker Larus smiles. "I'm sure we will. And I think we have seen enough to confirm our selection. But I will confer with the rest of the council and announce our decision tomorrow. Until then, both of you should go home and get some rest. You've earned it."

"Thank you, sir," Ari says.

Seeker Larus bids us good night and walks toward the arena. Ari and I head in the opposite direction, into the village.

We reach the path that leads to Ari's home, and he stops, giving me a sheepish smile. "Well. Um . . ."

"I'm glad you're going to be the new Seeker," I say. "Compared with Tomas and Johann, I mean."

"That's hardly a compliment. It's not hard to be better than Tomas and Johann."

I laugh. "True."

"And we don't know if I'm going to be the new Seeker or not," he adds. "They *could* pick one of them."

"Yeah right. You did great today, fighting the Vondur like that."

"Not as good as you," he says. "I'm sorry you didn't get to compete."

"Fortunately for you," I say, grinning, "because I would've *totally* won."

He smiles back. "In your dreams."

"See you tomorrow, Ari."

I walk the rest of the way to our hut alone. When I arrive,

the garden gate is flung wide open, and a candle burns in the window. I race up the path and rush inside.

Mama greets me with a bone-crushing hug. "Brynja! You were so incredible today. And so brave!" She pulls back and looks me up and down. "What were you thinking, jumping onto a dragon like that? You could've gotten yourself killed! Were you trying to give your mother a heart attack?" She pulls me close again.

I groan. "Can't. Breathe."

"Did you see the Vondurs?" Elisa adds, leaping up from the table and running toward us. "They came inside the arena!"

"Yeah, I saw them," I say as Mama finally releases me.

"But your silver dragon scared them away!" Elisa continues.

"I cannot *believe* you were riding the dragon without proper training," Mama says. "What were you thinking?"

"Your dragon was the prettiest of all," Elisa says.

A loud chuckle interrupts them both as Papa enters the kitchen and scoops me up into a hug. "I think what they're trying to say is that we're all very proud of you, Bryn."

I smile. "Does helping save the village from dark magicians mean that I'm not grounded anymore?"

"Absolutely not," Mama says immediately.

I sigh as Papa lowers me back to the floor. "Then would it be a good time to mention *this*?" I pull the jar of starflower paste from my pocket and hand it to Mama, along with her icefox-crystal necklace. "I might have happened upon some starflowers while I was in the Realm the other day."

Mama doesn't respond for a long moment, looking at the glass jar in her hand. Then she straightens and says, "Go wash up for supper. You've gotten absolutely filthy. And is that a rip I see in your shirt?"

But she smiles while she says it, and I know that's Mama's way of saying thank you.

The next morning every muscle in my body aches with exhaustion, but I leap out of bed early and help Mama with breakfast. As soon as possible, I excuse myself from the table and rush outside to the village square before Mama can remember that I'm supposed to be grounded.

Runa stands beneath the tree in the center of the square and frantically waves me over. As soon as I approach, she gives me a hug. "You were *unbelievable* yesterday," she says. "I had no idea you could ride Lilja like that! And the way you both scared off the invaders and fought Agnar and—and it was *amazing*!"

I laugh. "I did have *some* help."

Runa grins, throwing one arm over my shoulder. "The whole village has been talking about you. You're a hero!"

"Lilja's the real hero. She did all the work."

Runa rolls her eyes. "Right, and I'm sure she used her gift to free the red dragon from Agnar all by herself."

"Okay, I might have helped her a little."

"You have to tell me all about it. Every detail. I want to know *everything.*"

"Of course," I say. "And *you* have to tell *me* everything that happened in the arena before I got there. That golden dragon was part of the competition, wasn't it?"

"Yes. You didn't miss much—Larus had just announced the start of the trial. And when the Vondur came into the arena, Ari just charged into action. He leaped on the dragon's back like it was nothing and tried to keep the Vondur out. He was outnumbered, but he bought enough time for Seeker Ludvik to cast the shield to protect everyone in the stands, and then . . ."

Runa breaks off as three figures stride up the lane into the village square. The three remaining Seekers, each in their official green cloak, stop directly in front of the tree. Other villagers crowd around to listen, and several of the village criers stand at attention. Ari emerges from the bakery and walks over to my side. We share a wordless look of anticipation before turning our attention back to the Seekers.

"Good morning," Seeker Larus begins. He stands between Seeker Ludvik and Seeker Freyr, and all three of them are tightly masking their expressions. "As many of you are aware, there is quite a lot of work left to be done as a consequence of yesterday's events. The council is determined to ensure the safety of both the Realm and the village and make certain that our island will never be threatened again. To that end, we will begin using stronger defensive spells in the Realm to prevent anyone from stealing its creatures. But this will take time and quite a bit of spellwork, and we will need the council to be at full strength. Therefore, we must finish selecting a new Seeker."

The crowd around us is growing larger, and murmurs break out at these words. When the crowd falls silent again, Seeker Larus continues. "Obviously, the final trial of our Seeker competition did not take place. But the council has decided that we saw enough of our competitors' abilities, both during the competition and in the aftermath of the Vondur arrival, to make a decision. We have selected Ari, son of Petur, to become a Seeker."

A few cheers rise up from the crowd. Ari blinks, looking shocked, and I nudge him with my shoulder. "That's you, dummy. Congratulations." And despite the lump in my throat, I actually mean it. Ari will be a great Seeker, and he'll take good care of Lilja. He deserves it.

Seeker Larus raises one hand, and the crowd falls silent again. "However," he says, and Ari's eyes widen, "the council has also decided, in light of yesterday's events, to strip former Seeker Agnar of his title and place on the council. He will be exiled to the mainland along with the Vondur as penalty for his crimes. Therefore, the council is now short *another* member. Given the urgency of the situation, we have decided that we do not have time to attempt another round of competition, so we will make a second selection based on what we saw yesterday."

Several people glance around, looking for Tomas and Johann. As the only other competitors to make it to the final trial, one of them has to be the council's second pick.

"One person," Seeker Larus continues, "showed us something incredible yesterday. They demonstrated exceptional strength of spellwork, quick thinking during a crisis, and bravery in the face of danger, as well as an innate and remarkable ability to work with magical creatures. We are all truly indebted to her for her actions."

My heartbeat slams to a stop. Surely he can't mean . . . ?

"Therefore," Seeker Larus says, and he smiles directly at me, "we have selected Brynja, daughter of Jakob, as our fifth Seeker."

For one moment, everyone in the village is silent.

Then Runa lets out a loud whoop, and a few cheers rise from the crowd. Applause breaks out, and most of the people surrounding us join in.

Ari nudges my shoulder. "That's you, dummy. Congratulations!"

Runa hugs me again and yells something in my ear, but I'm so shocked I hardly notice. It's only when Seeker Larus tugs both Ari and me forward and presses folded green cloaks into our hands that it finally sinks in.

I'm going to be a Seeker.

I did it.

Ari and I can't help but grin as we turn and wave to the crowd, which continues to applaud. I spy my family—Papa, holding Elisa up on his shoulders, leaning one hand on his walking stick, and Mama, her eyes full of happy tears.

Elisa will never run out of starflower medicine now. And I've never seen my parents look so proud.

As the crowd disperses and word of what's happened flies through the village, Ari and I both spend a quiet minute with our families, accepting their congratulations.

"Am I ungrounded *now*?" I ask Mama as she hugs me for what must be the fifteenth time.

"Absolutely not," she says, but she smiles as she says it.

"When do I get to ride your dragon?" Elisa says. "And I want to see some unicorns!"

Papa laughs, swinging her down from his shoulders. "I guess you'll have to become a Seeker just like your big sister, El."

Mama glares at him. "Don't encourage her! I won't have *both* of my daughters running around getting into trouble. One is quite enough!"

From across the square, Ari leaves his mother's side and waves at me. Then he points up to the sky, almost questioningly, and I nod. I know exactly what he wants to do.

"Mama," I say, "can I go spend some time with Ari for a while?"

Mama and Papa exchange glances I can't read, and Mama nods. "Be back in time to help prepare supper," she says. "You're still grounded, remember."

"I will!" I say, already racing off. "Thank you!"

Ari grins at me. "Want to go see your dragon?"

"Always."

As we walk out of the square, a little girl, probably about Elisa's age, comes running up to me. "You're Bryn!" she says.

"Yes," I respond, smiling. "What's your name?"

"Inga," she says. "And I want to be a Seeker just like you when I grow up."

"Good. I'm going to need another girl up there with me to keep boys like this one in line." I point at Ari, and she giggles. "Keep practicing your magic, okay? And I'll see you in the next Seeker competition."

As she waves goodbye and runs away, the tears that have been threatening to emerge all day finally spill over. My heart feels so full I think it will burst.

"Are you okay?" Ari asks.

"Yeah," I say, rubbing my eyes. "Let's go get our dragon!"

At Dragon's Point, Ari and I both cast out our gifts so Lilja can sense us and whistle three high notes. As we stare up into the Realm, the shadow of a small silver dragon appears on the horizon.

"Everything's going to be different now," Ari says quietly. "The Vondur came way too close to being successful. They might try again. And others might too, once they hear what happened. We're going to have to defend the Realm more than ever."

Lilja descends rapidly, each beat of her wings stirring up a gust of wind, and I smile. "I think we'll be ready for it."

Ari and I climb onto Lilja's back, and she doesn't need any direction from us to know where to go. She soars over the Wild Realm, which is lit now by the red and purple rays of sundown. As we climb higher into the air, the land spreads out before us—the mountain peaks and low canyons, the glaciers and lakes, the enchanted forests and ashy volcanoes. All of it brimming with magic.

And we have the rest of our lives to explore every inch.

With Ari and Lilja beside me, I can't wait to begin.

Acknowledgments

This book started as a few sentences scribbled in a notebook four years ago. Bringing it to life would never have been possible without the support of many people to whom I owe my deepest gratitude.

My brilliant editorial team, Alyson Heller and Tricia Lin, gave me so much guidance and helped me find the heart of Bryn's story. I am also grateful to Cathleen McAllister, who created the stunning cover art, and to everyone at Aladdin for all that they do.

Endless thanks to my agent, Victoria Doherty Munro, who is my constant champion and guided this story through all its early stages until we found what it needed to be.

The unsung heroes behind this book are Alexandrina Brant, Rachel Done, and Allison Pauli, who faithfully read my long first drafts and provided invaluable insight. I couldn't have done this without you.

Many wonderful educators, librarians, booksellers, bloggers, and readers have graciously supported me and my books, and I am so grateful to all of you.

Thank you to Penny and Ivy, who both inspired Lilja in their own ways and brought me so much joy.

Finally, to Mom, Dad, and Katie: I love you. Thanks for everything.

About the Author

Alexandra Ott writes fiction for young readers, including her debut fantasy novel, *Rules for Thieves*, and its sequel, *The Shadow Thieves*. She graduated from the University of Tulsa and is now a freelance editor. In her spare time, she eats a lot of chocolate and reads just about everything. She currently lives in Oklahoma with her tiny canine overlord. Visit her online at www.alexandraott.com.